THE
INNOCENT
ANGELS

BOOKS BY ALISON BELSHAM

Detective Lexi Bennett Series

The Girls on Chalk Hill

The Girl's Last Cry

ALISON BELSHAM

THE
INNOCENT
ANGELS

bookouture

Published by Bookouture in 2023

An imprint of Storyfire Ltd.
Carmelite House
50 Victoria Embankment
London EC4Y 0DZ

www.bookouture.com

ISBN: 978-1-83790-516-4
eBook ISBN: 978-1-83790-515-7

ONE

Salt stung her eyes. Why was she sweating so much? She could taste it on her top lip, and feel it trickling between her breasts. She couldn't remember where she was. At a party? At somebody's house? It didn't stop her dancing. The music flowed around her, a tide of soft pastel colours swirling through the air – lemon, violet, sky blue and pink. She stuck out her tongue to see if she could taste them, but her mouth was too dry. She didn't feel at home inside her body.

Where was everyone else? If she was at a party, shouldn't there be other people?

Then everything changed. She couldn't hear music and the colours in front of her evaporated. She looked around. The room she was in was dark, lit only by a pair of fat, white candles on the floor. The flames whispered, casting silver and gold shadows on the walls. She felt damp cold prickling her skin and her dancing faltered.

She was holding something in her hand. A bottle of water. She unscrewed the cap and brought it to her lips. It tasted so good, and her mouth felt softer.

Where was she?

A tiny dark hole. She stumbled to a doorway and then sensed she was moving into a larger space. But it was all shadows.

She looked around again, turning a full circle as her eyes roamed the sparkling darkness. Metal and glass, fracturing what little light there was into tiny rainbows. Huge metal cages, stacked high with green glass bottles. As she stared at them, they became glinting emerald caverns, deep beneath the waters of a green and black sea. And she was a mermaid, swimming between them, searching for something...

She blinked and drank more water. She knew where she was now. In the vineyard's main cellar, of course. She'd been here before.

'Babe? Where are you going?'

Someone pulled her back into the small place where the candlelight suddenly seemed so much brighter.

The man who tugged on her arm wasn't who she expected to see. His footsteps rang loudly on the concrete floor, making her tremble. She wrapped her arms around her body defensively, belatedly realising she was completely naked. She looked round frantically for her clothes, but she couldn't remember what she'd been wearing. Or how she'd got here.

Fear bit into her gut with sharp teeth.

She heard herself gasp. 'I want to go home. I don't feel right.' She'd never felt like this before. What was happening to her?

'You're tired,' said the man. 'Stay here with me.'

As he came closer, she saw he was holding something. A syringe.

'You need to sleep.'

Panic churned through her, cold as sea water. She tried to back away, but he grabbed the top of her arm, fingers biting into flesh.

'There's nothing to worry about. You need this.'

The colours came back in a starburst, sharp and acidic. The colours of fear. He raised her arm and she felt a stab in her armpit. A rush of warmth spread through her.

'Lie down.' He helped her sink to the floor.

It was cold and hard, but then it became soft and yielding underneath her, as if she was sinking down into her own bed.

She stared at the nearest of the two candles. Its flame twisted sinuously in ravishing colours, hypnotising her as she slipped into a comfortable dream.

Somewhere nearby, she heard a baby crying. The sound made her chest tighten. It was her own baby's cry. 'Scarlett? Where are you? Mummy's here...'

She tried to push herself up on one elbow, tried to reach out for her daughter, but the man pushed her back down.

And the sound of her baby wailing drifted away into the distance.

TWO

SUNDAY

Despite the early hour, Will Steadman could already feel the heat of the sun as it struck the back of his head, just where his hair was starting to thin. At thirty-five, he was too young for this to be happening, but his father had been bald at forty and his older brother was heading the same way. It was going to be a hot day so at least the grapes would remain dry – the harvest was in full swing now and it was the only two weeks of the year when he didn't appreciate rain. Sodden grapes watered down the juice that ran from the presses.

Even though today was Sunday, the pickers would be working. It was imperative they got the crop in before the weather changed towards the end of the week, and as he made his way up the slope of Elvington Vineyard's largest field, he assessed what had been achieved the day before and how much still needed to be done. The pickers had worked fast but Elvington was one of the biggest vineyards in the county. There was still a long way to go.

He walked up the drive to get to the huge, corrugated steel production facility. Beyond it stood a smaller, wooden barn and the home paddock, where the team of foreign pickers camped

out for the duration of the harvest. He could hear the workers getting up – male and female voices and the hollow slamming of the door of the temporary ablutions trailer. Behind him, he heard snuffling at the side of a row of vines.

'Dylan!' he said, turning and squatting down at the same time.

The whippet ran towards him, sniffing for a treat, but Will had nothing to give him except a scratch behind the ears. It was Marietta's dog and was supposed to kept inside the fenced-off garden of the farmhouse during the harvest.

'Come on,' he said, straightening up.

The dog followed him for a few metres as he walked up the concrete drive to the winery, but then bolted towards the sounds of the pickers having breakfast. Standing at the door, Will texted Marietta to come and fetch him, then dug into his pocket for his keys.

The cavernous interior of the winery was pleasantly cool inside and, at this hour, still quiet. Later, it would be noisy as the steel-caged lift on the outside raised the crates of grapes up to the top level to be tipped into the giant presses. The clatter of machinery and the workers shouting to be heard over it would echo against the metal walls and roof. If they managed to pick well all day, the pressing would go on long into the night.

Although he'd checked over all the equipment when they'd finished up the previous evening, he climbed the spiral stairs to the top level to check again. The first grapes would arrive in less than an hour, and they had to be ready to go. Then he came down to the ground floor to check the giant fermentation tanks that lined the walls.

Touch wood – he tapped one of oak barrels which ran along the centre of the floor in a row – everything was going to plan so far. He was halfway through the busiest fortnight of the year, and just beginning to feel like he could breathe again. The whole operation was his responsibility.

His fiefdom, as he liked to think of it.

A noise distracted him from checking the last tank in the row. He stood still for a moment, head cocked to one side.

There it was again. It sounded like a baby crying. But that didn't make sense. Aurora, Johnny and Marietta's one-year-old daughter, had been taken to stay with Johnny's parents for the duration of the harvest so Marietta could work the presses. He shrugged – maybe she'd been brought home for some reason. He walked across to the row of tanks on the other side.

But as he reached the far end of the fermentation hall, the crying sounded louder. Surely he shouldn't be able to hear Aurora all the way in here?

Halfway along the rear wall of the hall there was an open doorway that led to a flight of stairs down to the cellars. They'd been dug out of the south-facing chalk hillside upon which the vineyard stood, and were used for storing the wines.

Will went to the top of the staircase and listened. The crying sound was definitely coming from the cellar, which meant it couldn't be a baby. Perhaps it was a cat or a fox, though he couldn't see how one would have got in. He went down the flight of stairs and unlocked the barred gate at the bottom. There were hundreds of thousands of pounds' worth of premier cru sparkling wine stored in the two chambers, and this gate and the various doors of the production facility were kept securely locked when no one was working there.

Everything was quiet as he flicked on the lights of the first cellar. It was a long, rectangular chamber, filled with rows and rows of metal cages, all stacked with bottles at various stages of second fermentation. His feet crunched on the rough concrete floor as he checked the spaces between each row of cages. He saw nothing out of the ordinary, and nothing had changed since he'd been down here briefly the previous day.

But he heard the crying again, this time louder and more

distinct. Closer. And it absolutely sounded like a human baby rather than any kind of animal.

'Hello?'

His voice echoed off the walls and the thousands of bottles, but there was no reply.

At the far end of the cellar, a large square break in the wall led into a second chamber. It was not quite as large as the first, but still had room for thousands of bottles of wine, as well as housing the small production line they used for corking and labelling.

Stepping into the darkness, he reached out sideways to feel for the light switches. Bright halogen light flooded the area, illuminating a maze of storage cages and crates.

'Is anyone here?' said Will. His question was met with silence. Then he heard a small gasp as lungs were filled, followed by a loud, sustained wail.

He ran through the cellar, frantically looking from side to side. There was no one here, but the crying continued. Standing in the centre of the floor, he listened hard, trying to ascertain the direction the sound was coming from.

Another piercing cry drew him to the very back of the cellar. At the end of the last row of crates, in the corner, he saw a wooden door he'd completely forgotten about. It led into a series of small, naturally occurring chalk caves, empty as far as he knew.

The door, however, stood slightly ajar, and another howl told him he'd come to the right place. He pushed against the rough wood to open it wider and stepped through. He sensed he was in a much smaller space, though it was completely dark. Something was gasping in front of him, low down on the floor.

'Hello, who's here?' he said softly. He didn't want to frighten the child.

He quickly pulled out his phone and switched on its torch. The small beam pooled directly at his feet. He changed the angle at which he held it, so the light swept across the floor, casting a pale circle which became larger, though more diffuse, as it moved further from him.

He sensed a movement just beyond its arc, then the light picked out a small human form.

It was a baby, sitting slumped forward on the chalk floor, head drooped. He or she was naked, apart from a nappy and a small pair of white feather wings attached to its back by red elastic straps round its shoulders. The infant looked up and let out another long howl.

Will ran towards the child and, as he did, the light of the torch washed across flat, white chalk until, just as he was bending to pick up the baby, he saw something out of the corner of his eye. His hand moved and the light revealed undulations of pale flesh. As he stopped in his tracks, the baby reached up for him with a loud sob.

But he was too busy staring at the woman's body to pick it up. Almost as white as the chalk she was lying on, lifeless, naked – her arms by her sides, her legs straight, pressed together. Her head was turned in the direction of the baby, eyes open but unseeing.

And like the baby, she had a pair of white feather angel wings on her back, now crushed underneath her body.

As Will realised what he was looking at, he snatched up the child and ran.

THREE

A half-marathon was hardly an Ironman triathlon and Lexi Bennett's final push over the line was propelled by fury. She stumbled past the remnants of the finish tape fluttering in the wind and immediately bent forward, hands on knees, to catch her breath.

Damn! Not good enough, Lex.

'Aunt Lexi, you were amazing!'

'Way to go, Lexi – you came seventh.'

Gritting her teeth momentarily, then swallowing her frustration, she looked up to see her sister Amber and her niece Tasha at the front of the spectators crowding the race's finish.

A runner she knew jogged easily over the line behind her and patted her shoulder as she passed.

'Well done, Annie,' Lexi said.

The other runner stopped abruptly and gave her a red-faced grin. She looked at her watch. 'PB,' she said.

Lexi turned to Amber and Tasha.

'PB? What's that?' said Tasha. 'Peanut butter?'

'No, silly,' said Lexi. 'Personal best. That was Annie's fastest time ever.'

'And you?' said Amber. 'A personal best too?'

Lexi gave a dry laugh. 'Far from it. More like a personal worst.'

The pressures of her job were beginning to show. Not enough training on the roads. Not enough time in the gym. This half marathon had been supposed to set her up for next month's triathlon, but a stabbing pain in the back of her thigh suggested otherwise. She grabbed a silver foil survival blanket from a crate near the finish and wrapped it round her shoulders. It wasn't a cold day, but she didn't need her muscles seizing up before she could find the box where she'd stashed her tracksuit ahead of the race.

'Lexi!'

She looked around. 'What are you doing here?'

Tom Olsen, her sergeant, was bearing down on her, accompanied by his husband, daughter and dog. Tasha immediately ran across to Billie and started chattering, while Amber briefly hugged both men and petted the Dalmatian.

'He couldn't miss seeing his boss's spectacular performance,' said Declan, with a wink.

'You mean her ritual humiliation,' said Lexi.

'You came seventh,' said Tom. 'That's great.'

'Not if you wanted to win,' said Lexi.

Tom turned to Declan. 'See? I told you she was competitive.' Something snagged his attention and he frowned, pulling out his phone. 'What? On a Sunday morning?'

'Leave it,' said Declan.

'Uh-uh, I'd better take it.' He put the phone to his ear. 'Yes... yes... sure. On my way.'

Billie looked up at him and pulled a face. 'Dad, no way. What about the film?'

'Dad will still take you.'

'But I wanted to go with you...'

Lexi watched the exchange. 'What is it, Tom? I could go.'

'No,' said three or four voices in unison.

'You need to rest,' said Amber.

Tom hustled her to one side, and they turned away from the others. 'Unexplained death. A young woman, doesn't look accidental apparently.'

'Where?'

'Elvington Vineyard, just outside the village of Elvington.'

'I know of it. Where are you parked? I'll just grab my tracksuit and meet you at the car.'

'Honestly, boss, I can go on my own...'

But she was already striding away to the tent where the runners' possessions had been stashed.

Detective Inspector Lexi Bennett knew her actions would annoy Amber, with whom she was supposed to be having dinner later. But she also knew Amber would understand.

A young woman was dead. And from what the first responder had told Tom over the phone, they were probably looking at a death due to unnatural causes. There was no way Lexi was going home to soak her weary limbs in a cold bath when there was a case demanding her attention.

As Tom drove them from Canterbury to Elvington, Lexi called in the CSIs, and left a message for Mort Barley, her forensic pathologist of choice. She instructed the uniforms at the scene to create a double cordon and told them to close off all access to the building where the body was still lying.

'There's a kid, too,' said the PC she was talking to.

'A second body?' Why the hell hadn't anyone mentioned this?

'No, boss. Alive. A baby girl. She was sitting next to the body, crying.'

God, if this didn't complicate matters, nothing would. 'Anyone there know whose kid it is?'

'No.'

'Okay, call social services for me and get someone to come for her.'

They were turning off a narrow lane into the vineyard by the time she finished the calls. An unpaved drive carved its path between rows of leafy vines, gravelly chalk crunching under the wheels of Tom's Jeep as he slowed to the required five miles per hour. To one side of the drive, set back some twenty metres, there was a traditional redbrick farmhouse with red roof tiles and green painted window frames. It was surrounded by a private garden, fenced off from the fields beyond. Once they went past it, they were driving between vineyards on either side and, as Lexi looked more closely at the crop, she could see bunches of green grapes, plump and heavy. Further up the hill in another field, a swarm of pickers were moving between the rows.

'Harvesting,' said Tom. 'That means people all over the property and more work for us to eliminate them if we need to.'

Close to the top of the slope, the driveway widened into a small parking area. To one side of it stood a squat redbrick building with floor-to-ceiling windows along its south façade and a wooden deck overlooking the valley. A metal sign on the decking advertised tastings and tours of the vineyard. They both climbed out of the car and looked around.

A little bit further up the slope towered the huge steel production facility. Even though the walls had been painted green, it still stuck out like a sore thumb – a jarring industrial structure inserted into a swathe of beautiful countryside. It was surrounded by flapping yellow and black police tape, which made it even more conspicuous.

'This way,' said Lexi, pointing towards it.

There were two police cars parked on the stretch of the

drive that led up from the parking area to the wide loading bay doors of the facility. Two PCs were standing just inside the cordon. They appeared to be arguing with a man standing on the other side of the tape.

Lexi experienced a sharp jabbing pain in the back of her thigh again as they strode up the hill. She gasped.

'You okay?' said Tom, turning back until she caught up with him.

'Just stiffening up after the run,' said Lexi. But it felt more like a pulled muscle if she was truthful with herself. She leaned back a little and massaged it with her hand. It didn't make any difference.

As they came closer, Lexi could hear what the man was saying. He sounded furious.

'You can't keep us out of the winery. The harvest has to happen now and the grapes can't be stored before going into the presses. If you keep us from processing our crop, you'll put our whole year's production in jeopardy.'

The woman PC gave him a pained look. 'I'm sorry, but...'

'We'll take it from here,' said Lexi, thankful that her police ID card had still been in her bag, even though it was the weekend. 'I'm DI Bennett and this is DS Olsen.'

'Thank God,' said the man, turning to address Tom. 'Can you tell your jobsworths to let us back in?'

Wow! He wants to make friends and co-operate.

'Firstly, sir, I'd rather you didn't refer to my officers in that way,' said Lexi. 'We'll all get along much better if everyone is polite. Can you tell me your name?'

The man glared at her. 'Will Steadman. I'm the chief vintner here, and I manage the vineyard.'

'You're the one who found the body, right?'

This, finally, shamed him into co-operation. 'Yes, I found the dead woman in our cellar, with a baby sitting next to her.'

'Do you know the woman?'

He shook his head.

'Where's the baby now?'

'She's in the back of one of our cars with PC Lacey,' said the male PC.

'Is she hurt? I assume you've called the paramedics.' Even if the poor little thing was physically okay, she must have been completely traumatised. After all, who knew what she might have seen?

'She appears to be physically okay, but an ambulance is coming to make sure.'

Lexi nodded. 'Good. Someone from the council's child safeguarding team will arrive soon.' She turned back to the vintner. 'Mr Steadman, you'll be given access to the building when we're satisfied we've recorded any evidence there might be. In the meantime, please help to keep the scene clear of your staff.'

Steadman scowled. 'You do realise that every hour you keep us out potentially costs us thousands of pounds?'

'And what value do you put on that woman's life?' she said.

Steadman backed off, shaking his head but still looking angry.

Lexi ducked under the tape and Tom followed. 'Now, can one of you two show us to the body?'

FOUR

Lexi instructed the male PC to wait outside for Mort Barley and the crime scene manager Emily Jordan, and called out to Will Steadman's retreating figure that he was to go nowhere until she'd questioned him. Then, after she and Tom had pulled on white scene-of-crime suits, the woman PC – PC McDonald, she told them – showed Lexi and Tom into the winery. Lexi looked around with interest. She'd been on a vineyard tour once in France, but it had just been a small, family-run affair. This was wine-making on a commercial scale, and Elvington wines were making a splash on the international market. So why was there a dead girl in one of their cellars?

As PC McDonald led the way through the fermentation hall and down to the first of the two cellars, Lexi checked on the information she had so far.

'What time did Steadman call it in?'

'He made a 999 call at 8.13 a.m.,' she said. 'Despatch alerted me and PC Cray and we arrived here at 8.39 a.m.'

'As far as you know, has anyone else been into the cellar since the body was found?'

'No. Steadman said he brought the baby upstairs and waited for us to arrive.'

'Once you've shown us where she is, can you set up a scene entry log and make sure no one comes down here without being in the appropriate kit?'

'Yes, ma'am.'

The two cellars were well-lit, with large halogen lamps hanging from the ceilings, but the caves beyond hadn't been wired.

McDonald stopped at the door and picked up a torch from the floor. She handed it to Tom. 'She's in here. There are a couple more flashlights already in there, but it's still pretty dark.'

'Thanks,' said Tom.

'Can you go up and tell the CSIs, when they arrive, that they'll need to bring lamps down?' Lexi asked.

McDonald nodded.

Tom stepped inside the cave and moved out of the way to allow Lexi in. It was a small chamber, and unlike the two big cellars, a natural cave rather than a hewn-out space. There were two large flashlights standing on the floor a little way in, their beams pointing upwards and bouncing off the chalk roof of the cave to light the area below.

They both stood stock-still while Tom shone the beam of the torch directly onto the body which lay in the middle of the uneven floor. There was not a second's doubt in Lexi's mind that the woman was dead. Her skin already had the waxy sheen of a cadaver. She was sprawled on her back, arms by her sides, legs straight, but her head was turned towards them. Her eyes were open and glassy – it appeared she'd been looking at something as she died. The baby? Was it her baby? Lexi's heart clenched at thought.

She took the torch from Tom, stepped forward and shone the light directly into one of the woman's eyes. There was no dilation of the pupil and a quick feel at the side of her throat confirmed there was no pulse. Her skin was cold to the touch already. Not that Lexi would hazard a guess at the time of death – she could leave that to Mort's expert eye when he arrived.

The woman was naked, but she was lying on something.

'What's that?' said Tom, pointing at her shoulder.

Lexi directed the light at it. 'Wings. Angel wings.' She swept the beam up and down the woman's body, looking for any sign of injury, but her pale skin was intact, and apart from a couple of faded bruises on her upper arms, there was nothing suggesting a violent end. Tom took a few photos from different angles using his phone, for reference until the forensic photographer provided them with better quality images.

'We'll wait for Mort to turn her over, but maybe there's an injury on her back.' She skimmed the torchlight round the sides of the body, looking for any sign of blood seeping from underneath, but there was nothing. Her head seemed to be intact and there was no blood in her long, black hair. With a gloved hand, Lexi swept a tress away from her neck, looking for signs of strangulation or ligature. It was clean.

She straightened up and shone the torch along the sides of the cave and into the darkest corners.

'Where are her clothes? She can't have arrived here naked,' said Tom.

The rest of the cave was empty, but then the light caught on a small patch of something shiny on the floor. Lexi bent down to inspect it.

'Candle wax.'

They inspected the rest of the floor and found other patches of wax.

'Candles are good for fingerprints,' said Lexi, but the stubs didn't seem to be anywhere in the cave. 'It's not suicide,' she went on decisively. 'Someone has removed the clothes she came in and the candles, so she definitely wasn't here on her own. And taking evidence suggests a knowledge of wrongdoing.'

There was the sound of clapping from the doorway. 'Bravo, Lexi Bennett, you've solved the case already.'

'First impressions count, Mort.'

'You're right. But early assumptions don't.'

Lexi rolled her eyes at the tall man with grizzled grey hair who had joined them in the small cave. Mort Barley, forensic pathologist – the man never arrived anywhere without an opinion, but he was usually right. She could hear footsteps and voices coming up behind him. The CSIs had arrived.

'We'll get out of your way,' said Lexi. She gave the cave a last sweep with the beam of the torch. 'Wait, what's that?'

Though small, the cave was irregular in shape and she'd just noticed the wall in the far corner had a slight curvature away from them. It was deep in the shadows, but when Lexi walked towards it and shone the torch directly at it, she realised the dense, dark black here was more than just shade. There was an opening where a fissure in the chalk widened to create a small gap. It looked too small to lead anywhere, but it might be a good place to hide the clothes or the candles. However, she knew better than to plough into it in a hurry. The CSIs would painstakingly check the whole area inch by inch for traces of evidence far tinier than she could spot, and they'd let her know as soon as they found anything that might be relevant.

She and Tom skirted back round the poor girl's body and out into the second of the two large cellars. Emily Jordan was just by the door, hurriedly briefing two CSIs, all of them in white suits and blue overshoes.

'Thanks for getting here so quickly,' said Lexi.

'Of course,' said Emily. 'I understand it's the body of a young woman?'

'Yes, and a baby, alive, was also found at the scene. No idea yet of the cause of death, but certain items – her clothes, candles – appear to be missing, so it needs treating as a crime scene.'

Emily nodded and looked around to check that her team was taking in these details. 'Was it her baby?' she said.

Lexi held up her hands, helpless. 'We've got no ID for the woman or the child,' she said. 'They were discovered by the head vintner here, and he says he doesn't recognise them. Perhaps you could get one of your guys to take a DNA swab from the little girl, in case we have to match it to her mother.'

Emily nodded but didn't say anything.

They were all used to dealing with dead bodies, but somehow an abandoned baby tugged on the heartstrings even more. If it was her mother lying here dead, Lexi had to hope that they'd be able to reunite the child with a loving father or at least some doting grandparents.

'Come on,' she said to Tom. 'Let's see if Will Steadman can get over himself for long enough to tell us about finding them.'

FIVE

As they came out of the building and walked down the drive in the direction of the car park, Lexi looked around for Will Steadman, but he seemed to have vanished.

When they reached the two police cars, she glanced into the back of the first. A woman PC was sitting with a baby on her lap, wrapped in a silver heat blanket similar to the one Lexi had taken at the end of the race.

She tapped gently on the window and the PC opened the door.

'PC Lacey?'

The PC nodded, stroking a lick of sweaty hair back from the little girl's forehead.

The child seemed drowsy now – after hours spent in a cold cave, it was no surprise that the warmth of the car would make her sleepy. Her cheeks were flushed and her long black lashes were clumped with tears.

'Thank you for taking care of her,' said Lexi. 'Child services should be here soon.'

'She could do with some clothes and a fresh nappy,' said PC

THE INNOCENT ANGELS
21

Lacey, crinkling her nose, and Lexi detected the smell of a soiled diaper.

'According to our information, she was found wearing a pair of wings?'

'Yes, ma'am. The elastic was cutting into her skin, so I took them off and put them in an evidence bag. They're in the boot.'

'Okay. Make sure you hand them over to the CSIs and record the chain of evidence.'

'Who are you?' It was a male voice, loud and brusque.

Lexi looked up to see a tall man, probably in his early forties, approaching up the drive. Everything about him smacked of monied ease – from his buttery suede loafers, designer jeans and logoed cotton shirt, to his deep tan and aviator-style sunglasses.

'I might ask the same of you,' said Lexi, straightening up and closing the car door. She realised she wasn't looking the part, in her tracksuit and trainers.

'You might, but this is my property and I have a right to be here.'

Heaving a tired sigh, Lexi pulled out her ID. 'DI Bennett and this is DS Olsen. Now, once more, who are you?'

His attitude changed. 'I'm Johnny Lycett-Boyd. I own Elvington.'

'And you know what's happened?'

'Not exactly. I received a message on my phone from Will Steadman, my vintner, saying something about a dead woman.'

'Where were you?'

He pointed down the hill in the direction of the sprawling farmhouse, just where the drive turned off the road. 'At home.'

'And you've only now decided to see for yourself what's going on?'

'I got up late and just checked my phone. I came straight here.'

'Right, what you need to know is that the body of a woman

has been discovered on your property, down in a cave leading off one of your cellars. There was a baby with her, who's thankfully still alive.'

Johnny Lycett-Boyd's mouth fell open but it took him a few seconds to formulate any words. 'Whose body? What baby?'

'We don't know yet.' Tom stepped forward and showed him an image on his mobile. 'Do you recognise her?'

Lycett-Boyd put out a hand to steady the phone, then gazed at the picture of the dead woman. 'No.' He shook his head and stepped back. Too quickly.

Lexi watched him carefully. A vein pulsed at the side of his forehead. A giveaway that he was nervous, possibly lying.

Why? What did he have to hide?

'Where's the baby?' he said, his eyes darting around.

Lexi wouldn't have told him, but Tom's glance at the back of the car gave it away. Lycett-Boyd peered through window. The infant was asleep in PC Lacey's arms now.

'Oh God, poor little thing.' He turned back to Lexi. 'Do you need some clothes for her? I have a daughter about the same age...'

'Thank you. That would be helpful. And a nappy.'

'I'll call my wife and ask her to bring some up. Meantime, when will I get access to my winery?'

Lexi shrugged and Lycett-Boyd grimaced. 'We're in the middle of the harvest – it's a critical time for us.'

'Mr Steadman has already made that clear.'

'The entire crop could be ruined.'

This sounded a little over-dramatic to Lexi. 'Sorry, Mr Lycett-Boyd. But a woman's dead, in suspicious circumstances. We'll give you access as soon as we're able.'

Both men seemed more interested in their ability to process the grapes than in the fact that a woman had died, and it left a sour taste in Lexi's mouth.

It took them almost a quarter of an hour to find Will Steadman, but Lexi needed to hear first-hand how he'd discovered the body. He hadn't left the vineyard, but it was a big place. Noises coming from beyond the winery led them to a large wooden barn where the crews of pickers were assembling. It became apparent that the seasonal workers either bunked down in the barn or brought their own tents and camped in the adjacent meadow.

'We'll need a list of everyone who stayed on the property last night,' said Lexi, 'and all of them will need to be interviewed. Can you call the station and get some more uniforms sent out here?' She could really have done with the rest of the team – her DCs, Ridhi Kulkarni and Colin Flynn – but it was a Sunday, and they'd already worked far too many weekends in the last month or two.

Tom nodded and started working his phone.

They finally found Steadman two fields away from the production facility. He was giving instructions to a team of pickers, which were then being translated into what sounded like an Eastern European language by their foreman. As soon as they waved him over, his phone rang and he took the call.

He turned his back on them to give himself some privacy, unwittingly allowing Lexi to inch closer to him and listen in on the call.

'No, sorry to message you on a Sunday, but we've run into a slight snag here and we've had to shut the plant down.' There was the squeak of a voice at the other end, but Lexi couldn't hear what the caller was saying. 'No, no, nothing serious. Just a technical issue with one of the presses. We should be up and running again later or tomorrow, but I just thought you might want to hold off picking for a day, as we'll have to knock back the date we'll be ready for your crop.'

Lexi stepped back. How Will Steadman ran the business didn't concern her. But he must have heard her feet crunching on the chalky ground at the edge of the vines. He whipped round, his brows low and his jaw jutting.

'I'd better go. A lot going on here. Yeah, yeah, see you next week...'

'If you're not too busy, we'd like a word now,' said Lexi, not bothering to mask the sarcasm in her voice.

Will Steadman's frown evaporated and he sighed. 'I'm sorry, but I'm firefighting here. Losing the production facility for even a day is disastrous.'

'I know. You and your boss have both made that clear. Our CSIs will work as fast as possible. Am I right that you only need the upstairs pressing and fermenting areas at this time?'

Steadman nodded.

'Tom, can you ask Emily to put a couple of guys on checking that part of the winery as quickly as possible so that Mr Steadman can get his crew back to work?'

'Sure.' Tom turned to go back to the production facility.

'And then maybe get the uniforms to show that photo of the woman's face around the picking crews to see if anybody recognises her.'

'Thank you so much. You've no idea how grateful I am,' said Steadman. He was at least a fraction more gracious than Johnny Lycett-Boyd had been.

'We try to minimise the inconvenience our work causes, but we have reason to believe it's a crime scene, so we need to be completely thorough.' She was aware that several of the pickers had stopped their work and were staring at them. 'Is there somewhere private we can go? I'd like to hear your account of how you found the body.'

'Of course. We'll use my office in the visitor centre.'

They walked back across the top of the fields in silence. Lexi took in the view, out over the vines and across the valley. It was a stunning location and she felt as if they could be somewhere in France. Then the sharp stabbing in the back of her leg brought her back to Kent with a bump. She was limping now, and it would only get worse if she didn't get some ice on it.

Will Steadman's office was a small room at the back of the squat brick building at the top end of the car park. It was cluttered and messy, but there was no mistaking his pride in his work. Award certificates adorned the walls – gold and silver medals won by Elvington wines at international shows. There was a potted philodendron on the windowsill that obviously didn't get its share of the love – its leaves were brown, and its soil had dried away from the edge of the pot.

'Coffee?' he said, pointing her to a hard wooden chair opposite his desk.

'No, I'm fine thanks.' Her thigh screamed otherwise as she gingerly lowered herself onto the seat, gritting her teeth. 'When you're ready.'

Will Steadman sat down opposite her and took a moment to compose himself. Lexi could see the shock of the discovery sweep over him as he began to recall the details – he fidgeted in his chair and his hands trembled until he clamped them together on the desk.

'It was the baby,' he said. 'I heard it crying.' He looked as startled as if he'd just heard it.

'Where were you?' said Lexi.

'I was checking that everything was ready for this morning's pressing. We don't have time for slip-ups or delays.' He blinked, realising the irony of what he'd just said.

Lexi got it – finding a dead body was a monumental delay in terms of getting the harvest in and processed.

'So you were checking the equipment?'

'Everything seemed fine, but I kept hearing crying. At first I thought maybe a fox or a cat had got into the building. I went into the cellars and it was louder. And I realised then that it was

human.' He suddenly sped up. 'The sound led me to the body.
As soon as I saw there was a dead woman there, I picked her up
– the baby, that is – and came outside to call the police.'

'You'd never seen this woman or the baby before? You've got
no idea who they are or how they came to be in the cave?'

'No. I'd like to help you, but I have no idea.'

'And, apart from bringing the baby out, you didn't touch
anything or take anything from the cave?'

Steadman shook his head.

'Was the building locked when you came here this
morning?'

He nodded. 'Yes. It's always locked overnight – there's a lot
of valuable wine in there. I locked up myself last night, just
after midnight.'

'You were working that late?'

'Yes, the whole pressing team worked late. We need to
crush the grapes quickly before mould can take hold.'

'Who else, besides yourself, can access the building?'

'Johnny and his wife, Marietta, have keys, of course. But no
one else.'

'Any sign of a break-in?'

'No.'

That cut down the number of suspects to three.

'Thank you. One of my officers will accompany you to the
station later today or tomorrow to make a formal statement.'

'What? I've been through what happened twice already. I
can't leave the vineyard in the middle of the harvest.'

Lexi frowned at him and stood up. 'I'm afraid you don't
have a choice, Mr Steadman.'

It was time to go and check in with Mort and Emily.

SIX

Back where the two police cars were parked, there was now a fast-response paramedic vehicle pulled up. A man in green scrubs and a hi-vis vest was just slinging his bag into the boot.

Lexi flashed her ID at him. 'You've checked over the infant?'

The man nodded. 'She's dehydrated and suffering from cold. I've left instructions for warming her and rehydrating. She should see a doctor later for a further check.'

'Thanks.'

The man got into his vehicle, and Lexi walked up to the car where PC Lacey was looking after the baby. Johnny Lycett-Boyd was still there, and had been joined by a petite, dark-haired woman, similarly dressed in jeans and a pale blue cotton shirt with the vineyard logo on it. Her face was sharp and intelligent, her dark eyes assessing Lexi as she limped up the drive towards them. Lexi could guess what she was thinking – she was all too aware of her messy hair and, close to, she probably smelled of stale sweat from her run.

But she reminded herself that it didn't matter. She was here to do her job, and that meant finding out how a young woman had died in the cave beyond the vineyard cellars.

As she got closer, she could see PC Lacey, still sitting in the rear passenger seat, but with her legs outside the car. The child in her arms was awake and now dressed in a pair of brown dungarees and a red T-shirt. She didn't exactly look happy, but at least she wasn't crying.

'I think she must be hungry,' said the woman. She had a strong French accent. 'I could fetch some formula.'

PC Lacey looked at her blankly. She was young and maybe had no experience with babies.

'Thank you, I think that's a good idea,' said Lexi.

The woman gave her a quizzical look.

'I'm DI Bennett,' she said. 'And you are?'

'Marietta Lycett-Boyd—'

'My wife.' Johnny Lycett-Boyd's voice cut across whatever his wife had been going to say, and she gave him a look which left Lexi in no doubt of what she thought of his interruption. But he ploughed on regardless. 'Marietta, can you get some food for the baby? And some water?'

He got another filthy look for his troubles.

'Boss.'

Lexi went towards Tom and was irritated when Johnny and Marietta both trailed behind her. She slipped under the outer cordon of police tape and turned back to them.

'Can I remind you not to cross this barrier. We'll let you know as soon as you can regain access to the plant.'

Marietta turned immediately and walked away, but her husband started to speak.

Lexi raised a hand. 'No. My team are doing their job and you'll just have to wait.'

She turned back to Tom and ushered him back inside the metal structure. She didn't need Johnny Lycett-Boyd trying to listen in. As the door swung shut behind them, she heard the voices of the husband and wife outside getting louder. It sounded as if they were arguing about something.

'Not happy campers,' she said.

'Can't blame 'em,' said Tom. 'Time is money in an operation like this.'

Lexi headed down towards the cave. She found Mort Barley standing in the narrow space at the entrance, dictating into his phone.

'Bring me up to speed,' said Lexi.

He looked up. 'She's in early rigor and, assuming she died in situ, at a constant temperature of ten degrees, that would put the time of death at between one and two in the morning.'

'And did she die in situ?' Lexi felt sure Mort would have an opinion.

'It seems likely, given the lividity on the back of her body. If she didn't die in the cave, she was moved there very soon afterwards – I'm not saying it didn't happen, but moving a dead body is a lot more complicated than moving a living one. What do you make of it, Emily? Died there or moved?'

Emily Jordan had just appeared at the doorway into the cave.

She shrugged. 'I haven't seen anything to make me think she was moved after death. Her feet are quite clean, so I think she came here wearing shoes. Especially if they gained access through the caves. If she'd come through there with bare feet, it would have shown.'

'Sorry?' said Lexi. 'Through the caves?'

'Yes – there's a narrow tunnel from the back of that cave, leading into another even smaller one.'

'Where does it go?'

'We haven't fully investigated yet – processing the immediate scene is more important at this stage.'

That was fair enough. 'Any sign of her clothes yet? Or the baby's?'

'Nothing so far.'

Lexi's leg was throbbing and she felt dehydrated.

'Ready to take the body, Mort?'

'Yes.'

'Okay. I'll leave you to it.' She hobbled along the narrow space between the last row of wine crates and the wall, Tom speeding ahead of her.

'I want to talk to Lycett-Boyd right now,' she said, as they made their way back through the cellars. 'He must know where that tunnel leads – it's his property.'

While Tom went to find him, Lexi went back to his Jeep in search of water and paracetamol. She was going to pay for this later, that much was certain.

Half an hour later, the body had been removed, though Emily's team were still at work collecting trace evidence from the floor of the small cave where they believed the woman had died, and from the two cellars.

Lycett-Boyd's temper had flared again when he realised that Lexi hadn't sought him out to tell him he could get his team working again, but instead was demanding to know where the tunnel led. The CSIs had gone a little way along it to look for the clothes the woman and the baby must have been wearing, but Emily had drawn the line at a full exploration for safety reasons.

'Honestly, I have no idea,' he said. 'Caving's not my thing. We occasionally store barrels in those two chambers, and they're too big to be taken out through that crevice, so I've never really worried about it.'

Lexi had to wonder at his lack of curiosity.

'Do you think the woman and child could have come into the cellars via the tunnel?'

Lycett-Boyd threw up his hands. 'I don't have an opinion on the matter. Your job is to work out what happened. Mine is to get my bloody harvest in, which you busies are preventing me from doing.'

How could the man be so unbelievably callous given what had happened here? Was there a chance that he actually had something to do with it?

They were standing outside the winery door. Lexi went over to the CSI van and helped herself to a fresh crime scene suit.

'What are you doing?' said Tom.

'I'm going to find out where that tunnel goes.'

He shook his head. 'No way – it could be dangerous. What if you get stuck?'

'Then you'll have to pull me out, won't you?'

Tom let out an exasperated sigh, but Lexi was higher ranking so there was nothing he could do. She pulled blue over-shoes over her trainers and tucked her hair inside the hood of the suit. She didn't want to leave trace evidence in what might possibly be a significant part of the crime scene. Because if there was a way in through the tunnel, it meant they'd have to cast a far wider net than just those who had keys and access to the winery.

'I'll go as far as I can along the tunnel. You two—' she pointed at Tom and Johnny Lycett-Boyd '—walk out in the direction the tunnel takes and see if you can find an exit point. Listen for me shouting.'

Lycett-Boyd rolled his eyes at first, but then obviously thought better of it. 'As far as I can recall, the tunnel initially heads east, underneath the far end of the plant.' He pointed out to one of the vineyards. 'But I have no idea how far it goes or if it changes direction.'

'We'll find out,' said Lexi.

She went back through the fermentation hall and down the

stairs into the cellars. The CSIs were taking scrapings from the floor and close-up photos of the wall by the cave entrance. Emily was inside the cave, supervising the wrapping of the feather wings to ensure that they didn't lose any fibres or other evidence that might be clinging to them.

'What do you make of it?' said Lexi, watching them work for a moment.

'Mort's initial feeling is an overdose, so you'll have to wait for the tox results.'

This didn't surprise Lexi – she hadn't seen external injuries on the body. 'Any sign of an additional person or people in here?'

'The temperature of the residual wax on the floor suggests that the candles were burned here last night, but there's no sign of the candle stubs. We've picked up some hair and fibres in the dust, but they might pre-date last night – and we don't have anything to match them against at this stage.' She looked at Lexi's CSI suit. 'What's going on?'

'The tunnel,' said Lexi by way of explanation.

'Really? Shouldn't you get a specialist in?'

She had a point, but that would take time and Lexi needed to know now.

'I won't take any risks, no squeezing through tight gaps. If it's too narrow for me, then it's unlikely someone could have brought a woman with a baby through.'

She slipped past the CSIs in the first cave, then shone her flashlight around the smaller second cave. There didn't seem to be any candle wax on the floor in here and the chalk surface didn't show any footprints, even though the CSIs had been through here to check for the woman's clothes.

She shone her light into the dark maw of the tunnel. With a deep breath that was as much about trepidation as the need for oxygen, she bent her head low enough to scramble into the gap. It was about four feet from the floor to the highest point of the fissure, beyond which it became just a narrow crack in the chalk above her. The ground beneath her feet was uneven, undulating up and down, and occasionally strewn with chunks of broken chalk which made her stumble or patches of gravel where her feet would skid and slide.

The stone was a soft grey rather than bright white, but the light bounced off the surfaces, illuminating a low passage that curved away to the left. For the first twenty metres or so, it sloped downwards, gently twisting as it became wider, then narrower by turn. It was dry underfoot, and the air was dusty, while the smell of the chalk took her back to the classroom.

It wouldn't have been easy carrying a baby through here, but perhaps if it was in a sling it might be manageable. However, she didn't think someone could carry or drag a dead or unconscious person along the tunnel, which suggested that if this had been the means of entry, the woman must have been alive and conscious when she came down here.

But did she come down here willingly? If that was the case, perhaps she knew the person with her. Or at the very least trusted them enough to come here, bringing her baby.

She scrabbled on and the tunnel opened out, making the going easier. It was hard to judge how far she'd come – progress was slow and she was limping – but about fifteen minutes after leaving the cave, she thought she could see a glimmer of light from somewhere above and ahead of her. She turned off the torch for a couple of seconds, and indeed, there was daylight in the distance.

As she turned the light back on, a flash of pink on the floor of the tunnel caught her eye. She moved forward, then squatted down to see what it was.

A baby's dummy.

She unzipped her crime scene suit enough to allow her to reach into one of her pockets for a clear evidence bag. She'd grabbed a couple when she'd suited up, just in case. She put her hand inside the bag and used it to pick up the dummy. If traces of saliva on the dummy matched the baby, they could be almost certain this was the way the woman and child had come into the cave. Which would mean it wasn't about who'd had a key but who had known about the existence of the tunnel.

She tucked the bag away and turned back towards where she'd seen the glimpse of daylight. As she got closer to it, the floor of the tunnel inclined steeply, and her feet slipped on the gravelly surface. She needed to use her hands to scrabble up the slope, so she turned off the flashlight and shoved it into the back waistband of her tracksuit bottoms.

'Hello?' she called, wondering if Tom and Johnny Lycett-Boyd had identified the tunnel's entrance from the outside.

There was no answer – just a slight echo of her own voice.

As she clambered uphill, the pain in the back of her thigh intensified and, without warning, her leg gave way underneath her. She gave a sharp cry as she slipped over backwards. Her back scraped on the pebbles and stones underneath her, as the torch flew out from her waistband and clattered to the base of the tunnel.

'Lexi, is that you?' Tom's voice came from above.

'I'm fine. I just slipped.'

She dug deep into the last reserves of energy that hadn't already been used in the morning's half marathon, reminding herself that she really needed to eat something once she was out of here.

The sliver of daylight from above was enough for her to locate the torch, and on her second attempt up the slope she made it to the top. There was an opening in the rocks that appeared to be masked by brambles.

'Tom? Are you there?'

'Where are you?'

'Can you see brambles?'

'Masses.'

She switched on the torch and waved it about above her head, hoping they would see it, or at least the light from it playing on the branches. 'I'm here.'

'Got you,' said Johnny Lycett-Boyd, somewhere close by.

He started pulling brambles out of the way.

'Wait!' said Lexi sharply. 'Does it look like anyone's been through here recently? Are there any broken or trodden down stems? Tom, take some photos.'

She waited a few minutes and then Tom pulled aside some of the tangle and gave her a hand to climb out. They picked their way carefully out of the bramble patch, the same way Tom had approached, to try to disturb as little of the surrounding area as possible.

'Hard to say. A couple of broken stems, but not much,' said Tom.

'There's a bramble pulled up here,' said Lycett-Boyd, pointing to one side of the entrance. 'Looks quite fresh.'

Which suggested someone knew there was a way in and out of the cellars via the tunnel, and the dummy strongly suggested that the baby had been brought in that way. But it wasn't something she was going express out loud while the owner was still with them. He had to be considered a suspect until they had proof otherwise.

However, there hadn't been any sign of the woman's or the baby's clothing in the tunnel. If they'd come into the caves that way, presumably there would be chalk dust and vegetation clinging to them – something Emily could analyse once the garments were found.

She looked around. They were at the top of the south-facing slope on which all Elvington's vines were planted, just on the northern edge of one of the largest fields. Rows of heavily laden vines stretched away down the hill, and she could see the village of Elvington in the bottom of the valley and the rolling Kent countryside beyond. But she wasn't here to appreciate the view, and a sharp tug in her hamstring acted as a reminder that she needed to get on with the job.

'We need to treat this area as a potential crime scene.' She pulled her phone out. 'Emily, I'm up in the field above the winery, on the north edge, where the tunnel from the caves emerges. Can you send a team up here to process the area, and also have some of your guys check the tunnel for evidence?' She would fill Emily in on the dummy later, once Johnny Lycett-Boyd was out of the way.

'Of course, we'll get right onto it.'

'I'm sorry – it's adding a lot more work – but we can't ignore the possibility that the woman, the baby and whoever was with them used it as a way of getting into the cave.'

They walked back towards the winery, and Lexi breathed a sigh of relief when Lycett-Boyd peeled away from them.

'What are your thoughts, boss?' said Tom, once the vineyard owner was well out of earshot.

Lexi didn't speak for a moment as she put things in order in her mind. There was a lot to process.

Tom slowed down, waiting for her.

'We've got a dead woman and a living child in what must be considered a secret location.' She pulled the evidence bag out of her pocket to show Tom the dummy. 'I found this in the tunnel, which suggests that was how the woman and the child got in. What we need to find out is who knows about those caves? Did the woman know about them herself or was it whoever took away the candles and the clothing? We know that Steadman and Lycett-Boyd know of their existence. Presumably other employees of the vineyard do too.'

'Both current and past,' said Tom.

'Good point,' said Lexi. They were nearly at the car park. 'One other thing, I got the distinct impression that Lycett-Boyd was lying when he said he didn't know who the body was. A complete change in his demeanour.'

'You think he's involved?'

'We've got to be open-minded to that possibility. Steadman, too. Anyway, we've done what we can here. Emily's got everything under control, and we'll have to wait for whatever the evidence tells us. Let's get back to the office.'

Like all cases, the first few hours were about evidence collection. Lexi needed to start putting that evidence together to find an emerging story. Who was the woman? How had she died? Whose was the baby? Where were their clothes? Who had they been with? Lycett-Boyd? Or Steadman? Or some person unknown?

The answers were out there, waiting to be found. And find them she would.

SEVEN

Yesterday's achievements

1. Washed car
2. Paid credit card bills
3. Killed B. All went according to plan – couldn't have worked out better. After so many dry runs and practices, I knew what I was doing
4. Updated X

Learning outcomes

1. Chalk dust shows up even on a pale-coloured car, and obviously on tyres
2. Using alcohol to relax B first was a good idea. Made her co-operative and compliant
3. Wonder about getting a dummy for the baby, maybe dipped in some kind of sedative to keep it quiet for duration...

Plans for today

1. Watch out for news coverage when they discover the body
2. Monitor the police investigation
3. Lay plans for my next angel

How are you feeling – in three words?

1. Happy
2. Proud
3. Fulfilled

Memory of the day

My most precious memories are of my mum – and they're precious because there are so few of them. I close my eyes and I remember a room, a kitchen with white walls and buttercup-yellow cupboards. I'm in a high chair, banging a toy on the rim of its table. Mum brings me a strawberry to distract me. The juice dribbles down my chin. I can smell the scent of the fruit, and when she bends over me, a curtain of dark hair brushing across my face, another smell, Mum's smell, of apples and lavender. I suppose now it was the scent of her shampoo, but for me then, it was just the smell of her. B's long hair reminded me of her. And the crying baby – that could have been me.

I remember Mum's voice saying my name. No one's ever said it like that since.

Motivation for the day
Opportunities don't happen – you create them

EIGHT

The incident room was deserted. No surprise – it was Sunday afternoon, after all, with no major case ongoing. Apart from the fact that now there was. While Tom made coffee, Lexi cleared the whiteboard of the detritus of past endeavours. She put all the documents and photos she detached into a pile on Ridhi's desk. It made her feel a little guilty and she would rather have dumped the thankless task on Colin, but she knew Ridhi would be conscientious about making sure everything went into the right file.

She rubbed the back of her leg – the pain seemed to be getting worse – as she contemplated what she had so far written.

Victim A

Baby A

'I'll download and print out the pictures I took,' said Tom, handing her a steaming mug.

'Got any biscuits?' Tom usually had either Hobnobs or

digestives in his desk drawer, and Lexi's blood sugar had hit rock bottom.

'Sure, I'll find some.'

While Tom went to search his desk, Lexi added what they knew so far under each of the two headings. There was precious little to write – where they'd been found, and what they'd been wearing, white feather wings. One dead, one alive and no visible injuries to either. Then she planted herself at Ridhi's desk and called Mort to check that he'd got the body back to the morgue in Maidstone.

'Of course.' He sounded affronted that she'd felt the need to ring.

'When will you do the autopsy?'

'In the morning. She's not going anywhere.'

Lexi sighed. He was right, but somewhere her family or partner or friends must be wondering where she was. Getting an ID on the body was critical – not only for her loved ones, but also because the investigation would flounder while they didn't know who they were looking at.

'Mispers, Tom?' she said, taking a biscuit from the package he offered her.

'On it.'

If someone had reported a mother and baby missing, surely it would be flagged up as urgent.

She had Chief Superintendent Maggie Dawson's number on speed dial. Her immediate superior wouldn't be working today, but Lexi knew she'd want to be kept in the loop.

'Hi, Lexi, what can I do for you?' Background noises suggested Maggie was in a pub or a restaurant – Sunday lunch with the family perhaps.

'Sorry to bother you on a Sunday, but you should know we've got a new case.'

'Give me a sec.' The line went silent for a few seconds. Then she was back, without the background noise. 'Fill me in.'

Lexi gave her the details as succinctly as possible.

'Next steps?' Straight to the point, as always.

'Mort's doing the autopsy first thing tomorrow. Emily's processing the scene. The team will interview everyone who was on the vineyard over the weekend – they're harvesting, so they've got a large contingent of seasonal workers on site.'

'If it was one of them, presumably they would have scarpered by now.'

'If someone's missing, we'll follow up on it, obviously. But it would be like an admission of guilt. Whoever did it might be hiding in plain sight.'

'Or they might not be connected with the vineyard at all?'

'They had to have knowledge of the caves. We think the woman and child entered via a hidden tunnel.'

'No possibility it's suicide or accidental?'

'Suicide, no. Who would kill themselves in front of their baby, assuming the little girl was actually hers? And their clothes are missing. Someone else was there, I'm certain of it.'

'Covering their tracks after an accidental death?'

'Then we still need to find them...' Tom was waving at her from across the room. 'I should go – I think Tom has something for me.'

'Okay. Keep me posted. By the way, how did the marathon go?'

'Don't ask.' As she finished the call, she went over to Tom's desk. 'What is it?'

'Missing persons report. Bethany Glover, twenty-three, and her daughter Scarlett Norris, fourteen months. Reported missing from their home in Elvington at midday today by her partner Liam Norris.'

Lexi's hand flew to her mouth. 'Oh no – we already knew about the body by the time he reported her missing. Have you got a picture?' It was unlikely to be anyone else, given the time-frame and the location, but she wanted visual confirmation.

Tom pointed to his screen and Lexi saw the blown-up image of a young woman with long, dark hair, holding a baby in her arms and smiling at whoever was taking the picture. They were standing on a beach in bright sunshine, the sky a deep azure, and she looked like she didn't have a care in the world. It was without doubt the woman whose body they'd found. The baby, however, was younger – about six months, maybe – so Lexi couldn't be sure. But then what were the chances of it being a different baby?

'Come on. We'd better go and break the news. I'll call for an FLO.' A family liaison officer, who'd have the unenviable task of picking up the pieces after Tom and Lexi left.

The village of Elvington wasn't one of Kent's prettiest. The approach to it was marred by an estate of 1950s redbrick semis crowded with more cars than there was space for. The main street had an air of abandonment, with only a Chinese take-away, a run-down hairdressers and a mini-supermarket. No village green, no church as the focal point of the community, no twee gift shops or tea rooms.

Tom took a left off the main street. They drove past more semis, this time built in the 1930s and pebble-dashed, and then on the eastern edge of the village, came to a couple of streets of boxy little 1980s houses. There was a dour-looking Pentecostal church that had bars on the windows – to stop people breaking in or the congregation from getting out? Lexi felt depressed on behalf of the inhabitants. The place seemed to have no soul. In its favour, however, it would at least be more affordable – a place for young, local families rather than retired bankers.

They passed a modern primary school, which bore out this thought, then Tom drew up in front of a shabby 1970s bungalow.

'This is it, I think.'

It had a garden in front, gravelled over at some point, but now grass and weeds were reclaiming their territory. There was a black wheelie bin, and next to it a pile of flattened cardboard boxes covered in brand names of nappies and powdered milk.

Tom stepped forward to ring the doorbell, and they waited in silence. Lexi hated the moment before having to break the news that a loved one was dead. Once the information was imparted, for her the hard part was over, though it would only be the beginning for the family of the victim. She would get on with the investigation while they mourned. But this moment in time always felt like standing on the edge of a precipice, heart in mouth, ready to jump.

The door opened. Narrow eyes assessed them from a puffy face. The man was in his early-thirties and already losing the flush of youth. A stained T-shirt struggled to hide a nascent beer belly. A drinker. But his haircut was sharp, and recent – a number one up the sides and back, much longer and swept back on top.

'Yeah?'

'I'm DI Bennett, Kent Police.' Still in the tracksuit, still unshowered – he surely had the right to judge her just as she had judged him. 'This is DS Olsen. Are you Liam Norris?'

'Yeah.'

'You filed a missing persons report earlier today?'

Liam Norris blinked. 'Have you found them? Where are they?'

'Can we come in?'

He rubbed his hand across his eyes, then pulled the door wider. It led straight into an untidy living room with an open-plan kitchen at the far end. There was a baby buggy folded against one wall and a high chair pulled up to the kitchen table. The living area was carpeted, the floor littered with bright plastic toys. By the window, which overlooked a scrubby back garden, a drying rack was hung with baby clothes. The smell of stale cigarette smoke hung on the air and there were empty beer bottles on the kitchen table.

Norris didn't invite them to sit down – the sofa and armchair were strewn with clothes and toys. He stood in the centre of the room, looking at them expectantly, his arms folded across his chest, slightly rocking forward on the balls of his feet.

'So tell me. Why are you here?'

Lexi took a breath to steady herself.

'I'm afraid, Mr Norris, that a woman's body was found this morning at Elvington Vineyard and we have reason to think it might be Bethany.'

'What reason? What about Scarlett?' Panic raised the timbre of his voice.

'Scarlett is okay. She was with her mother, but doesn't appear to have come to any harm. However, we will need you to formally confirm that it is Scarlett.'

Norris staggered sideways and crashed down into the armchair.

'You sure the body is Bethany?'

'Yes,' said Tom. 'Was there any reason that Bethany might have been up at the vineyard last night?'

Norris didn't answer. His world had imploded, leaving him blank-faced and confused.

Lexi went to the kitchen sink, quickly rinsed the dregs of beer out of a glass and filled it with water. She brought it to him, but he waved her away.

'Fuck that.' He got up and went past her to the kitchen, where he retrieved a close-to-empty bottle of whisky from one of the cupboards. He took a swig straight from the bottle and then looked from one to the other of them. 'Where's Scarlett? If she's okay, why didn't you bring her home?' The bottle in his hand shook.

'She's being looked after,' said Lexi. 'Someone from the child protection team has taken her to Canterbury.'

'Child protection?' He slammed the bottle down on the kitchen table. It rocked momentarily but didn't fall. 'Ah, I know what this is. Go on then. If you're going to do it, get on with it.'

'Get on with what?' said Lexi, keeping her tone neutral.

'You lot are all the same. Anything happens to a woman, and you always accuse the man. You've come here to arrest me, isn't that it?'

She noticed that he hadn't asked how Bethany had died. He was assuming she'd been murdered. Or maybe he knew.

'Should we be arresting you?' she said.

'I've done nothing wrong. I want my daughter back.'

'Social services are just checking that she's all right. Then they'll talk to you about her return.'

'Talk to me? What do you mean? I'm her dad. She should be with me.'

'Do you work at the moment, Liam? Would you be able to look after her?'

'That's my business.'

'That's exactly what the care team will ask you.'

'You can't take my kid away just because something's happened to Bethany.' Reminded of her death, he started to cry. 'She was such a good mum to Scarlett... She was my angel.' He put his hands over his face, unable to control his sobbing.

Tom gave Lexi a questioning glance.

His angel? Neither of them missed the significance.

Lexi stood up. 'I think the best thing is for you to come back to Canterbury with us. You can make a formal statement about when Bethany and Scarlett went missing, you can see Scarlett and talk to social services about the best way to proceed.'

Lexi knew she was kicking the can down the road, but it really would be social services' decision as to whether or not

Scarlett would be released into his custody. And he had to at least be considered a party of interest in Bethany's death.

He was right about one thing, though. They did always look at the husband or boyfriend first. Because when a woman was murdered, six times out of ten the killer was either her current or ex-partner.

NINE

Lexi felt bad as they drove back to Canterbury. Liam Norris cried noisily in the back of the Jeep the whole way, and she was torn between viewing him as a suspect or a bereaved partner. Currently he was both and, if she found he had any culpability in Bethany's death, she'd make sure they threw the book at him. But if it turned out he was innocent as he claimed, then this was a shoddy way to treat him at his moment of loss.

As they accompanied him across the car park and into the station, Tom gave Lexi a long sideways glance.

'You should go home, boss. Have a hot a bath and get a meal inside you. It's been a long day.'

His intention was sweet, but he was way off the mark.

'I'll think about resting when there's nothing more we can do today.'

Tom shook his head, but didn't argue with her. Instead, he took Liam Norris by the elbow and guided him through the double doors at the back of the station.

Lexi had called ahead and made sure that Linda Ellis, who'd been sent by the child services team to take charge of Scarlett, would be there to talk to Norris.

'No problem,' she'd said. 'I've arranged for her to stay with temporary foster carers, but if Liam Norris is her father, he'll be able to take her home.'

With Liam sitting behind her at the time of the call, Lexi couldn't go into details about his status as a possible suspect in Bethany's possible murder. She would need to bring that up once they were back at the office and Liam was out of earshot.

Inside the station, a further set of double doors led through to the ground-floor reception area, while corridors leading off to the left and right led to offices and interview rooms. Lexi's intention was to plant Liam in an interview room so she could find Linda Ellis and discuss the situation. However, as they came in, she could see Linda through the glass panels of the reception area doors. She was holding Scarlett, and when she saw them, she waved at Lexi.

'Wait here,' Lexi said to Tom.

She opened the door a crack, and stuck her head through. 'I've got Norris here, but I'd like to talk to you for a minute first.'

Linda Ellis's eyes widened and she swiped them to one side. Lexi followed her glance and saw Johnny Lycett-Boyd standing a few feet away.

'We've got a situation,' she said in a low voice.

Johnny Lycett-Boyd glared at her and then at Lexi in turn.

'Scarlett, darlin'.' Liam Norris pushed Lexi out of the way and barged into the reception with his arms wide. 'Dada's here now.'

'Dada,' cried the little girl, struggling in Linda's arms.

'Hold it a minute,' said Lexi, grabbing Liam by the upper arm.

'Get off,' said Liam. 'Give me my daughter.'

Johnny Lycett-Boyd coughed loudly. 'She's not.'

'She's not what?' said Liam.

'Your daughter. She's my daughter, and as Bethany's dead, I'm going to claim custody.'

'What the actual...?' Liam lurched forward, unsteady on his feet, and Linda took an instinctive step back from him. 'You're talking bollocks.'

'You know it's the truth,' said Johnny. His words were clipped and his cheeks flushed with anger.

Lexi stepped into the middle of the space, Tom at her shoulder. 'Quiet! Everyone be quiet.' She turned to Lycett-Boyd. 'When I showed you a picture of Bethany Glover's body, you claimed that you didn't know who she was. Now you're saying you're the father of her child?'

'He's lying.'

Lexi spun round to face Liam. 'Please don't interrupt.'

Liam Norris lunged towards Linda Ellis. 'Come on, Scarlett. Dada's gonna take you home now.'

Linda Ellis sidestepped him and Tom quickly blocked Norris's way.

'Who's named as the father on the birth certificate?' said Lexi.

'I am,' said Norris.

'Not so,' said Johnny. 'I've seen it. Bethany left the father's name blank.'

'So she didn't name you as the father?' said Lexi.

'I asked her not to. I didn't want Marietta to find out.'

'You had an affair with Bethany? Was it still ongoing when she died?'

'You bastard.' It appeared all of this was news to Liam. 'She would never have looked at anyone else. She loved me and she loved Scarlett. You're lying.'

Before Lexi could do anything to prevent it, he swung his arm back to launch a punch. His fist connected with the side of Johnny's jaw with a sickening thwack. Johnny stumbled sideways with a grunt, his hand going to his cheek. Then, as he regained his balance, he slapped Norris's face with the flat of his hand, accompanied by a loud string of expletives.

Tom threw himself in front of Linda Ellis to shield Scarlett with his body, and Lexi put herself in front of Lycett-Boyd to stop him hitting Norris again. She got a cuff on the ears for her trouble, but realising he was about to hit her rather than his intended target, Lycett-Boyd had at least tried to slow down his momentum and pull away.

Lexi needed to assert her authority. 'Stop now!' she bellowed.

There was silence, apart from the sound of the two men panting.

Lycett-Boyd was the first to speak, hissing through gritted teeth. 'I'll press charges against you and you'll never see Scarlett again.'

Norris's face reddened and if Tom hadn't caught hold of one of his arms, he would have launched another attack.

'It was you, wasn't it? You killed her. I'll get you for this.' The venom in Norris's voice made clear his murderous intentions.

'Tom, would you take Mr Norris to one of the interview rooms? Linda, I think you'd better place Scarlett in temporary care until it can be established who should get custody of her.'

'Absolutely,' said Linda.

'No bloody way,' said Norris. 'She's my kid and Bethany was my girlfriend.'

'She really isn't your daughter.'

Linda shot Johnny Lycett-Boyd a filthy look. 'I'm afraid in cases like this, paternity needs to be established by DNA test – and even then, it doesn't guarantee a right to custody.'

'I think you'll find it does,' said Lycett-Boyd, still rubbing his jaw, 'given that her mother's dead. Give me your card – you'll be hearing from my solicitor in the morning.'

Linda Ellis shifted Scarlett in her arms and stuck a hand into one of her pockets. The little girl was crying now as she watched her father disappear through the double doors. Linda thrust a card towards Lycett-Boyd and he snatched it rudely.

'Believe me,' he said, turning towards Lexi. 'Scarlett is mine. I've been paying for her upkeep since she was born and I'm not prepared to leave her in the hands of that thug.'

'It won't be my decision, Mr Lycett-Boyd,' she replied, and never had she been more thankful of anything.

'You know Norris did it, don't you?'

'Did what?'

'Killed Bethany, of course. The man's a drunk. He hit her more than once. I'd lay good money on it that he's responsible for her death.'

Lexi took a breath. She'd had enough of alpha males tossing punches and accusations at each other. 'Thank you for your opinion – I'll take it into consideration.' Then she turned on her heel and left.

Johnny Lycett-Boyd snorted with annoyance behind her, but she'd deal with him later.

TEN

Tom was leaning against the wall outside Interview Room One. He watched as she limped down the corridor towards him.

'You need to get that leg looked at. It's not going to go away just because you ignore it.'

'Thanks for your opinion, Dr Olsen.' She knew she was being tetchy, but the pain was a distraction. She raised an eyebrow and nodded towards the door. 'He okay?'

'Not really.'

No surprise there, then. 'That was enlightening. Wonder how Marietta Lycett-Boyd feels about her husband having a child with another woman.'

'Wonder if she even knows yet,' said Tom. 'I guess that's why he pretended not to recognise Bethany.'

'He literally panicked when he saw the picture. But now he wants his baby. If she actually is his.'

'Maybe she isn't. Maybe Bethany was shaking him down for money, even though it's Norris's child. Or possibly someone else's.'

'That would be a complication we don't need,' said Lexi.

'Lycett-Boyd gone home?'

'I hope so. Once the autopsy's done, we might know the cause of Bethany's death, and perhaps whether it was intentional or accidental. Then we can dig into where Liam and Johnny were at the relevant time and whether one of them might be implicated.'

'What about now?' said Tom, cocking his towards the interview room.

'Let's take a statement on when he last saw them and when he reported them missing. Then tomorrow we can see how that compares with whatever he comes up with as an alibi for the time of death.'

Norris was all over the place when they went into the interview room. Crying, railing angrily against Johnny Lycett-Boyd and demanding to see his daughter. They waited patiently until he ran out of steam and sat staring at them with wet, glassy eyes.

Lexi waited a few more seconds, rather than jumping straight in. When she judged that his breathing had slowed down enough to show that he was calm, she pressed play on the recording equipment and spoke.

'DI Lexi Bennett.'

'DS Tom Olsen,' said Tom.

'Please state your name,' said Lexi to Liam, 'so we have a record of your presence.'

Norris frowned. 'I should have a lawyer here. I got a right to a lawyer, yeah?'

This was going to be hard work. 'Of course, you always do. But this is just a witness statement. You're not a suspect at this time.'

'Then why're you recording it?'

'Because that makes more sense than having DS Olsen writing it down as you speak. It's in your interest. We won't be able to twist your words if it's recorded.'

Norris seemed to see the sense in this and gave a small nod, but he still looked far from happy. 'Liam Norris.'

'Liam, can you tell me when you last saw Bethany and Scarlett.'

'Yesterday evening, about five o'clock.'

'Where were you then?'

'At home. Bethany was giving Scarlett her tea. I left to go the pub.'

'Which pub?'

'The Stag...' He paused. 'No, wait – it was the Crown in Eythorne.'

'You're sure?'

'It was the Crown.'

They would check there to verify what he said.

'When did you return home?'

''Bout eleven.'

'But you didn't see Bethany and Scarlett then?'

'Bethany had already gone to bed. I didn't want to get an earful for waking her up. I fell asleep on the sofa.'

'So you assumed they were both upstairs, but you didn't go and check?'

'I had no reason to think they weren't there. I just went to sleep.' He was twisting his hands together on the table in front of him, and he couldn't meet Lexi's eye. Because he was lying or because he felt guilty over not checking up on them?

'What happened in the morning?'

'I woke up late, still on the sofa. The house was quiet. It seemed too late for them to still be in bed. Scarlett wakes early.'

'What time was it?'

'When I checked, a bit later, it was almost eleven.'

'Did you look for them?'

'I went upstairs to use the toilet, and I looked in our room. Bethany wasn't there. I thought she must have gone out some-where, and taken Scarlett with her.'

'Where did you think they might have gone?'

Norris gave a feeble shrug. 'Possibly over to her best friend's.'

'So you weren't worried?'

'I was worried, because I thought she might be pissed off with me for coming home drunk. I tried to call her mobile, but it just rang inside the house.'

'Did that worry you, that she'd gone out without her mobile?'

'It seemed odd. I called her friend, Karolyn. She hadn't heard from her. I couldn't think where else she would go, so then I called her in missing. It wasn't like her to have gone off without telling me where.'

'No other friends she might be with?'

Norris shrugged again, then shook his head. 'Not really.'

Tom gave Lexi a glance that spoke volumes. She assumed he was thinking the same as she was. It seemed a bit early to report your partner and child missing just because they weren't in the house when you woke up.

Unless you knew something had happened to them.

However, with nothing concrete to suggest he was involved, they had to let him go.

ELEVEN

MONDAY

Lexi's leg was on fire, and the pain became even worse when she tried to curl up into a ball. With a groan, she rolled onto her stomach and pressed a hand against the back of her thigh. It felt hot and swollen.

Damn!

She'd applied ice to it before going to bed the night before, but it didn't seem to have helped. Tom had been right. She was going to need to get this looked at, but it would have to wait. She had a dead woman and a contested baby on her hands, and they were more important. As she limped to the bathroom, she wondered how little Scarlett's first night without her mother had been. Taken by a strange person to a strange house. Not allowed to go home with her 'dada'. Everything would be different – the food, her cot, the clothes she'd been put in, meal-time and bedtime routines. She wouldn't even have the comfort of her favourite teddy or blanket. She made a mental note to check with Linda Ellis that she could go and pick up some familiar items for the poor little thing.

After a shower that ended with an icy blast, she tried a couple of stretches, but it felt like she was adding insult to injury and her leg protested with a sharp stab of pain. She gave up and got dressed.

Driving was torture, but instead of heading into Canterbury, fifteen minutes away, she turned out of the village in the direction of the M20 and headed northwest to Maidstone. She wanted to be there for Bethany Glover's autopsy, because it was still unclear if she was dealing with murder, manslaughter or an accidental death. Not that Mort would necessarily have the answers on the spot, but she always felt that showing her face was better at underlining the necessity of speedy results than any number of phone calls and emails.

She called Tom from the car and asked him to brief the rest of the team and organise them across a variety of tasks – interviewing the pickers at the vineyard, talking to Bethany Glover's family, finding out what sort of CCTV and ANPR coverage they had around Elvington and the vineyard, and checking out Norris's alibi. After checking with Emily Jordan that she'd finished at the scene, she also told Tom to call Will Steadman and give him permission to reopen the winery so he could start pressing the previous day's grapes.

On the outskirts of Maidstone, she stopped at a superstore and picked up some painkillers, for all the good they'd do. By the time she limped into the morgue, Mort had already started without her.

He gave her a nod but didn't stop dictating into his phone. 'Lividity on shoulder blades, buttocks, backs of arms and backs of legs suggest that the subject died in situ or was placed there very quickly after death.'

This matched Lexi's own thoughts – the small cave wasn't a place it would be easy to carry a body to. She would be working on the assumption that Bethany Glover arrived there alive.

'Any thoughts on the cause of death yet?' she said, when Mort paused for breath.

'She hasn't got any external injuries that would result in

death,' he said, carefully rolling her onto her back. 'That means you're going to have to wait for tox results. I've sent her blood to be tested for alcohol and all the major drug classes – opiates, amphetamines, marijuana and barbiturates.'

'So you think it's down to some sort of OD?'

'An overdose, accidental or otherwise, or poisoning of some kind. It might be suicide.'

'I can't buy that. Who kills themselves in front of their kid? And I'm certain someone else was there, either when it happened or maybe after – the clothes are missing and the wax on the floor means there were candles that were removed.'

'The candle wax could date from some earlier visit to the cave.'

'True, but not the missing clothes. Bethany Glover surely didn't arrive at the vineyard stark naked, wearing wings.'

Mort shrugged. Answering questions like that wasn't his remit. He picked up a scalpel and made a swift cut down the centre of her chest. 'The state of her lungs might tell me something, and likewise, I'll examine her stomach contents. If you can find out what time she ate her last meal, that will help me fix the time of death more accurately.'

Lexi thought back to what Liam Norris had told them. He'd last seen Bethany when he left for the pub at five. She was giving Scarlett her tea at that point, but they had no idea if she ate after that and, if she did, at what time. She could ask Liam if food was missing from the fridge, but she had a feeling his answer wouldn't be very reliable.

'Let me make a call,' she said. It also gave her an excuse to leave the morgue while Mort sawed open the cadaver's chest. It was a sound she hated, a hundred times worse than hearing a dentist's drill.

'Tom, can you send someone, maybe Colin, over to Bethany and Liam's place? I want to find out if Bethany ate on Saturday night before she went to the vineyard. See if there's washing up that hasn't been done yet and check the rubbish for packaging.'

'Do you think Norris will co-operate?' He'd been furious when they'd released him the evening before.

'He'd better – otherwise, threaten him with a search warrant.'

'On it.'

She went back into the morgue. Mort was leaning over Bethany's chest, studying her lungs at close quarters.

'Look here,' he said, pointing to her right lung, which he'd cut open.

Lexi looked. 'She was a smoker?' The tissue was speckled with dark smudges.

'Yes, a light smoker, but that's not what killed her.' He pointed at the bronchus, the main airway leading from the trachea into the lung. It had also been cut open.

'There's foam in her air passages. What would cause that?'

'Pulmonary oedema – a build-up of fluid in the lungs,' said Mort. 'There are plenty of things that could cause it – heart disease, pneumonia, sepsis and, what I think will be the case here, drugs. At least that's what I'm going to look for, given that her heart looks reasonably healthy for a smoker.'

'Can you tell from that what drug it might be?'

Mort shook his head. 'Plenty of them could create this sort of damage to the airways and the alveoli. If a drug was injected, it could cause increased pulmonary vascular permeability...'

'In English, Mort.'

'The capillaries within the lungs can leak fluid into the tiny air sacs, which then becomes frothy as the person struggles to breathe. Other drugs that are ingested or snorted, like cocaine and amphetamines, can raise the blood pressure in the lungs and have the same effect. On the other hand, opioids like heroin can result in excess histamine release – same result again.'

'Have you found any injection sites?'

'No, but they're easily missed. Given this oedema, I'll inspect her skin again, just in case. But the tox results are what we really need.'

'Have you seen anything to suggest she was a habitual drug user, and that this was an accidental overdose?'

'No, absolutely nothing. She doesn't have track marks or cocaine damage to her septum, and she looks too generally healthy to be an addict. But drug overdoses are much more likely in people who don't use drugs. Your habitual druggy knows how much to take and builds up a tolerance.'

'How long till you get tox results for me?'

Mort gave a dry laugh. 'You ask me that every time, and the answer's always the same. Two to four weeks. And now you'll say, "Can you expedite that?"'

'So, can you?'

'I'll see what I can do. If there are no drugs present in her system, I'll be able to give you a negative result pretty quickly. And we can narrow down which group of drugs it is just as fast – but giving you the specifics will take longer.'

'Fine. Whatever you can give me, as quickly as you can.'

'I'll do a hair analysis as well, just so we can be sure whether she was a longer-term user.'

'Thanks.'

Learning that Bethany Glover had probably died of a drug overdose came as no surprise at all. But did she take the drug willingly or did someone force it on her or trick her into ingesting it? The missing clothes suggested the latter and that, as far as Lexi was concerned, was murder.

Driving back to Canterbury, Lexi called Linda Ellis.

'How's Scarlett?' she asked, as soon as Linda picked up.

'I've put her with a family I know well, very experienced

foster parents. But that won't make it any easier for her. All she wants is her mummy and daddy.'

Lexi sighed. 'She probably should be with Norris, but to be honest with you, it's looking like he might be a suspect in Bethany's death, and he doesn't really seem to be in a fit state to look after his daughter. And we've got to consider that Lycett-Boyd would be quite within his rights to press for an assault charge against him. What are Liam's paternal rights?'

'Regardless of what Lycett-Boyd does, I share your opinion that Liam's not going to be a responsible parent at this point, so I've got an emergency placement and started proceedings for an interim care order.'

'How long will that last?'

'Initially, for up to eight weeks.'

'Does that give time for a DNA test to see who her biological father is?'

'It should do.'

'But presumably Norris can withhold consent for such a test?'

'I think it's going to be one for the lawyers. Usually, you need a mother's permission to do a DNA test on a child. If she can't give consent, the father can as long as he's either married to the mother or listed on the birth certificate. If what Johnny Lycett-Boyd claims is true, that there's no father listed on Scarlett's birth certificate, and if Liam and Bethany weren't married, then he doesn't have the say.'

'Who does?'

'The courts. It's most likely they'll want DNA from both Lycett-Boyd and Norris to check whether either of them is Scarlett's father. The whole thing might take weeks.'

'Poor kid. Will she stay with the same foster carers for the duration?'

'We'll try to make sure that she does.'

It was a rough start in life, losing her mother and now being made the subject of a tug of war between two men who both claimed to be her father. Scarlett wouldn't get to express an opinion, and Lexi supposed the court would favour whoever's DNA she was carrying. But what would happen to her if it turned out neither of them was her father?

She stopped at Emily Jordan's office before going to the station. If Bethany Glover had died of an overdose of some drug she wasn't habituated to – and it certainly appeared that she wasn't a regular user – then someone must have supplied her with that drug. The same person who'd been in the cave with Bethany and Scarlett? The person who'd taken their clothing?

'Have you found any trace evidence on either of those sets of wings?' said Lexi, as soon as she was sitting opposite Emily. 'They seem like something that could trap fibres or hair, and I feel almost certain there was someone else in that cave with them.'

'You're right,' said Emily. 'We've found a wealth of evidence on both sets of wings. But we've got nothing to match the fibres with. Of course, there's hair from both mother and daughter, and traces of mucous on the wings that Scarlett was wearing, almost certainly her own – snot and tears. But no fingerprints, and none either from the wax deposits on the cave floor.'

'What about fibres? If I could get a warrant issued for Bethany's house, could you see if you can find a match there, with either Bethany or Scarlett's clothing, or even Liam Norris's?'

'Definitely. But even if we get a match, it can't tell us that much. Fibres from Norris's clothing could have been clinging to Bethany and Scarlett's hair or clothes. It wouldn't be enough to prove that he was in the cave.'

Lexi sighed and sent up a prayer to the forensic gods that Emily and her team would come up with a solid lead, because so far there were too many unanswered questions. A woman and a child made to look like angels, but one dead and one alive.

What was the killer trying to say? And who was Bethany Glover? Lexi didn't have a fix on her yet. Scarlett's mother, Liam's girlfriend... but who was she beyond the roles she played in public? They needed to find out about her background and her family history if they were going to properly understand her, let alone have any chance at working out who her killer was and why they'd done it.

TWELVE

DC Ridhi Kulkarni stared at the images of Bethany Glover's body on the floor of the cave. She was contemplating the placement of the missing candles. One of the CSIs had placed small yellow markers beside each deposit of candle wax. They were numbered, one to five, and surrounded the body – one close to the top of her head, one at each point of the wings, and the remaining two on either side of her ankles.

What does the layout signify?

She looked up as Lexi came into the incident room.

'Boss, have you got a moment?'

'If it's something that allows us to move forward, I've got all the time in the world.'

Ridhi doubted that, but she wanted to pick Lexi's brain for a couple of minutes.

She stood up and took the photo over to where Lexi was studying the whiteboard.

'I'm looking into the staging of the crime scene,' she said.

'Staging or posing?' said Lexi.

'Ah, posing, isn't it?' Staging was when the perp tried to

make a crime scene mislead the police, posing was the positioning of the body and the use of props to leave some kind of message.

'That's right. He's used the wings to say something about what he's doing. He had wings for the baby, too. What does that tell us, Ridhi?'

'Premeditation? The killer knew the baby would be there. He left the baby as part of the crime scene.'

'But he didn't kill her. Just the mother.'

'Thankfully,' said Ridhi. She would have found it very difficult to look at the scene if he'd killed little Scarlett as well. 'The placement of the candles, right, all around the body. It makes me think that the person who did it was there in the cave with them for a while.'

'How so?'

'The amount of wax on the floor shows that they burned down quite a bit, but then they were taken away. I don't think he left them there burning unattended because of the baby. She almost certainly would have crawled over to her mother and she could have been burned or set those wings on fire. So I think he was present for as long as it took for that amount of wax to be deposited.'

'Well done – that's a good point,' said Lexi. 'So now, follow it up with Emily Jordan. She'll be able to tell you more about the candles and set up an experiment with similar candles to work out how long that was. Given the approximate time of death and the last reported sighting of Bethany, we'll be able to start building a more accurate timeline for the person's movements.'

Ridhi felt herself beaming at the praise, and tried to rearrange her face to look more professional. 'This thing with the candles and wings is his signature, isn't it?'

Lexi nodded.

'If we can work out what exactly he's trying to say with this, it might give us a lead to who he is.' Ridhi had been a detective for less than a year, but she was learning more with every case.

'And if he's done it before,' said Lexi. 'You should look into past murders on HOLMES 2, particularly unsolved ones, for similarities and patterns.' HOLMES 2 was the police database containing all the details of major crimes across the whole country.

Lexi's mobile rang, and Ridhi went back to her desk. She tried to imagine what it must have been like when the candles were lit. There was something church-like and ritualistic about the way the body was positioned and the inclusion of wings. Was it a reference to angels or to birds? And why did he put Scarlett in wings and leave her at the scene? Once the candles had been extinguished, the cave must have been pitch black. The thought of leaving a child alone down there with her dead mother – it was beyond cruelty. It was barbaric.

Ridhi looked round to see what Colin was up to. Scrolling on his phone and drinking coffee by the look of things. 'Colin, you've done HOLMES 2 training, haven't you?'

He glanced up momentarily, then looked back to his phone. 'Yeah. Aced it.'

'Can you give me a hand then? If that TikTok's not too pressing?'

He tossed his phone carelessly onto his desk and gave Ridhi his full attention. She explained about the candles and the wings and asked him if he could find any other murders with a similar signature.

'Looks like some sort of folklore stuff, doesn't it?' he said, studying the image of Bethany lying on the chalk floor with the wings spread beneath her. 'Reminds me of those two girls up on the chalk outside Wye.' That had been Ridhi's first case with the team, and it had been grim. Two girls murdered. Their sister

– they were a set of triplets – was kept alive. They'd caught the man who did it, and it turned out he was the man who'd murdered the boss's sister. She was also a triplet.

'Can't be connected to that, though,' said Ridhi. 'He's in prison.'

'You might want to find out what the folklore thing is all about,' said Colin. 'Could be a clue.'

While Colin scoured HOLMES 2 for matching or similar crimes, Ridhi googled all she could find on Kent folklore. She found a lot that was weird and interesting, but nothing stood out as relevant. No winged mothers or babies, no sacrificial rituals to the gods of wine. After nearly an hour of reading about the Green Man of Kent – half-man, half-cat apparently – and the Hooden Horse, now revived by Morris dancers, she was fed up. It made no sense to her, and she closed the folder as the landline phone on her desk rang.

'DC Kulkarni speaking.'

'PC Grey.' He was one of the team of desk sergeants that manned the station's reception area. 'I've got a gentleman here, says he'd like to talk to someone about the woman's death at Elvington Vineyard.'

'How does he know about it?' said Ridhi.

'It's been on the radio this morning. Calls from the public are starting to come in.'

'Any hint as to what exactly he wants to tell us?'

'No.' Ever helpful.

'Got a name?'

She heard him ask the man his name. 'Gideon Croft,' he reported back to her.

'Okay, put him in an interview room. I'll come down.'

Five minutes later she found herself sitting across the table from a man who was everything his name suggested. Hairy, bearded, round glasses, a preponderance of khaki in his choice of clothing and muddy hiking boots on his feet.

'Gideon Croft? I'm DC Kulkarni.'

'Hi.' He smiled at her with genuine warmth, and it made her realise he was younger than his crusty image at first suggested. Now that she was here, he started to empty the contents of a battered leather messenger bag onto the table – papers, books, leaflets, photos, all jumbled together, slightly creased and dog-eared.

'How can I help you?' she said. Viewing the papers on display, she had a feeling this was going to be a monumental waste of her time.

Croft looked up at her and blinked, as if he'd almost forgotten she was there, but then became more animated. 'I came in to help *you*, actually.'

'And how exactly might you be able to help us?'

He tried to draw the items from the bag into a neat pile. 'I heard on the radio that a woman had been found dead at Elvington Vineyard.'

Ridhi couldn't help but notice how long and dirty his finger-nails were. She cringed internally and returned her gaze to his face. 'Yes, that's right. Do you know anything about it?'

'Yes... I mean no. Not directly. But there's a precedent for women being found dead on that side of the valley.' He tapped the pile of papers with the back of his hand. 'I thought you should know about it.'

'I see.' She didn't really, but perhaps things would become clearer. 'Let's start with basics. Your name's Gideon Croft?'

'Yes, that's right.'

'What do you do for a living, Mr Croft?'

'I'm a lecturer in anthropology at Kent Uni, but I also study folklore in my own time. That's my real passion.' He leaned forward over the table as he said this, and there was something in the way he drew out the last word that made Ridhi's stomach turn.

'You think you have some knowledge that might be useful to our investigation?'

'I know I do.' He tapped his pile of papers again. 'You see, several women have been murdered in the area and their deaths had certain things in common.'

Ridhi was surprised. She hadn't heard about any other murders in the area recently. 'Can you tell me about them?'

'Yes. I would focus on four in particular. There are records of a fifth woman, who was beaten to death, but her husband confessed, so it's not really of interest.'

Four?

'Go on.'

'In all four cases, the women went missing and were found dead, several days later, on the northern slopes of the valley – where the vineyard is now located. They were found naked and garrotted, and the supposition is that they'd been sexually assaulted.'

'The supposition? What did the evidence show?'

Croft gave her a quizzical look. 'They didn't have any forensics back in those days,' he said. 'They didn't even have police. The county sheriff would have questioned anyone he thought relevant...'

Ridhi held up a hand for him to stop. 'You're talking about things that happened in medieval times, right?'

'The earliest of the four murders was in 1579, so, yes, absolutely for that one and the next two. But the last one happened in 1654...'

'Okay, you've been most helpful, Mr Croft, but I don't think these cases are going to be relevant to our investigation.' No wonder she hadn't heard about them.

Croft breathed out a heavy, almost an audible sigh. 'I haven't finished.' He sounded irritated. 'These four deaths were all linked to some of the local folklore...'

'No, really, Mr Croft. I'm afraid I need to be getting on.'

Ridhi stood as she said this, to indicate that the interview was over.

Croft stood too, but carried on talking. 'They were all linked to the Elvington Angel. Each woman had angel's wings marked on her back in charcoal.'

Ridhi stopped on her way towards the door and turned back to him. 'The Elvington Angel?'

'Ha – struck a chord, haven't I? I thought so. Tell me about this new death.'

Ridhi sat down again. 'What's the Elvington Angel?'

'Ever heard of it?'

'No, not that I recall.'

'I'm not surprised.' Croft looked smug, clearly delighted to have bought himself more time. 'It's an obscure story that has its roots in a number of villages in the North Downs, mainly centred on Elvington. It's local folklore, but these days there aren't many people that know of it. We're losing great swathes of our social history because everyone today's more concerned with social media.'

He'd gone into full college lecturer mode, but Ridhi didn't have time for it.

'What about the angel?'

'It's a grim story,' he said. 'Supposedly, back in the 1500s, an angel appeared to the villagers of Elvington one day, up on the hillside. It vowed to protect them from harm and bring them good fortune. But in return, they had to provide him with a virgin from the village.'

'An angel? Demanding a sacrificial virgin?'

'It's my private theory that it wasn't an angel at all. More likely a demon, tricking the people into giving him a young girl, whom he then spirited away for his own evil purposes.' Croft grinned. 'Supposedly everything went well for the village after that and they always felt under his protection. Until these women started turning up dead with wings drawn on their backs. The blessing seemed to have turned into a curse.'

'Angel, demon or predatory male?' said Ridhi. The question barely needed answering. But it seemed too much of a coincidence that the body they'd just found had been wearing angel wings.

'Tell me about what happened at the vineyard,' said Croft. 'I heard there was some sort of link.'

Ridhi raised her eyebrows. 'You heard? From who?'

Croft shrugged. 'Elvington is a small community. People talk.'

'What exactly are they saying?'

'That there are similarities between this case and some of the old ones.'

Ridhi waited for him to expand. If he had details that hadn't been released to the press yet, then someone at the vineyard must have been talking.

'One of the previously murdered women was found in the churchyard at Elvington. People claimed the angel had come back and was angry because people were forgetting about him.' He started flipping through his collection of documents. 'There's a treatise on it somewhere in here. You might find it interesting reading.'

'Sorry, I know you're trying to be helpful, Mr Croft, but these things are much too far back to be of interest to us. Even if the killer's harking back to the folklore, it's just a story.'

Gideon Croft looked momentarily affronted, but then tilted his head to one side. 'I would suggest that your current killer knows the old story of the angel. Maybe he's using it to deflect attention from the real reason that he killed the woman. And there can't be that many people around who still know the old tales. That could be a starting point for your investigation.'

'Thanks,' said Ridhi. He was clutching at straws, and she just wanted rid of him now.

'You mark my words – this is about the angel. But if you don't want my help...' He shrugged and got to his feet.

As she showed him out of the station, he skewered her with a steely look. 'You'll be knocking on my door.'

Ridhi felt as if someone had just walked over her grave.

THIRTEEN

Yesterday's achievements

1. Ironing done
2. Updated work diary for week ahead
3. Tidied garden refuse
4. Outlined plans for next operation

Learning outcomes

1. Next time, bring a bag for removing clothes, candles, etc
2. Worked out how to sync Google calendars
3. Stay calm and think things through

Plans for today

1. Work – so much to catch up on
2. Marketing stuff probably needs a look
3. Watch the girl – look out for way of making initial contact. How quickly can I set this up? Killing B

made me feel really good. I want to feel that again
as quickly as possible.

4. Check media for reports about B
5. Collect B's clothes – bring them back here for
   burning
6. Find out what leads the police investigation is
   following, if I can
7. Get an early night

How are you feeling – in three words?

1. Energised
2. Hopeful
3. Greedy

Memory of the day

That one time when I got lost. I hate this memory, but it's
always there, lurking in the shady corners of my mind. I don't
know where we were. All I remember is looking round, and I
couldn't see Mum anywhere. I remember the fear. I
remember crying – I was probably bellowing. A woman
spoke to me but I was too upset to say anything. I must have
been about three. I think I knew my own name, I could say it,
but all that came out of my mouth was howling for Mum.

We were at the shops, that much I think I remember. The
filthy pavement, grown-ups' legs going past, all in a hurry.
The woman took me by the hand and called out, 'Whose
baby is this? Whose child is this?' I hated that woman. She
tried to make me walk away from where I'd last seen Mum. I
pulled back, like a tug of war. I can still feel the fear – it's
something I can't forget.

And then Mum was there, running along the pavement
towards me. 'Hey, toots,' she cried. 'What are you bawling

about? Only been gone a second.' She had a row with the woman – I think the woman blamed her for leaving me alone on the pavement while she went into a shop. Or maybe I wandered out. I don't really remember the details. Just the fear. How scared I was when I couldn't see her. And I looked round and round. And she just wasn't there. That's what I remember most.

And that she was cross with me afterwards, when the woman had gone, and people weren't staring at us anymore. She was cross with me, so it must have been my fault.

Motivation for the day
A spark of every fire we seek is already within us

FOURTEEN

According to Will Steadman, the vineyard had eleven permanent employees on site and approximately thirty seasonal workers, who were currently harvesting the grapes.

'Approximately?' Lexi wasn't impressed. 'Surely you know how many people you're paying?'

'Yes, but it varies daily. Some pickers work right through – usually the ones from abroad who want to maximise their earnings while they're here – and some, the local workers, take days off. They're paid by the hour and Lydia in the office keeps the time sheets. Would you like to talk to her?'

They were standing outside the winery, and Lexi was watching the crates of grapes being loaded onto the lift and taken to the top floor to be tipped into the two huge presses.

'No, I don't need to talk to Lydia about the hours. I'd like you to provide me with a list of all the people who were on site over the weekend, working or not, so we can keep track of who we've interviewed.'

'Fine. I'll ask her to sort one out.' He seemed resentful at being asked to do an admin chore. 'I'd better get on before Johnny accuses me of malingering.' The words sounded bitter and Lexi sensed something wasn't right between the two men. Interesting.

She turned round to Tom. 'Can you organise the interviews with the pickers?' The whole team had come up to Elvington to interview the staff and workers. 'I'll go and take statements from the Lycett-Boyds.'

'I'd love to have been a fly on the wall in their house last night,' said Tom. 'Presumably he had to tell her about being the father of Bethany's baby.'

'If she didn't already know,' said Lexi. 'That's part of what I aim to find out.'

'Do you think it puts him in the frame?'

'Killing Bethany to get custody? I'm sure he can afford decent lawyers, which would be a far less risky way of going about it. But that doesn't mean it's not murder. Someone was there with her in the caves and the fact that they didn't come forward, did nothing to save her and left that poor baby alone down there, tells me that Bethany's death was no accident.'

She pondered that thought as she walked back down the drive to the old farmhouse at the bottom of the vineyard. Don't shit in your own nest – that was the saying. And if Johnny Lycett-Boyd had got a local girl pregnant and then killed her on his own property... Suffice to say, he wasn't even paying lip service to the homily. It seemed unlikely, but at this stage in the investigation, she could rule nothing out.

In a case like this, there were four possible hypotheses. Accidental overdose, administered by the victim. Accidental overdose, administered by someone else. Intentional overdose, administered by the victim. Intentional overdose, administered by someone else. Accident, manslaughter, suicide or murder?

The fact that someone else must have been there reduced the likelihood of Bethany having overdosed herself, accidentally or otherwise, and that person's failure to come forward pushed Lexi a long way towards thinking murder. No one would leave a baby alone in the dark with their dead mother by accident.

Now all she had to do was find the perpetrator and prove it.

The Lycett-Boyd farmhouse had obviously been extended several times over the years. She could make out the original part of the building – it was timbered, with flintstone walls on the ground floor and mottle and daub above. To the left, there was a redbrick wing that looked more Victorian, linking the house to what must have once been a stable block, but which now sported modern garage doors. On the right, positioned to catch the best of the sun, there was a vast glass conservatory which looked relatively new. She opened a wrought-iron gate and walked up the gravel path to the front door. There didn't appear to be a bell, just an ornate brass knocker in the shape of a stag's head.

She knocked, loudly, several times.

The door opened almost immediately, and a middle-aged woman in a cleaning overall peered out at her, blinking in the sunlight.

'DI Bennett, Kent Police.' Lexi flashed her ID. 'Is Mr or Mrs Lycett-Boyd in?'

The woman nodded but didn't speak.

'Can I come in?'

The woman pulled the door further open. Lexi stepped inside.

'If you wait here, I'll tell 'em.' She pulled the front door shut, and they were plunged into semi-darkness – all the doors leading off the hall were closed, and the only light leaked down from a crooked wooden staircase at the far end. The women shuffled away, barely picking up her feet on the uneven terra-cotta floor, and disappeared through a door on the right.

Lexi stood and waited. The old house creaked around her. The scent of lavender hung in the air and, as her eyes became accustomed to the poor light, she saw a blue-and-white china bowl standing on a warped wooden chest. Stepping closer and bending down, she could see it was full of the tiny purple buds and she breathed in deeply. As she exhaled, she heard the sound of voices from somewhere deeper within the house.

'...so what did you bloody expect? I'm not a monk, you know.'

'And that made it okay for you to screw around while I was carrying your child?'

Lexi straightened up and walked slowly, on silent feet, towards where the voices were coming from.

'I was drunk. It only happened once.'

'*Putain!* You expect me to believe that? And now you want me to lie for you and tell the world I'm happy for your bastard child to come here, into our home, with our daughter? The child of a common slut.'

'She wasn't a slut...'

'Sure – a really nice girl, huh?'

Marietta was definitely someone who might want Bethany out of the way.

A door slammed and footsteps approached. Male footsteps. Lexi dropped back towards the front door. Somewhere in the distance an infant cried. Their legitimate daughter.

'Yes, Mrs Goddard?'

A woman mumbled something.

'Damn!'

There was a moment's silence, then Johnny Lycett-Boyd came out of the doorway through which the cleaning lady had disappeared.

'DI Bennett, hello.' He was charm personified, his voice calm and measured. But Lexi didn't miss the slight flush to his cheeks.

'Mr Lycett-Boyd, sorry to disturb you, but would it be possible to take a statement from you now?'

'A statement? Of what?'

'I'll need to know what you were doing and all your movements on Saturday and Sunday.'

His face darkened. 'I was working all the time. I had nothing to do with what happened.'

'I'm afraid we still need the details of where you were and who you were with.'

Lycett-Boyd swore under his breath.

'We have to investigate every possibility. My team will be talking to everyone who was at the vineyard over the weekend, including you and your wife. No exceptions.'

'I see. Can it wait till later? I need to check in with my manager about restarting the presses.'

'Unfortunately, a murder investigation has to take priority – I'm sure you can understand that.'

'Understand what?' Marietta Lycett-Boyd appeared at the end of the hall. She had a little girl in her arms.

Lexi wasn't an expert but she guessed the infant was about eighteen months old, approximately the same age as Scarlett Glover.

'DI Bennett needs to talk to us about what we were doing at the weekend,' said Johnny.

Lexi caught an undertone of stress in his voice, and wondered if he was trying to warn his wife over what she might divulge.

'Now?' said Marietta. She was still angry.

'Yes, if you don't mind.' Not that she would give them any choice in the matter.

Marietta turned and went through another door leading off the hall, and Johnny indicated with a wave of his hand that Lexi should follow. She found herself in a large, airy living room that opened directly into the conservatory at the side of the house. There were two floral sofas framing a wide fireplace and every surface was crammed with silver-framed photographs – the Lycett-Boyds getting married, the baby's christening, Johnny in racing overalls standing next to a sports car, studio shots of Marietta when she was younger, both of them in the vineyard, skiing, sailing – the gilded life of a wealthy couple on display.

The cleaning lady who'd let Lexi in was passing a feather duster over the mirror above the mantelpiece.

'Mrs Goddard, would you mind taking Aurora up to her room for a little while? Johnny's mother will be here in a bit to collect her.'

'Of course.' The woman beamed. It was obvious she'd far rather play with the baby than do the cleaning.

As Aurora was handed over, grumbling and clinging to her mother for as long as she could, Johnny invited Lexi to sit down on one of the sofas.

'Marietta, would you talk to DI Bennett first? I need to make a quick call.' He beat a hasty retreat from the room, pushing past Mrs Goddard as she carried Aurora towards the door. It didn't give Marietta a chance to argue.

The man dripped with entitlement, but Lexi decided to let it go. She was just as interested to hear what Marietta had to say, given what she'd overheard.

Marietta sat down opposite her, smoothing her dark hair down after Aurora had mussed it up.

'I'm sorry,' she said. 'How can I help you?'

'I need to check everyone's whereabouts over the course of the weekend, so we can build up a picture of what might have happened.'

'To Bethany Glover?' She spat the name with contempt.

'Did you know her?'

'Of course I knew her. She's a local girl who has been sleeping with my husband.' Anger bubbled close to the surface. 'A whore.'

'Or maybe just a girl who was taken advantage of by an older man?'

Marietta frowned. 'One doesn't rule out the other.'

'Perhaps not. But one of them should have known better.'

Marietta shrugged.

Questions formed in Lexi's mind. *Did you realise your husband had fathered a child with Bethany? Do you think your husband had anything to do with her death?* But Marietta's emotional take on her husband's affair with Bethany Glover wouldn't constitute evidence. More importantly, first off she needed the nuts and bolts of where Marietta and Johnny were between the time when Bethany went missing and the time her body was discovered by Will Steadman the following morning.

'Take me through everything you did on Saturday and Sunday.'

'Pah, it's not that interesting.' She gave a shrug and pulled a face. 'On Saturday... we got up early, about seven o'clock. Usually, we sleep in later, but we're harvesting which means we're working weekends right now. We had coffee, then went over to the winery. I went upstairs to check that the presses were clean. Johnny was checking the fermentation tanks, I think. The first grapes came in from the fields a little bit after that – and then I was working in the winery all day, running the presses.'

'Did you stop for lunch?'

'I came back here briefly to use the bathroom, and I grabbed a sandwich. I think that was at about two o'clock.'

'What about your daughter? Where was she?'

'She was staying with Johnny's parents. She stays there most of the time during the grape harvest, so we can work. She was at home last night, as Johnny's parents were out for the evening, but she'll go back to them today.'

'They live nearby?'

'They have a house at Sandwich – twenty minutes' drive.'

'Were you with Johnny all of this time?'

'No, not at all. I was mostly at the top of the winery. He was working at the bottom with Will, directing the grape juice into the fermentation tanks.'

'So you can't vouch for his whereabouts during the day?'

'He's not tied to my apron strings.'

'What about when you finished working?'

'I was operating the presses until after ten p.m. It was a long day and I was exhausted. When the last of the day's grapes had gone through, I walked down to the house.'

'On your own?'

'Of course. Johnny hadn't finished yet.'

'When did he come back to the house?'

'Maybe about an hour after me. He left Will to lock up. We had a glass of wine together and some cheese. Talked about the day. He was angry with Will.'

'Why?'

'Will had been going on about biodynamics again – he's trying to persuade Johnny to let him turn Elvington into a biodynamic vineyard.'

'What's that?'

'It's like organic, but even more extreme. Planting and harvesting in line with the phases of the moon. It's all nonsense. My family has vineyards all over France, and we wouldn't waste a moment's thought on it.'

'They argued?'

'Disagreed, would be a better choice of word. Johnny ranted about it for a bit, then we went to bed.'

'And Johnny was with you the whole night from then?'

'Of course.' She picked up a coaster from the coffee table and attempted to balance it on its side. It fell onto the glass tabletop with a clatter. She was nervous.

'And Sunday?'

'We woke up late. And then Johnny found the message from Will, saying that there was a dead woman in the cave. He quickly got dressed and went to see what was going on.'

'You didn't go with him?'

'No. I was still half asleep. I had a shower, and then Johnny called me and asked me to bring up some baby clothes and formula.'

That was when Lexi had first seen her.

'How did you know Bethany Glover?'

'She worked in the Spar in the village on and off.'

'Is that where your husband met her?'

Marietta let out a sharp bark of laughter. 'In the Spar? I doubt it. Johnny doesn't do the shopping.'

'Where would he have met her?'

There was something about the way Marietta shrugged and rolled her eyes that was extraordinarily Gallic.

'I don't know. Perhaps in the pub, or maybe at the track.'

'The track?'

'Shepherd's Hill Race Circuit, over near Wooten. Johnny's hobby is racing classic cars. He spends most of his time up there, when we're not harvesting.'

'And he could have met Bethany there?'

'I have no idea. It's not something we discussed.'

Lexi could see why not.

'Did you know, before yesterday, that Bethany had given birth to his child?'

'I don't even know for sure if she is his child. I doubt it. But, no, he hadn't confided in me.'

'But you knew about the affair?'

Marietta glanced briefly from side to side, as if she expected to see Johnny lurking at the door or outside the window. 'I had guessed he was seeing someone, on and off. I didn't know exactly who it was, or if it was always the same person. But, you know, you can tell when your husband is being unfaithful. He's more attentive but wants less sex.' She glanced at Lexi's left hand. 'You're not married?'

'No.' Nor was she discussing it. She stood up to leave and

was momentarily unbalanced by a sharp pain in her leg. She took an experimental step – the muscle had seized up from sitting for too long.

'You're limping. You've hurt your leg?'

'Just a running injury.'

Marietta stood up too and Lexi could see her relief at the change of subject. 'I know of a good physio in Canterbury. I've used him a couple of times – Luke Evans. He works at the Synergy Health Club.'

Lexi nodded. She was a member of the club, but she didn't have time for physio with a murder on her hands. 'Just one last question.'

'Sure.' Marietta looked wary.

'Do you think your husband could have anything to do with Bethany's death?'

'I told you, didn't I? He was here with me all of Saturday night. At least as far as I know.'

'What do you mean by that?'

'Nothing, perhaps.' She paused, as if weighing up whether to speak or not. 'But I took a sleeping pill when I went to bed. I slept solidly and nothing would have woken me.'

Nothing at all?

It was time to talk to Johnny Lycett-Boyd. And Lexi decided she'd rather do it down at the station. The victim was his mistress and she'd died on his property.

FIFTEEN

Tom had also reached a decision that a formal statement down at the station was required, but his target was Will Steadman. The vintner had protested loudly at Tom's suggestion that he accompany him to Canterbury, but he wasn't getting any choice. The winery could manage without him for the couple of hours he'd be gone and, as Tom pointed out, it was important to get a statement properly filed. Steadman's evidence about discovering the body on Sunday morning was critical.

It was a warm day outside, but the interview room in the bowels of the station was like a cave – with no windows, it always maintained a constant temperature, no matter what the season. Steadman was surly as Tom showed him in and pointed at the chair.

'Can we make this quick?' said Steadman, as soon as Tom was sitting opposite him. He rested both his forearms on the table and leaned forward.

'We'll be as quick as possible,' said Tom, 'but we need to be thorough.'

Tom switched on the recording device and announced both their names, getting Steadman to confirm his.

'How long have you worked at Elvington Vineyard?'

'Wow! That's more thorough than I expected. What do you want – my bloody life history?'

'We'll be finished sooner if you just answer the questions.'

'Four years.'

'And before that?'

'Why's that relevant?'

Tom sighed. 'Please.'

'I worked in a number of vineyards in France and then Australia, learning how to produce sparkling wine.'

'And how did you come to get the job at Elvington?'

'When I was working in Tassie – Tasmania – I met Ben, Johnny's brother. He told me about Elvington, so when I came back here, I looked the place up. They needed a vintner and I needed a job – these things have a way of happening.'

'Why did you come back?'

'My parents are getting old. My father was ill, and I realised I needed to be closer to home to support my mother. I'm adopted and I don't have any siblings, so it falls on me.'

Tom wondered if Will Steadman was a little resentful of this need to relocate back home. He could understand that. France and Australia seemed far more appealing than a vineyard in Kent.

'Do they live locally?'

'No, they live in Essex. But I'm a lot closer than I was.'

He had relaxed a little as they talked about the mundane, so Tom felt ready to get to the meat of the interview. 'Tell me about Saturday. Who was at the vineyard?'

'Saturday was busy – we had a full team of pickers on site and the presses were running all day. I finally locked up the winery at approximately eleven p.m.'

'Did you go and check that there was no one still in the cellars?'

'Of course. We hadn't been working down there – but I went down and looked anyway. The lights were out and I shouted "Hello" just to be sure. There was no one there.'

Unless Bethany was hiding down there, but that seemed unlikely with a baby in tow.

'Where was Johnny at this point?'

'He'd left the winery – about half an hour before I locked up. He usually leaves someone else to tidy and check the premises.' There was a subtext here that was easy enough to decipher.

'Who else was working inside the building?'

'Myself, Johnny, Marietta.' He paused. 'Ina and Pierre – two of our permanent team. Mathéo Martin, who supervises the picking teams, he was in and out a bit as the grapes were brought up to the top.'

Tom knew that the team were busy taking statements from all the workers at the vineyard.

'Did you see Bethany Glover anywhere around the vineyard on Saturday?'

'No. I didn't know her, and the first time I saw her was on Sunday morning. Dead.'

'Tell me about Sunday morning.'

Steadman's body language became less comfortable and his voice less assured as he once again went over the details of how he'd heard the baby crying and then discovered the body. However, his retelling was the same in all the essential details.

'Did you know that Johnny Lycett-Boyd was having an affair with Bethany, and claims he fathered a child with her?'

'No, I had no idea.'

'But you worked with him closely?'

'He's my boss, and he doesn't work full-time at the vineyard, apart from during the harvest. He comes up for regular meetings and to check on the fermentation. But he mainly works down at the farmhouse on the sales side of the business. When he's not over at Shepherd's Hill.'

'Shepherd's Hill?'

'He part owns a car track over at Wooton. Classic car racing, driving experiences, test track – that's his real passion.'

It sounded like they didn't spend much time together at all, so if Lycett-Boyd was having an affair, no wonder Will Steadman had no idea.

'Are you close to Johnny? Would you call yourself friends?'

He shook his head. 'No, not really. I work for him, not with him. It's a professional relationship – so if you're wondering if he would confide in me, the answer's no.'

Steadman paused for a moment. Tom felt there was something more to come, so he stayed silent.

'Johnny can be a difficult man, if he doesn't get his way. His brother warned me of that in Australia, so I knew what I was getting into, coming here. He's the oldest son of a wealthy family, and his parents spoiled him – put him on a pedestal over and above his siblings apparently.'

'It sounds as if you were close to his brother.'

'Ben is much more easy-going, and talkative. We got on well when we worked together.'

'But Ben doesn't get on with Johnny?'

'There's a bit of friction between them. I think Ben would like to come and work here. But he knows he'd be treated like hired help, and he's got a good life out in Tassie. Married, a couple of kids. I'd say he's quite settled out there.' Now he was on a roll. 'Of course, it would make more sense for Ben to come and run Elvington. He knows far more about winemaking, and he has a far more sophisticated palate than Johnny. And it would free up Johnny to really develop Shepherd's Hill.' He shrugged. 'Not my place to tell them.'

Tom wondered if all this had ramifications for Steadman's

job. It sounded like he'd be far happier working for Ben Lycett-Boyd than for Johnny. Family politics of the wealthy – and now a murdered woman and an illegitimate child had turned up to muddy the waters.

SIXTEEN

Lexi sat down opposite Johnny Lycett-Boyd and waited while he fidgeted in his seat. He bit at a hangnail nervously, then rolled up his shirtsleeves. Something on the floor caught his attention. Why was he so nervous? Because he was guilty of something or because he didn't want her to think he was guilty of something? Both could have the same effect, and for some people, just being in a police interview room had them in pieces.

Somehow, she didn't think that would be the case for Johnny. A wealthy upbringing makes people confident, often overconfident. So there was more to his nerves than just the situation.

He finally broke the silence. 'Should I have a lawyer with me?'

'Naturally, you're entitled to one. But this is a witness interview, Mr Lycett-Boyd. I just need a formal statement of your whereabouts for Saturday and Sunday.'

Johnny nodded, his lips pursed.

'I'm going to record it for the sake of accuracy.'

'Go ahead.'

Once the formalities were done, Lexi launched straight into the questions. 'Can you tell me your movements on Saturday?'

'We're in the middle of the harvest, so I spent all day at our winery on the vineyard.'

'You didn't leave the vineyard at all?'

He shook his head. 'I started work at about seven a.m. and carried on through until we finished for the night.'

'What time was that?'

'Gone ten.'

'You didn't stop for meals?'

'I grabbed a sandwich on the hoof. Marietta brought one up from the house.'

'Did you see Bethany Glover at the vineyard on Saturday?'

'No. Nor would I expect to – there would be no reason for her to be there.'

'When did you last see her?'

'A couple of months ago. I dropped by her house to see Scarlett. My daughter.'

'But you were having an affair with her?'

'Had. We had an affair, though you could hardly call it that. More of a brief fling – a couple of years ago. Scarlett was the result.'

'And you're sure Scarlett is yours?'

'I am.'

'So's Liam Norris. Was Bethany living with Liam at the time of your affair?'

'Yes, she was.'

'So Scarlett could be his?'

'She looks like me. Could be Aurora's twin.'

Judging paternity by looks was far too subjective. 'Have you ever had a DNA test to prove the paternity?'

'No.' He cracked his knuckles. 'But I understand one is on the cards now?'

'That will be up to the child protection team to decide. I

won't be involved. Have you ever thought about suing for custody?'

'What, and take Scarlett from her mother? That would be an awful thing to do – disruptive to Scarlett, and disruptive to my own family. Bethany was a good mother and I was happy to help her out. But now she's gone, Scarlett should be with me.'

Lexi decided to change the subject. 'Do you know Liam Norris?'

'Yes. He worked for me for a while, a few years ago, but I haven't seen him since he left. We fired him, I can't remember why. I knew he was Bethany's boyfriend, but I avoided him – for obvious reasons.' He allowed himself a smile, which Lexi didn't return.

'Where did you go when you finished work?'

'I left Will to lock up and I walked down the drive to the farmhouse. Marietta will vouch for me – she'll tell you what time I arrived. We had a snack and went to bed.'

'I'd like to hear from you what time you got home.'

He shrugged. 'Half ten, eleven perhaps.'

'Do you take drugs?'

'Jesus, where's that coming from? I thought this was a witness statement, but now you're accusing me of being a druggy?'

'I'm accusing you of nothing. Please answer the question.'

'No, I don't. Tried pot a few times when I was at uni, but it wasn't for me. Can't stand smoking, so I never went down that route.'

'Tell me about Sunday morning?'

'You know about that already. I overslept, then saw the text from Will saying that a body had been found. Marietta will confirm it.'

'Did you ever consider leaving your wife and setting up house with Bethany?'

'Not that it's any of your business, but I didn't. Like I said, it was just a fling.'

Lexi stayed silent – the most effective way of getting people to spill things.

'Look, I couldn't leave Marietta if I wanted to. We have our ups and downs, but her family has invested heavily in Elvington. She owns shares in the company, so splitting with her would have business ramifications as well as personal ones.' He paused, frowning. 'She's my ball and chain. Like I'm hers. We understand the situation we're in.'

'What situation would that be?'

'Like I said, stuck together. We make the best of it.'

It sounded to Lexi like he was making excuses for playing away.

'Was Bethany blackmailing you for money for Scarlett's upkeep?'

'Of course not. She wasn't greedy. Not like my wife. Bethany was an angel compared to Marietta.' Lexi watched the emotions play across his features – sorrow, anger, contempt, indignation. But was it all a clever act?

'I would imagine discovering the dead body of your mistress underneath your winery is going to have some ramifications for your business, isn't it?'

Johnny passed a hand over his eyes. 'I haven't given that any thought yet. I'm more concerned about my daughter.'

'Scarlett? Or Aurora?' Lexi knew he meant Scarlett, but it would do no harm to rattle his cage.

'Scarlett, of course. Aurora is fine. But with Bethany gone, I'm not prepared to leave our daughter to be brought up by Liam Norris.'

'And how does Marietta feel about that?'

Johnny Lycett-Boyd slammed his fist down on the table, making Lexi jump.

'I don't give a damn how she feels. This is family. Scarlett's my kid and I'm her only parent. She'll come and live with me.'

He seemed so self-assured, so certain he would get what he wanted, but Lexi wondered if it would be that simple.

———

Tom was logging Steadman's statement when Lexi arrived back at the incident room. She'd sent Lycett-Boyd home and now it was time to take stock of what they'd learned. Tom offered her a chocolate digestive and she took three. One day she'd get back on track with healthy eating, but it wasn't going to happen in the middle of a murder investigation.

'What are your thoughts, boss?' said Tom through a mouthful of biscuit.

Lexi gave herself until she finished chewing to put her thoughts in order.

'Let's look at the possible hypotheses,' she said. 'My first theory is that Bethany knew her killer. And she trusted whoever it was. She went into the cellar with them, and she had Scarlett with her. It would have been difficult for someone to have forced them through that tunnel against her will, with her child. There was no sign of violence on the body, no scratches or bruising. Can you make a note to check with Mort and Emily as to whether there was any foreign DNA under her nails?'

'Of course.' Tom typed on his laptop. 'But what if the person took her down there first, and brought the baby later?'

'You mean after she was dead?'

'Or incapacitated?'

'Where would the baby have been in the meantime?'

'I don't know. In the person's car?'

Lexi shrugged. 'That would be risky. If she started howling...'

'Could have been parked in a remote place, after midnight.'

'We can't discount that,' said Lexi.

'And it still fits with her knowing her killer.'

'Wait – we're not even sure yet if the person who took the clothes and the candles away actually killed her. If she accidentally OD'd, they might just have wanted to hide the fact that they were there, that they were the supplier of the drugs.'

Tom nodded. 'True. But they might not even have been the person who supplied her.' He bit into another biscuit.

There were too many moving parts to what might have happened. They needed to find ways of ruling things out.

'Of course, we also can't discount the theory that she didn't really know the person. Maybe she'd recently met them. Perhaps they could have lured her there with the promise of drugs – though by all accounts so far she wasn't into drugs. But if person A, as we'll call them, wasn't someone in her life already, what made them pick Bethany? Why was Scarlett there? Would Bethany take her baby with her to meet a stranger in a cave in the middle of the night? And the wings – was that premeditation, knowing he was going to kill a mother and child, or did Bethany bring the wings? For what purpose?'

'However you theorise it, it looks less likely than the theory she was meeting someone she knew,' said Tom. 'So, who are we looking at if we believe she knew person A?'

'First, we've got to consider people already on the vineyard who might have known about the tunnel – Steadman and both Lycett-Boyds. And of course, there are all the other employees. Some of the seasonal workers might have known about it. Ex-employees, too. Apparently, Norris worked for Lycett-Boyd at some point. Could he have known?

'Let's see if there's any CCTV around the property,' Lexi went on. 'You'd think there would be with thousands of pounds' worth of expensive wine on the premises. We might catch some footage of someone behaving suspiciously. Perhaps the person she was meeting came into the caves through the winery.'

Tom made another note.

'But it seems likely that all three came in through the tunnel. We need to chase up Emily and see if the CSIs came across any concrete evidence on that front.'

'Suspects so far, boss?'

'Norris, of course. What if he found out about the affair with Lycett-Boyd? That would give him a motive.'

'Especially if he suspected Lycett-Boyd was actually Scarlett's father. But it can equally be argued that Lycett-Boyd has a motive or even two – he might have wanted Bethany out of the way, if she was threatening to tell Marietta about Scarlett. Or perhaps he wanted to gain sole custody of Scarlett.'

Of course, this had already crossed Lexi's mind too, but she wasn't so sure that these were credible motives. It could just as easily be argued that Marietta Lycett-Boyd had a motive – to remove her rival from the scene. But somehow it seemed unlikely that Bethany would have agreed to meet with her lover's wife in a secluded cave.

Lycett-Boyd had denied that he wanted to take Scarlett from Bethany, but he could have been lying. 'The man can afford top lawyers, and Bethany wouldn't have been able to, so I don't think he would need to resort to killing her. And even if he wanted her permanently out of the picture, it would be stupid to do it on his own property. However, if we look at it from the angle of opportunity – Will Steadman was the last person at the winery that night and the first person on the scene in the morning.'

'Motive?' said Tom.

'Good question. I don't think there's an obvious one. He claims he didn't know her. But she was a local girl who worked in the village shop, so maybe he's lying about that.'

'And what about the business with the wings and the candles?'

'Apparently Steadman is into some sort of weird farming by

moonlight stuff, so maybe he was making a sacrifice to the gods of wine.' But she shook her head as she said it – it was too far-fetched. If Steadman did have a motive, it was sure to be something less wholesome than appeasing Bacchus. Lexi had her doubts over the veracity of the signature anyway. The crime scene had been staged to suggest a ritual killing, but there seemed to be a number of suspects with genuine motives to want Bethany dead. The ritualistic nature of the scene might have been devised to throw them off the scent.

'Get onto Mort, will you? See if there were any signs of sexual activity in the hours before she died. We need to build up a better picture of Bethany's final twenty-four hours. Let's start digging with her family and friends. How was her relationship with Norris? Was she still seeing Lycett-Boyd? Could she have been seeing someone else? Did she secretly use drugs? Can we get hold of her phone, and contact the phone company to see if she had any calls on Saturday that could have been making arrangements to meet person A? Did she have her own car? Did it ping any ANPR points on Saturday evening? Has anyone managed to track down any of her family members yet? Surely Liam must know where her parents live?'

'I've asked Ridhi and Colin to dig into her background.'

'Good. We've got our work cut out, so let's get on.'

The adage was true. Find out how a person lived, and you'll find out how they died. And she was determined to get to the bottom of it – for Bethany's sake and even more so for little Scarlett.

SEVENTEEN

They were twenty-four hours into the case and they should have some firm leads by now, but they still had to wait to see what the evidence revealed. While contemplating where to turn next, Lexi called Linda Ellis for an update on Scarlett.

'I'd love to tell you she's settling in okay with her foster carers, but in all honesty I can't. When I handed her over, she was crying non-stop for her mother, she's barely eaten anything since we found her.'

This was hard for Lexi to hear. Perhaps Scarlett would be better off back with Liam Norris, the man she thought of as 'dada', but with Norris a possible suspect in Bethany's death she really couldn't sanction it. Plus, there was the question hanging over paternity, with no father's name on the birth certificate. All she could hope for was that the case and the paternity issue could be resolved quickly, so Scarlett's future could be sorted out.

'Linda, couldn't she go to Bethany's parents in the meantime? She must know them.' Ridhi and Colin were trying to track down Bethany's family.

'We're looking into it.' Linda Ellis wouldn't be drawn

further, and Lexi didn't know enough herself about Bethany's family circumstances to press the point.

Restless, she took Tom up to the vineyard to check how the evidence gathering was going. The CSIs were still busy, meaning the lower floor of the winery was still out of bounds.

'Let's see how they're doing up at the tunnel entrance,' she said, desperately hoping they'd found something that could prove useful.

As she and Tom walked past the winery, she paused. She could hear raised voices inside. Tom stopped beside her, and they listened. One of the voices was definitely Marietta – her French accent was distinctive. The other was a man. Putting her finger to her lips, Lexi moved silently towards the door of the facility, Tom right behind her. It wasn't fully closed – there was a gap of about a centimetre as the latch was resting against the edge of the doorframe rather than properly shut. Lexi put her ear against the space.

'But don't you see? If Johnny sells up, my job will be in jeopardy.' It was Will Steadman's voice.

'How can he sell the place on his own? I have my shares. Ben has his. We would all have to agree the purchaser and the price.'

'So what will you do when he presents a formal offer from one of the big drinks conglomerates?'

There was no answer forthcoming.

'Seriously, Marietta. You need to think about it. I know that's what he has in mind.'

'But you also know that Ben won't let go of his share without a fight. Johnny would need to offer him twice the market value. Ben is keeping Johnny trapped here.'

'Not that you mind, do you?'

'Pah! You don't know what you're talking about.'

Footsteps came towards the door. Lexi pointed with her finger and the two of them scurried around the corner of the building. As Lexi leaned back against the wall, trying to keep her breathing silent, she heard the door open, then swing shut, and footsteps moving quickly down the drive. She peered around the edge of the building. Marietta was marching down the drive brusquely on her own. It meant Will Steadman was still inside.

The door swung open again and slammed shut. Will Steadman made his way more slowly down to the car park and got into his car.

'Stay here till he's gone,' Lexi whispered. She didn't want him to know they'd been eavesdropping.

A few seconds later, when it was quiet, Tom and Lexi made their way towards the tunnel entrance.

'What did you make of that?' said Tom.

'Sounds like Johnny wants out. Will doesn't. Marietta's probably playing them off against each other. And now there's been a mysterious death on the property. How's that going to affect the share value of Elvington Wines?'

Could it be a motive for someone who didn't want the sale of the vineyard to go through?

———

There was nothing new to be reported at the tunnel mouth, so she and Tom came back to the station. She called the rest of the team into the incident room and stood in front of the white-board. It was time to give the investigation a sense of purpose and drive it forward. In her mind, she had a list of suspects and a clutch of theories – that Bethany either knew or didn't know her killer, that she knowingly or unknowingly took whatever drug had caused her death. She needed to assign tasks to the team to test out each theory and rule out competing suspects. It would be a group effort, but she had to steer their course.

Firstly, she updated them on what she and Tom had overheard outside the winery. Then she called on Colin for an update on the ownership of the vineyard.

'The company's split pretty neatly between Johnny Lycett-Boyd, his wife Marietta and his brother Ben Lycett-Boyd – the one out in Australia,' he said. 'They each own thirty per cent.'

'And the other ten per cent?'

'That belongs to Will Steadman.'

'That's interesting. If the vineyard is sold, he could lose his job but he would also be in line for a payout of ten per cent of the value of the company.'

'But does any of this have any bearing on the case?' said Ridhi.

'Good question.' It was something that didn't quite make sense. 'We've got a killing with ritualistic elements to it – suggesting a lone killer, maybe one that's killed before. But also it appears to be someone with specific local knowledge of the vineyard, where there's plenty of marital and financial strife.' She rubbed her eyes with both hands. 'A conflict of motives which could pull our investigation in different directions if we're not careful. So what does that mean, Colin?'

'It means follow where the evidence leads.'

'Absolutely. Anyone been in touch with Mort?'

Tom nodded. 'He thinks he'll have the tox results in some time tomorrow.'

'Good.' Finally, they might get something concrete to work with.

There was a single knock and the door swung open. 'All right if I listen in?' It was Maggie.

'Of course. We're nearly done, anyhow,' said Lexi.

She briefly brought Maggie up to speed. 'So we're starting by looking at either Liam Norris, her boyfriend, Johnny Lycett-Boyd, her erstwhile lover and possibly the father of her daughter, or Will Steadman, the vineyard manger. Lycett-Boyd's wife,

Marietta, has a possible motive, to get rid of her husband's lover, though I think it's a long shot.'

'And the motives of the others?'

'Norris – jealousy. Lycett-Boyd – to get rid of an unwanted complication. Steadman – the motive's not so clear cut. And, of course, we can't rule out an unknown suspect at this point.'

'Who's looking most likely?' said Maggie.

'I want to kick off by focusing on Liam Norris. If he found out about Lycett-Boyd being Scarlett's father, his motive could have been jealousy, a crime of passion. My priority for the team is to check out his movements on Saturday night and to see if any of the crime scene evidence can be connected to him. At the same time, we'll continue building a more detailed picture of Bethany's life by interviewing family, friends and work colleagues.'

'And what about you – what are you going to do?'

'My priority will be to work up a profile of the killer based on the crime scene and see how that matches our suspects.'

'Good. Why don't you run it past Ed Harlow? See what he makes of the posing and the wings.'

Ed Harlow was one of the country's top forensic psychologists, and he worked at the university in Canterbury. He'd helped Lexi get to grips with the killers' motivations on a couple of recent cases, and usually Lexi would be happy to consult him. However, now might not be the time.

'I'm trying to stay out of his hair at the moment. His wife, Charlie, has cancer and I think she's been moved to a hospice for palliative care, so he's taking time off.'

'Fair enough. Keep me posted, right?'

'You got it.'

EIGHTEEN

The first part of a murder investigation is always spent gathering evidence. Turning over every stone, following every lead, and keeping an open mind. It would be easy to let first impressions lead the way – Liam Norris cast in the role of jealous partner or Johnny Lycett-Boyd conveniently getting rid of the mother of the child he wanted to claim as his own.

But as Lexi packed up her things and went from her office to the station car park, she realised something was bothering her about these two scenarios. Norris had the motive and he had the opportunity – once he left the Crown at closing time, he had no alibi. Did he have the means? She needed to know the exact cause of death from Mort before she could answer that. A drug overdose seemed the most likely, so would Norris take his partner up to his rival's property and drug her there? Norris's potential motive was jealousy – a crime of passion. But Bethany's death looked like anything but that. Unless he had a set of keys from years ago, they would have to have used the tunnel to gain access into the cave. But would Norris have known it existed?

What about Johnny? Motive – to get Bethany out of the

way so he could claim Scarlett? Or perhaps she was in fact pressing him for more money for Scarlett, and he'd had enough. Opportunity? Once Marietta had fallen into her pill-induced sleep, he could have left the house and arranged to meet Bethany at the winery. As to means, Johnny had denied ever using drugs, but that meant nothing.

Will Steadman – he had the opportunity. And what about Marietta? She surely had the strongest motive, and she could have been lying about the sleeping pills.

With so many possibilities to stare down, Lexi needed to understand who she might be looking for. She had to get a handle on the killer – the type of person he was, what his motives might be, how he'd reached a point where he could kill a woman and leave her baby alone in a cave with the body.

What did she know about this person? Nothing for certain and any conclusions she could draw about him were so far based on assumptions. Even supposing it was a man rather than a woman was an unfounded assumption. But now was the time to start constructing a profile of them. In her mind, the suspect was a man. Why did she think this? Bethany's body was virtually naked, apart from the angel wings. This suggested a sexual element to the killing. Bethany was, as far as they knew, heterosexual – she lived with Liam Norris and had apparently had a fling with Johnny Lycett-Boyd. So if she went to the cave to meet a sexual partner, it seemed reasonable to assume the person she was meeting was a man. Though by no means certain.

Did Bethany know him? It would be odd to agree to meet a perfect stranger in such a private place, especially with your child. But maybe she met him somewhere else first, and he brought her to the cave. It seemed most likely that Bethany knew Person A, but that didn't mean that he'd come across the investigation's radar yet. It could have been a relatively new contact that no one else knew about.

Which of them picked the location? Did Bethany know about the cave from her dalliance with Johnny? Or did Suspect A have knowledge of the winery and the cellars beneath it? Why choose to come to the vineyard on a weekend when it was so busy? That suggested that perhaps Suspect A was at the vineyard already. Johnny Lycett-Boyd? Will Steadman? Talk about shitting in your own nest. Or one of the picking crew. She quickly left a voicemail for Ridhi asking her to check how long the pickers had been staying at the vineyard, and whether any of them had been in the local pubs or had shopped at the Spar supermarket in the village where Bethany worked.

She thought about the posing of the scene. Why the wings? Why the candles? What was the significance of both of them being turned into angels? To her, nothing about the scene had appeared accidental. If Bethany wasn't meant to have overdosed and Suspect A was her friend or lover, surely that person would have called for help. The fact that they didn't was criminal as far as Lexi was concerned.

But there was so much she didn't understand.

The men who seemed like clear suspects in terms of means and opportunity – Johnny Lycett-Boyd or Will Steadman, even Liam Norris – didn't appear to raise any red flags for the highly ritualistic posing of the death scene. They simply didn't fit the bill. Their possible motives were based on real-life issues rather than sexual fantasy. And Bethany hadn't, as far as Mort had concluded, been sexually assaulted.

She swung out of the car park and turned left to go up to the ring road, dialling Ridhi's number again. This time she picked up.

'Sorry to call you after work hours, but Tom said you'd had a weird encounter with a *helpful* member of the public.'

'Ah, he means Gideon Croft – I'm just writing up my notes on it now.'

'Anything of interest?'

'He came up with some story about an Elvington Angel protecting the village and women being murdered in its honour. But it's all ancient history, medieval times, not something of relevance to this case.'

'An angel? That's a pretty strange coincidence.'

'Yeah, he came up with the story, and I sent him packing. But I googled the Elvington Angel, and it is a thing. Just centuries ago.'

'And if he knew about it, so could other people.' It supported her earlier thought that whoever had killed Bethany wanted them to think it was a ritual killing. They were using a piece of ancient folklore to throw suspicion in the opposite direction.

'What did you make of the bloke?' Lexi wanted Ridhi's first impression, just in case he was someone they should take more seriously.

'I didn't take to him. Weird, probably a time-waster, but... I don't know. There was something off about him.'

Alarm bells went off in Lexi's head. 'He might be trying to insert himself into the investigation, so I think we need to find out more about him. Dig around a bit, Ridhi. See if we've had any contact with him before, if he turns up on HOLMES 2, and check where he was on Saturday night.'

'You think he's a suspect?'

'Until we rule him out, we've got to keep an open mind.'

Lexi was so lost in thought, it took her a moment to realise she'd reached her sister's house. If the ritualistic way the body had been posed, with the wings and the candles, was the killer's signature, it looked well-established, and that suggested to Lexi it wasn't the first time he'd killed. Another area to put the team on.

She parked her Crossfire behind her sister's Mercedes on the gravel drive and crunched up to the front door, which immediately swung open. Her niece and nephew must have been watching for her out of the window and ran down the front steps in their stocking feet to greet her.

'Aunt Lexi, Aunt Lexi,' cried Tasha.

She swept her niece into bear hug and raised a hand to acknowledge Sam's hello grunt. The teenage attitude was starting to show. Amber appeared behind them in the doorway.

'Not late for once – well done!'

Lexi laughed. 'You gave me such a hard time last time that I didn't dare.'

Amber led the way to the kitchen, and Lexi followed with her arm around Tasha. Sam darted off up the stairs – no doubt the PlayStation held more appeal for him than listening to his mother and his aunt gossiping.

'You're still limping,' said Amber, as Lexi settled herself onto one of the high stools at the breakfast bar.

'Yeah, it's pretty painful. I think I pulled my hamstring on a rough part of the course.'

'Glutton for punishment. Perhaps you should swap to something gentler – I go to a great yoga class.'

'Somehow I don't think being able to wrap my leg around the back of my head will be so useful during murder investigations as being able to run after villains.'

'Is that why you do triathlons?' said Tasha. 'To be able to chase the bad guys?'

Lexi laughed. 'Not exactly. But being fit certainly helps – my job can be unforgiving at times.'

Amber's husband Grant came into the kitchen.

'Good to see you, Lexi,' he said, coming across the floor to embrace her.

'You, too.'

'Glass of wine?'

'Just the one, when we eat.'

Amber was busying herself with the food preparation and something in the oven smelled delicious. Grant disappeared to his cupboard under the stairs, which he jokingly referred to as his wine cellar, then reappeared with a familiar looking bottle in his hand.

'Elvington?' he said, showing it to Lexi. 'I hear you're working on a case over there. You can tell us about it over supper.'

'Not in front of the kids,' said Amber. 'Tasha, go and fetch Sam – I'm about to dish up.'

Once Tasha had left the room, Lexi said, 'There's not much to tell at this stage.' The papers had reported that a woman's body had been found on the vineyard, but Lexi had made sure that they'd released no further information. 'We're not even sure yet if it's murder or an accidental overdose.'

'But wasn't there a baby, too?' said Amber.

'Yes, the woman's daughter was found with her, still alive.' She didn't mention the angel wings. So far they'd managed to keep that detail out of the public domain, and while she trusted Amber and Grant one hundred per cent, she wouldn't expect anyone on her team to blab to family members, so she wouldn't either.

The food was delicious. Chicken in a creamy bacon sauce that was complemented perfectly by the dry white wine Grant had opened. It was the first home-cooked meal Lexi had eaten for several days, reminding her once again that her diet of sandwiches and biscuits really wasn't good enough.

Tasha and Sam told her what was going on at school, doing entertaining imitations of their teachers that made Grant laugh and Amber frown. Over the apple crumble that followed, Tasha had more questions.

'Aunt Lexi, have you got a boyfriend?'

'No. I don't have time for one.'

'That's sad,' said Tasha.

'Don't you want to have kids?' said Sam.

'Wow, straight in there with the third degree. I think I

should get you two to come down to the station and question my suspects.'

She'd deflected the question easily, but it stung. Did she really have to choose between career and family? She looked around the table of smiling faces. This was her family and she was happy to be here.

'Boyfriends aside,' said Grant, 'didn't Amber tell me you were thinking about moving into town?'

Lexi currently rented a cottage in the village of Wye, eleven miles north of Canterbury. 'Sure, when I get time to go house-hunting.'

'Yes!' said Tasha. 'You could move here. We'd see more of you if you were our neighbour.'

'Ha – one of these giant houses would be too big for just me on my own.' Not to mention too expensive.

'But somewhere nearby, then,' said Sam. 'It would be great to have you around.'

That was pretty much enough to make Lexi do it. Since she'd rescued Sam from the clutches of a demented killer earlier in the year, the bond between them had grown fast, and she was relieved to see that he was bouncing back from the ordeal.

They chatted around the table for a bit longer, then Lexi looked at her watch. 'I'd better be going.' She wanted to go through everything they had on the case so far, so she could set new directions for the team at the morning's briefing.

'Hold on a moment, Lex,' Amber said, as Lexi made a move towards the hall.

She went into the kitchen and came back with a number scribbled on a piece of paper.

'My physio – you really need to sort out that leg, or you'll lose the rest of the season.'

'I know, I know.' Lexi took the piece of paper and glanced down at it. She recognised the name. 'Luke Evans?'

'Yes – he works out of Synergy. You know, the gym on Kingsmead Road.'

'Yeah, I know. You're the second person to recommend him. He must be good.'

'Brilliant. Sorted out Grant's back, and my frozen shoulder.'

———

Lexi keyed the number into her phone, then rang it from the car as she was driving out of Canterbury.

'Luke speaking.'

'You don't know me, but I've got a pulled hamstring and I'd like to make an appointment for an assessment.'

'Sure. Who gave you my number?'

'My sister, Amber Riley. She said you were good.'

'That's great. Happy to help you.'

'So when would be good?'

'Are you in Canterbury now?'

'Just leaving.'

'If you've got fifteen minutes to spare, I could take a look now – then we can set up a proper appointment later in the week. What's your name?'

'Lexi Bennett.'

'Oh yes, she told me all about you. See you in a minute.'

As she turned the car around and headed back towards the city centre, she couldn't help but wonder if this was her sister trying to set her up for a date... *'told me all about you'*. It certainly wouldn't be the first time.

NINETEEN

Luke, the physiotherapist, was certainly easy on the eye – tall and muscular, with a good tan and a smart haircut – making Lexi wonder why she hadn't noticed him around the gym before. And it definitely didn't seem beyond the realms of possibility that Amber would think him a suitable match for her, as it turned out he competed in Ironman events as well.

'So you pulled this yesterday, on the course?' he said, feeling the muscle at the back of her thigh with firm hands, once she was lying face down on his treatment bench.

'I think so. There's a bit of the course that goes up a hill, really rutted and stony.'

'Yeah, I saw a couple of guys go over along that stretch.'

'You were there?'

'I ran it.'

Lexi rolled her eyes. 'Probably miles up the field from me.'

He laughed and carried on with his assessment. 'Yup, it's pretty swollen here, just where your biceps femoris attaches to the side of your knee. That explains the pain that's radiating from your knee joint up the back of your thigh.'

'Is it bad?'

'Not too bad, despite how much it hurts. I think it's a strain, rather than a tear. You'll need to rest it until the swelling goes down, then we'll take a look at your training programme. Are you stretching properly before and after working out?'

Was she? She'd taken shortcuts in training and some weeks, when work was busy, she'd been lucky to train at all. But before she had to admit her own culpability, her phone rang. She sat up and dug it out of her bag. It was Tom. He wouldn't call her in the evening unless it was something important.

'Sorry – I'm going to have to take this.' She slipped off the treatment bench and picked up her jacket and bag. 'Can you text me about an appointment?'

It was a little rude, but he seemed to understand. 'Sure. Say hi to Amber, and thank her for the referral.'

Lexi nodded, but she was already at the door.

'What have you got, Tom?'

'Mort's on his way with the tox results.'

Mort arrived at the station at the same time as Lexi, and she ushered him into her office. The sight of Mort Barley in the Canterbury nick was a rarity – it must mean he had something important for her.

She sat down. 'Tell me.'

Mort placed a brown envelope on her desk. 'Expedited tox results,' he said.

'Thanks,' she said. Then she went quickly to the door of her office and yelled, 'Tom, d'you want to hear the tox results?' She sat down again and reached across for the envelope. 'What will I find?' It was quicker to get Mort to explain them than for her to work out which of the numeric readings was significant.

Tom appeared in the doorway just in time to hear Mort's answer.

'Fentanyl. She had lethal levels in her blood – enough to kill a horse, let alone a slip of a girl weighing a hundred pounds or thereabouts.'

'Damn! I thought I'd left that shit behind when I came back from America.'

'Fentanyl?' said Tom. 'Some kind of synthetic opiate, right?'

'Yes,' said Lexi. 'One hundred times stronger than morphine and fifty times stronger than heroin.'

Tom let out a low whistle.

Lexi turned to Mort. 'How was it administered?'

'There was no trace of it in her stomach, so not pills or lozenges. I think it was injected – I found a possible site for that, a tiny pinprick on her armpit. But you can take it via a nasal or sublingual spray, or patches, so the prick might be nothing. The killer could have injected her between the toes, above the hairline, in her cheek or gums... anywhere really.'

'So you won't be able to give us any indication of its source?' said Tom.

'Ha!' Mort's bark of laughter was all the answer they needed.

'Anything else we should know about?' said Lexi.

'There is actually. Stomach contents. A fair quantity of partially digested psilocybin. Someone sent poor Bethany on the trip of her life.'

'That's the active compound in magic mushrooms?' said Tom.

'Yes – so once she's tripping, the bastard administers a lethal dose of fentanyl,' said Lexi. 'Any way this could be self-inflicted or accidental?'

Mort cocked his head. 'Any drug overdose can be accidental. But there were no signs that Bethany habitually used drugs

– her liver looked pristine, certainly not the liver of someone with a drink or drug problem. She wasn't a party girl. Which means she'd have absolutely no tolerance for fentanyl, even in a much smaller dose. In theory, yes, she could have taken it willingly without realising how dangerous it was – or someone could have administered it to her with or without her consent or even knowledge. But you won't get the answers to that from the forensics. I can only tell you what chemicals are present, not how they got there.'

Lexi had heard this lecture from him before, but she still always asked because when Mort did have an opinion over how something had happened it was worth hearing.

'Do those results tighten up the time of death?' said Tom.

'Fractionally,' said Mort. 'Between one and two. Right, I'm off.'

'Where does this leave us?' said Tom, as Mort disappeared with a wave of his hand.

'Bye, Mort – and thanks,' Lexi called to his receding back. 'Someone's dealing fentanyl, maybe locally, or maybe our guy had to go further afield to source it. Would you talk to the County Lines team? See how prevalent it is in the area and if they have any names. Or better yet, perhaps they've got a CHIS who can help us.' A CHIS was a covert human intelligence source – an undercover officer or informant who had been given a criminal conduct authorisation, allowing them to participate in criminal activities so they could maintain their cover while feeding information to the police.

'I'll put Colin on that,' said Tom. 'He's mates with a couple of the guys in County Lines.' The County Lines team investigated the criminal networks which transported drugs out of the major cities and into the regions.

'Excellent,' said Lexi. 'If we find out who's been dealing fentanyl round here, we might get a lead on who administered it to Bethany.'

'Looks more like Norris than Lycett-Boyd, don't you think?'

'At face value, yes,' said Lexi. 'But I expect our Johnny knows just the right sort of people up at that racetrack of his. Could be either of them. Or neither.'

They'd find out.

TWENTY

MOTIVATIONAL JOURNAL – TUESDAY, SEPTEMBER 26

Yesterday's achievements

1. At work all day
2. Tried white noise device for insomnia – see learning outcomes below
3. Ordered wings for girl plus one
4. Booked car for MOT

Learning outcomes

1. White noise device – helped me get to sleep more quickly – that much was good. But didn't work a second time when I woke up at 1 a.m. Awake and churning till 5 a.m. The white noise couldn't push out the thoughts and the memories – they're becoming more insistent. Torment is getting louder. I feel surrounded by it in the dark, but if I turn on the light, I can't sleep. Will keep trying.

2. Taking a short sleep during the day at work might be counterproductive. And risky, if I get caught sleeping at work.

Plans for today

1. Try to catch up with the girl later on, build trust
2. Delete internet ID used to buy wings
3. Check for updates on police investigation into B – is there something I can throw in their path to send them in the wrong direction?
4. Scout suitable location – the caves will be too risky now
5. Arrange a catch-up

How are you feeling – in three words?

1. Tired
2. Distracted
3. Determined

Memory of the day

Before Mum went away, I had two parents. I remember being a family. We ate meals together around a table in a bright, sunny kitchen. I can remember being in a high chair, trying to reach what my parents were eating on the table, banging a spoon, crumbling a rusk into a mess of crumbs. Some days this would make Mum laugh. Some days it made her angry. I would never know which she was going to be. I didn't understand then that she had good days and bad days. Until she just had bad days.

Once Mum was gone, there was some time when it was just me and the man. I don't know now if he was my father or not. But mostly what I remember from that time is him handing me over to other people, women, who I didn't know. I was like a pass-the-parcel prize as he gave me to people who could look after me. I suppose he had to go to work. But I think it was more than that. He didn't want me. And one day he wasn't around anymore, and I was left with a stranger, then another, then another. Foster parents. A children's home. Care – that's what they call it. But that's not what it is.

Motivation for the day
Don't let yesterday take up too much of today

TWENTY-ONE

TUESDAY

Sandra Glover knew that her daughter Bethany was dead. Linda Ellis had been to see her about Scarlett and had magnanimously agreed to break the news of her daughter's death – it seemed it would be less stressful for a very sick woman than having the police arriving as well as social services. Because Sandra Glover was barely alive herself – she was in the palliative care wing of a hospice on the outskirts of Margate, lying in wait as stage 4 lung cancer slowly sucked the life out of her.

Tom felt bad for intruding into her grief for her daughter and her own death, but there were things they needed to know about Bethany and, given that Liam Norris was a possible suspect in her death, he couldn't be relied upon to answer honestly.

The smell of the building cloaked Tom with depression as he followed a care-worn woman up two flights of stairs and along a corridor to Sandra Glover's room. The silence was oppressive, and though there were pictures of landscapes and flowers hung on the wall, the desired uplifting effect seemed somehow hollow, given that most of the patients here would never experience the beauty of nature in the raw again.

The woman stopped outside a door and turned towards him. 'She tires easily and she's had an upset. Please be very gentle with her.'

Tom nodded. He wondered if it wouldn't have been better for Lexi or Ridhi to come on this mission, but that was old-fashioned thinking. There was no reason why this task should be more suited to a woman. They didn't hold a monopoly on kindness.

He went into the room, expecting to see an elderly woman – someone frail and broken by life's hardships. But Sandra Glover wasn't old. She looked sallow, hollowed out, tired, but not old. Bethany had only been twenty-three, and by Tom's guess Sandra must have been even younger than that when she gave birth to her. She was slumped back against a mountain of pillows, her eyes closed, breathing slowly in and out. Oxygen was being delivered through a nasal cannula and her chest rattled with each exhalation.

'It's okay, I'm awake.' Her voice was harsh and rasping. Her eyes opened and she blinked a few times. Then she raised a shaky hand and pointed at the plastic water beaker on the bedside table.

'Of course,' said Tom, glad to be able to do something rather than stand and stare.

'You from the police?' The last word dissolved into a flurry of coughs, as Tom placed the beaker into her outstretched hand.

'That obvious?' said Tom, while she had a sip of water.

'They said you'd be coming. Want to ask some questions about my Bethany.'

'If that's okay?'

'Not sure I can be much help to you. Haven't seen her in a couple of years. We fell out, me and Bethany. Over that bloke she was running around with.'

'Liam Norris?'

'That's the one. He got her pregnant. I said, "Don't go

throwing your life away on him. He's a wastrel." Bethany was smart. She could have done something with her life.' She sniffed. 'But she won't now. She didn't listen to me.'

'She didn't take kindly to your advice?'

'Kids don't, do they? You got kids?'

'A daughter.'

'Be careful what you say to her. It's too easy to push them away by doing what you think's right for them.'

'She's only nine.'

Sandra Glover shrugged. 'Be a teenager in a few years. No time at all.'

Tom supposed she was right. It would fly by.

'Was Bethany happy with Liam?'

Sandra's eyes brightened. The question had caught her attention. 'You think he did it, do you?'

'What do you know of their relationship?'

'Hooking up with him was the biggest mistake of her life.'

Tom waited for an explanation of this bold statement.

Sandra frowned. 'He was rough. Sure, she sometimes had a mouth on her. No filter – that's what they say nowadays, isn't it? But that doesn't make it okay for him to hurt her.' She shook her head wistfully. 'He thinks he's God's gift, and he's got a nasty temper on him. He took a swipe at her once, when they were first together. She knocked the kitchen table on the way down and broke a tooth. She'd been nagging at him over something. Maybe she learned over the last couple of years, but...' She paused, wheezing for breath. 'Maybe she didn't.'

So, Liam was physically abusive, but that didn't necessarily fit with the ritualistic aspect of Bethany's death. And of course, what Sandra Glover was telling him was all based on things that must have happened a couple of years ago. It wasn't much help as far as the current case was concerned. This was hearsay, and what they needed was forensic certainty.

'Did she report him to the police at the time?'

'Of course she didn't. That would have earned her another knock. But that's why I begged her not to have a baby with him. Why bring a kid into a relationship like that?' She started to cough. She looked exhausted. 'I wish Karolyn had never introduced her to him.'

'Karolyn?'

'Her best friend, Karolyn Small. She introduced them. She knew Liam growing up – they were in the same care home as kids.'

'Thanks for your time, Mrs Glover.' He would get Ridhi to check up on Bethany's medical records and the autopsy report to see if there were any other old, unexplained injuries.

Sandra Glover sank back into her pillow, the light in her eyes fading a little. 'The lady who came to see me…?'

'Linda Ellis? The social worker?'

She nodded. 'She asked me if I wanted to see Bethany's daughter.' She was racked with coughing for a moment, then took a few deep breaths to recover. 'I told her no.'

'Why?'

'What's the point? I'm dying. The baby won't even remember coming to see me. Or if she did, it would just be a scary old woman.'

'She might not remember,' said Tom. 'But you would. Scarlett's your granddaughter, Bethany's little girl. Of course you want to see her. She's family.' And for a little girl whose father was currently unknown, Sandra Glover might be the only family she had.

Sandra sniffed, tears filling her eyes. Tom could see her struggling not to cry out loud. He reached over to the nightstand for a box of tissues and gave her all the time she needed.

'Is it too late to change my mind?' She pressed her lips together to keep her emotions in check.

'No, of course not. I'll let Linda Ellis know and she'll make arrangements for Scarlett to visit.'

Sandra put a hand to her mouth and finally allowed herself to cry. 'I wish things could have been different.'

'How so?' said Tom, his voice soft.

'Bethany. Scarlett. The little one's setting off down the same path.'

'I don't understand.'

'I failed Bethany as a mother. Had me own problems, that's for sure. The council took her into care when she was four years old. They found her wandering along the front at Margate, all on her own.' She sniffed loudly. 'I'd been on a bender all night, still drunk, passed out. I'd left the door open and she wandered off.'

Tom didn't know what to say. He was appalled, but he couldn't help but feel a grain of sympathy for her at the same time. And a lot more for Bethany.

'After that, she was in and out of care all the time. I think she hated me, for what I did to her. I don't think she ever trusted anyone ever again, not properly.'

'I'm so sorry,' said Tom.

He poured her some water and watched her take a sip. When she handed the beaker back to him, he held her hand for a moment. 'I should go now,' he said softly. She needed to rest. And he didn't want her to see how close he was to welling up. Some people joined the police for the adrenalin rush of catching the bad guys. Sure enough, it was always thrilling. But this was another part of the job. Seeing people at their most vulnerable – victims of crime and their families. Cleaning up after the worst of what humanity wrought on itself. Not that far off from being a social worker, but in the immediate aftermath of tragedy and violence. And maybe, on days like today, this was what the job was really about. Making people feel safe again. Putting families back together.

Scarlett and Sandra shared genes. They shared blood. And it had to count for something.

TWENTY-TWO

Lexi had forgotten just how relaxing it could be to have someone else's hands working away on tired, sore muscles. Luke Evans was clearly gifted at his work and after forty minutes of stretching and deep tissue massage, Lexi felt like a new person.

'Wow – that was amazing. I could get used to this,' she said, as she got ready to leave.

Luke grinned. 'Another satisfied customer – what I like to hear. But you need to keep up with that stretching programme for the benefits to last.'

'Yes, sir.' She gave him a mock salute, but she was really going to try. She wanted to get back to training as quickly as possible. Inactivity made her twitchy, and somehow obsessing over her cases while sitting on the sofa never enabled her to join the dots in the same way that thinking about them on a run did.

'Same time next week?' he said, getting out his phone to log their next appointment.

'Absolutely.' She didn't add *if the case allows it*. She was determined to put herself first for a change, and taking a lunch hour wasn't too much to ask, was it?

'In the meantime, if you want to chat about Ironman strategy, what about a drink?'

He was easy on the eye. They certainly had a shared interest. And now he was asking her out? Amber's words rang in her ears... *you need to get a social life. Find some friends. Enjoy yourself.* It was true – for the past eight months since she'd been back in Canterbury, she'd focused on work and work alone, apart from building bridges with her sister and her family. She hadn't looked up any of her old school friends, and she hadn't found time to socialise with her new work colleagues, even though Tom had asked her round for dinner a couple of times.

'That would be good. I'm sure I could do with a fresh approach. More strategy required for my running as I'm getting older.'

'Right, you'll be a grandmother soon!' Luke laughed. She guessed he was a little younger than her, but not much. However, he was definitely way fitter, and she was sure she'd be able to learn a lot from him. 'Tomorrow evening?'

Lexi hadn't been ready for that. 'Um... I've just taken on a new case – it's hectic. Can I get back to you?' She hoped he wouldn't take it as a brush-off.

'Sure. Whenever suits you. I'll still be here.'

He smiled, and she realised these things didn't have to be difficult. She'd find time to meet him once the case was done. She walked back to the office appreciating the deep azure of the sky and the touch of the sun warm on her skin. Autumn was round the corner, so she might as well enjoy it while it lasted.

But... did she really need the complication of bringing a man into her life? Of course, it would be easy to go for a quick drink, maybe go for a run together. But what if it turned into something else? She didn't have time for a commitment like that. And she wasn't sure she wanted to make one. When she was working a case, she had to give it one hundred per cent, and there weren't many men who'd be able to understand that. So why start something she couldn't finish?

It's just a drink. Don't overthink it.

———

She needed to know more about Bethany. If she was going to get a feel for who might have killed her, she needed to know who she was and how she lived her life. Tom had come back with the information from Bethany's mother that Norris had been violent. But as far as they could gather, the relationship between Bethany and Sandra was highly dysfunctional. Could they really trust anything she said?

Find out how a person lived and you'll find out how they died. Harry Garcia, her old boss in America, had taught her that.

Time to check Bethany's medical records to see if there was any indication that she'd suffered abuse at Liam Norris's – or anybody else's – hand.

Elvington was too small to have its own doctor's surgery, and according to Google, the closest medical practice to the village was two and a half miles away at Shepherdswell. It seemed likely that Bethany might have been registered there, but the receptionist wasn't prepared to confirm it over the phone. The woman was quite right, of course – it could be anyone on the end of a phone line. The quickest way would be to go down there in person.

She arrived to find a busy waiting room. Jumping the queue to talk to the doctor wasn't going to make her popular. But after checking her ID, the receptionist referred her to the practice manager and a minute later she found herself sitting in a bright, functional office behind the reception area.

'I'm Sarah Watson – I manage the patient records here. How can I help you?'

Sarah Watson was the personification of efficiency – a brusque tone, tied back hair, neat navy skirt suit, sensible shoes, short nails – but the overall effect was leavened by her choice of jewellery, a bold statement necklace of oversized pink and gold beads around her neck and a chunky gold knuckleduster ring that spanned three fingers.

'DI Bennett, Kent Police. I'm investigating the murder of a woman called Bethany Glover. Can you check whether she was one of your patients?'

'To what end?'

'We want to establish whether she'd been subjected to intimate partner violence in the months leading up to her death. Her medical records might help us do this.'

Sarah Watson pursed her lips. 'You do understand that we still have a duty of confidentiality even to the deceased?'

'Of course.'

'Coroners have a legal right of access, but when it comes to a request from you lot, we have to determine whether disclosing the records is in the public interest or not.'

'With all due respect, I would imagine that solving a murder and bringing the killer to justice would serve the public interest.'

'Naturally. But will knowing the victim's medical history really contribute to achieving that?'

'I can't give you details of our investigation, but knowing whether Bethany Glover was a victim of domestic violence could well have an important bearing.' Lexi could feel herself losing patience with the woman.

However, it seemed that Sarah Watson was just being efficient. 'I can see your point, so if she's a patient of ours I'll be happy to release the records to you.'

'Thank you.'

'Do you have her NHS number or her date of birth?'

Lexi had taken those details from Mort's autopsy report, and handed a slip of paper to the practice manager.

'Give me a minute – I'll check.'

She opened the laptop on her desk and logged in.

'Yes, here she is.' She looked across the desk at Lexi. 'I can email them to you or print them out.'

'Email would be easier.' They would need to add the records to the HOLMES 2 database, and she didn't think the civilian staff in the incident room would appreciate having to scan them in page by page, rather than simply uploading them. She gave Sarah Watson the appropriate email address, thanked her, and took her leave.

Sitting in her car in the surgery's small parking area, she flipped open the email on her phone and skimmed through the pages and pages of details. A lot of it documented Bethany's pregnancy with Scarlett – blood test results, scans, the various routine appointments. She looked further back for the incident that Bethany's mother had mentioned to Tom, when Norris had knocked Bethany over, causing her to break a tooth. She couldn't find anything in the timeframe, but perhaps they should check her dental records. If the broken tooth was the only injury, she wouldn't have come to the doctor. But about a year earlier, there had been a visit to A&E. Bethany had presented with a bruised face and an X-ray had shown that she had a cracked cheekbone. There was also bruising on one arm and on her ribs. She claimed to have tripped on some stone steps, but a note from the A&E doctor confirmed that he was of the opinion someone had beaten her. Was she with Norris when this had happened or was it some other boyfriend or male acquaintance? The spurious tale of tripping over made Lexi assume it had been done by someone close to her.

She kept reading. Bethany had been registered at a practice in Dover before coming to the Shepherdswell surgery. She checked the home address listed for that time and recognised it instantly. Before Elvington, Bethany had been living in a hostel that catered for young people leaving the care system.

As she drove back to the office, she gave Linda Ellis a call.

'When you checked Bethany's files, did you come across any other relatives apart from her mother?'

'There was an aunt, but she died a few years ago. Bethany didn't have any siblings. She was fostered with a family for several years though, from when she was twelve through to sixteen. You might talk to them, see if they were still in touch with her.'

'Thanks – good idea.'

'I'll email their details.'

Maybe they'd have a clearer picture of Bethany's life, and so be able to give her a clearer picture of Bethany's death.

TWENTY-THREE

Tom felt like he needed a change of scenery. The incident room felt muggy and the clatter of computer keyboards was doing his head in. Ridhi looked half asleep in front of her screen.

'I'm going to the pub,' he said. 'Want to come along, Ridhi?'

Ridhi started and sat upright. She looked at her watch. 'What? It's only four o'clock.'

Tom laughed. 'Don't panic. I'm not proposing afternoon boozing. I want to go to the Crown at Eythorne, to check that Liam Norris was actually there on Saturday night.'

'Ah, got you. Sure, I'll come with you.'

The drive between Canterbury and Elvington was becoming increasingly familiar, and they took the same route to Eythorne as the two villages were just a mile apart.

'Do you think it could be Norris who killed her?' said Ridhi.

Tom thought for a moment. 'He wasn't averse to knocking her about by all accounts, but does that really fit with such a highly posed murder scene? And if he believes Scarlett is his daughter, would he really have left her naked and alone in the dark with her dead mother?'

'It doesn't make much sense, does it?' said Ridhi, as they

turned off the A2. 'I could see it if he came home drunk, got into a fight that turned physical, and she ended up dead in their house. But this business with the wings and the candles in the cave? You're right – it doesn't add up.'

The Crown was easy to find – it was on the main street of the village, and Tom pulled into the small car park to the right of the building. There were spaces for four cars, beyond which was a small beer garden squeezed onto a strip of grass between the car park and the next property.

They went up some steps at the side of the pub and Tom pulled open the door, allowing Ridhi to enter first. Although it was ostensibly open, there were no punters, and the barman, a sturdy specimen in his mid-thirties, was leaning on the bar, reading *The Sun*. He closed the paper as they came towards him, and straightened up.

Tom looked around. A typical village pub, not flashy, décor a little tired, the smell of stale beer and woodsmoke hanging in the air. There was a fireplace with the dead ash of the previous day's fire still waiting to be swept out.

'What can I get you?' said the publican.

Tom pulled out his police ID and placed it on the bar. 'We've got a few questions we need to ask you.'

The man looked at him askance. 'Such as?'

'Do you know a man called Liam Norris?'

'I do. He's one of my regulars.' There was no flicker of curiosity in his eyes, but he probably already knew about Bethany's death. Village news travels fast. No doubt he'd been expecting them to turn up.

'When was he last in here?'

'Sunday evening.'

'And before that?'

'A couple of weeks ago, maybe.'

Tom frowned. 'Are you sure? Because it's our under-standing that he was here on Saturday night.'

The publican raised his eyebrows. 'Saturday, you say?' He swiped a grey-looking cloth across the surface of the bar. 'Could have been.'

Tom waited while he rinsed out the cloth in a small sink behind him.

'You know, I think you're right. It was Saturday he was here. Days all seem the same when you work behind a bar.'

'Do you remember what time he arrived?'

'Early – between five and six, I'd say.'

'And when did he leave?'

The man's expression changed and his hand that was resting on the newspaper flicked at the corner of the front page.

Tom raised an eyebrow to encourage him to speak.

'Is he in trouble?'

'We're just establishing a timeline,' said Ridhi. 'What's your name?'

'Craig Williams.'

'So when did he leave, Craig?'

Williams paused again. Tom could practically hear the cogs whirring in his brain. Then he sighed loudly. 'Look, I don't want to self-incriminate...'

Tom exchanged a glance with Ridhi.

'We're not here to check up on you,' said Tom. 'It won't go any further.'

'We had a lock-in. Liam was here, a few of the other local lads. We've known each other since we were kids, and sometimes we just want to chill... I don't want to lose my licence, but Liam was here until just after midnight.'

'How did he get home?'

'I assume he walked after a session like that. It's not far. He's not that stupid that he'd get behind the wheel.'

'Thanks,' said Tom. 'And don't worry, we won't report you to the licensing board. Got better things to do with our time.'

They went back to the car.

'So?' said Ridhi. 'Seems a bit dodgy – not sure if Norris was in here on Saturday or Sunday.'

'I agree,' said Tom. 'You'd think he'd remember which day he had a lock-in. We'll be able to check CCTV and credit card payments to nail it down, so not much point in lying.'

'Okay, assuming he's telling the truth about it being Saturday night, does that get Norris off the hook with the timing of Bethany's death?'

'Say he left here at approximately midnight. Mort gave Bethany's time of death as between one and two. He'd have to walk the mile back to Elvington – about twenty minutes I should think. Then persuade Bethany to bring Scarlett out in the middle of the night, take them to the cave and give her the mushrooms and the fentanyl.'

Tom pulled out of the pub car park.

'He might just have time, if Bethany was completely co-operative. But it's a bit weird.'

'You're telling me,' said Ridhi. 'And he'd been drinking for seven hours – he must have been absolutely bladdered.'

Tom shook his head. 'Doesn't make sense, does it?'

The clattering keyboards had stopped by the time Tom and Ridhi got back to the incident room. Lexi was pacing up and down in front of the whiteboard, a look of immense concentration furrowing her brow.

'There you are,' she said, looking up as they came in. 'What have you got to add to what we know so far?'

Tom cleared his throat and told her what they'd learned from the publican. 'I guess Norris told us he left at closing time to protect the landlord, Craig Williams.'

'Who's now incriminated himself,' said Lexi. 'It would serve him right if we booked him for it.'

'Nothing we've learned so far has ruled Norris out as a suspect,' said Tom, 'but at the same time we haven't got anything yet that positively ties him to the crime.'

Lexi was frowning. 'Maybe we should turn our attention to the other most likely suspect – Johnny Lycett-Boyd. What was the exact nature of his relationship with Bethany? There must be a best friend in whom she confided. Someone who might have known who Scarlett's father actually is, and what really happened between Bethany and Johnny.'

'Norris mentioned calling Bethany's friend,' said Tom, 'on the Sunday morning when he realised Bethany and Scarlett weren't at the house.'

'Can you remember her name?' said Lexi.

He scratched the top of his head. There was a small patch there where his hair was starting to thin. 'Was it Karolyn he said? That's the name of Bethany's best friend, according to Sandra Glover. Karolyn Small.'

'That's it. Let's go and talk to Karolyn.'

As Tom drove, Lexi secured Karolyn Small's address from one of the civilian researchers. Lexi keyed it into Tom's satnav and they were soon cruising towards Dover.

'It's gone five,' said Tom. 'By the time we get there, she'll hopefully be home from work, depending on what she does.'

'But she'll only be useful to us if she's still friends with Bethany. We're not after ancient history. Was she happy with Norris? Was she still seeing Johnny Lycett-Boyd or did she have another lover we should know about?'

As a satellite village of Dover located on the main road from London, Whitfield very much catered to the needs of the long-distance lorry drivers about to head across the Channel. There was a large McDonald's on the roundabout and signs for a variety of budget hotels and the Dover Truckstop and Customs Clearance, where the drivers could fuel their vehicles and get to grips with the endless paperwork for taking goods to the Continent. Beyond the area which catered to the needs of those passing through, the village of Whitfield sprawled along the Sandwich Road – a mix of unattractive 1950s and 1960s housing interspersed with a single convenience store, a village hall, a tyre shop and a fire station. The address Michelle, the team's civilian investigator, had given them was Lenacre Avenue, a side street made up mostly of small bungalows, one of which was the house in question.

Tom parked the Jeep and they both went up to the front door. There was no bell, so Lexi knocked hard and then rubbed her knuckles as they waited. Tom could hear the sound of a baby crying somewhere inside the bungalow, then footsteps came towards the door and the crying got louder.

He and Lexi both instinctively took a step backwards as the door was opened, not wanting to crowd someone on their own doorstep. The woman standing in front of them was holding the crying baby on her hip, brushing its hair back from its forehead with her other hand.

'Yes?' she said, looking up at them. She looked tired. Her face was drawn, and her hands and wrists were pale and bony, the knuckles red and knotty.

'Are you Karolyn Small?' said Lexi.

The woman nodded, and Lexi introduced herself and Tom.

'Police? Is this about Bethany?'

'Yes,' said Tom quickly. 'Were you a friend of hers?'

Karolyn shifted the infant over to her other hip. 'I can't believe she died.' Her eyes filled with tears and she raised her free hand to swipe them away.

'Yes,' said Lexi. 'I understand that you and she were close when you went to school. Did you stay friends?'

Karolyn nodded. 'Yeah, we did. I used to see her every couple of months, for a drink or a coffee.' She looked down at her baby's head. 'We were going to have playdates when the girls got a little bigger. Scarlett's a month older than this one.'

'What's her name?' said Tom.

'Ronnie.'

'Can we ask you a few questions?' said Lexi.

'Sure.' She took them into a living room strewn with toys, baby equipment, and laundry. 'Sorry 'bout the mess. This one doesn't sleep and I find it hard to stay on top of things.'

There was a faint smell of dirty nappies and last night's pizza. Karolyn gently lowered Ronnie into a playpen, then handed her a naked doll with tangled blonde hair. 'Will you be quiet for Mummy, just for a little bit?' She started to cry and Karolyn gave them an apologetic look. It certainly seemed like she wasn't coping very well, and Tom felt sorry for her. He remembered when Billie was a baby and the looks he and Declan would get when she started to howl in public.

He bent over the cot and swept Ronnie up in his arms, jigging her up and down, spinning round the room with her, until her crying turned to giggling. Karolyn visibly relaxed. As he continued to humour Ronnie, Karolyn scooped up a pile of laundry from the sofa and invited Lexi to sit down.

Lexi turned towards her as she dropped the clothes on the floor and sat down too.

'Karolyn, we're trying to find out if Bethany was seeing anybody other than Liam Norris.'

Tom could practically see Karolyn trying to work out whether to tell them what she knew or keep her friend's confidence. He rubbed Ronnie's back so she wouldn't distract her mother.

'I... When I last saw her, she told me that Liam wasn't Scarlett's father.'

'Did she say who was?'

'Yes, she thought it was the guy who owns the vineyard at Elvington.'

'She was having an affair with him?'

'As far as I could tell it was on and off. He gave her money for the baby, but they weren't seeing each other regularly – it pretty much started as a one-night stand. He was just a bastard who took advantage of her after a couple of drinks. She wasn't a big drinker, even before she had Scarlett.'

'You said she thought it was him. As if she wasn't sure.'

'That's what it seemed like to me.'

'Between him and Liam, or was there another person it could have been?'

'I don't know.'

'And do you know if she's been seeing anyone else more recently?'

Karolyn shrugged. 'I haven't seen her for a few months – even though I've been over to Elvington to help with the grape harvest. We were supposed to meet up last week. She hinted there was something going on, but she wouldn't say anything over the phone, in case Liam heard. She was dead scared of him.'

'So why didn't she leave him?'

'She tried a couple of times and he just went crazy. Threatened to hurt Scarlett if she didn't come back and behave.'

'And you have no idea about whatever she hinted at?'

'She used to sometimes get a thing about some bloke or other in the pub, or someone who came in to where she worked. Like, if they flirted with her or something. But most of them never came to anything. It was probably something like that. It might even have been the vineyard guy again. I think he'd been sniffing round her.'

'Johnny Lycett-Boyd?'

'Yeah. He was bad news, as far as I was concerned.' She started to cry again – talking about Bethany was obviously painful, but then they'd been friends for a long time.

Lexi stood up.

'Thank you, Karolyn.' She did the usual – giving Karolyn a card and asking her to call if she thought of anything else. But in

Tom's experience, people never did call. They never remembered the vital clue that would solve the case. He suspected that most of the cards they gave out went straight in the bin.

Tom handed Ronnie back to her mother, and she immediately started crying again.

'What do you think?' he said, as soon as the front door had shut behind them.

'Maybe it was Johnny, maybe someone else. Which means we probably know even less than we did before.'

'So what do we do?'

Lexi shrugged as they both climbed into the Jeep. 'Maybe we need to come at it from a different angle. Let's see if Colin's made any progress with County Lines, and check with Emily about whether they got any DNA traces off Bethany and Scarlett's clothes.'

TWENTY-FOUR

The incident room was empty when Lexi and Tom arrived back at the station. Everyone had packed up and gone home for the evening, which was fair enough. Lexi sent Tom home, too. As the investigation proceeded, no doubt there would be overtime required, but she was conscious of the fact that he had a young daughter who had a right to at least some of his time.

Sitting alone in her office, she pondered over what to do next. Where was the case taking her? She dialled Colin's number.

'I'm about to go onto the pitch,' he said straight away. She knew Colin played football on Tuesday evenings, just five-a-side for fun, but it kept him fit.

'Sorry. One quick question, then we can catch up tomorrow.'

'Shoot.'

'County Lines – any joy?'

'Meeting Stan Garvie tomorrow for a rundown on fentanyl coming into the county.'

'Good. I want to focus on where the fentanyl came from. If we can trace the source of it and find out who was buying, it should give us a fresh pool of suspects. Now, go and score a couple of goals.'

Colin laughed. 'Yeah, right.'

Outside, it was already dark, but Lexi knew of one other person who would still be at his desk.

'Yes?' As abrupt as ever answering the phone.

'Hi, Mort. Just calling with a couple of questions.'

'No, we don't have a result yet on Scarlett's DNA test.'

'It wasn't that.' They were going to check whether Scarlett's DNA matched Liam's, as they had samples of both. A more formal paternity test, involving Johnny Lycett-Boyd's DNA, would have to be set up by Linda Ellis and her team. This one was strictly below the radar.

'What can I do for you then?'

'The magic mushrooms you found in Bethany's stomach – can you tell where they might have come from?'

'In a word, no. Not in terms of where they were picked – not my remit even if you could tell. But I can give you a few details.'

'Thanks.'

'There are literally hundreds of types of mushrooms around the world that contain psilocybin, the active component that gives people hallucinations. The two most commonly used in the UK are liberty caps – the small, light brown ones – and fly agarics – the red ones with white spots.' Lexi knew this already, but she let Mort continue with the explanation. 'The ones I found in Bethany's stomach were liberty caps and they were eaten fresh, rather than dried.'

'Meaning they were picked that day?'

'Or up to a couple of days before.'

'So whoever gave them to her either knew enough about shrooms to find them somewhere and pick them, or knew someone who was selling fresh liberty caps.'

'Bethany could have picked them herself.'

'That doesn't add up with what we know about Bethany's lifestyle. I think it's much more likely the other party brought the mushrooms and either persuaded her or tricked her into eating them. Then, once she was high, he administered the lethal dose of fentanyl. Whatever they were up to, the candles had time to burn down.'

'That's possible,' said Mort. 'Of course, there are other scenarios.'

'From what you know, can you ascertain the sequence in which Bethany took the mushrooms and the fentanyl?'

'Almost certainly. It can take up to half an hour to feel the effects of ingested mushrooms, and she'd certainly eaten them at least half an hour before she died.'

'How do you know?'

'From the progression of digestion. On the other hand, the dose of fentanyl evident in her blood suggests that she died fairly quickly after taking it. It was a huge amount and she clearly had no prior tolerance for opioids. So mushrooms first, fentanyl approximately twenty to thirty minutes after.'

'Not at the same time? Could someone have put drops of fentanyl onto the mushrooms and given them to her?'

'No, because she would have died of the fentanyl overdose before the mushrooms had reached that stage of digestion.'

Lexi was silent for a moment, thinking about the implications of what Mort had told her.

'Anything else?' said Mort.

'Yes, but this might be a long shot. Assume the person Bethany was with also took some of the mushrooms, maybe because they wanted to or maybe just to encourage her to take them.'

'Yes?'

'How long would we be able to trace the psilocybin in their system?'

'Not long at all. It doesn't show up on most common drug

tests and it doesn't stay in the blood or saliva for long. If someone took mushrooms with Bethany on Saturday night, there's no way you'd get a positive blood test from them now.'

'Damn!'

'It does show up for longer in a person's hair, but if you got a positive test on that, there's no way of pinpointing exactly when the person ingested it. And it's an expensive test to carry out.'

'Okay, I'll bear that in mind. Doesn't sound like it would be useful to us. Thanks, Mort.'

'You're welcome.'

After she finished the call, Lexi sat staring at her screen-saver for a few minutes. Somehow they had to be able to use the forensic evidence to narrow the field of suspects. She picked up her phone again.

'Hi, Maggie.'

'Hi, Lexi, what can I do for you?'

'Just wanted to run something by you.'

'Because it requires budget?'

Lexi laughed. ''Fraid so.'

Maggie sighed. 'Go on, then.'

'Here's my hypothesis so far. Bethany met with someone she knew in the cave under the winery. She had to take Scarlett with her, because there was no one home to babysit. I guess that means the meeting was important to her. Bethany, knowingly or not, ingested magic mushrooms. Once they'd taken effect, our suspect administered a lethal dose of fentanyl, then posed Bethany with the wings and the candles.'

'Why did they pose her like that?'

'I need to work on that – preferably with Ed Harlow.'

'So what's going to cost me money?'

'Mort tells me he can do a hair test for the presence of psilo-cybin, the active constituent of magic mushrooms. It's an expen-sive test.'

'Who do you want to test and what will it tell us?'

'If Suspect A took mushrooms with Bethany, it will show up in his hair.'

'Who do you think Suspect A is?'

'I've narrowed it down to three known suspects, of course with the proviso that there could still be an UNSUB. But testing Liam Norris, Johnny Lycett-Boyd and Will Steadman could give us the steer we need.'

'And what about the possible unknown suspect?'

'If we also test all the vineyard employees and seasonal workers who were at Elvington that night we might identify someone.'

'How many is that?'

'About forty in total. But some of the seasonal workers are women, and I think maybe we would just start with the men.'

'Was there a sexual element to the crime?'

'No evidence of sexual assault.'

'So Bethany could have been partying with a girlfriend and the drug-taking went wrong?'

'It's a possibility, but I don't see it as likely. An accidental overdose with a friend wouldn't result in that ritualistic death scene.'

Lexi waited. Maggie was obviously mulling it over.

'The seasonal workers will all leave in a few days,' said Lexi. 'If it was one of them, we'll need to act now.'

'Won't they be gone by the time the test results come back?'

'Sure, but we'll have their details.'

'Start with Norris, Lycett-Boyd and Steadman. I'm not so sure about the blanket testing of everyone on the property. What if your suspect didn't even take the mushrooms?'

Lexi was getting frustrated. 'Come on, Maggie. I can't not follow a lead just because of the possibility of it taking us nowhere. I've got to try everything to work out exactly what happened in that cave and who was present. This is one way of maybe finding out.'

'Like I said. Start with your three main suspects. Take hair samples from the rest of the workers and their details – then we can test later if there's an indication it might help.'

'Thanks.'

'I know it sometimes seems like I try to throw obstacles in your path, Lexi, but I also have a responsibility to the community that we use our resources in the most effective way possible.'

'I know, I get it. Sorry – I'll let you get back to your evening now.'

'See you soon.'

Lexi looked at her watch. It was after eight p.m. She was tired. But she knew she wouldn't sleep and the case would keep churning through her brain. She needed to exhaust herself properly, but with her hamstring issue a run was out of the question. Luke had suggested she try swimming, just to get things moving again, so she headed for the pool.

The cold water was a balm but even though she powered through fifty lengths, when her head hit the pillow the image of the dead woman in her angel wings stole any chance of sleep, and she could have sworn she could hear a baby crying somewhere in the distance.

TWENTY-FIVE

WEDNESDAY

Lexi had been last to leave the office the previous evening and now she was first in, sitting at her desk by half past seven. She'd been late to bed the previous evening, having spent almost an hour on the phone with Amber, who was firmly of the opinion she should go out with Luke whatever the state of the case.

'This one will finish and you'll be on to the next one. Then suddenly, one day, it'll be your retirement party and you won't have a date.'

Lexi had laughed, but there was an uncomfortable grain of truth in what Amber had said. It had kept her awake and as a result, mainlining coffee was going to be the only thing that would get her through the day. That, and frequent sugar fixes, starting with a squidgy pain au raisin she was already halfway through.

She studied her decision log, the dark red notebook in which she recorded each decision and action the team executed pursuant to the case. There were the three key suspects in Bethany's death – Norris, Steadman and Lycett-Boyd. Three possible verdicts – accidental death, manslaughter or murder.

But she was ninety-five per cent certain, at least, that it was the latter.

So what did the scene tell her about the suspect?

On a whim, she picked up the phone. She needed to knock heads with the one person in Kent who understood the importance of profiling and how to do it. Ed Harlow was a gifted forensic psychologist and they worked well together. Like her, he'd trained with the FBI at Quantico and, like her, he believed that to catch a killer, it was essential to get inside their mind.

'Hi, Lexi.' He sounded tired.

'Hey, Ed. Could you spare me maybe twenty minutes this morning? New case.'

'Of course.'

'I'll come to you.'

'Thanks, but I'm not at my office. I'm at the hospice with Charlie.'

Lexi had never met Ed's wife Charlie, but she knew she'd been having treatment for breast cancer.

'I'm so sorry, Ed. Another time will be fine.'

'No, it's okay. Phone me when you get here. We can meet in the café over the road. Charlie won't mind – she's sick of the sight of me moping around her room. She says I bring down the mood.' Lexi could hear a slight smile in his voice at the irony of this.

There was no answer from Ed's phone when Lexi parked up in the hospice car park half an hour later, so she made her way inside. Maybe she could find a nurse to fetch him when she got to the reception area.

However, there didn't seem to be anyone around. Breakfast had been served and cleared, and she couldn't find anyone to ask. She wandered along a corridor, looking around, but there was no sign of Ed. Eventually, she stuck her head around a door which was half open. There was just one bed in the room, and it was occupied.

'Hello?'

'Who are you looking for?' said the woman in the bed. She had spiky pale blonde hair and her skin had the slight grey tinge of someone seriously ill.

'I'm sorry,' said Lexi. 'I didn't mean to bother you.' She tried to back out.

'But who are you looking for?' Her voice was insistent.

'Ed Harlow. He doesn't work here, he's just visiting someone.'

'I know. I'm his wife.'

This caught Lexi off guard. She'd seen pictures of Charlie in Ed's office, but the woman on the bed looked completely different. The short hair, the ageing effect of pain and fatigue – her illness had taken a great toll. But now she knew it was Charlie, she could see the ghost of the youth and beauty she'd probably once taken for granted.

'You're Lexi, aren't you?' said Charlie. 'Ed's just gone to fetch me a newspaper.'

Lexi stepped into the room. 'I am. I just wanted a few minutes of Ed's time – I need his wisdom on a case. I hope that's okay?'

'Of course it is. I run out of errands to send him on...' She grimaced suddenly, and Lexi realised she'd been putting on a brave face. She must be in great pain.

'I won't keep him long, I promise,' she said.

'Have him for as long as you need him,' said Charlie. She fell silent, studying Lexi's face. Lexi stood awkwardly at the end of the bed, not sure whether she should sit down to wait for Ed or make herself scarce.

'He likes you, you know,' said Charlie. 'Talks a bit about the cases he helps you with. I should thank you for that – they're really the only thing that takes his mind off my illness, and things can get a bit intense around here.'

'I'm so sorry – it must be really difficult for both of you.'

'It'll be worse for him when I'm gone.' She paused, screwing up her eyes. Her breathing was a shallow rasp. 'You were out at Quantico, weren't you?'

'Yes. I worked with Harry Garcia, like Ed.'

'He said you just missed each other. We came home about a month before you went out there.'

'It's a small world,' said Lexi.

'You were there when Diamond River went down, weren't you?'

Lexi nodded cautiously. The Diamond River case, involving a serial killer called Leonard Crow, had been brutal. It was one of the reasons why she'd come back to England. 'I was a member of the team that brought him in.'

Charlie shook her head. 'What a monster. Ed's obsessed with the case. He wants to add it to his course.'

'I'll talk to him about it sometime.' A conversation she'd been trying to avoid ever since she met him. She liked Ed, but she didn't need to have him digging around in the most vulnerable parts of her psyche.

'Thanks.' Their eyes met and Lexi quickly looked away. 'Oh. You don't want to, do you?'

'It's difficult,' said Lexi. 'Things went wrong. People were hurt. Blame was thrown around. I'm trying to put the whole thing behind me, to be honest.'

'Don't you think others could learn from the mistakes that were made?'

Lexi's stomach churned. Her boss, Harry Garcia, who had also been her lover, had hung her out to dry. He'd used her as bait to reel in Leonard Crow, in a private conversation the rest of the team had known nothing about.

Lexi had nearly died that day, but Harry Garcia had been

unrepentant. In his book, catching the killer before he struck again was paramount – and that's what they'd done. The ends had justified the means.

But would they have done if Leonard Crow had killed Lexi?

She couldn't forgive him for it.

In a split second, the razor-sharp memory caught her off guard. She was back in Virginia, wintertime, and her vision blurred as the icy waters of the Diamond River rushed in over her face, turning the man who stood above her, holding her under, into a black shadow...

Charlie was staring at her with wide eyes. 'Lexi, are you okay?'

Lexi shook her head to dislodge the picture. 'Yes, sorry, I'm fine.'

'Will you do something for me?'

'Of course.' What could she want?

'Will you look out for Ed in the first few months after I'm gone? Pull him in on any cases you can? It'll make a difference.'

Ed. So soon to be a widower.

Lexi nodded. She could feel a lump bulging in her throat. It was unspeakably cruel. 'I will,' she said, her voice cracking.

'Lexi, there you are.' The door swung open, and Ed came into the room. He tossed a newspaper down on the bed, and Charlie snatched it up, scanning the headlines and snorting at one of the stories.

'I'll take Lexi over to the café,' Ed told his wife. 'She needs to pick my brains. Will you be okay?'

'Well, I won't be going anywhere, if that's what you're worried about.'

Ed gave her an apologetic smile and led Lexi out of the room.

'Keep him as long as you want,' Charlie shouted after them as they left.

'Did she moan about me?' said Ed, as they fell into step with each other.

'I think she feels a little bit crowded at times.' Lexi tried to be diplomatic.

Ed sighed. 'I just want to be there for her, to spend as much time as I can with her before...'

The unspoken words hung silently in the air between them as they crossed the road to the café. Inside, they were able to return to the mundane, ordering coffee and wondering if the cakes on offer might taste better than they looked.

'What's your case?' said Ed, as they sat down at an empty table.

'It's a murder. I've got three possible suspects, as well as having to consider an unknown killer. I need to build a profile from the details at the scene to get a steer on which might be the most likely suspect.'

She described what had happened and how the body had been presented. She also explained the tox results, but deliberately didn't tell him anything about Bethany's background or anything at all about the suspects. 'I'd like to hear your interpretation of the scene and what you can read from it.'

Ed chewed thoughtfully on a dry-looking flapjack for a moment. 'The baby wasn't there by accident,' he said eventually. 'Your suspect posed Bethany in those wings and the fact that he had a second, smaller pair means that he expected Scarlett to be present.'

'I agree. Unless Bethany brought them – fancy dress for whatever sort of party she was expecting.'

Ed shook his head. 'If Bethany had brought the wings and the baby unexpectedly, there wouldn't be an element of the posing. Scarlett has literally been used as a prop.'

'Which suggests to me this is a progression, not the first time this person has killed or attempted to kill. Do you agree?'

'I do. This doesn't look at all like a first attempt. The killer has planned the whole scenario in advance – the location, the wings, the candles, ensuring that Bethany had Scarlett with her.'

'So we're looking at a very organised killer. Even though we're only aware of one victim, this appears to bear all the hall-marks of a serial killer quite far into his progression.'

'I think you'll have to go with that assumption.'

'I'll put one of the team onto looking for earlier killings in the series. We'll have to widen our sweep, because I don't think there's been anything similar in Kent within the sort of timescale that we're looking at.' It was the sort of detail that would have been fed into the HOLMES 2 database, so she would ask her civilian investigator Michelle to look into it.

'If Scarlett is part of the posing, he's using her to send a message. He could have killed both mother and daughter, but he left the baby alive. What's he saying to us?'

Lexi thought out loud. 'The mother deserves to die, but the baby can live.' She drank a mouthful of coffee. 'Or, "Look at me. I have the power over life and death." One's alive, the other's dead. He can show mercy where and when he wants. He's in control.'

'All of those things are going to be feeding into it,' said Ed. Lexi noticed that his eyes looked brighter and his face less drawn. Charlie had been right – getting to grips with a case gave him some respite from the dire situation he was facing. 'But where do the wings come into this message?'

'This is interesting. We had a visit from a self-proclaimed local folklore expert. He told Ridhi some cock and bull story about an angel which was believed to protect the village of Elvington from harm, seemingly in exchange for the sacrifice of young women. It's clearly nonsense – angels and human sacri-fice?' She shook her head.

'Did he mention the angel story first or did Ridhi tell him about the wings?'

'He just came out with it.'

'Seems like too much of a coincidence. He might be your unknown suspect.'

Lexi had to agree with him. 'I've got the team digging into his background.'

'What about your other suspects? Does any of this strike a chord with them?'

'The reason why they're suspects is because either they have more conventional motives for wanting Bethany dead, or simply the local knowledge and opportunity to kill her. Which wouldn't explain the posing of the scene.'

'In other words, one of them could be hiding his true nature – almost always the case with serial killers.'

'Or the posing is an elaborate smokescreen to make us think we're after a serial killer when it's actually something much more mundane. Either way, none of them are overtly matching the profile at the moment.'

Ed paused for a moment, deep in thought. 'I think this has to be more to do with the killer's own worldview and experiences than some sort of elaborate cover-up.'

'So is it telling us something about his relationship with his own mother – which would actually make Scarlett a proxy for himself?'

'Quite possibly.'

'Something must have happened to him when he was an infant, something that's traumatised him ever since, and now he's playing it out with other mothers and babies. Or perhaps that's just what he wants us to think.'

Ed nodded. 'Faking it to make things seem more complex than they really are? Getting back to the suggestion that the posing is simply a smokescreen... Look, I'd better go,' he said.

'Of course. I shouldn't have taken up so much of your time.'

'It's okay – Charlie will thank you for it. A moment of peace and quiet.'

They stood up and Lexi embraced him. Ed's hug felt a little bit tighter than normal, and she blinked back tears as she watched him crossing the road to return to the hospice. In her pocket, her phone buzzed.

'Yes, Tom?'

'There's another dead girl.'

Her heart stopped for a moment. Then she ran to her car as fast as she could, gasping at the sharp stab of pain up the back of her leg.

TWENTY-SIX

MOTIVATIONAL JOURNAL – WEDNESDAY, SEPTEMBER 27

Yesterday's achievements

1. Good progress on infiltration plan
2. Wings delivered – just in time
3. This stupid journal doesn't have a list for yesterday's failures – but still failing to sleep
4. Killed angel number two

Learning outcomes

1. The police are all over Elvington but don't seem to have a suspect yet
2. The postman commented on the size of the wings package. Next time get them delivered to a collection point
3. When I lay on the charm, anyone will succumb
4. Killing is cathartic, but also tiring

Plans for today

1. Sleep
2. Haircut
3. Work

How are you feeling – in three words?

1. Fulfilled
2. Excited
3. Exhausted

Memory of the day

The reason I don't sleep well is because of the dreams, and the reason I have the dreams is because of the memory. I can't hope to forget – that will never happen – but perhaps if I can park it here, on the pages of this journal, it will become less vivid for a while. I'll try anything that might allow me to have an uninterrupted night's sleep.

Of course, it's the memory of the last time I saw Mum. I know I was three. Not because I remember my age, but because of my care record when she died and when I was taken into care. This memory terrifies me. It has done all through my life. Night terrors and bed-wetting that was too much for a succession of foster parents to deal with. I would be handed back, but it wasn't my fault. It was because of what happened to me.

I was only three when I saw what I saw. I relive the moment every single night. Over and over. I was just three.

I'm alone in the dark. I know I'm in Mum's bedroom. I'm not sure if I knew that at the time, but of course I now know that's where it happened, so my memory is coloured by that knowledge. I'm sitting on the floor, clutching the edge of the duvet that spills off Mum's bed. The house is silent – it's nearly dawn. There's no traffic. Gradually the dark shadows take on the outlines of familiar furniture. Outside, a bird trills and I'm scared. More scared than I've ever been in my life. Too terrified to call out or cry.

I can only hear myself breathing, shallow and fast. On the bed, Mum's sleeping form. The man doesn't seem to be here. He often stays away at night, coming home to tears and recriminations in the morning. Is that what I'm scared of? That he'll arrive and there'll be shouting?

It's light. I shake my mother and pull on her arm, but she won't wake up. I hold up my hands in front of my face. They're covered in blood.

Motivation for the day
Follow your dreams

TWENTY-SEVEN

As Lexi ran across the hospital car park, Tom filled her in.

'We just got the call about the body.'

Lexi's stomach lurched and a hundred questions bubbled up in her mind. 'Where?' This was the most important. She had to get there right away.

'At the vineyard. One of the pickers found her and Will Steadman immediately rang me.'

'Was she in the cave?'

'No. There's a pergola they use for wine tasting, out among the vines. Apparently she's there.'

Lexi remembered seeing an ornate pergola in the distance as she'd walked through the vineyard with Will a few days earlier.

'Did he call 999?'

'No. He called me first. I've alerted first responders to get there.'

'Good.' They needed the scene secured as fast as possible. 'And he's certain she's dead?'

'Yes. I told him not to touch her and to keep everyone else away.'

'Fine. Meet me there.'

'I'm on my way now. Can you call Emily to bring her team, and let Mort know?'

'Next on my list.'

There were no shortcuts to get from where she was to Elvington. Lexi had to drive right through the middle of Canter-bury, but thankfully it was well past rush hour. She swung out onto the ring road to take the A2 towards Dover, drumming the heel of her hand on the steering wheel as she waited for the traffic lights to change.

She rang Tom to give him her estimated time of arrival.

'Blue light it,' he said. He was already halfway there, having set out from Canterbury as soon as he'd got the call.

'It's not going to save any lives.'

'No, but it might save the crime scene.'

'First responders should be there by now.' The light went green, and she was finally able to put her foot on the gas. 'And you'll be there in, what, ten minutes?'

Twenty minutes later, she slid the Crossfire into an empty space next to Tom's Jeep. The vineyard was already busy. Apparently, the fact that a second body had been discovered on the property didn't interfere with bringing in the grapes. Lexi wondered if anything would deter Steadman from getting his harvest into the presses. And how was the news of a second suspicious death on the property playing out with Johnny and Marietta? Did Marietta suspect Johnny was involved? Would he be persuading her that he wasn't, or was he past caring what his wife thought of him? Someone at the vineyard had to know what was going on.

She could see blue lights flashing across the field that lay west of the car park. There was a narrow, rutted track between this field and the one to the north of it, and she used it to make her way across to the pergola area. Tom waved at her from the edge of a blue-and-white tape cordon, where he was talking with Steadman.

'You can't close off the lower part of the track,' Will Steadman was saying as she came into earshot. His voice was whiny, and his features drawn tight. 'We need tractor access down there to bring in the grapes.'

Tom ignored him and turned to Lexi. 'Let's suit up.' He pointed at the CSIs' van and they went across to get themselves ready before entering the inner cordon.

Two minutes later, they approached the wrought-iron pergola. It stood at the junction of four fields, commanding a stunning view over the valley beyond. But they were looking into the structure, rather than out, and as she got closer, Lexi could make out the shape of a dead body lying on the ground inside.

Tom let out an audible gasp and as Lexi saw the woman's face, she realised why.

It was Karolyn Small.

Bethany's best friend since childhood, the woman they'd spoken to only the previous day. Now she was dead. Cold fear rooted itself inside Lexi's gut.

'No... this can't be. Oh, Karolyn...' Her voice faltered. Then she took a deep breath to get control of herself. Had their visit put her in danger? If it had she would never forgive herself, but for now, she had to be the consummate professional.

Tom looked ashen but said nothing.

A paramedic, kneeling next to the body, was just closing his bag. As he stood up, Lexi saw a pair of white feather wings extending from behind Karolyn's shoulders.

Oh, no.

'She's cold,' he said. 'Been dead some time. We would never have been in time to save her.'

'Can you see any cause?' said Lexi.

The man cocked his head to one side. 'Looks like a drug overdose to me,' he said. 'There's foam in her airways. Pupils fixed and dilated. You'll get more from the pathologist.'

Too right they would. As the paramedic went back through the double cordon to his ambulance, Mort Barley approached.

'Lexi, Tom,' he said, with a vague salute of his arm.

'Shhh...' snapped Lexi.

'What?' Mort was instantly indignant and ready to take offence.

'I heard something. Shhhh...'

Mort and Tom looked at her with puzzled expressions.

Lexi heard it again. A high-pitched keening, somewhere down the slope amid the vines. She set off between two of the rows. Tom followed her. Mort shrugged his shoulders and turned back towards the body.

'Oh my God,' said Tom, catching up with her. 'Are you thinking what I'm thinking?'

Lexi stopped and listened again. There it was again, maybe a row or two over from where they were. She didn't say anything, just carried on scanning the ground on either side of the rows. It got louder as she got closer, and she knew what it was. Through the vines, she saw a flash of white.

'Ronnie!' she called.

Karolyn Small's baby let out a blood-curdling shriek as Lexi shoved through a gap in the vines to appear in front of her.

There was Ronnie, in just a nappy, with a pair of white feather wings askew on her back, the rest of her body caked in dirt and chalk dust, crawling away from Lexi as fast as she could. She howled again.

Lexi caught up with her and bent down to pick her up, but

as soon as she placed her arm around Ronnie's waist, the infant turned her head and bit down hard.

'Ow!' Lexi nearly dropped her.

Tom stepped up to them. 'Let me take her,' he said, and at the same time the baby extended her arms to him.

Lexi handed her over to Tom, and Ronnie immediately stopped crying.

TWENTY-EIGHT

They went back through the rows of vines to where Karolyn's body still lay.

Lexi glanced around at Tom, who was coming up behind her. 'Don't let Ronnie see her mother.'

But she spoke too late.

'Mama!' She wriggled in Tom's arms and let out a long howl. He turned his body to block her view, and Lexi felt her heart splitting. Not that Ronnie would understand that her mother was dead, but now she'd be handed over to strangers and she'd never see Karolyn again. It was beyond brutal to put a child through this.

'I'll find someone to take her,' said Tom.

She sent Tom back to the car park and told him to find a PC to look after Ronnie until one of Linda Ellis's team could arrive to collect her. As he strode off through the vines, Lexi turned back to Karolyn's body. She needed to consider the posing of the scene, before the CSIs trampled all over it and Mort removed the body. Then she quickly texted Ridhi to find out the name and address of Karolyn Small's next of kin.

The pergola was an elegant wrought-iron structure – a circle of six arches, topped with a filigreed cupola. There were vines growing up each of the columns, but they only reached halfway up, making Lexi guess it was a recent instalment. Once they covered the cupola, the leaves would provide a shady canopy overlooking the rows of vines. It would have been a lovely prospect, but from now on it would forever be associated with Karolyn Small's death.

The ground it stood on was the mixture of chalky gravel and earth she was used to from the hills that loomed up behind her own cottage. It was dry now – there'd been no rain for a couple of weeks – and that meant they wouldn't get any useful foot-prints from it.

Karolyn was lying on her back in exactly the same position as Bethany had been in, and with both mother and daughter wearing wings, Lexi had no doubt the two deaths were connected. This was a killer with a strong signature – the wings and the inclusion of the women's own babies as part of the scene. What sick message was he trying to impart? She moved in closer to the body and checked the ground for candle wax, which she found in the expected places. No doubt Emily would be able to compare it with the wax from the cave, and it would surprise no one if there was a match.

'Lexi!'

She raised her head and saw Emily coming along the track towards her. They met at the tape that marked the inner cordon. Emily's team were right behind her, putting down foot-plates as they came within the outer cordon, and the photographer got to work quickly so they would have a record of the scene before it was disturbed further.

'Hi, Emily.'

'Twice in a week. We must stop meeting like this.'

Lexi gave her a wry smile. 'I wish we could.' Then it was

onto the business at hand. 'First appearance is that whoever killed Bethany killed this girl, Karolyn Small, so anything you find here that matches something from the other scene will be significant.'

'Who found the body?'

'One of the seasonal workers, then Will Steadman called it in.'

'So Steadman is a commonality between both scenes.'

'You think he did it?' Lexi was surprised, as Emily didn't usually venture an opinion. She was all about the facts and the facts alone.

'No. What I mean is that he could have contaminated both scenes, so we'll watch for that. We'll need his clothes and the clothes of the person who found the body, so I can take fibre samples for comparison with any fibres we find at the scene.'

'Right.' Lexi made a note on her phone so she would remember to follow this up.

Mort looked up from where he was bent over the body.

'The paramedic suggested she died of an overdose,' said Lexi.

He stood up. 'Right, I'll be heading off then, if you don't need my services.'

'Oh, for God's sake, Mort.'

'No, you clearly have all the information you need about the time and cause of death, and I've got some paint I need to watch drying.'

Emily exploded with laughter, and Mort scowled at her. But Lexi could see he was trying not to smile.

'Would the promise of a packet of Hobnobs persuade you to stay?'

Mort snorted indignantly, but he dropped his bag on the ground and turned his attention back to Karolyn's body. Lexi waited patiently while he worked, not wanting to annoy him again. She listened to the notes he dictated into his phone for a minute, but then he glared at her, so she stepped back to the outer cordon. Bloody man. He made being difficult into an art form.

While he got on, she called Colin. 'Can you come out here with a few uniforms and organise interviews of all the seasonal workers on the property?'

'That'll go down well. We already pulled them off work on Sunday and Monday to ask about Bethany's death and we got bugger all for our troubles.'

'This one's different. Karolyn's body was left out in the open, amid the vines. More chance that someone might have seen something.'

'All right, I'll get it sorted. What timeframe do we want to cover with the interviews?'

'Yesterday afternoon and evening, and through the night. The body was discovered just before eight this morning. I haven't got an estimated time of death yet.' She stared at the back of Mort's head and he must have felt it, because he turned round and gave her a wave.

She went back under the cordon as she finished the call with Colin.

'Your paramedic was right,' said Mort. 'There's foam in her airways, which can be indicative of a drug overdose. Obviously, I'll confirm this with a tox screen.'

'Approximate time of death?'

'Taking temperature, lividity and rigor into account, I would put it between midnight and three a.m. I might be able to tighten that up when I get to examine the contents of her stomach.'

'Any sign of assault, sexual or otherwise?'

'No obvious injuries or fresh bruising. I can't say yet whether she had consensual sex within the last twenty-four hours, but I'll be able to check for that during the autopsy.'

'Thanks, Mort.' She saw Tom talking to a uniformed PC at the outer cordon and went across to them.

'We need to find her clothes and the baby's clothes, if they've been left here,' she said, as the PC strode off on whatever errand Tom had sent him on.

'Probably easiest to get a dog out here for that,' said Tom.

Lexi nodded, and he tapped something into his phone.

'Let's go and talk to Will Steadman. See if he knew Karolyn Small or saw her on the property last night.'

They stripped off their CSI suits and bagged them up for Emily Jordan – just in case they'd picked up any traces of evidence.

As they walked back in the direction of the winery, Lexi saw Johnny Lycett-Boyd hurrying towards them.

'Stop right there,' she called. She didn't need him trampling over any evidence nearer to the scene, or seeing the position of the body, the wings or any of the other details. He was a suspect and needed to be treated as such – if later it turned out that he knew things about the scene, it could be critical to their case.

'What the hell is going on?' he said, grim-faced. 'Steadman's a gibbering wreck and I can't get any sense out of him.'

'I'm afraid there's been another suspicious death.'

He made a move to go past them.

'I'm sorry, but you can't go there.'

'It's my bloody property – I'll go where I want.'

'I don't want to arrest you, but that's exactly what'll happen if you don't follow my instructions.'

Lycett-Boyd let out a frustrated sigh and took a step back. However, it didn't escape Lexi's notice that his jaw jutted forward aggressively, and his hands were balled into fists by his sides. He was certainly a man capable of physical violence.

'Do you know who the woman is?'

Lexi hadn't mentioned that it was a woman, but he could

have learned that from Steadman or the worker who found the body.

'Her name's Karolyn Small. Did you know her?'

He shrugged. 'Should I have done?'

'She was a local woman, known to us as a friend of Bethany's. I just wondered if you'd come across her?'

'No. Bethany Glover and I didn't mix in the same social circles. I'm sure you understand.'

That you're a stinking snob and think yourself above these girls, apart from when it comes to sex?

His simmering aggression had evaporated, and his body language indicated that he wanted the conversation to be over. Perhaps he did know her. Perhaps he'd slept with her. Could he be Ronnie's father too? It was an interesting thought. A killer who impregnated women, then killed them for their children.

Her thoughts were galloping out of control. Evidence first. Hypotheses later.

'We'll be taking statements from everyone who works here about their whereabouts yesterday afternoon and last night. Can you please make sure that you and your wife are available to speak to one of my officers later on?'

'Of course. But you need to pull your bloody finger out and catch whoever's doing this. My business and my family are being victimised – and if you can't find them, I'll have to do something myself.'

'I strongly suggest that you don't try and take the law into your own hands,' said Lexi. She'd had enough of his preening arrogance. 'That could end up with you behind bars rather than the killer. All I need you to do is co-operate with my team and let us know of anything that happens out of the ordinary.'

Lycett-Boyd grunted in lieu of a reply and turned on his heel, striding off along the path ahead of them as they made their way back to the centre of the vineyard.

'I don't trust him,' said Tom. 'I think he knew her.'

'If he did, we'll find out. He's lied to us once already in this investigation. He's a man with something to hide.'

Lexi had a strong hunch about Johnny Lycett-Boyd. But now she needed solid evidence. And she was determined she was going to find it.

TWENTY-NINE

Will Steadman was at the winery, trying to oversee a grape harvesting that had been railroaded by not one, but now two, unexplained deaths. He was shouting out instructions to various employees as Lexi and Tom came into the fermenting hall, and he frowned when he saw them. There was a palpable tension in the air.

Lexi could understand the stress he was under, but that didn't negate the fact they needed to question him. 'Mr Steadman, I'm afraid we need a few minutes of your time.'

'Can we speak later?' he said. He looked pale, his face drawn. 'I need to ensure things are running smoothly here. We've already lost time, and if the grapes get backed up there's a risk of mould.'

'No, we really need to talk now.'

'Then it'll have to be here. I can't stop working.' He turned away from them to check the dials on one the huge stainless-steel fermenting tanks.

Lexi looked around. There were a couple of employees busy at the other end of the area, but most of the activity was taking place on the upper floors.

'Did you know Karolyn Small?'

'I recognised her as one of the local pickers.'

'But you didn't mention that when you called to say her body had been discovered. Why was that?'

'I couldn't remember her name. I don't know the names of all the seasonal workers.' His eyes darted round the hall, as if he was worried about being overheard.

'Did you know the man who found her body?'

'Yes. Mathéo Martin. He's in charge of the pickers who've come over from France.'

Lexi texted the name to Colin and asked him to seek out Martin first.

'When was Karolyn last here, as far as you know?'

Steadman's face took on a pained expression. 'I'd need to check the rota in my office. The foreign picking team work every single day while they're here, but the local pickers are sometimes part-time. Can I send you that information at the end of the day?'

'No, we need to pin down her known movements as quickly as possible,' said Lexi.

'You need to appreciate that this is a murder investigation,' said Tom, 'and if you don't co-operate we can take you to Canterbury for questioning.'

Steadman sighed, and Lexi stepped into the role of good cop to Tom's bad.

'Look, it'll only take a few minutes to check the rota and then I promise we'll get out of your hair until later.' She indicated the door with her hand, and Steadman sullenly moved towards it.

'Back in five,' he called to the staff who were within earshot.

As they walked down to the visitor centre where Steadman's office was located, Lexi recognised Colin's car arriving in the car park. He and Ridhi emerged, and she waved them over.

'Colin, this is Will Steadman, head vintner. He's going to give us the details of Karolyn Small's work rota.'

Colin nodded hello.

Lexi turned back to Steadman. 'In fact, I think it would be useful if we had the complete work rota for all the seasonal workers, so we can track people's comings and goings.'

'For yesterday?' said Steadman.

'For the whole harvest. It might help us to make links between the two deaths.'

Steadman now seemed to be resigned to doing what he needed to keep them happy. He led them up the wooden steps to the visitor centre's deck and unlocked the door.

Colin followed him in, with a barrage of questions about how many seasonal workers there were on site, and how many were staying in the barn or camping in the field behind it. Ridhi went in after, taking notes.

Lexi placed a hand on Tom's arm as he made to follow.

'Let them get on with it. It doesn't need four of us in there.'

Tom stopped, then went to the railing at the edge of the deck. The view was stunning, with fields of vines rolling down the hill below, the village of Elvington at the bottom of the valley, with the north-facing slopes rising up beyond. Lexi joined him and looked across to the fields beyond the winery. She could just see the pergola in the distance, with the mortuary's black van parked close by. Mort was obviously preparing to remove the body.

'Same killer,' said Lexi, thinking out loud. 'But was Karolyn murdered because she knew Bethany, and so maybe knew something about her last hours or who she'd been seeing? Or is it just a coincidence – if the killer's targeting local girls?'

Tom turned to look at her. 'I think we need to assume the former until we know otherwise.'

Lexi nodded. There was something very cosy about what was going on. Karolyn worked at the vineyard. Bethany had been in a relationship with the owner of the vineyard. Both were killed on the property. Daughters of the same age. Childhood friends. A spider's web of connections that they would need to untangle until they could identify the killer at the centre. Lycett-Boyd or Steadman? Liam Norris or Gideon Croft? Or someone else, still lurking in the shadows?

After a couple of minutes, Colin and Ridhi emerged from Steadman's office, Ridhi clutching several sheets of paper.

'Got it,' said Colin, nodding at the printouts. 'I've arranged for four uniformed officers to come up here to interview the workers.'

'Excellent,' said Lexi. 'And once you've set that in motion, you and Ridhi can go and break the news to Karolyn's next of kin.'

'What? Us?' Colin looked horrified.

Lexi nodded. 'That reaction is exactly why it needs to be you, Colin. All part of the job.' She'd been waiting a while for an opportunity like this. It was all very well being an expert in interpreting CCTV and ANPR records, which to give him credit, Colin was. But Lexi felt that sometimes he lacked empathy for the victims of the crimes they investigated – and nothing would bring home the human cost of violent crime more than spending time with a victim's next of kin.

Colin grimaced. 'Okay.'

'And don't make Ridhi do it on her own,' added Tom.

This finally made Colin smile. 'Thought wouldn't have crossed my mind.'

He turned away to go down the steps from the decking, leaving Ridhi standing behind him, rolling her eyes.

THIRTY

'Please tell us your name,' said Ridhi, having snapped on the recording device they'd brought with them for the interviews.

'Mathéo Martin.'

'Your position here?'

'I work here temporarily, for the harvesting.' Martin spoke with a pronounced French accent, dropping his Hs on here and harvesting. He was a good-looking man, and Ridhi made a point of reminding herself not to be too charmed by the combination. 'I bring a team over from France each year. You would call me the foreman, I think.'

'How many in your team?' said Colin.

'It varies, depending on availability and how many people I need for the size of the vineyard. Here, I have twenty-five working at the moment.'

'How do you recruit them? Do you know all of them personally?'

'Most of them work for me year-on-year, some are students. They come from different countries. Some I know well. For others, it's the first time.'

'Can you tell us about this morning?' said Ridhi.

Martin's expression clouded. '*Mon dieu*, it was a great shock.' He paused, perhaps putting his thoughts in order. Ridhi let him take his time. 'I got up at six, like every morning.'

'Where are you staying?' interjected Colin.

'I stay up in the barn with my team. I like to keep an eye on them.'

That was interesting. Did they need someone keeping an eye on them?

'I had a shower, then made coffee. I wanted to work out how many more days we would be needed, because there are a couple of smaller vineyards who want us to pick.'

'So you went out into the fields?' said Ridhi.

'Yes, I wanted to double check exactly how far we had got yesterday, and how much remained to do. I was walking down to the bottom field and I came to the pergola. When I got closer, I saw the woman lying there.' His voice faltered – the memory was clearly distressing.

'Can you remember exactly what time that was?'

'Not exactly. Some time after seven o'clock.'

'What did you do when you saw the body?'

'I ran to her. I thought she might be still alive, but as I came closer I realised she was dead.'

'How did you know?' said Colin.

'Her eyes were open. The way she was lying seemed stiff.'

'Did you touch her, try to revive her?' said Ridhi.

'*Non*. I put a hand an inch in front of her nose and mouth. As I suspected, there was no breath. Then I stepped back quickly. I didn't want to disturb anything... just in case.'

'In case of what?'

Martin shrugged. 'I didn't know how she died.'

'What did you do next?'

'I phoned Will Steadman to tell him what I'd found.'

'Why didn't you ring the police first, or call for an ambulance?'

Martin raised his hands, palms up, in a gesture of supplication. 'I don't know the emergency numbers in your country.'

It seemed fair enough. Ridhi wouldn't know what to dial if she was in France, although maybe she'd just try 999.

'Did you recognise the woman?'

'I had seen her working in the fields. I knew she was one of the local pickers, but I didn't know her name. Also, she'd stayed late on a couple of evenings, when the pickers were barbecuing after working. In fact, she was here last night. She seemed to be getting friendly with one of the other pickers.'

'Someone from your team?'

'No, one of the locals.'

'Would you say they were together?'

He shrugged. 'I saw them talking. The next time I saw her she was dead. I don't know what happened in between.'

'Would you be able to identify the man she was with?'

'Yes, of course.'

'What did you do after calling Will Steadman?'

'Monsieur Steadman asked me to stay by the body until he arrived. He called the police and came to the pergola.'

'At any time while you were there, did you see a baby?'

'A baby?' Martin's face registered shock. 'Was there a baby there? I didn't see another body.'

'The baby, thankfully, is alive,' said Ridhi. 'She was found crying in the vines. You didn't hear anything like a baby crying?'

Martin shook his head.

Maybe Ronnie had fallen asleep at some point and woken up again as people started to congregate. There was no way of knowing.

'And you saw no one else up and about anywhere on the vineyard?'

'No. I saw no one else.'

'Thank you, Mr Martin. If you think of anything else that might be relevant, no matter how small, please get in touch with us. I'm afraid we'll have to interview your team again this morning, so please ask them to co-operate.'

If Martin was annoyed about having his workforce disrupted by another series of interviews, he had the good grace not to show it, and he left the visitor centre with a look of relief that he'd be able to get back to his job.

———

'Please tell us your name,' said Ridhi. The recorder was already switched on and they had the subject's permission to record the interview. The young man in front of them was apparently the one that Mathéo Martin had seen talking with Karolyn Small the previous evening. He had a square face with a strong jaw and wide-set eyes, and dark, curly hair that was in need of either a comb or a cut.

'Alex Robinson.'

'How old are you, Alex?'

'Twenty.'

'Tell us a little about yourself, how you came to be working here.'

'I'm studying viticulture at Plumpton.'

'Plumpton?' said Colin.

'Plumpton College, just north of Brighton. I'm doing an MA as I want to go into the wine business. I'm helping with the harvesting here for work experience.'

'Where are you staying while you're here?'

'I'm camping in the field up by the barn. There's quite a few of us from Plumpton here. We're sharing a tent.'

'Did you know Karolyn Small?' said Ridhi, watching his face carefully.

'The girl who died? Yeah, I knew her.'

'How well?'

'Not well. I mean, I just met her here, this week. But we chatted a few times. She seemed nice.'

'We understand that you spent some time with her last night.'

'Who told you that?' Robinson caught his breath. His eyes darted from side to side.

'You were seen talking to her at the barbecue.'

'There were a load of us there last night. We cooked some sausages, drank some beer. Karolyn was there so, sure, I probably talked to her.'

'Nothing more than that?' said Colin.

'No.' He shook his head. 'W-what are you implying?' He stuttered slightly, and, realising he was twisting his fingers together on the table, snatched his hands down to his lap.

'We're not implying anything,' said Ridhi gently. 'We just need to find out when people last saw Karolyn alive, and how she spent the evening.'

He nodded, but he didn't look any more relaxed. 'We shared a couple of beers. I liked her.'

'What time would that have been?'

'I don't know.' He raised both hands. 'We finished working pretty late, after nine, so maybe between nine and eleven.'

'When did you last see her?'

'Like, when everyone turned in – about eleven. We all get up early to work, so no one was really caning it.'

'You said goodnight to her at eleven and she left?' Colin was pressing for more detail. 'Was she going home? Or was she staying on site?'

'I don't know. We said our goodnights and I went back to the tent with the guys. I didn't watch where she went.'

'Did you see her again at any point after you'd said goodnight?'

'No, that was it. That was the last time I saw her.'

'You stayed in your tent all night?'

'Yes. I was knackered. Harvesting is hard work.'

'And your mates will vouch for you?'

He nodded. 'There are six of us in there – like sardines. You can't go in or out without treading on somebody.'

'Thanks. You've been very helpful.'

They let him get back to work. Colin had received a text from one of the civilian researchers in the incident room, giving them the details of where Karolyn's parents lived. Time for the death knock.

'What did you make of him?' said Ridhi, as they walked down to where Colin's car was parked.

Colin tilted his head to one side. 'If his mates back him up, I'd say he's out of the picture.'

So if it wasn't Alex Robinson, who was it?

THIRTY-ONE

Having taken over the vineyard's visitor centre, much to Johnny Lycett-Boyd's disgust, Lexi called a team meeting to piece together what they knew so far about Karolyn Small's final hours. She'd managed to blag a small whiteboard from Will Steadman, before banishing him from his own office. This hadn't gone down particularly well, but as he was busy in the winery, he wasn't in need of it anyway.

Lexi set out the facts.

'According to the vineyard's work rota, Karolyn did an early shift yesterday, which was why she was home when Tom and I called on her. She must have returned later on for the party.' She scanned the previous day's times. 'Early shift the day before that. Off at the weekend.'

'We need to find out who was looking after Ronnie while she was working,' said Tom. 'They'll be able to confirm when she dropped off and picked her up on each of those days.'

'Colin and Ridhi are with her parents now. I've asked them to check with Mr and Mrs Small – it's something they'd probably know.'

'Where's Ronnie now?' asked a young DC, Maya Blackwood, with a red ponytail and a generous covering of freckles on her face.

'Linda Ellis is looking into who her father is, or next of kin. She'll be in temporary foster care until a responsible relative is identified,' said Lexi. 'She might be able to go to Karolyn's parents.'

'Do we even know who the father is?' said Tom.

'Not yet.' Lexi didn't want to get sidetracked, so she went to the board and listed the known timings for the day before.

- 7.00 *Karolyn starts work*
- 15.00 *Karolyn's shift finishes*
- 21.20 *late pickers released from work*
- 21.20 *onwards - the barbecue, Karolyn talks with Alex Robinson*
- 23.00 *left barbecue*

'So she finished working at three,' said Tom, studying the board. 'We need to work out when she came back.'

'Maya, will you chase up on that and see if you can find anyone who saw her between three and when the barbecue started? Particularly sightings of her leaving or arriving back.'

'Yes, boss.'

Lexi added another time to the board.

- 7.30*ish – Mathéo Martin discovers body*

'So we've got a six to seven hour gap, in which Karolyn fetches Ronnie from whoever's looking after her and then meets with someone at the pergola, ending up with her naked, winged and dead. Given the similarities between the scene where Karolyn was found and the scene where Bethany was found – the candles, the wings, the presence of their baby daughters, still alive – I'm expecting to have the same cause of death confirmed, which we know in Bethany's case was a fentanyl overdose. It's highly likely that the same person supplied or administered the drug.' She looked round at the assortment of uniformed PCs and detectives in plain clothes. 'However, you know the danger of making assumptions, so all minds entirely open until we get official confirmation of these facts.'

Tom raised a hand.

'Yes?'

'You speculated that she fetched Ronnie. But perhaps the killer brought the baby here to her?'

'Good thought. That would mean that she knew the person, and that they also had access to Ronnie. Or alternatively maybe they snatched Ronnie – but if that was the case, whoever had been babysitting would have reported her missing. We'll follow up on that when we know who was looking after her. In fact, Tom, can you task someone to make a timeline for Ronnie Small over the twenty-four hours leading up to Karolyn's death?'

'Of course.'

'Thanks.' She surveyed the room once again. 'Motive – that's the next thing we need to consider. With Bethany, we wondered about a crime of passion or jealousy committed by her partner, Liam Norris. However, the posing of the scene required a degree of premeditation, so that seemed unlikely. Now we have a repeat of the crime with Karolyn, that particular motive seems even more unlikely, although that in itself doesn't necessarily rule Norris out.'

Tom took over. 'We're also considering Johnny Lycett-Boyd, given his history with Bethany. He claims not to have known Karolyn, but he said the same of Bethany at first.'

'With Bethany, he had an obvious motive. We don't know what his motive might have been with Karolyn – possibly these are sexually motivated crimes, although there's no evidence of sexual assault. He definitely had the opportunity. He's here all the time and his presence anywhere on the vineyard doesn't arouse suspicion in the way that Liam Norris's might. Of course, that goes for Will Steadman, too.'

'What about means?' said one of the civilian researchers.

'Access to drugs – so far, we have no idea where the fentanyl that killed Bethany came from. And no suggestion that any of our suspects have particular links to drugs or drug dealing.' Lexi shrugged. 'It's critical that we find the source, because that might lead us to our killer.'

'Colin's fixing up to meet with a contact from County Lines,' said Tom. 'Hopefully that will shed more light on possible areas of enquiry.'

It was time to throw open the floor.

'Anyone hear anything of particular note in their interviews this morning?'

'Such as?' said one of the uniformed PCs.

'Conversations people had with Karolyn, observations about her, reports of anything out of the ordinary. Come on, constable, I shouldn't need to be prompting you on this stuff.'

The PC nodded. 'Sure, sure, I get it.'

'I've got something.' Maya Blackwood had raised her hand.

'Shoot,' said Tom.

'I interviewed one of the local pickers, a woman called Suzy Sutton. She was a friend of Karolyn's. They knew each other well, from what she said.' Maya hooked her little fingers round each other to denote the level of closeness. 'A couple of weeks ago – she couldn't be more precise than that – Karolyn told her she was seeing someone new, a bloke.'

'Did she know who it was?'

'Karolyn wouldn't say. Went all coy about it, which made Suzy think it might be a married man. She let slip the guy was a bit older.'

Lexi instantly thought of Johnny Lycett-Boyd – he seemed to have a track record of playing away. He might even have met Karolyn through Bethany.

'This Suzy couldn't make a guess who it was?'

'She didn't venture any names, but I could talk to her again if you like?'

'Please do that. Good work, Maya. And track down her other friends, and people she worked with, and find out if they knew anything about this mystery man.'

At that moment the door of the visitor centre opened, and Colin and Ridhi came in. They both looked sombre. Telling Karolyn's parents that their daughter was dead would have been a tough experience.

'All right, you two?'

Colin screwed up his face.

'Yeah. It didn't exactly go well, though,' said Ridhi.

It never did.

'You've left them with a family liaison officer?'

'Yeah, Philippa's there.' Philippa Reid was one of the FLOs working out of Canterbury. 'And as they looked after Ronnie when Karolyn worked, Linda Ellis is going to place Ronnie with them until full custody is settled.'

'I don't suppose they told you who Ronnie's father is?'

'I don't think they know. I started to ask and Mr Small shut down the conversation before I finished my sentence,' said Ridhi.

'They were looking after Ronnie yesterday while Karolyn was working, and again when she went out to the barbecue,' added Colin. 'Usually, if Karolyn worked late into the evening or went out, she would leave Ronnie with them overnight, rather than disturb her. They'd assumed that would happen last night, but then at about eleven, after they'd gone to bed, they heard Karolyn come into the house. Mrs Small went downstairs to ask her what she was doing, and she said she'd come for Ronnie. Was going to take her home.'

'Did Karolyn give them a reason why?' said Lexi.

'Not much – just something about wanting to see her,' said

Ridhi. 'I think there was a bit of an argument. Mrs Small said Karolyn smelled like she'd been drinking, so she asked her not to take Ronnie in the car. She said she wasn't driving. A friend had given her a lift and was waiting outside.'

'A friend?' said Lexi. Her heart rate rose.

'Karolyn didn't give a name,' said Colin. 'And even though Mrs Small looked out and saw a car outside, engine running, she couldn't tell us anything about it. "It was dark. I couldn't see what car it was, just the side lights."'

'Where do they live?' said Tom.

'Elvington.'

'So, no CCTV to help us. Karolyn could have been driven from the vineyard to their house in a few minutes,' said Lexi. 'Do we know what make and model of car she drove, and if she was using it yesterday? If so, where is it now? If they were in the killer's car, it's going to be harder to trace.'

'I'll get on it,' said Colin. He seemed keen to get back to something mundane after his brush with the more emotional side of an investigation.

Lexi updated Ronnie's timeline on the whiteboard.

- 7.00-23.00 *with grandparents*
- 23.00 *collected by Karolyn, apparently driven there by a 'friend'*

'How precise were they about the time that Karolyn picked up Ronnie? We need to work out if she went straight from the barbecue down to her parents' house, or if there was an interval before she met up with this unknown person.'

'Sorry, boss,' said Ridhi, 'they were a bit vague. But they were expecting to look after Ronnie again today. Mrs Small had phoned and got no answer. She assumed Karolyn was still sulking after their argument.'

'The big question is, why did she go to her parents and

collect Ronnie?' said Lexi. 'Was it her idea? Or was she being directed by the killer? And was he the older man that she was secretly seeing? Could he have been Johnny Lycett-Boyd? We need to move fast, because this is beginning to look a lot like the first two out of three.'

'What do you mean by that?' said Maya.

'Three kills and we'll have a serial killer on our hands.'

THIRTY-TWO

A serial killer meant they had to brace themselves for another murder. It meant throwing everything at the case to get between the killer and his next intended victim. And they would only be able to do that if they could identify either the hunter or the hunted. Lexi had been in this situation a dozen times before, and she knew the feeling of helplessness that came with it.

She sat at her desk, rubbing her face with her hands. Somewhere, probably not very far away, there was a woman with baby, completely unaware of the dark clouds brooding on her horizon. A child who would be motherless unless Lexi and her team could protect her.

She wrote a list of tasks to assign in the morning. Find out if two more sets of wings had been ordered. Dig deeper into Karolyn's life to find intersections with any of the current suspects. Did she know Johnny Lycett-Boyd or Will Steadman? Did she have any sort of connection to the vineyard?

Her phone pinged. A reminder that Luke Evans had texted earlier and they'd arranged to go for a drink. She opened her contacts, intending to phone and cancel. But something stopped her. Amber's words – that she was forever putting her life on hold for whatever case she was working on. She always had a case, and it was always more important than anything else in her life. That much was true. But what could she really achieve this evening, at her desk for another hour or two? She'd be churning through the same stuff over and over like a hamster on a treadmill. Sometimes stepping away for an hour or two would allow her to come back to the case with a fresh head.

She didn't have time now to go home and change, but there was a make-up bag in her desk drawer, so she went to the bathroom to see if she could make herself look more human and rather less exhausted.

As she freshened up, Lexi couldn't remember the last time she'd been on a date. Definitely not since she'd come back to Canterbury. She'd thrown herself into her new job as head of the Major Investigation Team and had allowed that and her triathlon training to take up all of her time. Casting her mind back further, she supposed the last time she went on a date would have been in Virginia...

She didn't want to think about Harry Garcia. That bastard.

Her complicated feelings about him weren't a can of worms worth opening just before she was due to meet Luke Evans. But this wasn't a date, just a quick drink. Not something to get gut-twistingly nervous over. Just making friends, widening her circle of acquaintances, which was something she really needed to do. Just to get Amber off her case. She could report back that she'd been out with a man and maybe that would shut her up for a bit.

She swiped her lips with a neutral lipstick and dabbed them with a tissue. Now mascara.

Butterflies fluttered inside her, making her feel stupid. She had no trouble when she was called to the most horrific murder scenes – nerves of steel. But now, the prospect of having to make small talk in a pub for a couple of hours was making the mascara brush in her hand shake. She'd probably take out an eye if she wasn't careful.

She wasn't cut out for this stuff at all.

By the time the main courses arrived in the little Italian restaurant they'd moved on to after the pub, Lexi realised that driving home was going to be out of the question. A glass of red in the pub, another glass of red here – she wasn't drunk but she was definitely over the limit. So that would mean a taxi all the way back to Wye, or maybe... Twirling a piece of spaghetti round her fork, she wondered absently if she could turn up at her sister's house and commandeer the spare room for the night.

It would make it quicker to get to work in the morning, and she was already racked with guilt for taking an evening off. What had she been thinking?

'Mmm, this is good,' said Luke. He had chosen a wild mushroom pasta dish. 'I'll have to remember this place next time I'm carb loading before a marathon.'

'Without the Chianti,' said Lexi. She was starting to relax – chatting with Luke was easy. The fact that they both competed in Ironman competitions and triathlons meant they had plenty to talk about. But half of her mind was still on the case. Why Karolyn? What had brought her into the killer's scopes?

'If you follow the training programme I've outlined, you should be ready to compete again once the spring schedule kicks off,' said Luke. 'The key to it will be giving your leg plenty of rest and recovery time before you hit any intensive training.'

'It's already feeling much better,' said Lexi. 'The swimming helped. Though with this current case, I'm not getting much time for it.'

Luke topped up her water glass and asked the waitress for another bottle of fizzy water. It was nice that he wasn't pressing more wine on her, which she'd experienced on some dates in the past.

'Yeah, tell me about your work. How much of it is like the detectives we see on TV?'

'Car chases every day? Tick. Consulting with serial killers in subterranean cells? Tick. Finding the solution to the murder at the bottom of a bottle? Tick. That's it. My life in a nutshell.'

Telling families their loved one was dead. Watching Mort slit a body from sternum to pubis. Late nights and gritty eyes from watching hours of CCTV. No one wanted to hear about the realities of the job.

Luke laughed. 'But seriously, how do you go about deciding who might be a suspect and who's not?'

'It's the same in every case. You follow where the evidence leads. You look for solid facts, because guesswork won't cut it when you get to court.'

'So it's the forensic team rather than you that solves the crime?'

'I suppose that's one way of looking at it. Sure, they confirm the physical facts. But I have to investigate more than that. These days we get plenty from technology – traffic cams, people's mobiles. And old-fashioned eyewitness testimony. My job is to put it all together to determine the truth.'

'What are you working on at the moment?' He was gazing straight at her, and Lexi felt a ripple inside.

'I can't really talk about it. Nothing interesting,' she said to bring the temperature down a notch.

'But every day's different, right?'

Lexi nodded, her mouth full of spaghetti.

'See, I'm a bit envious of that. My day starts and finishes within the four walls of my treatment room, unless I'm doing a home visit for a client. But it's never exciting.'

But also not so emotionally gruelling, Lexi thought to

herself, feeling guilty all over again about taking a couple of hours off.

'We should call it a night.' She flagged down the waiter and they split the bill. He didn't even suggest that he should pay for her, which was a relief.

'Can I give you a lift home?' he said, as they came out of the restaurant.

'It's fine,' said Lexi. 'I live out at Wye. I wouldn't expect you drive that far at this time of night.'

'No, let me,' he said. 'A taxi out there will cost you a fortune. If you can get someone to take you at all, given that they won't get a return fare.'

'It's really kind of you,' said Lexi.

'It's not far.'

Of course, it meant that her car would stay in Canterbury, where she'd left it in the station car park. But depending on what they were doing in the morning, maybe she could ask Tom to come and pick her up.

Luke drove a little Mazda sports car that felt much lighter than the muscle car Lexi drove. Probably guzzled a lot less fuel, too. He put some jazz on the stereo, removing the need to talk without leaving an awkward silence. Lexi relaxed in the bucket seat, staring out of the window at dark trees and lit houses, pushing back against thoughts about the case that had started to bubble up.

Luke slowed down to stay within the thirty-mile speed limit as they came into the village.

'How long have you lived out here?' he said, turning the music down.

'Almost a year. Since I came back from the States.' They glided through the silent streets. It was if people went to bed earlier out in the countryside. 'I'm thinking about moving into Canterbury, though. Less hassle for the commute and closer to my sister and her family. Or put it this way, my sister's thinking about it on my behalf.'

'More people and more lively, too. Would I be wrong if I guessed that nearly everyone who lives here is pushing retirement age or more?'

'Well, not *everyone*... This is me.' Lexi pointed at the driveway of her small cottage and Luke pulled in. 'Coffee?'

'Got decaf?'

'Yes.' She wasn't going to tell him that the packet of decaf pods for her coffee machine had been sitting unopened for months. They'd be fine.

She put him in the living room and went through to her kitchen to make the drinks – coffee for him and a camomile tea for her. She wondered whether he was expecting her to offer him something stronger, but she wasn't going to. He still needed to be able to drive home, after all.

Damn – no milk.

'Black all right?' she called through to the other room.

'Fine.'

When she brought the coffee through, she saw he'd chosen to sit on the sofa, and she wasn't quite sure whether she was supposed to sit next to him or opposite him in the armchair. And she despised herself for the slight flutter of panic this dilemma caused. She put the coffee cups down on the low table, giving herself a swift ticking off as she did so. Sofa. That was the right choice. Sitting in the chair would look stand-offish. Dating – absolutely excruciating. It reminded her why she tried to avoid the whole business.

'I would say I love what you've done with the place, but this is rented and you haven't done anything, have you?'

Lexi laughed. 'Spot on.' The rented furniture was all a little tired, a little faded, but Lexi had long since stopped noticing. 'It's not exactly my dream home, but as I spend so little time here, I haven't got around to changing anything.'

'Your sister's right. It's too quiet out here for someone your age.'

'But it's great for running. Out of the front door and up onto the Downs in minutes.'

Luke's eyes widened. 'Isn't that where those two girls were found murdered?'

He was referring to the Carter sisters – it was the first case Lexi had worked on her return to Kent.

For the next half hour, she told him a bit about the case and then they talked about which parts of Canterbury might be good for her to look at.

'I think the Old Dover Road area might just be a bit too close to work.'

'What about north of the city centre – you'd be just round the corner from me.' He gave her a roguish grin, and Lexi realised that somehow, over the course of the conversation, they appeared to have moved closer to each other.

'We could go out running together.'

'Mmm... and maybe other things.'

When did someone last move in on me for a kiss?

The thought was fleeting as Luke's lips sought hers, and she kissed him back hungrily, her arms wrapping themselves around his neck.

Seconds later, a loud banging on the front door made them spring apart.

'Lexi? Lexi? Are you there?' Someone outside was shouting her name.

'What the hell?' said Luke.

Lexi recognised the voice. What was Ed Harlow doing here at this time of night? She glanced at her watch. It was past eleven. Why not phone?

'I'm sorry,' she said to Luke, standing up.

'Lexi?' Ed's voice sounded anguished. Something must have happened – and in a heartbeat she knew what.

'Who is it?' said Luke, also springing to his feet.

'A friend.' There wasn't time to explain more than that. She went to the front door, aware that Luke was close behind.

As she opened the door, he pushed past her.

'Do you know what time it is, mate?' said Luke.

Ed Harlow was standing on the step. His clothes were rumpled, and his face was puffy. Lexi could tell he'd been crying. She pulled on Luke's arm to make him move back.

'It's okay, Luke.'

Luke stepped back, confused.

Lexi pulled Ed into an embrace. 'I'm so sorry.' She knew exactly what had happened. Charlie must have died. She stroked his hair and held him tighter. 'I'm so sorry, Ed.'

Luke stood staring at them. 'What's going on?'

Lexi pulled Ed into the cottage and gently pushed him to propel him towards the living room. Then she turned to Luke and whispered, 'I think his wife has just died.'

Luke raised a hand to his mouth. 'Oh God – I'm so sorry. I didn't realise.'

'It's fine, honestly.'

'I'd better go.'

Lexi nodded. 'Thank you for a lovely evening. And sorry it got cut short.'

Was she?

Once Luke was gone, Lexi went into the living room. Ed was standing by the window, staring into the darkness with unseeing eyes. Lexi embraced him from behind for a moment, then went to the kitchen and fetched him a whisky.

'When did it happen?'

'This afternoon.' He drank the whisky in one gulp. 'I wasn't ready for it. I thought we had more time.'

She guided him to the sofa, all too aware that just moments before she'd been wrapped in Luke's arms. He seemed to read her thoughts.

'I'm sorry. I interrupted something.'

'It was nothing. He just gave me a lift home. I hardly know him.' Why did she feel the need to make excuses? It meant nothing to Ed if she'd been on a date with someone. But for some reason, she didn't want him to get the wrong impression.

Ed wasn't even listening to her. 'She meant everything to me, from the moment I met her.'

'And I'm sure you did to her.'

Ed shook his head. 'Not really. Just before her diagnosis, she told me she was going to leave me. She'd had enough. Wanted to lead a different life.'

Lexi could feel the pain radiating from him.

'When we found out she had cancer, I persuaded her to stay, to let me nurse her through the illness. Then, if she recovered, she could choose to stay or go. I thought her getting cancer would give me a second chance to prove myself. It's not how it worked out. I think she was seeing someone else, and he scarpered when she was diagnosed.' He put his hands up to his face. 'It was all such a bloody mess and I thought I could make it right again.'

There were no words that wouldn't seem trite. Ed's grief was overwhelming, and all Lexi could do was reassure him with her silent presence that he wasn't alone. And so they sat, Lexi with an arm around his shoulders, until dawn streaked the sky outside and Ed finally fell asleep slumped against her.

THIRTY-THREE

THURSDAY

Lexi's phone buzzed, its loud ringtone amplified by the rattle of its vibration on the wooden coffee table. She pulled her arm out from behind Ed's sleeping form, but her hand was completely numb and shooting pains tore from her elbow to her shoulder.

'Ouch!'

She picked up her mobile with her other hand. The screen told her it was Tom. It also told her it was nearly ten a.m.

Oh, shit!

'Yes,' she said softly.

'Lexi, is that you? I can't hear you.'

'It's me,' she hissed. She didn't want to wake Ed.

'You're not in the office.'

'No, clearly not. I'll be in shortly.' She didn't have to tell Tom why she was late. But then he wasn't the problem. It was her own conscience that was going to crucify her.

'Head for Sherperdswell instead.'

'Why?'

'Meet me at the track at Shepherd's Hill.'

'What are you not telling me?' A sense of foreboding made her feel suddenly cold.

'Johnny Lycett-Boyd. He's dead.'

She let out an audible gasp and, beside her, Ed started to stir.

'What the hell?'

'He was up at the racetrack – came off on a sharp corner, apparently. Rolled his car. I'm on my way there now.'

'He's definitely dead?' She couldn't believe it.

'Yes. No doubt about it.'

'When did it happen?'

'Just now. Twenty minutes ago, maybe.'

Lexi stood up, and then winced at the sharp jab of pain in her leg.

'I'm on my way.' She rubbed the back of her leg. She needed a shower and a change of clothing, but there wasn't time for that. She raked through her tangled hair with her fingers and avoided catching sight of herself in the mirror over the fireplace.

Ed was watching her from the sofa, fully awake now.

'I'm so sorry, Ed. I have to go.'

'I understand.' Of course he did.

'Have you got someone you can call? You're welcome to stay here if you can't face going home on your own.'

Ed stood up. 'No, I can't impose on you.' He shook his head. 'I'm sorry about last night. I screwed up that date for you, didn't I?'

'It was nothing. He would have been leaving anyway.' Was that true? Whether it was or not, she didn't have time to think about it now.

Luke had driven her home the previous evening, so she had to call a cab to take her into Canterbury where her car had been left. Once she was behind the wheel, she tried to put her muddled thoughts in order. There was no reason, from anything Tom had said, to suspect it was anything other than an accident. But given he was a possible suspect in Bethany's death and now

Karolyn's as well, it couldn't be a coincidence. She needed to know exactly what had happened.

When a prime suspect in a murder case inexplicably died, it was hard to see it as anything other than connected.

A couple of miles west of Elvington, the Shepherd's Hill Race Circuit was a twenty-minute drive from Canterbury. It was only a few minutes off the A2, and the main gates were open, so Lexi was able to drive straight in. She followed the signs along the edge of a huge grass car park – empty on a weekday morning – and followed a curve to reach the side of the track where the vehicle bays and spectator stands were located. Now she could see the track itself, a huge looping circuit of smooth concrete, bounded by banks of used tyres and black-and-white crash barriers. At the furthest point from her, on a tight bend, flashing blue lights advertised the presence of police cars, a fire engine and an ambulance.

Unable to work out how to gain direct access to the track with her car, Lexi drove into the area of vehicle bays and pits at the nearside of the track. She spotted Tom's Jeep pulled up at the back of a low brick building with a number of doors. Signs on each door identified the circuit office, the team viewing area and the first aid room. She parked and got out the car, dialling Tom's number as she did.

A man in grease-stained overalls waved at her. 'Sorry, love, you can't stop there. Could you make your way back to the car park?'

Lexi dropped her phone into her pocket and got out her police ID instead. 'Police. I understand there's been a fatal accident?'

The man peered at her ID, then nodded.

'Did you see what happened?'

'No, I was in the workshops.' He pointed towards a large, open-sided hanger, in which Lexi could see cars with their bonnets open or up on lifts. No one seemed to be working on

them, but she expected they would have gone round to the front
of the building to gawp.

'Your colleague,' he said, pointing at the Jeep, 'he's just
headed across to the accident site. It's on the far side of the
track.'

'Thanks,' said Lexi. A narrow alley down the side of the
building led to the trackside and she could see the backs of a
couple of men in overalls, talking in hushed tones as they
squinted at what was happening in the distance. They turned
round as she came towards them, ashen-faced with shock, one
of them clutching a cigarette in a shaking hand.

'Did either of you see the crash?' she asked.

'I did,' said the man with the cigarette.

'Put that out,' snapped the man she'd just spoken to, coming
up behind her. 'For God's sake, Terry.'

Terry took a quick drag, then dropped the cigarette and
ground it out with his heel. Lexi looked round – there were 'no
smoking' signs everywhere, as they were near the refuelling pit.

'Tell me what you saw,' said Lexi.

He took a deep breath. 'Johnny was out on the track. He
wanted to test his Porsche's setup for racing – he'd been driving
on the roads, so it needed some attention.' His eyes widened
with fear. 'He was going to retune it himself.' Did he think she
was going to try and blame him for the crash?

'Was anyone else on the track at the same time?'

'No, just Johnny. He was really caning it, pushing the car to
its limits. After last night's rain, I think the track was a bit greasy
at Shepherd's Crook – that's what we call the bend where he
came off. He braked at the wrong spot and the rear wheels slid
out, then he spun out of control, hit the barrier and flipped.'

'He should have braked earlier,' said the other man. 'He was
off the line before he even hit the bend.'

'I understand he was an experienced driver who knew the
track well?'

'He part-owned it. He drove here all the time,' said Terry. 'He must have taken that corner thousands of times – he knew what he was doing.'

'Could there have been a problem with the car then?' Lexi looked out across the track and saw Tom walking towards the wreckage.

The men shrugged. None of them answered. Clearly it was an idea no one wanted to consider.

'Can one of you take me over to the other side of the track?' she said.

Investigating the crash would fall under the Roads Policing Unit, but she needed to ensure the results would come straight to her, particularly if there was anything irregular.

One of the other mechanics, not Terry, said he would, and led her to the other end of the team viewing area where there was a support car parked. They drove out onto the track and around the circuit until they reached the Shepherd's Crook bend. Lexi thanked the mechanic and got out. Tom was there already, talking to a uniformed policeman. Behind him, the fire crew were busy removing the roof of a crumpled blue Porsche 911 Turbo to retrieve Johnny Lycett-Boyd's body. Lexi could see blood on the caved in windscreen, but she didn't go any closer. Seeing his broken and crumpled body would tell her nothing.

She went to join Tom and the policeman, whose insignia confirmed he was a member of the RPU.

'We'll ask the coroner to check his blood alcohol levels,' the policeman was saying, 'although no one has suggested that he was driving under the influence.'

'I'm DI Lexi Bennett,' she said. 'The victim, Johnny Lycett-Boyd, was a person of interest in a murder we're currently investigating.'

'Sergeant Kevin Malthouse,' he said. 'Your colleague was just filling me in.'

'Could you also ask them to test his blood for drugs as well as alcohol? Including psilocybin. It features in the case we're working on.'

The sergeant's eyebrows went up, but he nodded. 'Sure. We'll also have an engineer check the car for faults. By all accounts, he knew the track and should have been fine to handle this corner. Of course, he may have suffered some sort of cardiac event. We'll have to wait for the autopsy results.'

'Has anyone been dispatched to tell his wife?'

'Not yet – I'm overseeing things here and my partner hasn't arrived.'

'Okay,' said Lexi. 'I know her – Marietta Lycett-Boyd. I'll go and break the news.'

'Glutton for punishment,' muttered Tom, as they walked back across the centre of the circuit to return to their cars.

THIRTY-FOUR

Lexi drove straight to the vineyard. Marietta needed to hear the news in person, and the fact that there had been a fatal crash at Shepherd's Hill wouldn't remain unknown for long. The people working at the track would tell friends and family and, somehow, local newshounds always heard of these things even faster. For Marietta to find out that her husband was dead from a local radio newsflash was unconscionable.

Parking in the vineyard's small car park, she guessed that Marietta would be working in the winery. She could see even from here that the place was a hive of activity as crates of grapes were being unloaded from a tractor trailer and being stacked up by the goods lift on the side of the building. As she walked up to the facility, she could hear the hum of machinery and the rattle of the lift cage, and shrill voices shouting to be heard above the din. Will Steadman came out of the open doorway as she arrived.

'Is Marietta in there?' she said, as soon as he came within earshot.

'She was, but I think she's just popped back to the house. Do you want me to call and check?'

'If you don't mind. Could you ask her to wait for me down there?'

'Sure.' Something in Lexi's countenance must have alerted him. 'Everything okay?'

Lexi kept her expression neutral. 'I just need a word with her.'

His fears allayed, Steadman got out his phone. Lexi went back to her car and by the time she reached the farmhouse further down the hill, Marietta was standing in the front door, a questioning look on her face.

'Will called and said you were coming down.'

'Can we go inside?'

'Of course, but I can only spare a moment. I need to get back up to the winery.'

Lexi followed her through to the kitchen, rehearsing the words in her mind.

Marietta leaned against the breakfast bar. 'What's this all about?'

'Maybe you should sit down, Marietta.'

The woman glared back at her. Marietta wasn't going to be told what to do in her own house.

'Another dead girl?' Her tone was hostile.

Lexi took a deep breath and readied herself for the fallout. 'There's been an accident over at the track. Johnny was involved.' Lexi saw Marietta's knees flex, but she quickly supported herself by placing her palms flat on the counter.

'Johnny? Is he okay?'

Lexi pressed her lips together, but she had to answer. A slight shake of her head was all that was needed.

'*Merde!*' Marietta stepped back and stumbled.

Lexi rushed round to her side of the counter and put an arm round her. She looked around quickly for somewhere to sit.

Only when she'd lowered Marietta onto a hard wooden chair she'd pulled out from the kitchen table did she dare to continue. 'I'm afraid he died at the scene. An ambulance attended, but he was pronounced dead while still in the car.'

Marietta's face had turned the colour of ash and her whole body was trembling.

'You were there?' She began to cry, loudly, grabbing at a roll of kitchen paper on the table to stem the tide.

'Briefly, then I came straight here.' She looked around. 'Let me fetch you some water.'

Marietta ignored her, stood up and went to one of the cupboards opposite the breakfast bar. She found a glass and a bottle of brandy. Once she'd poured herself a generous measure with shaking hands and had downed half of it, she turned back to Lexi.

'How did it happen?' Her French accent seemed stronger, her voice more tentative. She'd lost all semblance of her icy cool.

'I spoke to one of the mechanics. He'd been retuning the car and he took it for a test lap. He came off on that very sharp bend on the far side of the track.'

'Shepherd's Crook.'

Lexi nodded.

'Johnny knew that track like the back of his hand. That shouldn't have happened.' Her face crumpled again. 'Something was wrong with the car?'

'It's too early to say, but that possibility will be thoroughly investigated.'

Marietta threw back the rest of the brandy. She looked shaky on her feet.

'Sit down. Breathe.'

This time she did as she was told, and Lexi sat down opposite her.

'What was he doing at the track?' she asked.

Marietta shrugged. 'I didn't know he was there. He should have been here, working. We're still in the middle of the harvest.' She frowned at Lexi's raised eyebrows. 'I don't keep tabs on him all day long. I have my own job to do – and now it's going to be double the work.' She sounded tired beyond belief. She gripped the edge of the table with white knuckles, as if trying to suck strength and stability from the solid wood.

'Can I call someone for you?' Lexi presumed the rest of Marietta's family were all in France. 'Johnny's parents? A friend?'

She took a deep breath and straightened her spine. 'I will call Johnny's parents and let them know. I'd better tell Will.' She got up and tidied the glass into the dishwasher.

Lexi admired her strength of character, but the enormity of what had happened probably hadn't sunk in yet. It would no doubt hit her later, maybe in the small hours, when she'd find herself alone in the bed she'd shared with Johnny.

Marietta picked up a notebook and pen from beside a phone charger on one of the counters, and sat down at the table. 'What happens now? Where have they taken his body?'

'To the morgue. I'm afraid, because of the way he died, there'll have to be an autopsy.'

'I understand.' She made a note. 'Can I go to him?'

'Of course.' Lexi gave her the necessary details and again asked if she could call someone. It didn't seem right to leave her here on her own or to let her drive to the mortuary alone. But then she heard the sound of a key in the front door. She looked around towards the hall.

'Hello? Anyone home?'

Marietta was on her feet in an instant. 'Johnny? Is that you?'

It sounded like Johnny's voice, even to Lexi. But it couldn't be.

Then the owner of the voice came into the kitchen. Dressed in cargo pants and a denim jacket, he was tall and lean. His brown hair had been kissed blond by the sun and his skin was tanned dark. But in every other respect, she could have been looking at Johnny Lycett-Boyd.

Marietta ran to the man. 'Ben! What are you doing here?' She flung her arms around him and started crying again against his chest.

'Marietta, what is it?' He looked down at the top of her head, shock and concern wiping the smile of greeting from his face.

So this was Ben Lycett-Boyd, the brother who supposedly lived in Australia.

And, to her mind, his entrance couldn't have come at a more interesting moment. His brother only just dead, and here he was, turning up out of the blue.

THIRTY-FIVE

'Marietta, what's going on?' he said when she didn't answer him the first time.

Lexi sent him a warning look over the top of Marietta's head. He disengaged from the embrace and stepped back so he could look at his brother's wife properly.

'What is it?'

'Johnny... Johnny's dead. He crashed the Porsche on the track.'

Ben literally reeled. He stumbled sideways until he bumped into the open kitchen door. 'No. No way. I spoke to him on the phone an hour ago. He said he'd meet me here.'

'It only just happened,' said Lexi.

'Who are you?' said Ben, turning to look at her more intently now.

'DI Bennett, Kent Police.'

Marietta went to the cupboard again and got out the brandy. She handed the bottle and a clean glass to Ben. 'What are you doing here? Why didn't we know you were coming?'

Ben put the glass and the bottle down on the kitchen table and dropped heavily into one of the chairs. 'I meant to surprise you both. I'm on a flying visit to London, a business thing. I found I had a bit spare time today and I thought I'd come down. See how my niece is doing.' He looked around the kitchen. 'Where is she?'

'She's with your parents. You should know – it's the middle of the harvest. We're too busy... and now this.'

They both fell silent.

Lexi cleared her throat. 'I'll arrange someone to be in touch with you about viewing the body,' she said. 'And I expect the accident investigators will want to talk to you, Marietta, about Johnny's movements this morning.'

Marietta nodded.

At least she would have someone with her now. Assuming Ben could extend his flying visit, given the circumstances. Lexi hadn't liked the thought of leaving her alone.

'I'd better go,' she said.

'Wait,' said Ben. 'I need to know exactly what happened.'

'Like I said, the accident investigators will be in touch, and when they've worked out the reason for the crash, they'll share it with you.'

'So you're not an accident investigator?'

Marietta put a hand to her forehead. 'You don't know, Ben?'

He frowned at her.

'Some women... two women have died, here on the vineyard. DI Bennett is investigating their deaths.'

'What the hell?' This time, he helped himself to some brandy. 'When did this happen?'

Lexi went towards the kitchen door. 'It's an ongoing investigation. Not something I can talk about.' She looked at Marietta. 'We'll be in touch if we need any more information.'

She left the kitchen and went down the hall to the front door. Then she heard Ben's voice and paused. He sounded flustered and confused.

'Jesus, what's happening here, Marietta? What women? How did they die?'

Lexi paused. She couldn't hear Marietta's answer, just Ben's reaction to whatever she said.

'A kid? What does this mean for Elvington? Does Johnny's thirty per cent go to you or to Aurora? And what if this kid turns out to be his? Does she have a claim?'

Lexi shut the front door quietly behind her.

It seemed like the shock of his brother's death had already worn off. Ben Lycett-Boyd appeared to be more concerned about the implications for the business than what Johnny's death meant for his family.

And that, in itself, was very interesting indeed.

Back at the office, Lexi had instructions for Ridhi.

'Do me a favour and check what flight Ben Lycett-Boyd came in on, how long he's been in the country and when he's booked to return to Australia.'

'I'll get right on it.'

Tom gave Lexi a hard stare. 'What exactly are you thinking? That he's a person of interest in his brother's death? He was nowhere nearby at the time of the crash.'

'I don't know where he was at the time of the crash, actually,' said Lexi. 'I'm not really thinking anything – just going on a fishing expedition. He just seems very concerned with what happens to his brother's shares in the vineyard, and he's arrived in this country just as there are rumours circulating that Johnny was planning to sell up.'

'All of which coincides with a couple of murders on the property,' added Colin. 'Coincidence? I don't buy it.'

Lexi shot him a look. He'd just said exactly what she was thinking. 'If it was anything other than an accident, we have to assume that Johnny's death was linked to the other two deaths. It just might be of interest if we find out that Ben Lycett-Boyd has been in the country all this time. Maybe the whole ritualistic murder scenes are just a smokescreen for someone who has a financial interest in what happens to the vineyard.'

She thought about the discussion of the killer's profile she'd had with Ed Harlow, and wondered how much of it was applicable to Ben Lycett-Boyd. Despite his blustering in Marietta's kitchen, could he have actually known about Bethany and Karolyn's deaths? He was very quick to ask whether Scarlett would have any claim on Johnny's estate. It suddenly made the matter of Scarlett's paternity all the more pertinent. If it turned out that Johnny was her father, it meant both her parents were now dead. Lexi sighed. While the adults fought over the money, who was going to look out for this poor orphaned child? She suspected the answer to that would depend upon Johnny Lycett-Boyd's will and for a moment, she very much disliked the world.

'Ridhi, can you also dig into Ben Lycett-Boyd's financial situation?' Will Steadman had suggested that the younger Lycett-Boyd was doing well in Australia. But what if he wasn't? Maybe he had his eyes on the prize – the successful vineyard in which his brother seemed to be losing interest.

Her phone rang and the thoughts chasing circles in her mind evaporated.

'Hi, Maggie.'

'I just heard – Johnny Lycett-Boyd is dead?'

'He is. His car came off the track at Shepherd's Hill. Total write-off and he was dead before they could get him out. It seems weird, given how well he knew the track and the car.'

'Hmm...' Maggie paused for a moment. 'Then it looks like your case is all wrapped up.'

'What?' Had she heard right? 'How do you come to that?'

'He was your prime suspect, wasn't he? You've got to be considering suicide.'

'It's too early to know the cause of the crash. And he wasn't the only suspect.'

'Two women dead on his property, one of whom he fathered a child with. Bethany's body found in a secret cave that virtually nobody else knew about. For all we know, he might have been having an affair with Karolyn, too. Sexually moti-vated murder. Urges he couldn't control. If he decided he didn't want to kill again, suicide would have been the only way out.'

'Hang on a minute. This is all supposition.'

'Tie up the loose ends, Lexi. It's Occam's razor.'

The simplest explanation is usually the best one.

But was it in this case?

Not in Lexi's opinion. In fact, it had just blown the whole case wide open. Because she was beginning to wonder if in fact she had a third murder on her hands.

'Let's just wait and see what the accident investigators come back with,' she said.

Maggie let out a frustrated sigh.

THIRTY-SIX

Skipping lunch, Lexi headed up to Maidstone. She'd secured a promise from Mort that he'd do the autopsy on Karolyn Small as quickly as possible, because she needed to know if the cause of death was the same for both girls. Bethany had been given magic mushrooms to mess with her mind and then, when she was tripping, the killer had found it easy to administer a strong enough dose of fentanyl to kill her. If they found that Karolyn had died in the same way it would confirm what Lexi already knew – that they were dealing with the same killer. And if it was the work of a true serial killer, rather than someone pretending to be a serial killer, then they might be running out of time before the next death.

The more she thought about it, the less likely she believed that Johnny Lycett-Boyd's crash had been suicide. In her opinion, he didn't have the personality type and, even if he did, crashing your car wasn't a good way to guarantee death. What if he'd been pulled out of the wreckage to face life with crippling injuries?

Mort was grumbling about something as she walked into the

morgue, and when he saw her, he easily segued to make his grumbles about her in particular.

'Jump she says, and I raise the bar and add hoops just to make my own life more difficult.' He slid the body he was examining back into its refrigerated drawer.

'Oh, stop it, Mort. You never do anything to make your own life more difficult. And you know full well why I asked for this autopsy to be expedited.'

'Yes, but you're not the only one in a hurry.'

'I'm sorry, honestly.' She wasn't. 'You know I appreciate it when you pull out all the stops for me.'

Ego massaged, Mort led her across the room to a covered body on one of the stainless-steel mortuary tables. When he folded back the white rubber sheet that was covering it, Lexi saw Karolyn Small's body. She looked tiny and fragile – almost a different woman to the one Lexi and Tom had spoken to only forty-eight hours earlier. Her skin tone was grey and her make-up was smudged. Black smuts of mascara littered her cheeks, beneath open, unseeing eyes. Her long brown hair was knotted and tangled.

Mort was all business, expertly folding the sheet and putting it to one side. He checked the tag attached to Karolyn's big toe and sorted his phone to record his observations. Lexi smeared Vaseline under her nose and put on a mask, while Mort adjusted a strong arc lamp to shine directly over the body.

While Lexi patiently waited, Mort made a close examination of every inch of Karolyn's downy skin. He made occasional observations about a fading bruise here, an old scar there, but he didn't log any recent injuries or signs of a struggle. Every now and then, he plucked some minuscule piece of fluff or fibre from her skin with tweezers, popping them into small, clear plastic evidence bags which he quickly labelled. Lexi pulled on latex gloves and helped him turn Karolyn's body over. Her back, buttocks and the backs of her legs showed dark purple patches of lividity, where the blood had pooled after her death. Mort studied it and his lips moved slightly as he made closer calculations as to the time of death. Lexi waited in silence. She knew better than to question him too early. He'd reveal all the information she needed when he was good and ready.

He picked off quite a lot of grit and dirt that was clinging to her skin, then asked Lexi to help him turn her back over. Then he took a speculum and angled the light so he could assess whether she had been sexually assaulted.

'No sign of injury or sexual violence,' he reported. He took samples that he would check for the presence of sperm or spermicide, so they could tell whether she'd had sex with someone in the hours leading up to her death.

'Anything there?' She couldn't restrain herself from asking, as Mort slipped the samples under a high-powered microscope on the side bench.

He took off his glasses and screwed his eye up against the eyepiece. He took his time, maybe on purpose. Lexi tried not to crowd him.

'Yes, a few dead sperm, which indicates the presence of spermicide. She had sex, and the man wore a condom.'

'Can you tell when exactly it happened?'

'Not precisely, but there are some considerations. With unprotected sex, we can look at what percentage of the sperm is still alive and make an estimate. When a condom comes into the picture, there are usually precious few spermatozoa in the vagina and those there are will have been killed by spermicide. However, semen contains enzymes, as well as sperm, which degrade over time. I'll do a few tests and see if I can narrow down the timeframe for you, but it'll take a couple of days at least.'

'Thanks, Mort. And can you get a DNA reading from the sperm for comparisons?'

'Of course.' He went back across to Karolyn's body. 'I'm going to open her up now. You staying?'

Lexi usually ducked out of autopsies at this point. It was such a brutal process and to her mind the victims had already suffered enough. However, this time she was going to have to stick it out.

'Yes, I need to know what's in her stomach – if she ingested magic mushrooms and if they were the same or similar to the ones you found with Bethany Glover.'

Mort nodded, but he was already making a long straight cut from the top of her chest down to her pubis. Lexi looked away, not because of the blood. Dead bodies don't bleed. But it seemed so impersonal, like an animal on a butcher's slab being gutted. Even though she went to the most gruesome of murder scenes, she knew she could never do Mort's job.

'I'm going to nip out and check my email.'

Mort grunted.

Her inbox was overflowing, and she needed to get back to the office to deal with it. Or at least some of it. There were text updates from most of the team, and several messages from a number she didn't recognise. She opened the first one.

Sorry about last night – hope yr friend ok now. Luke x

That was thoughtful. She smiled to herself, but a reply could wait until she got back to the office. And she should give Ed a ring, too, to see how he was doing.

When she went back into the mortuary, Mort was once more looking at something under the microscope. She glanced towards Karolyn's body. It was still open, the skin peeled back on either side, so she looked away quickly.

'Mushrooms,' said Mort, without looking up from the microscope. 'Same type as the one's in Bethany's stomach.'

'And fentanyl?'

'That's a blood test, but I'll mark it urgent.'

'Thanks, Mort.'

She'd been right. Two murders didn't make a serial killer, but they were two-thirds of the way there. And if it had been Johnny Lycett-Boyd, he surely would have hung around for a third one. She was more convinced than ever that his crash hadn't been self-inflicted.

THIRTY-SEVEN

Ridhi ripped open the packaging and took as big a bite of the falafel and avocado wrap as she could fit into her mouth. It was well beyond lunchtime and she'd been running on empty for hours – if she didn't eat it now the damn thing would qualify as dinner rather than lunch.

This, of course, was the cue for her phone to ring.

She put down the wrap and studied the mobile's screen as she hurriedly chewed. It was the desk sergeant downstairs. 'Hi?' was all she could manage.

'Ridhi?'

'Yeah.'

'Got a bloke here at the front desk, would like a word with you.'

Finally she swallowed. 'What's it about? Does he have a name?'

'A Mr Gideon Croft. Something about the Elvington cases.'

'Oh good grief – him again.' But the boss had told her to find out more about Croft, and how better than from the horse's mouth. 'Okay, I'll come down.'

'Thanks.'

She finished her wrap at a speed she knew would invite indigestion later, and hurried down to see what Gideon Croft felt was important enough to tell the police this time. She felt sure he was just a chancer with nothing to do with the murder, but they hadn't ruled him out. This time, though, maybe he'd show some knowledge of the second murder that could place him at the scene. Perhaps she'd be able to crack the case…

Dream on, you silly girl.

She couldn't bring him into the incident room – there were pictures of the murder scenes up on the whiteboard – but the boss was out, so she could use her office.

'PC Kulkorni, good to see you again,' he said, as she came into the downstairs reception area.

'Hello, Mr Croft, what can I do for you?' She didn't bother to point out that she was a DC, not a PC, let alone correct his pronunciation of her name. Sometimes it just wasn't worth it.

'I wanted to talk to you again about these two dead women at the vineyard.'

'Okay, let's go upstairs.'

Once they were in Lexi's office, Gideon Croft opened the battered briefcase he was clutching and pulled out an ancient-looking book with a green woven cover. 'This is what I wanted to show you,' he said.

He thumbed through the pages for what seemed like forever. A page dislodged itself and drifted to the floor, followed by another. He leaned down and picked them up, then had to flick back through a couple of chapters to replace them where they belonged. Ridhi waited patiently without saying anything.

'Sorry, it's a very old book,' he said. 'I shouldn't have really brought it out of the university, but it might be relevant to your case.'

'Perhaps it would be easier if you just told me what's on your mind.'

Gideon Croft sighed, closed the book and held it tightly on

his lap. 'This is a compendium of Kent folklore and folktales, published in 1840.' He paused.

'And?'

'It goes into a lot more detail about the Elvington Angel than I was able to tell you. And, you see, I think your murdered women being brought up onto the hill above the village of Elvington... I think it's someone trying to re-awaken the old tale.'

Although there was no way he could have known that Karolyn Small had also been found wearing wings, he was still trying to link the murders to the folklore.

'Re-awaken? What exactly do you mean by that?'

At that moment the door opened, and Lexi appeared.

'Oh!'

'Sorry, ma'am,' said Ridhi, jumping up from Lexi's chair, and feeling a rush of blood to her cheeks. 'Mr Croft wanted to talk to me, and the incident room is a bit noisy.' She noticed Ed Harlow, the forensic psychologist who'd helped them before, standing at Lexi's shoulder.

'No worries,' said Lexi. She took her chair and Ed followed her in and perched on the edge of the desk. He looked pale and drawn.

Ridhi wondered if Lexi was bringing him in. Colin had said that Lexi had been told to shut the case down, now that Johnny Lycett-Boyd was dead. This certainly didn't look like she was doing that.

'What were you talking about?' said Lexi.

Gideon Croft warmed to having a larger audience. 'It's this,' he said, holding up the book. 'The Elvington Angel was a persistent belief in the village of Elvington and the surrounding areas until well into the middle of the nineteenth century. And what those of us who study folklore tend to find is that even when a widespread belief like this dies out, there will still be little pockets that endure.'

'I'm not sure I follow you,' said Lexi.

'From what I know about the first murder...' He glanced at Ed.

'It's all right, you can speak freely in front of Mr Harlow.'

Croft nodded. 'I'm guessing the scene contained some reference to an angel – and if it did, you have a clear indication that the cult of the Elvington Angel is still going strong somewhere in this valley. If I were to guess that your second murder scene also had an angel reference, I'd be right, wouldn't I?'

It was a lot of guesswork. Or did he actually know more than he was letting on?

'But why would people who believed that a benevolent angel was watching over them see fit to kill women and pose them wearing angel wings?' said Ridhi.

'Ah ha, I was right,' said Croft triumphantly. 'Same again.'

Ridhi bit her lip, realising she'd just let the cat out of the bag.

Damn!

But on the other hand, it suggested that he maybe didn't have prior knowledge of the scene, so there was that.

'It's evidence of cult activity,' Croft continued in a conspiratorial tone.

'Cult activity?' said Ed Harlow. His voice was abrasive.

'The remaining believers in the Elvington Angel have come together and they're making sacrifices to ensure continued beneficence. It's clear to me that their choice of location, high on the hill to the north of the village, is significant. This is where the Elvington Angel was first supposed to have appeared.'

'I see,' said Ed. 'And how many people do you think belong to this cult?'

Croft raised his hands, leaving the book balancing precariously on his bony knees. 'Not many. I wouldn't have thought more than half a dozen.'

'And they would all be in on this ritual sacrifice?'

Croft nodded.

'Of two local girls, women who they might have known?'

'I think it would be essential that the girls were of the village. Born in Elvington preferably.'

Ridhi thought about what they knew of Bethany's early life. She certainly hadn't been born in Elvington.

'And that book tells you all about this cult?' Harlow wasn't bothering to disguise the disdain in his voice.

'No, no, you misunderstand me. This...' He tapped on the cover with a long fingernail. '...contains the original story of the angel. The cult is something I've surmised, given my expertise in the field. We've seen things like this happen up and down the country.'

Lexi started to say something, but Ed cut in. 'I don't think I've misunderstood anything. I think that you don't understand crime scenes, criminology or forensic psychology. These killings have none of the hallmarks of a cult, and plenty to suggest that they're the work of a lone killer. That's my opinion, based on *my* expertise in the field.'

Croft's eyes widened with shock. This clearly wasn't the reception he'd expected. He stood up hurriedly. 'I'm sorry, Miss Kolkrini. I came here in good faith to help you with your case, but obviously you have other experts advising you.'

'I...' Ridhi started to speak.

'Thank you for your input, Mr Croft,' said Lexi. 'We'll keep it under consideration. Ridhi, could you show Mr Croft out and then come back here?'

The tone of Lexi's voice made Ridhi nervous, but she quickly ushered Gideon Croft out of the office and down the stairs.

'Thank you for your help,' she said, as she delivered him through the double doors into the reception area.

He said nothing but glared at her briefly, before turning and walking out of the station.

THIRTY-EIGHT

Lexi turned and looked at Ed. 'Wow! That was a bit harsh...' Then she saw the desolate expression on his face, and she wished she could bite back the words. She'd momentarily forgotten the pain he was in. And that she'd brought him back to the office with her after phoning him and realising he was still lying on her sofa at home, in pieces.

'Sorry. It just spilled out of me.'

'No, it doesn't matter. You were right. Gideon Croft is just a busybody who wants to insert himself into the investigation. There's always one.'

'He's not a killer – you can rule him out. My read on him is that he's hungry for privileged information. It makes him feel special to be in the know. He wants to trade his information for ours. If he was the killer, he wouldn't need to do that.'

Lexi shook her head. 'That's one take on it, Ed. But it's not exactly unknown for serial killers to try and insert themselves into the investigation.' She thought about how creepy he'd seemed, but pushed that from her mind. Killers more often than not appeared completely normal. 'I think I'll have Ridhi dig around into his background a little.' She paused. 'Anyway, how are you doing?'

Ed sank down into the chair that Croft had just vacated and put his head in his hands. 'I forget for a moment, then it all crashes back in. I can't believe she's gone.'

Lexi watched him. There was nothing she could say to assuage his pain. She remembered that feeling exactly when she lost her sister, Rose. Time wouldn't heal it – it just meant you got used to the hole in your heart.

He'd told her that his brother was driving up from Exeter to be with him, but it would be a few hours yet until he arrived. Lexi didn't want to leave him on his own, but at the same time, with two women dead, she couldn't abandon the case.

Like always, he could practically read her thoughts. 'You want me to leave, don't you? I've got no business being here in this state.' He managed a weak smile. 'I messed up your date last night, you don't need me messing up your day today.'

'It wasn't a date,' said Lexi quickly.

'Sure, of course not,' said Ed. 'But there was definitely a vibe...'

'What d'you mean?'

'I sensed he was jealous when I turned up.'

'No way. He was totally understanding.'

Ed stared at her long and hard. He was building up the courage to say something.

Lexi waited in silence, a technique she used when interviewing suspects.

'He's not really your type,' he said at length.

'You'd know all about my type then?' She kept her voice light, but it made her remember how much she hated the whole business of dating. She decided not to give him the chance to answer. 'I assume you share my opinion that that was a whole load of twaddle from Croft.'

'Oh God!' He let out a dry laugh. 'Monstrous rubbish.'

Ridhi appeared sheepishly in the doorway, shooting a worried glance at Lexi. 'Sorry about that.'

'Nothing for you to be sorry about,' said Ed. 'The man's an idiot.'

Lexi frowned at him. 'Ridhi, can you do a background check on Croft? See what contact we've had with him in the past. And run a search through the local press – see if he's given his opinion on other cases, perhaps.'

'I would guess the Elvington Angel story is absolute nonsense,' said Ed.

'I'll look into that, too,' said Ridhi.

'Okay, let us know what you find.'

'Sure, boss.' She disappeared in the direction of the incident room.

'You're suspicious of him now?' said Ed, his voice laced with disbelief.

'I think whoever is doing this is posing the bodies to create a signature. And when we see a signature like that, what do we think of?'

'Serial killers.'

'Exactly. But I've suspected from the start that the killer is posing the bodies as misdirection – in other words, he's staging the scene to look like a serial killer signature, to hide the fact that it's something else entirely.'

'Some sort of double bluff?' said Ed.

'Yup. That was my initial thought – that's what made me think Johnny Lycett-Boyd might have been behind it as a way of getting custody of Scarlett. But he's dead and now we have Gideon Croft turning up and muddying the waters further with his fake theory about a sacrificial cult.'

Ed shook his head. 'It's not enough to make him a suspect.'

'Perhaps. I'll see if Ridhi comes up with anything, and then maybe we'll check his alibis.'

'You're right – if only to rule him out. I don't think this business with the wings has anything to do with this mythical angel, whatever Croft says. If it's a true signature, it's something much more personal to the killer. And if it's a misdirection, there will still be things that we can learn from the way he chose to misdirect us. There are no babies in the folk story, but both these scenes featured living babies. Dead mothers, living children. I think there's a lot more to unpack right there. Ronnie and Scarlett might just be the key to these killings.'

Lexi understood now why Charlie had asked her to bring Ed in on some cases. With his mind engaged on a murder case, Ed could escape, at least momentarily, from what he was going through. But even if it would bring him some temporary relief, it couldn't be healthy. He would have to face up to his grief at some point. But for now, she would take his help. He always brought such clarity to her thoughts – and this time he was right. They needed to work out what drove the killer to include living children in his signature. Something in his past, without doubt, and certainly the key to the whole case.

Ed's phone rang and he took a brief call.

'That was my brother,' he said, disconnecting. 'He thinks he'll get to me in an hour or so. I should get going.' Ed lived in a converted oast house just outside Sandwich. 'I'd better get some food in and sort out the spare room.'

'Ed, I'm so sorry about Charlie, you know that.'

Ed's face fell and he breathed out heavily. 'Even if you know it's coming, it still bloody hurts.'

She wrapped him in a hug and he clung tightly to her for almost a minute.

'Let me know when the funeral is,' she said. 'I'd like to come.'

'That would be nice.' Then he was gone, and Lexi had to bite down hard on her lower lip. She'd barely known Charlie. It was Ed she felt for.

THIRTY-NINE

Tom could tell by the look on the PCs' faces that they were fed up with searching the vineyard, first for Bethany and Scarlett's clothes, then for Karolyn and Ronnie's clothes, none of which had yet to come to light. So they weren't going to greet his latest request with joy.

'We're looking for a used condom,' he said.

A couple of the male PCs smirked at this. The rest of them ran the gamut from bored to repulsed.

'We know that Karolyn Small had sex a few hours before she died. The presence of spermicide indicates that a condom was used and, if we can find it, we'll have a wealth of genetic material and possibly even a finger mark or two from its removal.'

'But we don't know where she had sex?' said one of the woman PCs.

'No, not specifically. We know she was drinking with some of the other seasonal workers, in particular Alex Robinson. He claims he didn't have sex with her and we've already searched the tent he slept in. However, we need to do a fingertip search of the field above the barn where he was camping, and extend it out from there.' He pointed at one end of the gaggle of uniforms. 'You four take that area.' Then he looked at the others. 'The rest of you, start at the pergola where the body was found and work your way out from there. And, of course, bear in mind that the condom might have been dumped at some place other than where the act happened. For all we know, it could have been taken off the property. Or maybe Karolyn had sex at home before coming up here.'

'In other words, a wild goose chase,' someone muttered.

Tom didn't see who it was, and he didn't much care. He had a certain amount of sympathy for that view – but if the evidence was there to be had, they needed to find it.

The PCs divided into their teams and set off to search. Realising that he hadn't tasked anyone to check the bin area at the back of the visitor centre, he donned a white crime scene suit and latex gloves and went round there himself. There was a row of vast, multi-coloured commercial wheelie bins, into which all the rubbish and recycling of the vineyard was sorted. The bins, not surprisingly, stank, and for a moment Tom considered retreating and giving the job to someone more junior. But that would waste precious time. With two women dead and the prospect of pressure from the press, not to mention their superiors, the boss was looking for fast results.

He spread a polythene sheet on the ground in front of the bins and tipped out the first bin full of landfill waste, the most appropriate bin for the disposal of a used condom. Trying not to retch at the stench, he started to carefully sift through the repulsive haul. Food packaging, dead flowers, half-eaten food, dirty tissues, non-food packaging, wodges of soggy blue kitchen roll, a dirty nappy...

Half an hour and three bins later, he had trophies – two used condoms, from different bins, and now in separate evidence bags. He divested himself of the white paper suit and latex gloves, and went to check on how the uniformed searchers were getting on. They had less to show for their efforts. The team checking the area around the pergola had found nothing, which wasn't surprising given that the CSIs had already been all over that ground. The other team had found one used condom in the wheelie bin that served the campers. But still no sign of Karolyn or Ronnie's clothing.

He told them to keep at it a bit longer while he went to deliver the three condoms found so far to Emily Jordan for forensic processing and DNA testing. It gave them enough reason to request DNA samples from all the male employees and seasonal workers, which along with their fingerprints would hopefully lead to the identification of a suspect, if indeed one of them was the killer.

'Excellent work,' said Lexi, when he rang her on his way back to the station. 'Could be just the break we need, especially if they can get a finger mark or two from any of the condoms.'

'Where are you?'

'On my way to the Crown in Eythorne. Apparently Karolyn Small occasionally worked behind the bar there – I want to see if the landlord can shed any light on her social life.'

'Wasn't that where Liam Norris was drinking on the night Bethany died?'

'It was. Want to meet me there?'

'Sure. What are Colin and Ridhi doing?'

'Karolyn's parents told them she was enrolled at MidKent College to take a diploma in beauty therapy. They've gone to talk to the lecturer and see if they can find any friends she might have made on the course.'

'Okay, I'll see you outside the pub.'

The landlord looked at them and sighed. 'You again,' he said, as he recognised Tom. 'I don't have any more to say.'

Lexi nodded, showing her ID. 'You clearly know my colleague.'

'If you say so.'

'I asked you about Liam Norris – whether he was here last Saturday night,' said Tom.

'I told you.'

'We're not here about that this time,' said Tom, leaning forward on the bar.

The landlord took a step back.

'Mr Williams—' Lexi had got his name from Ridhi's interview notes '—I understand that Karolyn Small worked here.'

He looked at them warily. 'Yes, that's right. Couple of times a week.'

'I'm sorry to have to inform you that Karolyn is dead. We believe she was murdered.'

Craig Williams passed a hand across his forehead and stared at them disbelievingly. 'Murdered? I heard on the radio that a woman's body had been found. Was that her?'

'Yes.'

He was rendered speechless. His mouth opened, then closed. He turned away from them, his shoulders slumping. Then he took a glass from a shelf and poured a measure of whisky from an optic. He'd drunk it by the time he turned back round.

'Tell us about her,' said Lexi, to help him steady himself.

'She was a nice girl. Worked hard when she was here. Why would anyone do that to a young woman with a baby? That poor nipper – she hasn't got a dad, anyway, and now this.' He seemed to have surprised himself by saying this much and clamped his mouth shut.

'When did you last see her?' said Lexi.

'She was in at the weekend,' he said. 'Did the Saturday and Sunday evening shifts. She was tired – she'd been working up at the vineyard earlier in the day.'

'A hard worker,' said Tom.

'She wanted a better life for her and Ronnie. The kid's dad left her before Ronnie was even born, so it was tough.'

'Do you know who Ronnie's father was?' asked Tom.

'No clue. She didn't talk about him much.'

'And after she finished work on Sunday, you didn't see her again anywhere?' Lexi wanted to keep the questioning focused.

Williams frowned. 'I only ever saw her here. We didn't have a relationship outside of work.'

'You never shared a drink once the pub was shut, or gave her a lift home?' said Tom.

'I don't care for what you're implying, mate.' Williams leaned forward over the bar, emphasising his superior height and build. 'I'm a happily married man. Karolyn Small was just one of my bartenders.'

Lexi soothed his ruffled feathers. 'Of course. We didn't mean anything. We're just trying to piece together her last hours.'

'When exactly did she die?'

'Tuesday night, or early Wednesday morning.'

'At the vineyard?'

'Yes.'

'You know she was working up there?'

'We do, thanks. What about you, where were you two nights ago?'

'Here, till closing time – eleven o'clock. Then home with the wife.'

'Where do you live, Mr Williams?'

He pointed towards the window. 'That cottage opposite.'

Lexi didn't bother to go and look.

'Karolyn worked here on Saturday night. Was she friendly with Liam Norris at all?'

The landlord shrugged. 'Seemed to me they knew each other. But friendly? Not quite. I got the feeling that she avoided serving him when he came up to the bar. Let one of the others do it.'

This came as no surprise. Karolyn had been Bethany's best friend. She was the one who knew Bethany was seeing someone else, and she knew Bethany was scared of Liam. If Liam had killed Bethany, maybe Karolyn suspected him, or even had proof to back it up. Maybe she needed to be shut up, too.

'Thanks for your time, Mr Williams. You've been most helpful.'

Williams shrugged and turned back to his bar, downing another shot of whisky as Lexi and Tom made their way out.

FORTY

Yesterday's achievements

1. Next target identified
2. Some information gathered. I'll keep chipping away until I know what I need to

Learning outcomes

1. Not all babies are cute
2. Double check the elastic on the wings before setting out next time
3. Feel sure the police were considering Johnny L-B as a suspect until his unfortunate crash – interesting

Plans for today

1. Work appointments
2. Follow next victim
3. Floss teeth – get on top of this gum issue. Maybe buy mouthwash

4. Pay council tax
5. Dispose of K and R's clothing

How are you feeling – in three words?

1. Tired
2. Tired
3. Tired – it was a long night

Memory of the day

Mum disappeared. I didn't know then that she was dead. I thought she'd stopped loving me and gone away. I thought she was angry with me. I did things that annoyed her, so I couldn't blame her for wanting to go off somewhere and just leave me behind. But I thought she'd come back.

Needless to say, she didn't. The minutes stretched into hours. The hours into days. The days into weeks. The weeks into months. The months into years. And all the time, I'd have half an eye on the door. Listening for her footfall on the stair. Staring at strangers' faces on the bus or on the pavement, even when I'd practically forgotten what she looked like.

The people who looked after me in the wake of Mum's death were many and varied. It always started the same way – they'd be smiley and solicitous of my well-being. 'Here's your new room. You'll be happy here.' I was fed and clothed, bathed and put to bed at a reasonable hour. They succeeded at things that Mum had failed at. But they weren't my mother, and they couldn't step into her shoes. Slowly their empathy would fade to nothing, their eyes becoming cold. I would be passed on to the next. Sometimes a care facility, sometimes a foster home.

I remember one woman who told me over and over and

over not to be sad. She said my mummy was an angel now, looking down from heaven. Another smacked my wrist for taking a biscuit from a plate without asking. Sometimes there were other kids and mostly they bullied me, until I learned to bully back, and then I'd find myself on the move again.

And always I was waiting for Mum to come back. The woman who said she was an angel told me she was always with me, always watching out for me. I believed that for so long. Always by my side, better than when she was alive. She spoke to me sometimes, like she was really there. I believed she would come back. I only learned the details of her death a couple of years ago. That she'd been stabbed to death by a drug dealer she owed money to. Now, I'll never forgive her.

Motivation for the day
Keep your face always towards the sunshine – and shadows will fall behind you

FORTY-ONE

Lexi got back to the station feeling wrung out. They just didn't seem to be making any progress. Any thoughts that Bethany's death might, by a long stretch of the imagination, have been accidental had been flung out of the window once they found Karolyn's body posed in the same way and her winged baby nearby.

'Why? Why? Why?'

'Why what?' said Tom, following her up the stairs.

'Why the wings? Why the babies? Why the vineyard?'

'That's a new one.'

'What?'

'Why the vineyard? We haven't even considered that.'

Lexi thought about it as she took off her black blazer and hung it on the back of her chair. 'Bethany was having – or had had – an affair with the owner. Karolyn was working on the harvest.'

Tom stood leaning on the doorframe. 'Karolyn makes sense – she was actually on the property anyway. But Bethany wasn't.'

'As far as we know. Though Karolyn left the vineyard with someone, presumably the killer, to fetch Ronnie.'

'Both girls had links at Elvington.'

'Possibly the killer did, too. Emily's taken DNA samples from all the men who are working on the harvest. If we can get a match to one, or better yet both, of the murder scenes, we'll have our man.'

'But what if we can't?'

Lexi shrugged. 'We keep on digging.'

Tom turned away from her without speaking. There was someone in the corridor behind him, saying something.

'Yes, this DI Bennett's office,' said Tom.

He stepped to one side and a uniformed officer appeared in the doorway. Lexi recognised him immediately – it was Sergeant Kevin Malthouse of the Roads Policing Unit.

'Sergeant Malthouse, what can we do for you?' She included Tom, and waved them both into the room.

'I wanted to come and talk to you about the crash at Shepherd's Hill.'

'Go ahead,' said Tom.

'Our mechanics have been all over the wreck and you should know that we can't rule out foul play.'

It was exactly what Lexi had expected to hear. How could it not be connected, given that two women, one of whom was his mistress, had been murdered on his property? It had crossed her mind at one point that if Johnny had killed the women, he might have traces of magic mushrooms in his system, or even fentanyl – which might have been a reasonable explanation for the crash. But this sounded like something more.

'What do you mean you can't rule it out?'

'It means we have reasonable grounds to suspect that the car he was driving had been tampered with. And as it was his car, and by all accounts no one else ever drove it, we also assume that he was the target of whoever messed with it.'

'So it's the view of the RPU that Johnny Lycett-Boyd's death was murder?'

'We thought you should know, given your current cases are linked to Elvington Vineyard. I assume you'll get your Chief Super to request that you take over this one.'

'I think it would make sense,' said Lexi.

Malthouse nodded. Running a murder investigation was well beyond the remit of the RPU. 'I'll get the files over to you as soon as we get the nod, and you can have a meeting with the mechanics about the suspected sabotage.'

'What was it?' said Tom.

'Looks like someone messed with the rear spring rates.'

It didn't mean much to Lexi, but no doubt the mechanics would spell it out to them. Suffice to say, if they could show someone had tampered with Johnny's car before he went out on the track, they could prove at the very least a manslaughter charge, and maybe murder.

'Thanks for coming by,' she said to Malthouse. Once he'd left the office, she turned to Tom. 'Come on, let's get on it. We've got a couple of hours till knocking off time.' *If you don't mind working late.*

Tom glanced at his watch.

'You want to get home?'

He shook his head. 'No, it's fine. Billie's got football practice after school. We're good.'

They went in separate cars, so Tom would be able to pick up Billie when they finished, and half an hour later they were both pulling off the road through the gates of the Shepherd's Hill Race Circuit. Their first port of call was the circuit office to see which mechanics had been rostered on the day of the crash, and which in particular had worked on Johnny Lycett-Boyd's Porsche.

The track manager was a man called Stephen Flannery, who they hadn't met on their previous visit. He was a tall man of about fifty with an Irish accent, and Lexi couldn't begin to imagine how he folded himself up to fit into the cockpit of a racing car.

'Sergeant Malthouse said you'd be paying us a visit,' he said, once they'd introduced themselves. 'Though I think he's wrong, you know.'

'Why do you think that?' said Lexi.

Flannery shrugged. 'Those police mechanics – they're used to dealing with road vehicles. You set a car up for the racetrack very differently.'

'But Johnny Lycett-Boyd drove his Porsche on the road as well as the track, didn't he?' said Tom.

'Sure he did, but he had it race tuned. Malthouse's men are suggesting the rear spring rates were set too high and that made it more likely the car would come off on a sharp bend at high speed.'

'You don't agree with them?'

Flannery raised a conciliatory hand. 'Look, they're not wrong in that having the spring rates set too high can present problems. But it's a matter of judgement. How high you have them depends on the driver, the car, the track – and Johnny knew just how the car handled and how he liked to set the springs.'

'So doesn't it seem rather strange that he had such a severe crash on a track he knew inside out, in his own car?'

Flannery shrugged. 'It just takes a split-second misjudgement, a tiny error, and you can end up in a spin.'

'But if someone wanted to sabotage the car on purpose, adjusting the springs could be a way of doing it?' said Tom.

'An experienced driver would know straight off that his suspension was different.'

'Didn't Johnny crash on his first lap of the day?' said Lexi. 'So even if he realised something was off, he'd need to get round to come back to the pits. Did you examine the car after the crash?'

'No, your guys immediately took it away for assessment.'

'So you can't say for certain that the spring rates were set as Johnny would have wanted them?'

'That's true. But nothing the police mechanics have said makes me think the car was sabotaged. Aren't you considering human error? Johnny was a good driver, but he was by no means perfect. What if he'd had a drink the night before?'

'That'll be looked into as well.' In fact, she'd asked his blood to be tested for fentanyl and magic mushrooms already. But she got the feeling that Flannery was pushing back against the suggestion that anyone at his track might be to blame.

'Our mechanics do a great job here. They know their business and none of them would do anything to mess with someone's car. I can vouch for every one of them.'

Lexi could understand the guy being defensive, but he had to accept something had gone wrong, and that it was their job to find out exactly what. 'Who was working on the cars the morning when Johnny crashed?'

'Cameron Johns and Terry Mercer were in the workshop. Both highly experienced, had worked with Johnny for years. But Johnny checked the tuning himself – he did a lot of his own tuning.'

'Are they here now?' said Lexi. The mechanic who'd been smoking by the side of the track after the crash had been called Terry. Presumably the same man.

Flannery checked his watch. 'Maybe. We've got a corporate racing taster day scheduled tomorrow, so they might still be setting up the cars for it.'

He led them out of the circuit office and across to the huge open-fronted workshop. It was still a hive of activity, even at six p.m., and Flannery walked down the length of it peering into each of the bays. Then he pointed. 'That's Johns,' he said, pointing at a young mechanic in grease-stained, dark blue overalls, sporting an overgrown Afro, 'and that's Mercer, two bays down.' Mercer was in orange overalls, just as filthy, but all they could see of him was two legs sticking out from underneath a sleek-looking Mercedes coupe.

'Thank you,' said Lexi. She went over to Johns and pointed Tom to Mercer, as Flannery wandered back to his office.

'Cameron Johns?'

The man looked up from whatever he was doing under the bonnet of a souped-up Audi R8. 'Yeah.'

Lexi flashed her ID and gave her name. Johns straightened up and started wiping his hands on a greasy rag that he picked up off the car's front wing.

'I understand you were working here this morning?'

'Yes.' He looked her steadily in the eye, but he wasn't going to expand on his answer.

'Whose car did you work on?'

'You want to know if I worked on Johnny's car before he crashed. The answer is no. Johnny was here and he liked to deal with his own car.'

'Did you see him make any changes to the rear spring rates?'

'Not particularly. I was working on another car at the other end of the shop.'

'Did anyone else work on Johnny's car?'

'I couldn't say – had my head under a bonnet most of the morning.'

'Who else was around?'

'Terry was working, but not on Johnny's car while I was here.'

'Did you see any strangers wandering round? Anybody back here who shouldn't have been?'

Cameron Johns shook his head. 'Not that I can remember but, you know, people wander around...'

'And these workshops are always open like this?'

'Yeah.'

And that was it. She tried a few more questions but got nothing useful out of him. Tom got even less out of Terry Mercer.

'He was completely vague as to who'd been around and at what time,' said Tom.

They went back to the office and asked Flannery for a list of all the people who'd been anywhere on the track that morning, as well as at any time on Wednesday. He said it would take him a while to compile and that he'd email it to them.

'Can you also provide us with any CCTV footage from around the track?' said Lexi.

Flannery nodded as if the whole business was becoming tiresome. 'We've also got cameras on the gate and around some of the perimeter,' he said. 'A lot of expensive cars here so we take security seriously. I'll download the footage and send it over to you.'

'Thank you,' said Lexi. 'You've been a great help.' She gave him her card, so he'd have her email address.

'I gotta go and fetch Billie,' said Tom as they emerged back into the early evening sun.

Lexi had no call on her time, so she headed back to the office. Driving into Canterbury, she slapped the heel of her hand against the steering wheel.

Damn!

Were Cameron Johns and Terry Mercer lying when they said they hadn't worked on the car?

Could Malthouse be wrong about the spring rates causing the crash?

Maybe Johnny Lycett-Boyd was still under the influence of drugs or alcohol from the night before. Did that mean when he adjusted the settings himself, he got it wrong and caused the crash? But she didn't believe for one minute his death was accidental.

He was a suspect in a murder case, and Maggie wanted her to prove he was the killer, that the guilt had got to him, and that the case was now closed.

Who benefitted from that?

The real killer. Of course.

This case was far from closed.

FORTY-TWO

FRIDAY

The early morning rush hour traffic slowed Lexi's progress into Canterbury, but it gave her time to think about her next priorities. Set up the different hypotheses for each of the deaths, then knock them down like bowling pins till only one was left standing. It conjured a nice image, but at the moment all her balls were sliding into the channels on either side of the lane.

She needed to get her shots on target now, and she had some ideas on how to do it.

Her phone rang.

'Emily, please tell me you have some news.'

'I do.' Lexi could tell from the way the crime scene manager said the words that she was smiling. 'Those condoms that Tom sent over yesterday – one of them matched the spermicide that we detected inside Karolyn's body, so I pulled strings and got an immediate rapid DNA analysis.'

'Thank you,' Lexi cut in.

'The results have just come back to me, and you're not going to believe what – or rather, who – we found.'

'Who?' Lexi found herself wishing Emily would get to the point.

'There were cells on the outside of the condom that matched Karolyn's DNA, so this was the condom that left the traces of spermicide inside her.'

'And you got a match for the sperm inside the condom?'

'We did. It matched one of the vineyard employees, but not who you might think.'

It came to Lexi in a flash. 'It was Steadman, wasn't it?'

'Wow – way to steal a girl's thunder. How did you know?'

'Just a hunch.'

It hadn't been just a hunch, but she didn't have time to explain it to Emily. She had to act fast.

'Tom,' she said, arriving in the incident room almost out of breath from running up the stairs. 'Send a couple of uniforms to bring in Will Steadman, right now.'

'On what grounds?'

'On the grounds that his semen was found inside a condom that had Karolyn's cells on the outside of it.' She perched on the corner of Ridhi's desk, as Tom put in the call.

As soon as Emily had said it was one of the vineyard's employees, things had slotted into place. There had been something off about Steadman's response to Karolyn's death. He'd seemed more shaken by it than Bethany's, even though he'd been the one to find Bethany's body. And he'd claimed not to have known Karolyn's name, when in fact it now turned out he'd actually had sex with her a few hours before she died.

Yes, he certainly had some questions to answer.

She went into her office and powered up her laptop. Tom followed her through and sat down opposite her.

'I'm just checking if Emily's emailed those results through,' she said. 'It would be good to know where exactly that condom was found.' The details would be on the evidence log.

'Two were in the bins behind the visitor centre and one was in the bin up in the field where the pickers are camping.'

'Got it.' She scanned the screen for the details she wanted.

'It was one of the ones from the visitor centre bins. A ribbed Durex, flesh coloured.'

'The one I found first,' said Tom, 'nearer the top of the rubbish.' He looked slightly bilious at the memory. 'This moves him up to the top of the suspects list, doesn't it?'

'It has to,' said Lexi. 'I'm assuming Karolyn left the barbecue because she had an assignation with Steadman. And the result was she ended up dead.'

'And Bethany?'

'His alibi for that night is unprovable. He was home alone.' She tapped a biro on the edge of her desk, thinking it through. 'Tom, while we wait for him to arrive, apply for a warrant to search his cottage and his car. There might be fibres from the missing clothing in his car or his house.'

'I'll get right on it.' He got up and went to the door, turning back to talk to her. 'But if he was sleeping with her, she might have been in his car or to his house before anyway.'

'Of course. But we'll have to build the case against him one little bit at a time.'

Will Steadman could hardly contain his fury at having been snatched away from his work.

'Couldn't this have waited a couple of days?' he said, as Lexi and Tom came into the interview room. 'The grapes might be in, but the work isn't over – once the wine is in the tanks you can have as much of my time as you need.'

He was obviously assuming he was just here for another witness interview. Lexi had told the PCs to imply this as she hadn't wanted him to guess he was under suspicion. It was important to assess his body language when that particular penny dropped. She would have liked to have had Ed sitting by her side for this interview, but now wasn't the time.

'There are some things we need to clear up right away, Mr Steadman,' she said. 'I'm afraid a double murder investigation trumps your winemaking.'

She didn't mention that the RPU had suggested a third murder. That wasn't in the public domain and she still hadn't worked out in her own mind how Johnny Lycett-Boyd's death fitted within the whole scenario. Particularly if it was now looking likely that Will Steadman had killed the two women.

Steadman said nothing, but she noted the jut of his lower jaw. He didn't agree.

'You told us yesterday that you didn't know Karolyn Small.' A muscle twitched in Steadman's cheek. 'So would it interest you to know that we have recovered a used condom that has DNA traces that match both you and Karolyn?' Steadman's eyes widened momentarily. 'Would you care to explain that?' His whole body went tense.

Lexi waited for him to answer. Perhaps he was dumb-founded. Perhaps he was sifting through his options. But his mouth remained tightly closed. Of course, it didn't need explanation. What happened was perfectly clear.

'To put it another way,' said Tom, 'you knew perfectly well who she was when Mathéo Martin came to you and showed you her body. And then you lied to us about knowing her.'

Still Steadman didn't speak. His hands were shaking and sweat glistened on his upper lip and forehead.

'Okay, I'll tell you what I think happened,' said Lexi. 'After you locked up the winery Tuesday night, you either called Karolyn to meet you or met up with her by pre-arrangement – I'm sure we'll be able to determine which if we check the relevant phone records.' Steadman's body language confirmed this. 'What's troubling me is why you then took her to pick up Ronnie.'

Steadman stayed silent, not denying what she'd said so far.

'Why did you need both Bethany and Ronnie to have their daughters with them when they died?'

The man in front of her finally seemed to come out his trance. 'This is madness. I admit that I had sex with Karolyn...'

'We can prove it anyway,' said Tom.

'But you're suggesting I had something to do with her death.' He shook his head vigorously. 'No way. She and I had sex, very quickly, in my office at around eleven and that was it. She walked out of there alive and well. I stayed working a little longer, so people wouldn't see us leaving together. That's all there is to it.'

'What time did she leave the visitor centre?'

Steadman rubbed his face with his hands. 'I don't know. She didn't stay long. It was maybe eleven thirty by the time we finished.'

'Why did she come and have sex with you? Had it happened before?'

Steadman frowned and his voice betrayed anger as he answered. 'We were seeing each other. No one at work knew and we just wanted to keep it quiet for a bit longer.'

'So you sneaked about having sex in the office? Wow, I bet she found that irresistible.'

Steadman scowled.

Lexi skewered him with an intense stare. 'I'm afraid I don't believe you, Mr Steadman. I think you met her out by the pergola and drugged her in the same way you drugged Bethany Glover. Was she high when you had sex with her?'

'You're wrong.'

'You were responsible for the deaths of both young women, and you posed their bodies with the wings, and used their infant daughters as props, to suggest there was a serial killer at work. But I'm afraid I think this has more to do with scaring off any potential buyers of the vineyard. Johnny's plan to sell put your job at risk.'

'You've gone completely mad.' A spattering of saliva landed on the table between them, such was the force of Steadman's words. 'I didn't kill either of them. D'you really think I would murder two young women to save my job? How would that even work?'

Perhaps that wasn't his motive. No doubt she could uncover the true motive with the right question. Whatever it was, Lexi had physical evidence that he had sex with Karolyn shortly before she died. If they could uncover physical evidence linking him to Bethany, it would be enough to build a case on.

'Then maybe it had more to do with your belief in biodynamic farming,' said Tom. 'Planting and harvesting according to the cycle of the moon? What next? Sacrifices to mother nature to ensure a good vintage?'

Steadman switched his gaze to Tom. 'Bloody lunatic,' he muttered, tugging at the collar of his shirt. 'I don't have to put up with this.' He stood up, pushing his chair back from the table.

'Sit down.' They hadn't charged him or read him his rights, so he was free to go, but Lexi still had questions.

Steadman ignored her order, but he placed his hands on the table and leaned forward, giving Lexi a hard stare.

'I lied to you before,' he said, waiting a moment to let his words sink in.

Lexi met his glare, her face impassive, unimpressed.

'I do have an alibi for the night Bethany died. A rock solid one, actually.'

'You said you were alone in your cottage,' said Tom.

'I wasn't alone.'

'Who was with you?' said Lexi.

'Marietta. We weren't going to say anything, but if you're looking to pin these murders on me, she'll speak up. She was with me all night.'

FORTY-THREE

'Do you believe him?' said Tom, as they went back up the stairs to the incident room.

Lexi was fuming. 'What is it about these men? Steadman, Lycett-Boyd... were they in competition to see who could get the most notches on their bedpost?' She shook her head. 'Yes, I believe him and it turns my stomach.'

Tom looked slightly taken aback at her reaction.

'Sleeping with his boss's wife. Having sex in his office with one of his workers, probably just an hour or so before she was murdered.'

'Complete failure at zip control,' said Tom. 'Elvington's very own man-whore.'

'Lycett-Boyd wasn't any better. Both of them taking advantage of young women like that.' She grimaced. 'But there would be no point in saying that unless he's certain Marietta will come through for him.'

'If she does, she could be lying. After all, wasn't she supposed to have been home in bed with Johnny the night Bethany died?'

'She can't provide an alibi for both men. But now Johnny's

dead, maybe she thinks he doesn't need one. I'm guessing she doesn't know about Will sleeping with Karolyn. In fact, that's probably why he and Karolyn were keeping their relationship secret. I think it's time we had a word with Mrs Lycett-Boyd.'

'Over at Elvington?'

'No, we'll bring her in here for questioning. Make it seem more formal – perhaps that'll focus her mind on who she was actually sleeping with that night.'

'But why should we trust anything she says?' Tom threw his hands up. 'It turns out that the supposedly grieving widow was shacked up with the vintner. So where was Johnny that night? Did he know about her and Will? Or was he down in the caves with Bethany and Scarlett?'

'One thing it does explain is the palpable level of tension between all three of them. And possibly Johnny's early demise suits Steadman very well. After all, what better way to secure his job than to marry the woman who probably now owns sixty per cent of the vineyard?'

'Maybe they were in it together...'

There was only one way to find out, and half an hour later, Lexi and Tom were in the same interview room again, this time with Marietta Lycett-Boyd opposite them. Unlike Steadman, she seemed calm and composed, making Lexi suspect that she'd received a call from him, warning her of what he'd told them.

'I understand you need to ask me a few questions,' she said, as soon as they sat down. 'Please can we make this quick – I have a funeral to arrange and family members arriving.'

'I'm sorry,' said Lexi. 'It's a difficult time for you. However, new information has come to light that casts doubt on something you told us earlier.'

'I will do my best to help you.'

'When I spoke to you on Monday, you explicitly told me that you had been at home, with your husband, on the night that Bethany Glover was murdered. However, this morning Will

Steadman claimed that you were with him at his cottage that night. One of you must be lying.'

Marietta took a deep breath. 'I was the one who was lying. What Will said is true – I was with him the night that Bethany died.'

'So why did you say you were with your husband?'

'Is it not obvious? Our marriage was crumbling. We each sought solace elsewhere. That's not something we wanted to share with the world, so we agreed to say that we were at home together.'

'So where was Johnny that night?'

'I don't know. I didn't ask him where he was going when he left work. Maybe he went home, maybe not.'

'You didn't ask him where he was that night, despite knowing that a woman was murdered in the caves underneath your winery? Didn't it occur to you that he might have been with Bethany? That he might have been responsible for her death?'

'Will believes that you hold him responsible. Now you think it's Johnny?'

'You weren't concerned at all that it might be your husband?' said Tom.

Marietta shook her head and pushed out her lower lip like a sulky teenager. Much as Lexi hated to pass judgement on people, she couldn't help herself from being sickened at the revelations they were stumbling across. Yes, some people had open marriages, but here it seemed bed-hopping was the norm. That must have affected the relationship between Will Steadman and Johnny Lycett-Boyd, who was also his employer.

'Did your husband know you were seeing Will Steadman?'

A one-shouldered shrug. 'I never told him explicitly, but Will and I didn't exactly hide it either. To be honest, Johnny didn't care if it gave him the freedom to go whoring.'

'Did you know about Bethany?'

'I didn't want to know the names of his girls.'

'And you had no idea that he'd fathered a child with another woman.'

Marietta's brow creased and her cheeks flushed with anger. '*Putain!*'

'Please answer the question.'

'No, I had no idea there was a child. He was a shit.'

'You were angry when you found out about Scarlett?'

'Of course I was. You would be too, if you found out your husband had a child by another woman.'

'Did you tell Will Steadman how angry you were?'

She rolled her eyes. 'Now you think Will might have had something to do with Johnny's death. Oh my God, you are letting your imagination run wild, Inspector.'

'Imagination doesn't come into it,' said Lexi. Time to change tack. 'Were you aware that Will Steadman was sleeping with Karolyn Small?'

'*Merde!*' Shock registered on her face before she managed to hide it.

'Was he also sleeping with Bethany Glover?'

'I'm not his wife. Or his mother. I don't keep tabs on him.'

'But you were with him the night Bethany Glover died?'

'I told you I was.'

Lexi didn't particularly believe or disbelieve her. She was beginning to feel that she couldn't trust anything that Marietta said, any more than she could trust what Will Steadman said. Could they have jointly committed the murders? Some perverted sex game that required a third party? A ménage à trois? And then literally have thrown Johnny under the bus?

'Were you with Will on Tuesday night?'

Marietta paused a fraction too long to make her answer reliable. 'Yes... No... Some of the time, not all night.'

'You know he had sex with Karolyn that evening?'

'I don't believe you.'

It was Lexi's turn to shrug. 'That's up to you.'

'He had sex with her in his office after finishing work,' said Tom. 'Did he come to you after that?'

Marietta looked furious. Her small, elegant hands clenched into fists on the table in front of her.

'Please answer the question,' said Lexi.

'No. I got it wrong. I didn't see him that night at all.'

They were wasting their time. Marietta was a snake, changing her answers whenever it suited her. And an unreliable witness in court would be worse than no witness at all.

———

Maggie was in Lexi's office when she got back upstairs. She looked up from the screen of her mobile as Lexi came into the room.

'Ah, here you are.'

Lexi smiled. She was always pleased to see Maggie, even though she could guess what was coming. *Why haven't you closed the case yet?*

'I've scheduled a press conference in twenty minutes,' she said. 'Can you be ready in time?'

'Of course.'

'Can you report on any progress?'

'I'm not sure I want to go public on where we are at the moment.'

'Which is where?'

'Everyone at the vineyard appears to have been sleeping with everyone else. Alibis are changing from minute to minute. Will Steadman was sleeping with one victim. Johnny Lycett-Boyd had an affair with the other. Steadman was sleeping with Lycett-Boyd's wife, who seems to be a compulsive liar. And Johnny Lycett-Boyd's accident wasn't an accident. And it wasn't suicide.'

'How do you know that?'

'He doesn't fit the profile, psychologically, and he's too intelligent to take a risk like that – there's no certainty of death in a car accident. And the RPU say they can't rule out foul play. I think someone tampered with the car.'

'Hmm.' Maggie considered what Lexi had said. 'But no arrest anytime soon?'

Lexi wasn't sure for a second if she was being ironic or serious. She settled for pulling a face that made the answer clear.

'Who's in the frame?'

'Johnny was – it's entirely possible he killed the two girls. But would that make his murder a revenge killing on their behalf? Norris wanting revenge for Bethany's death? At this point anything seems possible. Will Steadman had sex with Karolyn in the hours before she died, but now Marietta Lycett-Boyd has stepped forward with an alibi for him on the night Bethany died. I'm not sure I believe her, but what would be her motive for lying? To keep her lover from being charged with murder?'

'It's a possibility. What about the French guy who found Karolyn's body?'

'I don't have a reason to think that was anything other than innocent. But we've taken DNA samples from all the male vineyard workers, both permanent and seasonal, so I'm hopeful we'll get more clarity if we can find a DNA match from both scenes.'

'And Johnny Lycett-Boyd? How was it done?'

'Like I said, the RPU think his car could have been tampered with. The mechanics at the track don't agree – they say it was race-tuned the way he liked it. Though Johnny was the only person who worked on it that morning.'

'Which points to the suicide theory.'

'I still don't buy it. Someone else could have messed with his car – and it stands to reason that they'd be careful not to be seen doing it. Johnny wasn't a trained mechanic. Perhaps he overlooked something. The RPU have got the vehicle, and I've asked them to check it for prints. We should find Johnny's and the mechanics who worked on it, and possibly Marietta's – but I'll be interested to see if there are any other prints, particularly on the parts that Malthouse has suggested were sabotaged.'

'The big question – same or different killer?'

'Different cause of death, and presumably a different motive, so on the face of it, it could be a different killer. But the coincidence of three murders linked to the vineyard in a matter of days... I think it's likely to be the same killer. He would never have killed Johnny in the same way as Bethany and Karolyn – their deaths appear to have had some form of sexual motivation.'

Maggie nodded. 'You need to wrap this up, Lexi. Two girls dead, two babies orphaned – the press are baying for blood.'

'And you're just about to throw me to the wolves.'

Maggie grinned. 'It's nothing you can't handle.' She stood up. 'I'll see you downstairs for the presser in ten minutes. Karolyn's murder has taken this from the local papers up to the nationals, and they're scaremongering shamelessly. Make them think you've got things under control.'

'Okay, I'll make the point that it's very localised to Elvington and that the net is closing in. That might even push our perp out of the woodwork, force him to make a mistake. Do you want me to make the drugs element public – warn young women away from men bearing mushrooms?'

'Yes, and steer the journos away from any questions about the seasonal workers. I don't want this turning into a field day for xenophobes.'

'Got it.'

'And, Lexi, just hurry up and solve the bloody case, will you?' There was a slight sting in her words. 'I'm fully confident that you can do it.'

'Yeah, I'm confident I can do it, too.' And she meant it.

FORTY-FOUR

The presser took place in the large conference room on the ground floor of the police station. It was more crowded than Lexi could ever remember. Maggie had been right – the nationals had jumped on the story like flies on manure, and regardless of what Lexi told them, they were determined to twist the facts to their own ends.

'Should single mothers barricade themselves in their houses?'

'Should we send all seasonal workers packing back to the continent?'

'Can you guarantee the safety of local people working on other vineyards?'

'When will you know who did this?'

'When are you going to make an arrest?'

'When can we feel safe in our homes again?'

Lexi desperately wanted to tell them all where they could get off, but she maintained a cool exterior, answered their questions patiently and politely, while all the time she was boiling with anger inside at their irresponsibility.

'To anyone working at Elvington, or feeling nervous, just stick together and don't wander around on your own at night.'

'If you'd done your job properly, you wouldn't need to be issuing warnings like this,' called out a young woman journalist in the front row.

'We're working flat out and sending extra uniformed patrols to Elvington and the surrounding area.' Now she'd have to get someone to arrange these. Rash promise number 563 made at a press conference.

Bloody morons, she thought as she was finally able to step down from the dais and head back in the direction of her office.

'Well done, boss,' said Tom, falling into step behind her. 'I don't think I could have kept my temper with that lot.'

'Nothing they would have liked better,' said Lexi. 'They're having a field day with this as it is, and a DI losing their cool would have been the icing on the cake. By the way, can you organise the extra patrols I so stupidly promised?'

'Of course. Overtime in the budget?'

'What do you think?'

'Probably not?'

'I'll talk to Maggie.'

Her phone rang. A number she didn't recognise.

'DI Bennett,' she said. 'Who is this?'

'Marietta Lycett-Boyd.' She sounded stressed. 'The press are here. They're blocking the gates to the vineyard. Some of them have come nosing round the house, pressing their faces against my windows. Please, can you make them go away?'

'The ones up at the house are trespassing,' said Lexi. 'I'll send a couple of PCs to stand at the gate. We can't make them leave the lane outside the gate, but they'll soon get bored if there's nothing to see.'

'Thank you. I'm here on my own with Aurora, and it feels like we're trapped.'

Despite the complications of Marietta's varying accounts of

where she was on the night of Bethany's murder, Lexi felt some sympathy for her. She'd just lost her husband and the father of her child, and at the busiest time of year, the vineyard had suddenly become the focus of a triple murder investigation.

'Do you have any family or friends you could go to stay with for a few days? Maybe Johnny's parents?'

'And who will run this place?'

'Mr Steadman?'

'No. I must remain here and oversee the end of the harvest.'

Lexi's phone signalled another call incoming.

'I'll sort out those PCs, Marietta, but I'm afraid I have to go.' She switched to the other call – the screen told her it was Linda Ellis. 'Linda, hi. What can I do for you?'

'I've got the DNA results back. Scarlett Glover was indeed Johnny Lycett-Boyd's daughter.'

Lexi put a hand to her mouth. 'Oh no – that means she's an orphan. What will happen now?'

'She'll stay where she is at the moment, with the foster carers, while we work out her next of kin on either side. Bethany had no siblings, but her mother's still alive.'

'In a hospice.'

'It's complicated, because she has no relationship with her father's family, while Liam Norris, who she does have a relationship with, will now have no claim to keep her.'

'Even though he's been her de facto father since she was born?'

'If he wants her, there'll be a court battle – assuming that the Lycett-Boyds also want her. Or maybe no one will want her.'

It was a heartbreaking thought. Another call buzzed in. Luke Evans. He would have to wait.

'Aurora is her half-sister, but I can't see Marietta taking her on,' she said.

'It might take a while to sort out, but we'll try to ensure she ends up in the best place. Even if that turns out to be adoption.'

Lexi hung up. The fallout from Bethany's death would spread further. If Scarlett was Johnny's daughter, could she claim a share in the vineyard? How would Marietta handle that? Would the prospective sale of the vineyard, something she understood to be mostly driven by Johnny, still be on the cards?

Those questions weren't her concern. Her problems were more immediate.

———

She sat at her desk wrestling with motive, wishing she had Ed Harlow sitting opposite her to bounce ideas off. She needed to work out who benefitted from Bethany and Karolyn's deaths, for there was no doubt in her mind that they had been given the fentanyl that killed them by the same person – Mort having confirmed that there had been fentanyl in Karolyn's system. Then she needed to consider who would benefit from Johnny's death. And if a person appeared on both those lists, would that necessarily make them the killer of all three?

But there was something more to this case. A person who was killing for financial gain or to remove a love rival wouldn't stage the murder scene with such complexity. Sure, killers staged scenes as often as not – to hide their motives and to misdirect the police. But this case went beyond the usual Serial Killer 101 basics. She'd never seen a living infant used as a prop before. This had to have a very specific meaning.

Everything she'd learned about profiling from her time in the States suggested one thing. That this wasn't staging by a killer who wanted to lead the police astray. This was posing. It was a very specific signature, somehow rooted in the killer's childhood. A dead woman and a baby. What could it mean?

And who could it relate to?

Childhood trauma was practically a given when it came to this kind of highly stylised or ritualistic killing. But which of her suspects had something relevant in their background? Something that had happened to them as a child or a teenager that could trigger the need to create such mayhem.

Liam Norris, Bethany's long-term partner, was without doubt a violent man. Lexi had reason to believe that he'd physically abused her on more than one occasion and he might have killed her in a temper. But was there something in his early life that might have pushed him from straightforward domestic violence to the fetishist posing of Bethany and Karolyn's death?

What about Johnny Lycett-Boyd? On the surface, his motivation to kill Bethany might have been to hide his relationship with her, or the fact that he had a child with her. But was it more to do with an urge to kill? Did this explain why he might have gone on to kill Karolyn in the same way?

Then there was Will Steadman. There was definitely something 'off' about him – his weird theories of biodynamic agriculture suggested a level of credulity fixed during puberty. A man child who'd never grown up. Could this be because of some childhood trauma that was now playing out in the way he posed the death scenes? Lexi considered his relationships with women. He was sleeping with his boss's wife, while at the same time carrying on what seemed to be a solely sex-based relationship with Karolyn. It suggested an objectified view of women that was common in men who killed repeatedly.

Johnny's death didn't fit with the ritualised deaths of the two women, but that didn't mean it wasn't the same killer. He killed the women to satisfy his ritualistic urges. But the motive for killing Johnny was likely something more pragmatic. Had Johnny worked out who the killer was?

Or maybe it was a different killer? Who benefitted from Johnny's death? Marietta would benefit financially, of course, and she'd admitted herself that their marriage was a sham. She might easily have had access to Johnny's car, but would she have the technical knowledge to make changes that would result in a crash? Lexi supposed she was being sexist to assume that she didn't, so this was a hypothesis that deserved further investigation.

Will Steadman's job was under threat if Johnny sold the vineyard. But was that enough to make him kill Johnny? Presumably he could get a job somewhere else. English vineyards, once a rarity, seemed to be ten a penny these days, and he was an experienced vintner. Who would inherit Johnny's share of the vineyard? She made another note to follow up on checking whether Lycett-Boyd had left a will. He had a wife, a daughter, a brother – and now a second daughter.

Was Ben Lycett-Boyd in line to inherit some of Johnny's shares? Enough to put him in control of Elvington? Ridhi had discovered that he'd been in the country when both of the women had died. But did he fit the psychological profile for the two murders? Or should they be looking for someone with no connection to the vineyard? Someone to whom the angel wings held meaning, someone with a knowledge of the local folklore. Gideon Croft? Ed thought it was safe to rule him out as an interfering busybody. But Lexi wasn't quite ready to do that yet. They knew too little about his past to discard him out of hand.

She closed her notebook. She needed some lunch.

FORTY-FIVE

On her way back to her office with an uninspiring supermarket sandwich, Lexi stuck her head into the incident room. Ridhi was sitting on her own, studying her computer screen with a look of intense concentration.

'What're you up to?'

'Going through the CCTV footage from the track on the morning of Johnny's crash.'

'Anything of interest?'

'Well... there's something I don't quite get. I mean, it feels to me like some of the timing on the different cameras isn't in sync.'

'How do you mean?' Lexi came round to Ridhi's side of the desk and pulled a chair across so she could sit next to her.

'See here?' said Ridhi, pointing at the screen. 'This footage starts at 9.04 a.m. and shows the Porsche driving into one of the mechanic bays, and there's Johnny getting out of it.'

Lexi watched. Johnny stopped to talk to one of the mechanics – she recognised Cameron Johns – and stayed there for a few minutes. Then he left the workshop and walked towards the track office. The time stamp on the footage was by then showing 9.15 a.m.

Ridhi loaded the feed from a different camera. She fast forwarded to 9.15 a.m. and Lexi saw Johnny going into the track office. He emerged at 9.25 a.m. and then reappeared at 9.27 a.m. in the feed of a camera angled at the trackside, where he spent the next twenty or so minutes watching some other drivers doing practice laps.

'It all seems quite straightforward to me,' said Lexi. 'But it shows us he was away from his car at that point. Maybe that's when someone messed with it.'

'Give me a second – let's take a look.' Ridhi reloaded the feed from the camera that faced the mechanic bays. Lexi could see Cameron Johns working on a Mercedes next to the Porsche.

'Nothing to see,' said Lexi.

'No, but this is where the timing gets odd. See here, the time stamp says 9.32 a.m., and here comes Johnny and says something to Cameron, then disappears again. But here...' She switched back to the trackside feed and rewound it to 9.32 a.m. 'He's at the track at the same moment.'

'So the clock's wrong on one of the cameras,' said Lexi.

Ridhi shook her head. 'That can't be it, because a few minutes before, when he leaves the workshop, goes to the track office and then to the trackside, all of the cameras are in sync. And later when he goes back to the workshop and opens the bonnet, they're all in sync again. It's just this one bit, where he seems to be in two places at once.'

'Run it by me again,' said Lexi. She studied the footage that seemed to prove that Johnny was in two places at once. 'Wait, look here. Trackside Johnny's got a white shirt on under his jacket.' He was wearing one of the green waxed jackets so favoured by the rural rich. 'Get the other one up.' Ridhi swapped the feeds. 'Look, this time he's wearing a denim jacket. So that's not Johnny – that's his brother Ben.' The grainy quality of the video made them seem incredibly alike, and with no expectation of Johnny having a brother there, it would have been too easy to assume they were one and the same.

'God, how could I have been so stupid?' said Ridhi, putting a hand to her mouth.

'Not stupid. It's the way the eyes work – recognising something and letting the brain fill in the blanks. I only spotted it, because I bumped into Ben Lycett-Boyd at the farmhouse shortly after the accident.'

'So you knew he'd been up at the track?'

Lexi thought back to the conversation with Ben Lycett-Boyd. 'No, he didn't say that. He said he'd spoken to Johnny on the phone – and I suppose that could be true, because it doesn't look like they actually came face to face.'

'But given what happened a few minutes later, why wouldn't he say he'd been at the track?'

Ridhi had a point. It seemed suspicious it. But the footage didn't show him going anywhere near Johnny's Porsche. They watched as Ben Lycett-Boyd finished talking to Cameron Johns and then went back towards the car park, now talking to someone else on his phone. Johnny perhaps?

'See if Johnny's on the phone at this point – 9.37 a.m.'

Ridhi swapped back to the footage of Johnny at the trackside. 'Yes, there he is taking a call.'

So Ben had been at the track, and had spoken with Johnny's mechanic, a very short time before the crash occurred. And yet when she told him about the crash a while later at the farmhouse, he'd seemed genuinely shocked. As had Marietta. Responses that would be hard to fake. However, he had the motive – to stop Johnny selling the vineyard – and the means – he spoke to the mechanic – and the opportunity – he was in the workshop.

It was time to call Ben Lycett-Boyd into the station for a more formal interview. She wanted to know why he hadn't admitted he'd been at the track shortly before the crash, and what exactly he'd said to Cameron Johns. Could he have been putting the mechanic up to tampering with the car?

'Why didn't you tell me that you went to the track before coming over to the farmhouse yesterday morning?' Lexi was pacing from side to side in front of the interview room table where Ben Lycett-Boyd sat with his head in his hands.

He looked up at her. 'It looks bad, doesn't it?'

'Why do you say that?'

'Honest to God, when you said that Johnny was dead, everything I'd done that morning went clean out of my head. I was in shock.'

'But later, you must have realised...'

'Realised what? Yes, I'd been to the track, but I hadn't even seen Johnny there. I didn't think it was relevant.'

'With all due respect, it's up to us to decide what's relevant with regard to our investigation into your brother's death.'

Ben had nothing but a shrug for this.

'You were caught on CCTV footage talking with Cameron Johns, standing next to Johnny's car minutes before the accident happened. Could you recall that conversation for me?'

'It was short. I just asked him if that was Johnny's car, and he said it was. We talked about it for a couple of minutes, then I left.'

'Can you be more precise?'

'Not particularly. He quoted some stats at me and talked about the setup. It's not my bag, so I didn't really listen.'

Lexi had to wonder – if that was the case, why would he have made a point of talking to the engineer at all? They would need to get Cameron Johns' account of this conversation.

'Tell me, do you know the details of your brother's will?'

'Everything will go to Marietta and Aurora.'

'You know that for sure?'

'Before he married, his share of the vineyard would have come to me. But naturally once he had his own family, he changed his will, just as I did. My shares in the vineyard all go to Julia – my wife – if and when I die.'

'Have you seen his new will?'

'No. You'll need to ask Marietta about that.'

Lexi paused for a moment, then moved on. 'You didn't agree with his plan to sell the vineyard, did you?'

'If you're suggesting I came back here to kill him to prevent that from happening, you're way off the mark, lady. I came here to talk some sense into him about what would be best for the family. The whole family. He was being a selfish bastard, and I wanted to point that out to him, face to face. Now, if you'll excuse me, I'm grieving his death.'

He stood up and went towards the door.

'Don't leave the area without informing us.'

Lexi did nothing to stop him. She couldn't. Because so far, she didn't have physical evidence to tie him to any of the scenes of the crime, and given his recent arrival in the UK it seemed unlikely to her that Bethany and Karolyn would have known and trusted him enough to meet with him. The case against Will Steadman still looked stronger.

FORTY-SIX

The harvesting never stopped. Despite the two dead women, despite the death of the owner, it appeared that Will Steadman was a steady hand on the tiller – the pickers kept picking and grapes continued to be tipped into the presses. Lexi suspected he had something to prove. The future of the vineyard must be more up in the air than ever. Perhaps he wanted to show the new majority shareholder – Marietta? – that he was more than capable of keeping it going.

If he didn't end up being arrested for murder.

'When were you last up at the track?'

Steadman looked up at her from his desk in the visitor centre. 'I don't know. I don't go up there. It's probably been a couple of years.'

If he was lying, they presumably would have spotted him on the CCTV footage from the track, and so far they hadn't. But if she was going to build a case against him, she would need to put him in the vicinity of Johnny's Porsche at some point.

'Can you account for your whereabouts on Wednesday night?'

'That's easy – I've worked here late every evening since the harvest started.'

'What time did you knock off?'

He thought for a moment. 'Wednesday... I think I locked up here just after ten.'

'Then what did you do?'

'Drove back to my cottage and went to bed.'

'Was anyone with you? Marietta, perhaps?'

'I was on my own.' He was terse. The vineyard Lothario clearly didn't care to be called out for what he was.

'When you left work, were there any other cars still in the car park?'

He frowned up at her. 'Of course there were. Some of the pickers who stay on site have cars.'

'What about Johnny's Porsche? Was that there on Wednesday night?'

Steadman blinked as he realised the implication she was making, and it reminded Lexi of a snake's eye membrane flashing across its eyeball. 'I have no idea.'

'But Johnny was here on Wednesday, working, wasn't he?'

'Yes. But sometimes he just walks up from the farmhouse. I'm afraid I don't keep track of his comings and goings, much less his car. Maybe Marietta could help you with that.'

'Maybe she could.' Can't answer a question? Refer the questioner back to Marietta. First Ben, now Steadman. Time to beat a path to her door.

Marietta seemed even less pleased to see her than Steadman had been. She stood at the front door of the farmhouse without inviting Lexi in.

'I'm in the middle of a meeting with my solicitor,' she said. 'Now isn't a good time.'

'Just a couple of quick questions, then I'll let you get back to it.'

Marietta peered past her. There were still a few members of the press nosing around the area. 'I can give you one minute.' She pulled the door wide and shut it quickly behind Lexi. But then she stood her ground in the hallway, glaring.

'Marietta?' called a man's voice from the living room. He said something in French and she answered him, speaking too quickly for Lexi's school-level understanding. But she was obviously talking with a French solicitor. Was she planning a return to her native country?

'Mrs Lycett-Boyd, can you tell me where you were on Wednesday evening?'

'The night before the crash? I was here, of course.'

'Did you see Will Steadman that night?'

'No. Like I said, I was here.' There was a finality to her tone.

'Can you remember whether Johnny drove the Porsche up to the vineyard or whether he walked up that day?'

'Wednesday? He took the car up there – I remember because he gave me a lift.'

'And in the evening, he drove down and the car was parked here overnight?'

'I suppose so, but I can't be sure. I walked back down here when I stopped working.'

'Was he here?'

'No, he was working later that night and came back after me. I don't know if he walked or drove down the hill.'

Which meant the Porsche had either been in the vineyard car park all night, or parked at the house. Lexi wondered how much was involved in tampering with the spring rate. Was it something that would have needed to be done in the workshop, or could someone with the right know-how and the cover of darkness have adjusted it during the night?

She called Kevin Malthouse, the RPU sergeant, from her

car as she drove back to Canterbury. When she asked him if someone could have changed the spring rates in the car park overnight, Malthouse sucked air between his teeth. 'Good question.' There was a moment's pause before he answered. 'I suppose so, in theory. But first off the person's got to have the knowledge. Changing the spring rates just enough to make the car dangerous suggests it was someone who knows a thing or two – a mechanic. And they'd have to have the right kit with them.'

'Which is what?'

'A couple of spanner wrenches of the right size. Again, suggests a pretty high level of knowledge. It's definitely more likely to have been done in the workshop by an experienced mechanic.'

'Or could Johnny have accidentally done it himself? He was the only person who worked on the car in the workshop, and he wasn't a trained mechanic, was he?'

'I've spoken with the guys from the track,' said Malthouse. 'They reckon he knew what he was doing when it came to adjusting the springs – and when we looked at the wreck, the springs were some way off his usual setting. Too far off for it to have been an experiment.'

'So maybe it was someone who wasn't quite so knowledgeable perhaps?' Another thought came to Lexi. 'If someone with the right skills and the right kit had made the changes at the vineyard during the night, wouldn't he have had an accident as he drove from home to the track on Thursday morning?'

'It's not that likely, actually. Driving on the track is very different to driving in normal road conditions. On the track, the car is under immensely more pressure on every bend because of the speed – and that's where the setup becomes critical to how well the car stays on the road.'

'So if I had a hypothesis that someone tampered with the

Porsche at the vineyard or at Lycett-Boyd's home at some point during the previous night, you wouldn't laugh me out of court?'

'No, I wouldn't. I still think it's more likely to have been done in the workshop – for ease of access and so on – but it's not impossible it could have been done elsewhere.'

'But if it was done earlier, Johnny surely would have spotted it when he worked on the car that morning?'

'Not if he was only looking at the engine. The rear springs are at the other end of the car.'

'Thanks, Kevin. You'll let me know when you get any forensics off the car, right?'

'You'll be the first person I call.'

She hung up and dialled Maggie.

'I think I've got the beginnings of a case against Will Steadman,' she said, without preamble.

'Beginnings is good,' said Maggie. 'But you need more?'

'We're waiting on some forensics – they could make or break it.'

'When will you know?'

'Maybe twenty-four hours. Maybe longer.'

'Don't pull him in yet, or you'll run out of custody time. Put a tail on him. Make sure you know where he is and what he's doing every minute of the day.'

'Overtime?'

'Do it for forty-eight hours. Then we re-assess.'

'Got it. Thanks, Maggie.'

'The thanks will be entirely mine if you can get something that will stick before this bastard kills again.'

But could she?

FORTY-SEVEN

Another long day at the coal face seemed to have yielded little, but Lexi knew she was on the right track. She was familiar with the way investigations ebbed and flowed, and she was starting to feel the inexorable tug of a solution that was only just beyond her sightline, almost within reach.

She drummed her fingers on the desk. She was waiting for the HOLMES 2 database to spew out its search results on murders of young women with babies or infants left at the scene. Ridhi had checked this already at the start of the investigation, but she admitted she hadn't gone very far back in time. Lexi wanted to dig deeper and widen the search beyond Kent to take in the whole of the southeast. There was something about this case that wasn't hanging together. None of her suspects seemed to be slotting into place, and the signature was the key. She wasn't expecting the query to turn up anything of particular use, but she also knew better than to leave any stone unturned. A few minutes later, she was rewarded with references to a couple of cases. She studied the screen.

Then she practically ran to the incident room.

'Tom, you need to see this.'

'What have you got?'

'HOLMES 2 has thrown up two cases that could be of interest. First, a woman was murdered in North Benfleet and was found with a baby crying by her side.'

'North Benfleet? Where's that?'

'Near Basildon, in Essex.'

'Nothing in Kent?'

Lexi shrugged. 'The Benfleet one isn't one for us anyway,' she said. 'The woman's husband was convicted of strangling her. Now serving life.'

'And the other case?'

'Has more potential. The victim died of a drug overdose, though not fentanyl. She was found in a squat in Bromley, with her baby daughter asleep next to her. First put down to suicide but, according to the records, they're still looking for the dealer.'

'And what makes it of interest to us?' Tom raised an eyebrow.

'The woman had ingested mushrooms as well as barbiturates and ketamine.'

'Was she wearing wings by any chance?'

'No. But the coincidence with the mushrooms makes it worth a deeper look. Do you think you can fix up a meeting with the SIO?'

'Will do.'

Lexi sighed. 'Let's call it a night. See you in the morning.'

'Night, boss.'

She was tired and a range of aches and pains – the back of her leg, the small of her back – reminded her that if she didn't take some care of herself, she'd burn out. A swim, followed by a sauna, followed by a solid night's sleep would do her the world of good. And while chewing up lengths of the pool, her mind would be free to wander, one of the best ways to see connections that would lead her to the answer.

Driving from the station to the health club, she called Ed

Harlow. He'd been on her mind on and off all day, and she wanted to make sure he felt that she was there if he needed support.

'How are you?' she said, when he grunted hello.

He sighed. 'Up and down. Mostly down, when I'm not distracted by the overwhelming admin of it all. It's the thing you don't count on – endless tasks like closing bank accounts, cancelling direct debits, providing death certificates. It just reduces someone's life to office chores. Ugh!'

'Is your brother helping you?'

'He's doing a bit. Frankly I wish he'd go away and leave me alone. He's always hovering at my shoulder. Being the subject of endless sympathy can be exhausting.'

'Delegate some of the practicalities to him.'

'I would but, as executer of Charlie's will, most of it falls on me. And all I want to do is curl up in bed and pretend it hasn't happened.'

'Do you want me to come over?'

'No, not this late. You're busy, and to be honest I'm exhausted.'

'Okay. Let's see if we can go for a walk at the weekend.'

'Thanks, Lexi.' He let out a dry laugh. 'I know Charlie put you up to this... but really, you don't have to.'

'I would have done it anyway, Ed. I know how hard it is, what you're going through.'

There was a moment's silence on the other end, then Ed coughed. Damn – she hadn't meant to make him cry.

'How's the case going?' His voice sounded a little shaky.

'I get the feeling it's about to break. There are so many strands, and varying motives, but somewhere there's going to be an intersection. And when we shine a light on that, it'll all become clear.'

'And what's preventing that from happening?'

'Right now? It's this issue with the motives. On the one

hand, you've got a highly ritualistic kill with a strong signature, which points to a sexually motivated serial killer – at least in Bethany and Karolyn's deaths. But if you look at who benefits from all three deaths – money, family politics, the future of the vineyard – that brings in a different range of suspects. At first, I thought the ritual – the wings, the candles, the deserted babies – was just a distraction tactic to throw us off the scent of the real killer. But now I'm not so sure. I've a gut feeling it's genuine and I think it's the key to the case.'

There was a pause at the other end of the line as Ed considered what she'd said.

'And I came across something else odd today. A case from a couple of years ago – I found it on HOLMES 2.' She filled him in on the details. 'What do you think? A close enough match to consider it the same killer?'

Ed exhaled. 'Any posing of the body?'

'Nothing recorded. But if it was a first kill, the signature would develop later. So could it be the same?'

'Hard to say. Any of your suspects got links to Bromley?'

'I'll have Ridhi go over that in the morning. Tom's going to contact the SIO.'

'See what turns up. It could be an early kill, maybe even his first kill, before he had the nerve to position the body after death. The first murder often terrifies as much as it sates an individual's need to kill. After the first it becomes easier, and that's when you see a killer developing his signature.'

'Plenty of food for thought.'

Ed cleared his throat. 'Who's still on your list?'

'Gideon Croft, but he's a rank outsider.'

'Agreed.'

'Will Steadman, the vintner. He's got some weird farming-by-the-phase-of-the-moon views and his job will certainly be on the line if the vineyard is sold. Furthermore, he had sex with the second victim in the hours before she died.'

'Anything circumstantial at the scene?'

'Not yet. Her clothes haven't been found.'

'And no traces of him at the first crime scene?'

'I'm waiting for results.'

'Going back to the issue between posing and staging. The wings, the babies – classic posing. The killer's unique signature, with special personal meaning. I think you're on the right track to be putting it in the spotlight.'

'We need to find the intersection between the suspects with pragmatic motives and someone who has the sort of background that would result in a need to recreate this unique posing. What makes it unique is the inclusion of the babies. Abandonment issues? He's setting up each scene with the mother abandoning their child.'

'It's a good shout. You might want to dig into Steadman's past on that score. And at the same time, check where he might have been when the woman in Bromley was murdered.'

'Him and Ben Lycett-Boyd, Johnny's brother. He's recently arrived from Australia, and just as all this kicks off which is definitely interesting. I've got Ridhi checking out his alibis for the relevant nights. I'll add the old case to that, as well.' She was sitting in the sports club car park. 'Listen, Ed, I gotta go.'

'Sure. Thanks for the call. Good to get out of the headspace I'm currently in.'

'If you think of anything, get in touch.'

'Of course.'

She got out of the car, anxious to feel the cool balm of the water enveloping her.

After forty minutes of vigorous front crawl in a virtually empty pool, Lexi was ready for the welcoming heat of the sauna. She'd brainstormed the case thoroughly as she'd cut through the cold water, and while she hadn't come up with a breakthrough, she now felt she had everything ordered in her mind. Whatever came next, she would be ready for it.

It was after nine o'clock. The club shut at ten on weekday nights, so she would just have time to relax, then a quick shower before heading home. The sauna itself was empty. A blessed relief. Sometimes it was busy with men, talking loudly about football – not really what she wanted at that moment. Instead, with the place to herself, she was able to lie full length on the wooden slats and bliss out as the heat cocooned her and relaxed tired muscles. She put the case to one side and emptied her mind. This was her time, floating on the edge of consciousness, luxuriating in the heat.

She dozed, every sinew soft, the tension seeping out of her. Aches and pains at bay, troubling thoughts put to sleep...

She woke up with a jolt, her head swimming. She'd been in here too long and now she was overheated. Pulling her towel up around her body, she sat up slowly. The hot air stung her eyes and her mouth was like dry board. With a grunt, she pushed herself to her feet and staggered towards the door, imagining the gush of cool air once it opened.

But when she pushed against it, she was brought up short. The door didn't open as she expected it to. Had she pushed it instead of pulling it? No, she knew it opened outwards. She pressed harder against the glass, leaning on it with her whole body. But still it didn't budge. Gasping, she stepped back and stared at it. What the hell was going on? Surely a sauna door couldn't be locked.

Maybe something outside was in the way, jamming it shut.

She peered through the smoked glass that made everything beyond appear dark and dull. She couldn't see anything blocking the door. There didn't seem to be a keyhole in the door plate. But maybe there was some way of shutting it, if there were times they didn't want people going in there.

Whatever. She needed to get out. The heat was making her woozy. Maybe there was a switch inside for turning it off. She looked around but couldn't see one. Nor could she see an emergency button or pull cord anywhere. Surely there had to be one in a public sauna?

Then she saw a small plastic fitting, high up on the wall, close to the door. It had a hole in the middle. Clambering onto the bench below it, she studied it. She could just make out a few red fibres sticking out of the hole. There had been an emergency cord in here, but it had been cut off. Why?

Her breathing was becoming more laboured, her mouth ever drier. She blinked. Her eyes felt dry and gritty. Skin slick with sweat. And a soft flutter of panic in her stomach.

She pushed against the door again. It still didn't open. She shouldered it forcefully. The glass shuddered but the door remained closed.

'Hello? Is there someone out there?' She positioned her mouth close to the edge of the door and shouted as loudly as she could. The place was practically deserted. The club would be closing in a few minutes. Someone would come round to check that all the changing rooms were empty, wouldn't they? She shouted again and banged her fists on the glass, desperate to attract attention.

What was keeping the door shut? She staggered a couple of steps back to the nearest bench and sank down. Heat rises, so should she lie on the floor? She dropped down to her knees, but the floor seemed as hot as every other surface in the wood-lined cabin. Head pounding, she was unable to think straight. What was happening?

She crawled back to the door and bashed on it feebly with one fist. It left a sweaty smear on the glass.

'Help!' Her voice cracked and her throat felt like dry tree bark.

Something was preventing her from opening the door. She

squinted up through the glass. On the outside, there was a looped metal handle for people to pull the door open from the outside. Now, from this angle, she could see that something was jammed through it, something that must somehow also be attached to the doorframe or wall beyond it to stop the door from opening.

With the realisation, her mind clicked back into gear. This wasn't an accident. Someone had shut her in here. While she'd been dozing on the bench, someone had done this. It wasn't a joke – or they would have let her out by now. She'd been shouting and banging for long enough. She had to believe there was never any intention that she should get out. Was it the same person who'd snipped off the emergency pull cord?

What happens if you stay in a sauna too long? She racked her brains. Heat exhaustion. Loss of consciousness. Could you die?

She wasn't going to die in here.

She was dizzy. Black floaters in front of her eyes. It seemed hotter than ever – the temperature was actually rising. She had to break out. Taking a deep breath to summon all her strength, she wrapped her towel around her foot, knotting it at the ankle. She positioned herself in front of the glass door, planted her supporting foot firmly on the floor and swung back her padded foot. She kicked the glass as hard and fast as she was able. Her foot crashed against it, sending a streak of pain up to her knee as she fell backwards onto the tiled floor. She bounced hard on her coccyx, jarring her spine and making her teeth slam shut.

But she doubted anyone heard her yelp.

'Damn!' She sat up, eyes watering with the pain, blinking back tears of frustration. The toughened safety glass was too thick, and the aborted kick had sapped most of what energy she had left. If she didn't find a way out quickly, she was going to pass out. And if she was lying silently on the floor, anyone giving the sauna a cursory check as they locked up for the night would miss her. Even if they switched it off, it would take hours for the cabin to cool down.

Just. Hold. On.

She took a few slow breaths. Like breathing fire. She needed something harder, something sharper, to shatter the glass. But there was no handy hammer in here. No tools of any sort. Nothing but flat wooden slats, forming stepped benches rising up the walls.

One slat, on one of the top benches, was buckled up at one end.

It took a supreme effort, but Lexi climbed up to the bench below it. She grabbed at the piece of wood that had warped in the heat. She was able to get a good grip, and she moved along the bench to lever it up. A deep breath. Double-handed grip. She pulled hard, trying to rip it from its mooring. Splinters pierced her palms and fingers, but then a couple of nails holding it in place pulled loose. Then a few more. It snapped away from the bench and Lexi slumped back against the wall, dizzy with exhaustion.

There was no time for rest – she probably had minutes before she passed out. If she woke up at all after that, it might be with brain damage or heat stroke. She had to act now. She bit down hard on her lower lip, hoping the pain would fix her focus and help her to concentrate.

This time, she used her towel to fashion a handle at one end of the wooden slat. When it was wrapped around and knotted as tightly as she could manage, she was ready.

It had to work.

It was her last chance.

She took the slat in a double-handed grip. Then she stepped back, twisting at the waist, raising the slat above one shoulder as if she was wielding a baseball bat. With a ferocious yell, she swung the wood hard at the glass door, pouring all her strength into the trajectory, not allowing her momentum to stop when the wood made contact with the glass.

There was an ear-splitting shatter and the safety glass splintered into tiny pieces and fell to the floor. Lexi was propelled forward by the force of her swing, launching headlong through the gap where the door had been. She landed on her belly and right side, skidding across the floor on a torrent of spiky glass pebbles.

But the floor was cold. The air was cool.

She could breathe.

She wasn't going to die.

FORTY-EIGHT

MOTIVATIONAL JOURNAL – SATURDAY, SEPTEMBER 30

Yesterday's achievements

1. Watched the press conference on television
2. Checked up on DI Lexi Bennett. Maybe she is my new obsession. And why not?
3. Went to work – okay day
4. Trapped Lexi in the sauna. It was so satisfying to hear her crying for help
5. Watched from the outside as an ambulance and the police arrived. She was carried out on a stretcher and blue-lighted away. She didn't die

Learning outcomes

1. People are resourceful. I thought I'd jammed that door well enough, but she managed to get out and raise the alarm
2. Acting on impulse isn't clever. What if I'd left some DNA traces?

Plans for today

1. Working this morning
2. Make plans for the end
3. Visit Mum's grave

How are you feeling – in three words?

1. Elated and regretful
2. Fierce
3. Ready for what's next

Memory of the day

This afternoon, I'll take a bunch of thistles to Mum's grave. The flowers that sum up our relationship so perfectly. When I think about her, I think about love – but not in the normal way. I wonder if there was any love between us, in the short time we spent together. I know there was hate, on both sides. I hated her for deserting me. I hated her for her inability to look after me properly. I hated her for putting grown men, strangers, ahead of me. I hated her for placing her desire for drugs and alcohol above my need for food. And I hated her most for not loving me enough to understand the harm she was doing. She simply didn't love me enough.

I loved her, because I didn't know any better. I didn't understand that the relationship between a mother and a child could be anything other than this. I didn't understand that my life wasn't 'normal', for want of a better word. To me, it was just the way life was. I loved my failure of a mother. She was pretty. She had a laugh that sounded like silver bells. All I wanted to do was earn her praise, and her approval, and most of all her love. And then I loved her because she was an angel, always at my side, always watching over me, protecting me from the horrors of my small life. Only she wasn't an angel, just a woman who failed me. So today I'll take thistles to her grave and punish more bad mothers.

Motivation for the day
The heart of a mother is a deep abyss ~~at the bottom of which you will always find forgiveness~~

FORTY-NINE

SATURDAY

Lexi blinked and looked around the room. She didn't know where she was, but definitely not at home. Bedroom furniture she didn't recognise, striped curtains she'd never seen before. Where was she? She ran an inventory of the spare rooms she knew – Amber's fourth bedroom, the room she'd stayed in at her grandparents' house as a child – and drew a blank. This wasn't the bedroom of any man she'd ever slept with, unless...

A sharp pain stabbed her in the ribs as she tried to sit up, and she remembered in a rush what had happened. The sauna. The hospital. Tom driving her home. Ah, that was it – this was Tom's spare room. There was a jackhammer working on the inside of her skull and her tongue felt like sandpaper. She looked around and was rewarded with the sight of a glass of water on the bedside table. She was still dehydrated. Her hand stung as she picked up the glass, but she drank greedily. When it was empty, she put it down and stared at her palm, her wrist and her forearm, the length of which was peppered with small cuts and grazes.

The moment replayed in her mind as sharply as when it had actually happened – her body surfing across the tiles on pebbles of broken glass, gasping for air, too winded for a few moments to call for help.

She pulled back the duvet she was lying under and looked at the rest of her body. All the cuts, all the grazes, all the bruises. Her front and her right side looked as if someone had taken a cheese grater to it. None of the cuts were deep – the door had been made of safety glass, which had dissolved into scratchy pebbles rather than sharp shards – but it looked horrible. She remembered how much it had stung when they'd cleaned her up in A&E, and then coming back here in a hospital gown as the swimming costume she'd had on in the sauna had been ripped to shreds. Tom had lent her a T-shirt and a pair of boxer shorts.

With a sigh, she sank back onto the pillows.

There was a knock at the door. 'Lexi?' It was Tom's voice.

Before she could answer, the door opened and Billie, Tom's nine-year-old daughter, burst into the room.

'Wait, Billie,' said Tom, behind her in the hall.

'I can't believe what happened,' said Billie in a rush, planting herself on the end of the bed. 'That you had to go to hospital and then come and stay here. Did it hurt a lot?'

From the doorway, Tom shrugged apologetically. 'Tea?' he said over his daughter's chatter.

'Hi, Billie,' said Lexi. 'Yes, it hurt, but I'm okay now.' She glanced up at Tom. 'I should get going.'

He shook his head. 'You're not going to work. It's Saturday, and doctor's orders are rest and rehydration. You were dangerously dehydrated. I only stopped them from keeping you in by saying that I'd personally see to it that you got a few days' rest and drank plenty of water.'

'I promise I'll drink water all day.' She looked around the room and it dawned on her that her clothes were still in her locker at the pool.

'We're going to cook you breakfast,' said Billie. 'Bacon and waffles.'

'If you eat breakfast with us, then I'll drive you home,' said Tom. 'But promise me not to go into work.'

Lexi forbore from pointing out that she was his senior officer and didn't have to promise him anything. He knew that already. Just as he knew perfectly well she'd be back in the office just as fast as she could be. Bethany and Karolyn couldn't be brought back, but maybe, if she was lucky, she could prevent another name being added to that list. She didn't have time to lounge in bed drinking water all day.

Still grumbling, Tom drove Lexi home and they arranged to meet in the office an hour later. A couple of painkillers and some salve, along with the softest items of clothing in her wardrobe, would hopefully be enough to dampen the sting of the multitude of scratches and the crushing headache.

Most of the team were in already when she arrived – word had spread quickly that she'd been attacked.

'That was attempted murder,' said Ridhi, hardly able to keep the fury out of her voice. 'We'll find whoever did it, boss.'

Up to now, Lexi had pushed away all thoughts of who might have done it and why. She knew it had been no accident, but considering who might want to end your life was more than a little disturbing. Now she had to confront it face on. Whenever someone was attacked or murdered, what did she ask? Who benefitted. She felt certain she was closing in on whoever had killed Bethany and Karolyn, and it was a certainty that that person didn't want to be caught. They'd be only too happy to get her out of the way, whether temporarily or permanently.

Tough! They'd failed, and she was more determined than ever to discover their identity.

Tom had called in the CSIs as Lexi had been wheeled out

by the paramedics, and apparently they'd worked the scene for most of the night. Colin had been liaising with them.

'Emily's been in touch this morning,' he said. 'They dusted everywhere for prints. The door had been jammed shut using the metal bar from a single arm barbell, so there's no way you could have bent or broken that to get out. But whoever stuck it through the handle knew well enough to wipe it clean.'

'They will have got hundreds of sets of prints from the spa area,' said Lexi. 'It's always busy. The only prints that might prove useful would be on the metal bar – and there weren't any.'

'Who do you think did it?' said Tom.

Easy to answer. 'Whoever's afraid that I'm coming for them.'

'It has to be linked to the current case,' said Ridhi. 'You did the presser yesterday morning, and that identified you as the SIO on the Elvington murders. Maybe the killer thinks the best way to avoid detection is to pick off the detectives.' Lexi saw her shudder.

'Okay, Ridhi, you run that hypothesis,' said Lexi. 'Check out the whereabouts of our current suspects last night – see if any of them were near the health club. Colin, go to the club and see who was there yesterday evening – you have to swipe in, so I assume that information is logged.'

'Does that mean whoever did this had to be a member of your gym?' said Tom.

'Probably not. I know people can check guests in, and prospective members can have taster sessions. Also, people come to see the various therapists that work there. Let's face it, security at these sorts of buildings is usually pretty lax. You wouldn't need to be a rocket scientist to sneak in.' Lexi thought about who she'd seen there when she was changing and swimming. It had been almost empty. 'I suppose someone could have been following me. It had to have been an opportunistic crime, because I only decided to go on the spur of the moment.'

As the victim of this particular crime, Lexi couldn't lead the investigation of it, so she had to turn her attention to something else. One thing she felt unsettled about was the tampering with Johnny's Porsche. All the time it was up at the track before the crash, it had mostly been in the view of the CCTV and they'd seen no one other than Johnny working on it. It had been at Elvington overnight before the practice session, but to her mind it seemed unlikely that someone at the vineyard would have risked working on the car there. Far easier and less suspicious to tinker with the car up at the track, as long as whoever did it was a regular. If it was done at the track in the short time the car spent in the workshop before Johnny drove it, it couldn't have been a stranger.

Unless it was a stranger who could pass himself off as a regular. Someone people wouldn't necessarily take any notice of, if they saw him.

Someone who, when they saw him working on the car in the CCTV footage, they'd just assume was Johnny.

Ben Lycett-Boyd.

They knew he'd been there. They'd seen him in the footage talking to one of the mechanics. And he'd tried to cover it up, failing to mention it when Lexi reported Johnny's death to his wife.

She left the office and drove out to Shepherd's Hill on a hunch. Maybe there was some video footage they hadn't seen, or maybe if she looked at the video again, she'd see Ben where confirmation bias had shown her Johnny before. Or an eyewitness who had slipped through their net. She parked in the public car park and showed her police ID to gain access to the track, then walked along the front of the workshop. The bays were full and busy with people – drivers and mechanics in overalls, men in team T-shirts, women who were clearly more interested in the drivers than the vehicles, a couple of local journalists. There was a buzz of excitement in the air and, from beyond the track office and the spectator stand, Lexi could hear the roar of engines.

She knocked on the door of the office and tried the handle. It was locked. Perhaps Stephen Flannery was trackside watching the action.

The spectator stand was crowded with people – families, young men, fathers with small sons, a few gaggles of young women – all with eyes glued on the half-a-dozen souped-up saloon cars battling for position. Lexi scanned the faces, not interested in who was winning whatever race it was. Eventually she spotted the track manager deep in conversation with a portly middle-aged man near the finish line. They weren't paying attention to the race either, their heads bowed close the better to hear each other speak. Lexi made her way through the throng to get to him.

'Mr Flannery?' Her voice was drowned out as a Sierra Cosworth flew by with a high-pitched roar. 'Mr Flannery?' She shouted his name loudly, then put a hand on his shoulder.

He looked round, alerted by her touch.

'Inspector Bennett,' he appeared to mouth.

The man he was with gave him a nod, raised a hand in a wave and walked away.

There was a gap in the cars. 'Let's go to my office,' said Flannery, his voice louder than it needed to be.

Lexi nodded and followed him from the track, her ears still ringing.

'What can I do for you?' he said, as he unlocked the door.

Lexi followed him inside. 'I just wanted to check we'd had all the footage from the day of the accident,' she said.

Flannery frowned. 'Indeed you have.'

'I'll take you into my confidence, Mr Flannery,' she said. 'I'm almost certain that Johnny's car was tampered with, and equally certain it was done while the car was being tuned up here before his practice session.'

'Now that's quite an accusation, Inspector.' Flannery's body language transmitted hostility. 'Are you suggesting one of my mechanics was responsible?'

'From what I understand the issue to have been – a problem with the spring rates – it seems unlikely that someone would have managed to do that while the car was parked at the vineyard. Access would be tricky, tools required, as well as technical knowledge. Doesn't that suggest to you that a professional mechanic must have been involved?'

'I don't even necessarily accept your theory that the car was tampered with. There might have been a fault in one of the springs, or Johnny could have mistuned it himself. It might have been down to driver error on the track.'

Lexi didn't think she was going to make any headway with Flannery. She stared up at the photos on the wall behind, trying to think of a way to convince him of what she believed to have happened. The pictures showed various race teams, posed on and around the bonnets of various styles of race cars. There were drivers holding up trophies or bottles of champagne, managers and mechanics, and the obligatory sprinkling of pretty girls in tight clothing. Johnny Lycett-Boyd featured in more than a few of them, as did Stephen Flannery and the mechanics she and Tom had spoken to on their last visit.

But there was another face she recognised.

'That's Liam Norris, isn't it?'

He looked younger, his hair was shorter, but there was no mistaking Bethany Glover's boyfriend in a set of Shepherd Hill mechanic's overalls.

Flannery turned around to look at the picture she was pointing at.

'Yes, that's Norris. What of it?'

'Does he still work here?'

'No. Johnny sacked him, couple of years back.'

When Johnny had told her Norris had once worked for him, she'd assumed it had been at the vineyard – and the assumption had been wrong.

'When did you last see him?'

Flannery shrugged. 'Not for months.'

'Do you mind if we look over the video footage for the morning of the crash again?'

It seemed he did mind. 'I sent it to you already.'

'Yes, but I'd like to take another quick look now.'

He grudgingly opened up his laptop and logged into the track's security system.

'Which camera did you want to check?'

'The one facing the mechanics' bays, showing Johnny's Porsche.'

He loaded the appropriate footage.

Lexi watched, hardly daring to breathe. But she was wrong. There were only the current mechanics who worked at the track. No sign of Liam Norris.

'What about trackside?' she said. She was grasping at straws now and she knew it.

Until she saw him.

'Look, there – that's him, isn't it?'

Liam Norris, in deep conversation with one of the other mechanics at the side of the track. And in the background, Johnny Lycett-Boyd driving past in his Porsche, making his fateful last journey.

Back in the Crossfire, she quickly called Kevin Malthouse.

'Were you able to lift any prints from the working parts of the car besides the regular mechanics and Johnny's own?'

'We were – we got several partials from a greasy area underneath the wheel arch. We think it's where someone might place their hand if they were adjusting the spring rates.'

'Have you run them through the police database to find a match?'

'Not yet – we've just ruled them out against Johnny and his own mechanics.'

'Okay. I've got a suggestion. See if they match a man called Liam Norris. His prints are on the database already.'

'I'll let you know if we get a hit.'

'Thanks.'

Liam Norris. He had the means – he'd worked at the track as mechanic. He had the motive – if he'd found out that Scarlett wasn't his daughter, but was Johnny Lycett-Boyd's. And he had the opportunity – he was present at the track when Johnny crashed.

But did that put him in the frame for Bethany and Karolyn?

He supposedly had an alibi for when Bethany had died. But Lexi couldn't categorically rule him out yet...

Walking from the car park to the back door of the police station, Lexi heard someone calling out her name.

'Lexi!'

She turned in the direction of the shout and saw Luke Evans hovering by the gate. Changing course, she gave him a wave.

'Hi, Luke.' A brief embrace and a swift kiss on the lips felt entirely natural.

'Sorry, I know this looks like I'm stalking you,' he said with a grin, 'but I was just heading to your office and I saw your car going into the car park.'

'You were going to my office?'

'The guys at the gym told me what happened to you last night, and I wanted to drop off these.' He held up a small, rectangular Tupperware box. 'Home-baked protein brownies. I made a couple of batches last night – thought they might make you feel better.'

'Wow – thank you, they look delicious.' She took the box from him, her mouth watering.

'When do you knock off? I wondered if I could cook you dinner this evening.'

It was a Saturday, so in theory she shouldn't be working at all. But things were coming together and she didn't want to lose the momentum. 'I'm not sure, Luke,' she said. 'I've reached a critical point in the case.'

He looked disappointed, but then hid it with a smile. 'No worries. We can catch up once you've got more free time.'

'That would be nice.' And she meant it.

An evening with a friend. A nice normal thing to do. Wonders never ceased.

FIFTY

If it wasn't death by a thousand cuts, it was certainly agony by a thousand cuts. Every time Lexi shifted in her chair, little darts of pain reminded her of skidding across the floor on broken glass. She took a couple of painkillers, hoping they would dampen the pain and stop the loop that kept replaying in her brain.

A knock on the door made her jump. After what had happened, she felt totally on edge.

'Who is it?'

The door opened and Ridhi appeared. She stared at Lexi from the doorway.

'Are you okay, boss?'

'I've had better days, it has to be said.' Judging by Ridhi's expression, she must look as bad as she felt.

'Got a couple of things for you.' Ridhi came in and took the chair opposite the desk. 'First, I just talked to a DS in the Maidstone MIT. Apparently, they had a case a couple of years back in which Gideon Croft appeared. Proposed a link between the murder and some folklore nonsense. Had them going for a bit, until they found the real killer and worked out that everything Croft said was jackshit.'

'No surprise there,' said Lexi.

'I also checked out his story about the angel. It seems clear that he invented that. Just your run-of-the-mill fantasist wanting to get involved.'

'Good work. Let's not waste any more time on him. Anything else?'

Ridhi held up a thumb drive. 'It's a list of club members who were signed in while you were swimming.'

'Thanks.'

When Ridhi had gone, Lexi scanned the thumb drive. None of the names were familiar, either from the current case or cases she'd dealt with in the past. It didn't surprise her. No one who was out to harm her was going to check into the club and leave such an obvious trail. To use a false name, someone would have had to have joined the club using false ID – and that seemed unlikely, given that her visit had been spontaneous. However, they could have borrowed or stolen an existing member's ID card. All you had to do was swipe it through a turnstile, and the person on reception was usually busy talking to someone or on the phone – not scanning people to check that they matched their ID photo.

Or perhaps whoever did it could have come in another way – broken in maybe? The CSIs would look out for anything like that.

Tom put his head around her door. 'You wanted to brainstorm?'

'Come in – oh, you've brought coffee. What a hero.' She pulled the flash drive out of her laptop. 'We need to get a fix on our killer. To my mind, he's all over the place, in terms of MO and signature. Are we looking at one killer for all three murders, or two different people with different motives and motivations? I'm starting to think the latter.'

'And does the person who attacked you have anything to do with it?'

'I think that has to be the case. I've got Ridhi and Colin checking Steadman's, Norris's and Ben Lycett-Boyd's alibis for the time I was in the sauna, and for the unsolved historic case. So far, apparently, both Steadman and Lycett-Boyd were in the country, not in Australia then. No fix on Norris's whereabouts yet, but he wasn't in prison or out of the country when it happened, so he's still a possibility.'

'When exactly was it?'

She pulled up the file she'd printed out. 'Just over two years ago – August 2021.'

'That's a long gap to now.'

'Sure, but he might have killed in between, somewhere else. I've asked one of the civilian researchers to look for murdered women with children at the scene – although it's dangerous to assume there's always a child.'

Lexi's stomach rumbled. It was late afternoon, and as usual she'd been too focused on work to think about food. Then she remembered the box of brownies that Luke had brought her. It gave her a warm feeling that he'd done that. She grabbed the box from the bottom drawer of her desk and opened it. They smelled so good.

'Brownie?' she said to Tom, offering him the box.

He shook his head and patted his stomach. 'Declan has banned me from eating cake.'

'Seriously?' She helped herself to one of the brownies. 'Sounds a bit mean. But all the more for me then.'

Tom laughed.

She finished the little square of chocolate heaven and got back to business. 'I think our killer has abandonment issues.' She held up one hand. 'I know – it sounds like a cliché, but leaving the child at the murder scene is making a point. A very deliberate point. It's definitely pre-meditated, because he has the wings for them. So what's he saying? The babies are angels, the mothers are fallen angels? Bad mothers?'

Tom cut in. 'He takes the bad mothers to save the babies. Could this stem from a belief that his own mother was bad?'

'He leaves the babies, trusting that society's safety net will catch them.'

'Like it caught him? When his own mother was taken?'

They were talking over each other now.

Lexi opened up HOLMES 2 and typed words into the search bar.

'What are you looking for?' said Tom.

'Murdered mothers with infants, but going further back. I think our killer's maybe recreating the past.' She shrugged. 'It's what they do, isn't it? He's an adult now, so a dead woman with a child from twenty to forty years ago.'

She scanned the results quickly – there weren't exactly many of them once she'd filtered out the solved cases. Most of them related to domestic violence cases with an identifiable killer. Of those left, a black-and-white photo stopped her in her tracks. It was dated 1991, location Levenshulme, Manchester, according to the tag. A woman's naked, bloody body lying on a crumpled bed, her head hanging off the edge, long hair sweeping the floor. A nearly naked toddler sitting beside the bed, craning its neck over its shoulder to look squarely at the person taking the photograph, mouth open in a ferocious howl, holding up two tiny hands covered in blood.

She felt suddenly sick, and twisted the laptop so Tom could see the image.

'Find out what happened to that baby. Try Manchester social services.'

Tom frowned. 'Boss, it's a long shot. Where's the connection?'

She scanned the text accompanying the image. 'They reckon the child had been sitting by the body for nearly twenty-four hours by the time they were discovered. When young kids see the death of a parent, they very often wipe it from their memory. It's the brain's way of protecting itself. But if the memory resurfaces, the trauma can be acute. What this baby experienced looks intense. I can't believe that something that horrific wouldn't resurface. And the consequences of something like that could be...' She didn't need to finish the sentence.

'Does it say what happened to the kid?'

'Baby D, as he was named to preserve his anonymity, was taken into care, and no other family members were found. Eventually he was adopted by a family who quickly moved out of the area.'

'Didn't you tell me Steadman was adopted?'

'Yes, I did. But Norris also came through the care system. I don't know what his background was, or how old he was when he was taken in by the state.' She would have to ask him. She looked at the date on the picture. 1991. 'This baby will be thirty-five now. Just like Norris. Just like Steadman.'

'And Ben Lycett-Boyd?'

'He wasn't adopted, and he looks incredibly like Johnny, so I think that rules him out for now.' But the others... could Steadman or Norris be Baby D? They needed to find out urgently.

Her phone rang. She looked at the screen. It was the man they'd just been talking about.

Will Steadman's voice sounded panicked. 'One of the pickers, Irina – we can't find her.'

'When was she last seen?' Lexi glanced at her watch – it was gone five.

'I don't know. I think she was around when we brought in the last of the grapes. That was at lunchtime.'

'And since then?'

'The harvest is done. The pickers are having a barbecue to

celebrate. But Irina's friends say they can't find her anywhere. She isn't answering her phone. They're scared for her.'

'How old is she?'

'I have no idea.'

'Over eighteen?'

There was a pause. 'Yes... I think definitely over eighteen.'

So not a minor. Lexi took a deep breath. 'Stay calm, keep them calm. Start a search of the property. And ask her friends if she was seeing anyone, or if there's anywhere she might have gone once she finished work.'

'She doesn't know anyone here – she's one of the seasonal workers.' He sounded exasperated. 'What about you? Won't you do anything?'

'She's an adult, and she's only been missing a few hours. Usually we don't open a missing person report until someone's been gone for longer – but given recent events... I'll come over, but if she turns up in the meantime, please let me know.'

She briefed Tom and grabbed her bag. The last thing they needed was another woman to turn up dead at Elvington. 'Can you send some PCs over to help search for her? And in the meantime, put one of the researchers on finding out who that Baby D grew up to be.'

As she drove to Elvington, another thought crossed her mind and she called Will Steadman back. 'She doesn't have a child with her, does she?'

'No. You couldn't do the grape harvest with a child in tow.'

That at least was something. But if the killer's urge to kill was growing stronger, he might not be able to wait until he found a woman with a baby.

Pulling into the vineyard's car park, Lexi realised she'd driven the whole way on autopilot. She had no memory of the journey – it was a route that was becoming so familiar it seemed like she could drive it with her eyes closed. Something that told her she needed to get this case solved and off her desk before there was another dead body.

She left the car and walked up to the visitor centre, where she found Steadman in his office, in deep conversation with Mathéo Martin and a couple of the other seasonal workers. He was trying to persuade them to form teams to search for the missing girl, but it appeared that Martin was resistant.

'She's probably gone off with one of the guys,' he said. 'My workers have been picking non-stop for a couple of weeks. They need a break. They need their time off.'

One of the other workers chipped in. 'Irina's a big girl – she can look after herself.'

'Come on, guys,' said Lexi, and they all turned to look at her. 'It won't take long if everyone joins in. I'm sure you'll find her quickly and then everyone can get back to the party.'

'Inspector Bennett, thank you for coming,' said Will Steadman, no doubt using her title as a way of persuading the others to get on board.

Grumbling, the seasonal workers left to round up some searchers.

'I need a coffee,' said Steadman, getting up.

'I need to ask you a few questions.'

He ignored her and left the office, reappearing a moment later with two small cups of black coffee. Lexi took one gratefully, despite her annoyance. The bitter liquid scalded her throat.

'What can you tell me about the missing girl?' she said.

'Only what I said on the phone. Her name's Irina Fischer, she's Romanian. That's really all I know.'

'You weren't sleeping with her then?'

What? Where the hell had that come from?

Steadman's face told her she'd spoken out of turn, and he was right. She'd surprised herself. She might think these things, but it was very rare for her to let her mouth run away like that.

'Of course not.'

'Where have you been since the girl went missing?'

'You can't be serious, Inspector Bennett?' He was angry now. 'I've been in the winery all day, right up until Mathéo came to me and said Irina's friends were worried about her. Just because the grapes are in, it doesn't mean my work is over. Far from it, in fact.'

'And there are witnesses who can vouch for that?'

'Yes, there are witnesses. I have a whole crew working in there with me.'

'Fine. I'm sorry, but I have to establish where everyone was when she went missing.'

He wasn't mollified. 'I need to get back to work.'

'One more thing.'

He frowned at her.

'You told me you were adopted. Can you tell me where you were born?'

'What's this to do with?'

'Please, just answer the question.'

He threw up both hands, showing his frustration. 'Somewhere up north. I don't remember the name. I need to go.'

She wasn't going to get any useful information out of him now, but no doubt they'd be able to dig up his social services records.

'I need to talk to Irina's friends. Where are they?'

He shrugged. 'I expect they're back with the rest of the seasonal workers, at the barbecue in the camping field.'

As he strode off, Lexi looked around, scanning the vineyards and peering down into the valley below. Where could the missing girl be? Long, straight rows of vines stretched away, as far as the eye could see. Not a soul to be seen now that the picking teams had finished their work. The geometric patchwork they formed was almost hypnotic, the straight lines undulating as the ground rose and fell, becoming sweeping curves, lines that swooped...

What the hell?

The rigid rows of vines had become twisting sinews, flowing down the hillside in ripples, creating formations which dissolved and reformed into twirling, spinning patterns in front of her eyes under a sky that went from blue to violet to lilac to white, waves of colour that made no sense.

The air was hot and heavy, her head was spinning.

There was something terribly, horribly wrong.

FIFTY-ONE

Tom worked the phone while researching on the laptop. Multitasking was a thing he particularly despised but he needed to get a team of uniforms organised to search the vineyard, as well as follow up on the boss's frankly crazy hunch that a blood-spattered baby in Manchester from thirty-two years ago might have something to do with their case.

Another call incoming.

'DS Olsen,' he said, not bothering to look at the screen to see who it was.

'Tom, it's Emily.'

'Emily, hi. Please tell me you've got something for us.'

'I have got something, and I think it'll make a huge difference. We managed to retrieve a couple of finger marks from the rear wheel arches of Johnny's car and we've got a match.'

'And?' Why did people always pause just before they were about to tell you something big?

'They belonged to Liam Norris.'

'Jesus – that is big. That pretty much implicates him in tampering with the car, doesn't it?'

'It's where you'd expect to find prints from someone

adjusting the spring rates – but you need to bear in mind we can't date them.'

'How long would you expect them to last?'

'Motor oil is designed to maintain its integrity in a wide range of conditions. That means the prints might last far longer than one would normally expect. If it becomes important to the case, we could run some comparison tests.'

'We might need that,' said Tom. He knew from Lexi that Norris had worked up at the track in the past, but they also had video footage placing him there on the day. 'It's circumstantial, which won't on its own prove much, but it all builds the case up into something that might stick, so thanks for that.'

'No problem. I'll get back to you if we find any more.'

He disconnected. He needed to speak to Lexi. He dialled and she picked up straight away.

'Uniforms should be with you shortly – can you direct them once they arrive?'

'Amazing.'

'And Emily called. They got prints off the Porsche, rear wheel arch, which matched Liam Norris. It really puts him in the frame for the sabotage.'

'Amazing.' Lexi's voice sounded a little distant, as if her attention was caught by something else.

'Lexi? Did you hear what I said?'

'Yes. What? Sorry, can you say again?'

Tom recounted the call he'd just had with Emily.

'Okay, let's bring Norris in for questioning. Can you go pick him up, Tom, while I run things here?'

'Of course.'

'Amazing.'

'Also, Baby D – he was placed with foster parents while they searched for other relatives. Then a year later he was put up for adoption and was placed with a family fairly quickly.'

'Great. Could you track him further?'

'He ended up in south London somewhere – Lewisham or thereabouts. Are you okay? You sound a bit...'

'I'm fine. Actually, I think I'm a bit dehydrated. I'm just on my way to find some water.'

'You sure?'

'I'm fine, Tom. Bring Norris in. Let's see if we can make some progress.'

Tom hung up. She definitely didn't sound well, but he wasn't surprised. She'd done the Ironman less than a week ago and since then there'd been the incident in the sauna. She needed to learn to take time off, not push herself so hard.

He reminded himself of Norris's address and went down to his car. They'd all be due a few days break once this case was sorted. Maybe he'd head somewhere warm and sunny with Declan and Billie.

The bungalow that Liam Norris had shared with Bethany Glover and Scarlett looked much the same as when he'd visited it with Lexi the weekend before, although the flattened boxes by the recycling bin now bore the logos of beer companies rather than nappies and baby milk.

A lot had changed in a week.

Tom walked up to the front door slowly, taking time to peer in through the sitting room window and to look down the pathway that ran down one side of the house. No signs of life.

He pushed his index finger on the doorbell and heard it ring inside.

No sounds from within, so he rang again. And waited.

After a couple of minutes, he gave up and went around the side of the bungalow along the path to the back. The garden was unkempt and the grass needed mowing, apart from where it had been scuffed away underneath a low-hanging baby swing.

There was a narrow patio at the back of the house, and a back door that needed repainting. He went up to the window and squinted into the kitchen. It was untidy – he would have been surprised if it wasn't – and the remains of someone's breakfast was still on the small table. Liam Norris didn't eat his toast crusts.

Had he scarpered? Tom thought about what Emily had told him. What if Norris had tampered with Johnny's car? He'd been furious to learn that Scarlett was actually Johnny's daughter – that anger could have driven him to do something stupid. And if he hadn't meant for Johnny to die, he might now be panicking. On the run from a potential murder charge.

'He's not in, love.'

Tom looked round in the direction of a woman's voice.

An elderly woman in a canvas sunhat was standing in the next-door garden. She had a pair of secateurs in one hand, but she was far more interested in Tom than her rose bushes. Tom walked over to the low fence that separated the properties.

'I'm looking for Liam Norris. Do you know where he is?'

'And who are you when you're at home?'

'DS Olsen, Kent Police.'

'Is this about poor Bethany? She was such a kind girl. Tell me, what's happened to baby Scarlett?'

'She's being looked after.' Tom didn't want to get side-tracked. 'Liam – do you know where he is?'

The woman pursed her lips into a look of disapproval. 'Went off about ten minutes ago – that way.' She pointed out over the fields that the back gardens abutted.

'That way? Literally, or drove off in that direction?'

'Walking. There's a path along the edge of the fields.' She waved her hand.

'Where would he be going?' Walking didn't sound like someone fleeing the police.

The woman gave him a sharp look. 'I'm not his bleedin' mother. I wouldn't know.'

'I mean, where does the path go?'

'Up the valley. Then it depends if you stay on the path or go off where it meets the road.'

Tom peered across the fields. They sloped gently upwards. He hadn't seen Norris's car outside the house, so perhaps it was parked somewhere else and he was going to get it.

'That's the direction of the vineyard, isn't it?'

'Like I said, depending on which path you take. But, yes, you would go that way to get to Elvington.'

The woman turned her attention back to her pruning.

Could that have been the route Bethany and Scarlett took on the night Bethany died? Perhaps Liam was going up to the vineyard for an assignation with the missing girl. Or perhaps he'd seen Tom's Jeep approaching and had scarpered. No, he must have been gone before that or he'd still be in sight in the distance.

At the back of the garden, there was a dry-stone wall, no gate, but the wall wasn't high. In a split-second decision, Tom scaled it and set off at a jog along the side of the field. Norris was ten minutes ahead of him, but probably wasn't running, so maybe he could catch up. Of course, it might have been easier to go back to the car and drive around by the roads, but that meant he'd have to make an assumption about where Norris was going. This way, hopefully, he'd get a sight of him somewhere ahead.

The ground was uneven and stony – it wasn't a proper path – and Tom wasn't wearing suitable shoes. But he had a gut feeling that something was going to give. Something that could break the case wide open. And if Norris was on his way to meet the missing girl, he might be the only one who could prevent another murder.

FIFTY-TWO

Lexi stared at the phone in her hand. Had she just spoken to Tom? She couldn't remember a word of what had been said.

Her mouth was dry. She needed water. She needed to get out of the sauna. She looked around. No, she wasn't in the sauna – she was at Elvington, standing at the edge of the car park, with a field of vines stretching out below her. But she felt so hot, and her heart was racing. She wasn't making sense of what she was seeing and hearing.

She was dehydrated. After what had happened in the sauna, the doctor at A&E had told her to rest for a couple of days and drink plenty of water. She'd done neither, just ploughed on with the case. Of course she had. Women were dying and children were being orphaned. She couldn't lie around in bed all day and hope that the killer would wait for her to recover before carrying on his grisly work.

Now there was another woman missing. She had to pull herself together.

She blinked and stared. The rows of vines in front of her were sliding down the hill, moving smoothly and swiftly in neat, ordered lines. The leaves shimmered and changed hue, then liquified and dripped from the branches.

'No.' She looked away and looked back. It was still happening. 'No way.'

What was still happening?

This wasn't dehydration, or at least not dehydration as she knew it. It must be far more severe than she realised. And having a black coffee wouldn't exactly have helped. There was a bottle of water in her car. She would drink that and then go in search of some more.

She turned round but all the cars in the car park looked the same. Same make, same model, same colour, same year. Where was the Crossfire?

Oh God, this isn't dehydration. I'm hallucinating. I've been drugged.

She tried to catch hold of the small glimmer of lucidity. Somehow, she'd ingested something hallucinogenic. She had no experience with hallucinogens, so she had no idea what it might be or how long these hideous effects would last.

Water.

Water should help, but she was miles from the pool and she shouldn't drive. No, water to drink, not to swim in.

Her thoughts weren't making any sense.

I need help.

Another flash of lucidity, but help from where, from who?

She stared at her phone. All the apps had changed and were revolving around the screen. She had to call Tom, but she couldn't work out which of the candy-coloured icons to press, and if she could, they kept swapping places, making it impossible for her to track the one she wanted.

She closed her eyes and took a deep breath. She wasn't going to panic. She opened her eyes and the sky was much darker, almost purple.

Stay calm. Close your eyes.

Where was Tom?

Where was she? She looked around. She wasn't in the car park anymore. She was out in the middle of a field of swaying, multi-coloured vines.

'Help! Somebody help me...' But it only came out as a whisper. There was no one here, no one close by. Had she been here for seconds? Or maybe days? She tried not to panic.

Her phone, already clutched in her hand, rung. Instinct kicked in. Muscle memory in her fingers answered it.

'Boss? Where are you?' She knew the voice. She knew this person. 'Boss? It's Ridhi. What's going on?'

'Ridhi.' Her voice sounded deeper, distorted – she was speaking in slow motion. She tried again. 'Ridhi.'

'Is something wrong?'

'Yes, something is wrong.' She knew she wasn't making sense. She bit hard on the inside of her cheek, hoping the pain would sharpen her focus. After what seemed like an eternity, she managed to speak. 'I've been drugged.'

She heard Ridhi's sharp intake of breath at the other end of the line. 'Where are you?'

She looked around. She was clueless.

'Are you at the vineyard?'

Yes, that was it. 'Yes.'

'Do you know what drug you took?'

She giggled as the answer mushroomed in front of her eyes. 'Shrooms.'

Ridhi didn't appear to find this funny. 'Who gave them to you?'

'Coffee.'

'Stay where you are. I'm going to call for help.'

'Help, yes, I think I need help.'

'I'll get someone to you, and I'll look up antidotes and call you back.'

The phone went silent and she dropped it on the ground. It was no use to her if she couldn't talk.

He hadn't even told her where he was or what he was doing. She was supposed to be the one in charge. What was she even doing here? She couldn't hold a coherent thought in her head and was constantly distracted by the ebb and flow of shapes and colours that seemed to impose themselves on everything she looked at.

She spun around slowly, trying to find an anchor.

The car park came into her range of vision. Now she could see the Crossfire. A Crossfire, anyway. It wasn't blue, so it wasn't hers. But maybe it would be by the time she got to it. Something glinted on the ground in front of her and she bent down to look closer. Someone had dropped their phone. Must belong to one of the pickers. She picked it up and shoved into the pocket where she usually kept hers.

Her feet crunched noisily on the stony ground, echoing behind her as if she was being followed by an army. She looked over her shoulder to check. She wasn't – it was just her and an army of vines. If she could make it to the car park, and if she could find her key, then she would have access to water.

She walked and walked and the car park seemed ever further ahead of her, never getting nearer. The sun grew hotter. The land became a desert, the glinting cobalt blue of her car a mirage, shimmering in the heat. Her mouth was dry, tongue like parchment, but her body was wet with sweat. The hill seemed steeper and steeper, a vertiginous drop falling away behind her, her feet slipping and sliding on the gravelly surface. She felt exhausted, every ounce of energy drained with the effort, and still she didn't get there.

But finally she did. And what seemed like hours later, she found her car key in her pocket. The first car she tried to open wasn't the Crossfire. Nor the second. But, eventually, by a process of elimination she came to a car that did open, and there was the bottle of water, lying on the passenger seat like a lottery win. She'd never been so grateful to see anything ever in her life.

She snatched it up, not caring that the water inside the bottle was blue, no, pink, no, green. It was water and she drank it down, hard and fast, finishing the bottle in one long draft. She leaned back on the bonnet, savouring the cool relief. She closed her eyes to escape from the visions, but that just replaced the psychedelic vineyard with swirling patterns on the inside of her eyelids. When would it ever end?

Opening her eyes again, she could see the path that led up to the winery. A man and a woman were walking up the slope. She studied their backs, wondering who they were and then realised – that was Marietta, her long black hair in a thick plait. Or was it? The man by her side was Luke. Wait, what? Luke Evans, here? Then she remembered. Luke was Marietta's physio, too. She blinked. She'd been wrong. That wasn't Marietta at all. It was Bethany. With Liam Norris. Only that couldn't be...

She started up the path to follow them, realising that the woman was actually Karolyn. Will Steadman turned to look back at her. But his face morphed into Luke, then Liam, then Johnny, then Ben. The girl was a stranger. The girl that was missing?

The couple disappeared into the winery and Lexi wondered if she'd seen them at all.

FIFTY-THREE

The water had helped. It didn't stop the hallucinations, but Lexi definitely felt better. She tried to conjure up what she'd just seen – who it was that had been walking up to the winery, but she still felt confused. Had Will Steadman drugged the coffee to give himself time for a getaway?

Whatever his motives, it had taken effect quickly, but from what she could remember it would only wear off slowly. Just when she needed her wits about her, her brain was addled and she couldn't trust her own eyes. Perhaps that was motive enough.

Taking a deep breath, she looked at her phone screen. It was still a blur of moving colour. She narrowed her eyes and focused hard. The apps fell back into their normal places, still shimmering, but a second later they were all over the place again. It started to ring and she almost dropped it.

'Yes?'

'Boss?' It was Ridhi. 'I've looked up psilocybin poisoning. Do you know how much you took?'

'Will Steadman gave me a coffee. No idea of the dose.'

'How are you feeling?'

'Not great. It's been... weird.' She paused. 'Is weird,' she added, watching the sky turn into a vast rippling rainbow.

'Hang on, I've got some stuff about it.'

Lexi heard the tapping of her keyboard and waited. On the brow of the hill beyond the visitor centre she watched the branches of a row of tall beech trees merging and separating in spiral patterns.

'It's not that helpful,' said Ridhi's voice in her ear. 'The best I can find is that the person should be given sedatives to make them less anxious...'

'Not going to happen. I need a clear head.' Though currently she had anything but.

'Well, it's either that or a zen-like suggestion to surrender to the experience. You know, embrace the flow, man.'

'For the love of God, is that it?'

'That's about it.'

'Damn. How long till it wears off?'

More tapping on the keyboard. 'Six to eight hours.'

'What time is it?' What time had she drunk that bloody coffee?

'Ten to seven.'

'In the morning?' No, of course it wasn't.

'Um... no. It's the evening.'

'But I got here at about six-ish.' It seemed like she'd been tripping for days. Nothing made sense. Nothing apart from the absolute fury she felt at Steadman. Maybe she could use her anger to help her focus.

'You've been there less than an hour.'

Lexi shook her head. 'Sorry, Ridhi. This stuff is really messing with my head.'

'You're at Elvington?'

'Yes.'

'Do you want me to come out there?'

'Yes, and bring backup.'

'Sit tight. I'll be with you shortly.'

'Can you bring some water?'

'Absolutely.'

Lexi disconnected the call and looked around. Down here by the visitor centre, things seemed quiet, though she could hear the distant blare of music coming from the field above the barn where the seasonal workers stayed. She remembered they were having a barbecue to celebrate the end of the harvest.

She looked up towards the winery and thought about what she'd seen, presumably just a few minutes before. She'd been muddled as to who she saw walking up the drive, but now she felt she had more of a grip on things. Applying logic, it must have been Marietta and Will. With Johnny gone, it would have been a lot easier for them to pursue their affair – if the revelation about Will sleeping with Karolyn hadn't derailed it. And though the pickers could relax now all the grapes were in, work in the winery would still be ongoing, with Will and Marietta overseeing it.

She needed to get Steadman into custody fast, before he got away or killed again. She glanced at the sky – intense turquoise with a few ripples, but at least it wasn't a rainbow anymore. Maybe the effects of the psilocybin were beginning to recede.

He'd incapacitated her, so what was his intention now? Who was next on his list?

And suddenly it was as clear as day.

'Marietta!' she yelled.

She ran up the slope towards the hulking production facility. It loomed above her and, as she came closer, the green painted corrugated steel walls took on the texture of moss. If she reached out to touch them, would they feel soft? She blinked and they returned to normal, but the structure seemed bigger than ever. But getting further away with each step. The tricks in her perception were making her feel nauseous. She desperately wanted it to stop.

After what seemed like an epic run, she reached for the door. It wasn't locked, so she stepped inside. Her eyes were immediately assaulted by the glare of the lights. Were they shining right at her? They weren't. She realised she was hypersensitive to every stimulus. Neon colours ran down the sides of the stainless-steel fermentation tanks and the sound of the grape presses was louder than thunder. A man's shout from somewhere on the floors above made her jump, every muscle in her body pulled tight.

Breathe. Stay calm.

But that simple thought flooded her with anxiety. Panic swelled in her chest. She should wait for Ridhi, and where was Tom?

She stepped outside and leaned with her back against the door, panting.

Get a grip.

She slowed her breathing enough to slow down her heart rate. She felt calmer. She let some time pass.

Going back inside, she drew on all her strength of will to ignore the colours and the lights. She looked around. There was no one down here. The work was being carried out on the upper floors. She walked slowly through the hanger-sized room. At the end, the door leading down to the cellars was open.

She stood in the doorway, at the top of the stairs, listening.

Voices.

A man and a woman.

Familiar voices.

The woman had a French accent. Marietta.

The man's voice had a distinctive south London twang. It wasn't Will Steadman's voice, but it was familiar. She listened for a bit longer, but she couldn't quite make out the words.

But then the voices were drowned out by a sound that made her blood run cold.

A baby howling. Not just crying for its mother, but terrified or in pain.

She started running down the stairs, pausing at the gate at the bottom as she heard Marietta's voice.

'Aurora!'

There was the sound of footsteps on the stone floor. Marietta running towards her child? Lexie peered around the corner just in time to see Marietta disappearing through the gap from the larger cellar into the smaller one.

Who was she with?

'Aurora!' There was a sharp yowl, then the baby's cries became less agonised. Her mother was here.

Lexi strained to hear what was going on.

'What is Aurora doing down here?' Marietta's voice was laced with fear – probably because she knew as well as Lexi did what the implications were.

'I thought you might want to say goodbye to her.'

Lexi recognised the voice and a tangle of information began to unravel.

His accent – distinctively south London.

The baby from Manchester with blood on his hands, who'd grown up somewhere in Lewisham.

The woman who'd died from a fentanyl overdose with her baby beside her. In Bromley.

The physio who had staff access to come and go at the health club.

The chocolate brownies, laced with psilocybin.

A man stepped into view from behind a row of crates.

Luke Evans.

FIFTY-FOUR

Tom ran through the vines as if his life depended upon it. Only it wasn't his life that was at stake. There was a girl missing from the vineyard and the man he believed to be the killer of the previous missing girls was making his way there now. Did he have an arrangement to meet Irina somewhere on Elvington's grounds? Would she become the third girl to die? He couldn't let that happen.

He was running uphill, towards the centre of the vineyard, in the direction of the pergola where Karolyn Small's body had been found. As the slope got steeper, he began to pant, cursing himself for not keeping up his fitness regime. Being a dad cut into the time he had for the gym and he was carrying almost half a stone around his middle that shouldn't be there. But he had no choice. He had to catch up with Liam Norris before he could spirit Irina away. To the caves? Or somewhere else? It would need to be somewhere out of sight if he was going to act in broad daylight.

Now he could see the top of the wrought-iron pergola, bobbing above the rows of vines ahead of him as he ran. He went faster, giving his everything to get there in time. As he got closer, he heard voices, a woman laughing. Thank God, his hunch had paid off and he'd come to the right place. He slowed down, so they wouldn't hear his approaching footsteps, and he crouched low as he moved forward, so they wouldn't see his head over the vines. That was no guarantee that they wouldn't see him – the vines at Elvington were well pruned and tidy, and now that the harvest was over, the man and woman at the pergola might easily see a flicker of movement. He just had to hope that their attention was on each other so he could get close enough.

Close enough for what? He needed a strategy. Hopefully, his appearance would put paid to the plans Norris had for Irina, but then what? He wondered if he had grounds for an arrest and, if he did, whether it would be wise to attempt that without backup. Norris was a burly individual and not afraid of using his fists. At least they knew he wasn't averse to being violent towards women – Bethany's injuries were testament to that. But would he fight if Tom attempted to detain him?

There wasn't time to wait.

He paused, just two rows of vines from the pergola. Between the ironwork, he could see the figures of a man and a woman. The man he recognised as Norris, in tight jeans, a dark T-shirt and trainers. The woman was pale and slender, ash-blonde hair falling to her shoulders, dressed in a pale yellow sun dress and flat sandals. If not exactly pretty, there was a certain appeal to her features, and when she smiled at something Norris said, her face became radiant. He was pulling a blanket out of a backpack and spreading it out on the ground. When it was done, he gestured for the woman to sit on it.

As she dropped to her knees and sank sideways into a sitting position, Tom stepped forward.

'Are you Irina Fischer?'

The woman looked surprised, but she nodded. 'Yes, that's me.' She spoke with a strong Eastern European accent.

'What do you want?' said Norris. From the hostility he attached to the word 'you', he clearly remembered that Tom was with the police.

'Irina, come over here.'

Irina frowned and Norris's body language signalled aggression – his head jutted forward, and his fists curled at his sides.

'Why?' said Irina. She stood up, but she made no move to go to Tom.

Tom's hand went to his hip, where he had a pair of cuffs in his pocket. 'Liam Norris, I'm arresting you for the murder of John Lycett-Boyd. You do not have to say anything...'

Norris lunged at him, but Tom dodged to one side. 'Come on, mate, don't make it worse for yourself.'

Norris took a deep breath and stood still. Irina was looking from one to the other of them, her eyes wide. 'What did you do?' she said to Norris.

'Nothing. It's rubbish.'

'Irina, we have reason to believe that Liam was responsible for the deaths of two women here, Bethany Glover and Karolyn Small. By coming here to meet him, you put yourself in danger.'

Irina Fischer rolled her eyes with an exaggerated movement of her head. 'No way. I can judge character. Liam is a good man.'

'He beat up his girlfriend, Bethany, then killed her.'

'I never killed her,' said Liam, taking a step back. 'I loved her.' But he didn't deny the beating.

Tom inched forward. He guessed Liam was about to make a break for it.

'And you killed Karolyn Small.'

'No.' His eyes flashed from side to side. He was looking for an escape route. The pergola had arched openings all around it. Liam dashed for the one that faced down the hill and started to run.

Tom sprinted after him, only too aware that he'd barely

recovered from running across the fields from the village. Norris was younger than him, probably fitter, so the chances were that he'd get away. But at least Irina was safe.

They pounded down the steep hill, Norris between one row of vines, Tom running in the next row over. Norris was fast and the gap between them was growing, but there was no way that Tom was giving up, despite the heaving of his lungs and the burn of lactic acid in his legs.

'Stop, Liam. Things will be... worse for... you if you run... You know we'll... get you... no matter what.' The words came out between great rasping breaths, so disjointed that they hardly made sense. Liam Norris wasn't listening anyway.

But luck was on Tom's side. With a yelp of pain, Liam was down on the ground. He must have tripped. Tom crashed through to the next row of vines, ducking his head to avoid the top wire that ran between them, and raising his feet to stop himself falling over the lower one. He almost stumbled as he emerged into Liam's row, but he managed to keep his balance and rapidly covered the ground between them.

Swearing loudly, Liam was struggling to his feet, but he was winded and he couldn't move quickly enough. Tom was upon him in a second and had the cuffs on him in ten. As he finished the caution, Irina hurried down towards them.

'Let him go.'

Tom looked over his shoulder and saw her barrelling towards him, fists flying. He shoved Norris down to his knees, then put up his hand, palms outwards, to fend off the furious woman.

'Irina, stop it.' He caught both her wrists and she hissed at him. 'I can arrest you too, if I have to, but there's no reason for you to get caught up in this.'

'This? You're arresting an innocent man.'

'You don't know him.' Tom let go of her wrists, and Irina

stepped back from him, sulky, with downturned lips and a jutting chin.

He grasped Norris's shoulder and pulled him to his feet. 'Come on.' He looked at the girl. 'I'll show you something, Irina – then you'll believe me.'

Running down the hill had only taken a couple of minutes. Climbing back up, pushing a recalcitrant Norris ahead of him, took longer, but ten minutes later they were back at the pergola. For safety's sake, Tom unlocked one side of the handcuffs, passed it behind one of the iron columns of the pergola, then snapped it back into place on Norris's wrist. He couldn't run now – he was locked to the pergola. Tom got out his phone and called for backup to transport him to the station for booking.

'You said you would show me something,' said Irina.

He quickly pulled on a pair of latex gloves and bent down to pick up Norris's backpack, which was still lying where he'd left it after unfurling the rug.

'It's my belief that Liam was going to give you magic mushrooms to eat, then force you to take an overdose of fentanyl, which is how Bethany and Karolyn died.'

Irina looked shocked, but said nothing as Tom methodically emptied the bag onto the rug. There was a bottle of white wine and three cans of beer. Two bags of crisps. A packet of supermarket sausage rolls. House keys. Car keys. Mobile. A variety box of miniature chocolate bars. A plastic pod containing Bluetooth earbuds.

No magic mushrooms.

No fentanyl.

No angel wings.

'Not found what you were expecting?' said Norris.

Tom ignored him and turned to Irina. 'Why did Liam invite you here?'

'He didn't,' said Irina. 'I invited him. I said, "Let's have a picnic, away from the others. Somewhere we can have a bit of privacy." He suggested here.'

Tom bit his top lip. His assumptions had been wrong. At least as far as Norris's intentions towards Irina were concerned. A few drinks, a quick shag, but there was nothing here to suggest he meant her any harm.

Did that let him off the hook for tampering with Johnny's car?

Tom didn't know. He would still take him in for questioning. They still had his print on the wheel arch of Johnny's Porsche.

But if Liam Norris wasn't responsible for the deaths of Bethany Glover and Karolyn Small, it meant someone else was. Someone at the vineyard.

Where Lexi was on her own, without backup.

He'd made a terrible mistake.

FIFTY-FIVE

Squatting down on the bottom step, Lexi's head spun as both cellars were plunged into darkness. She felt dizzy, as if she was swaying on the brink of a precipice. She took a deep breath and grabbed hold of the gate for support. She stood, feeling unsteady on her feet, unable to anchor herself visually in the dark, but she had no choice.

Why had she eaten that bloody brownie?

She stopped. She had to warn Ridhi – she'd left the box of brownies open on her desk. If anyone else helped themselves... She quickly sent Ridhi a text.

DO NOT EAT BROWNIES – DRUGGED

She hoped it made sense, and that Colin hadn't needed to pop into her office. There was no way that he wouldn't have helped himself if he'd seen them.

Momentarily distracted by her concern for her team, she needed to refocus on what was happening between Marietta and Luke. Their voices had become more distant. They must have moved through from the cellars into the cave. She tried the gate, but it was locked. Luke must have locked it behind them so he was free to do whatever he was planning.

Lexi knew what that was, even though she could hardly bear to think about it.

In her frustration, she slammed her fist against one of the metal bars. The gate rattled, the sound skittering through the cellars beyond, bouncing off the walls, magnifying and repeating.

Damn! Slow down. Think.

Her senses were still distorting everything – sound, vision, touch – perception gone haywire. Just because she'd heard the rattle like a clap of thunder didn't mean that anyone else had. She strained her ears in the silence that followed. There were no voices now, and no response to the noise she'd just made. The light in the far cellar was flickering and becoming more distant. She guessed it was the light of a torch, and that Luke and Marietta were in the caves beyond. In the cave where Bethany Glover had been found dead with Scarlett crying beside her.

An image flashed up in her mind. Bethany's dead body, but the face was Marietta's and the baby at her side was Aurora.

She couldn't let that happen.

She ran back up the stairs, choking down the feelings of shock and nausea that surged through her. If the gate to the cellars was locked, she knew another way into the caves and she had to get there before Luke Evans staged a repeat of what he'd done to Bethany.

He was the baby who'd been abandoned by his murdered mother. And now he was about to repeat history. The knowledge felt like ground glass paralysing her gut.

She emerged into the dazzling brightness of the fermentation hall and ran its length to the outside door. She had to shoulder her way past a couple of the winery employees. They shouted after her, but their words morphed into confetti on the

air. She burst out of the door and raced around the side of the
building.

Which way? Which way?

She ran along the lee of the wall, then stopped at the corner.
The vineyards stretched out from here in every direction – and
of course, they all looked the same. She cast her mind back to
the previous week, when they'd found the hidden entrance to
the caves. Catching her breath, she mapped out the subterranean spaces in her mind – the two large cellars, the caves
beyond, and how they lay in relation to the ground level. They
stretched beyond the footprint of the building in the direction
she was now facing.

She stared out over the vines. There was a narrow path
along the edge of the closest field, and where it met the field
beyond, she could just see a fluttering of blue crime scene tape,
a remnant from when the area had been cordoned off by the
CSIs searching for traces of the killer's entrance and exit from
the caves.

She ran along the path towards it.

This was the place. She remembered the small, bramble-
covered hillock that concealed the narrow entrance to the
natural tunnel. As she reached the spot, the twisting, tangled
stems became a nest of snakes, slithering over and around one
another, determined to impede her progress. Clamping her jaw
tight to push back against the sensation of panic sweeping
through her, she tugged at the canes with no thought for the
sharp thorns that tore at her hands and arms. She had to find the
way in before time ran out for Marietta.

Mindless of the blood dripping down her forearms, she
scrabbled through the brambles to the gaping black maw which
led to the caves. She dug her phone out of her pocket and
turned on its torch. The chalk walls at the entrance of the small
tunnel were green with moss, some of which rubbed off on her
clothing as she bent down and turned sideways to squeeze her

way inside. Fuelled by fear and adrenalin, she hurried forward, directing the beam of light onto the uneven floor so she could avoid tripping.

Although she'd scrambled through here once before, it seemed entirely unfamiliar, winding up and down, almost seeming to change direction before her very eyes. She rounded a corner and almost struck her head as the ceiling of the tunnel suddenly sloped down in front of her, leaving only a crawl hole for her to wriggle through. She dropped to her hands and knees as the space became tighter and tighter. Was she going the right way or had she branched off at some point without realising it? What if she got stuck down here? No one knew she was here and there was no way that there would be a phone signal so she could call for help.

Don't surrender to the fear. Marietta needs you. Aurora needs you.

It was so narrow now that she had to put down the phone in front of her and use both hands to lever herself between a small crevice in the chalk, but as she emerged into a wider area, she at least remembered having done exactly that before. She was going in the right direction, and it couldn't be much further.

When she came around the next bend, she saw a flickering light ahead of her. Candlelight in the smaller of the two caves? She quickly turned off her torch and proceeded as quietly as she could on her hands and knees.

A baby screamed.

'Put her down.' Marietta's voice was shrill with panic. 'Help!' It rose in volume as she called out. 'Can somebody hear me? Please, I need help.' This was followed by a string of French expletives and the sound of a struggle – feet moving on the gritty floor, the sound of a blow, a gasp from her, a grunt from him. Aurora screamed again.

Lexi rushed forward. She could see what was happening as the cave opened out ahead of her. She stopped dead in her tracks. She didn't want Luke to realise she was here. Flattening herself against one side of the tunnel, she peered around a jutting outcrop of chalk to watch.

Luke Evans was struggling with Marietta. It looked as if he was trying to tear her clothes off. Aurora was lying on the floor on her back, howling loudly as she struggled to turn herself over. Marietta was fighting back, clawing at Luke's face.

'Please, Luke, it doesn't have to be like this.' Marietta was gasping, hardly able to form the words. 'I don't want my daughter to see this. Let me take her out to the main cellar and then I'll come back. We don't need to fight.'

'We're not fighting. You're fighting,' said Luke. 'If you do as I say, everything will be fine.'

Don't believe him.

There was a scuffle and Aurora screamed again.

'Put her down!' Marietta was terrified.

'I won't hurt her, but you need to take off your clothes and put on the wings.'

'Why? Why are you doing this to us? Why must Aurora be here?'

'You know why, Marietta. So she can be the innocent angel to your guilty one.'

'*Merde!* You've gone mad. You killed those other girls, and now you kill me?'

There was the sound of a blow and Marietta yelped.

Then Luke said, 'Now shut up and eat this.'

Lexi's blood ran cold.

FIFTY-SIX

'Don't eat it!'

Lexi scrambled through the tiny mouth of the tunnel into the cave. The nearest candle guttered with the rush of air she brought with her. It went out, leaving just a single candle, high up on a ledge, hardly banishing the darkness, while creating even blacker shadows behind each figure.

Marietta, half dressed, her clothes in disarray, gasped as she looked round at Lexi, but Luke's reaction was instant. He grabbed the back of her head with one hand and rammed part of a brownie into her mouth with the other, clamping his hand over the lower half of her face to stop her spitting it out. Marietta started coughing, struggling to breathe, choking on the dry brownie shoved violently down her throat.

Lexi sprung forward and tried to tug Luke's arm away.

'Don't swallow it,' she said. 'It's laced with magic mushrooms.'

She couldn't tell if Marietta had understood what she said. The three of them locked in a struggle, pushing and pulling against one another as Lexi tried to free Marietta from Luke's grasp.

Luke took a step forward, shoving the two women up against the wall of the cave. Lexi's head went back and slammed against the chalk, sending shards of pain radiating through her skull. Marietta sank to her knees, but raised her arms to push Luke away as hard as she could. He stumbled to one side, treading on Aurora's outstretched leg. She let out a piercing scream.

Lexi blinked and snatched the baby up from the floor. 'Come on, get up,' she said to Marietta. They had to get out of here and raise the alarm.

But Marietta was still struggling to breathe, choking and vomiting at the same time.

Luke eyed the two women and the child in front of him. This was clearly more than he'd bargained for, and Lexi saw indecision in the way he blinked back and forth between them. She had to make a split-second decision. She could make a run for it with Aurora and save the baby for certain, leaving Marietta behind, or she could give Aurora to Marietta, pull her to her feet and push her out of the cave, while she stayed back to delay Luke as long as possible.

But then she remembered that the security gate at the bottom of the stairs was locked. But the cellars weren't the only way out of the caves. There was also the tunnel through which she'd just crawled. Though it seemed unlikely that Marietta could manage that on her own while carrying Aurora and holding a torch.

'Take Aurora,' she hissed to Marietta, lowering the baby into her arms, 'and stay behind me.' Then she flicked the single candle off its ledge, plunging the small space into darkness.

In the pitch black, every breath and every movement sounded louder. Luke, panting, made a grab for her. But she'd anticipated this and ducked to one side. Aurora's whimpers told her where the little girl and her mother were, so she moved as silently as she could in the opposite direction, feeling for the wall with an outstretched hand.

Instead, her hand hit Luke's chest and he snapped his fingers round her wrist.

'You ate one of the brownies, didn't you?' he said. 'How else would you know they were drugged?'

Instead of answering, Lexi twisted her wrist sharply, bending at the waist to give her arm a wider range of movement, until it popped out of Luke's grasp. He grunted with annoyance.

'Are you still tripping?'

As if triggered by his words, the room spun wildly and Lexi realised that she was. The adrenalin as she'd burst into the cave had overridden the lingering effects of the psilocybin, but the drug also made her suggestible and the moment Luke reminded her that she was still under its influence, it kicked in again powerfully. A sprinkling of coloured stars dazzled her – Luke had a torch and he was shining it directly into her eyes.

'Oh yes, look at the size of those pupils.' He laughed.

She turned away, biting the inside of her cheek again in the hope that pain would bring focus.

As she turned her head, within the flash of colours she saw a glistening silver snake. It slithered through the air towards her, weaving from side to side, blind without eyes, no line where its mouth should have been. It wasn't a snake. It was a blade.

Luke had a knife.

She did the only thing she could think of. She raised one leg high, knee bent, weight back, ready to slam it forward to where she assessed his groin to be. It was a huge risk. She was aiming in the dark, and if she didn't get a direct hit, he would be able to grab her leg and flip her onto her back. She had no idea whether or not he'd have the guts to use the knife he was holding, but she had to assume that he would. Taking a deep breath and holding it, she kicked hard at where she thought her target was, and his

sharp cry told her she'd hit home. The knife clattered to the
floor.

Luke's deep, heaving breaths told her exactly where he was,
curled on the floor in a foetal position in front of her. And now
she had a few precious minutes to get Marietta and Aurora
away from him.

'Who has the key for the gate? You or him?'

Marietta sniffed. 'He has it.'

'Where?'

'I don't know. His pocket, I suppose. He took it from me
when we came in, and locked the gate behind us.'

Lexi needed to search Luke for the key, but she didn't trust
him – if he made a fast recovery, the tables could turn again.
She needed to find the knife to give herself the advantage.

She found her phone and switched on her own torch. Marietta blinked up at her, dazed by the bright light and what had
happened to her. She was clutching Aurora so tightly that the
little girl wriggled and gasped in an effort to get free.

'Look out!'

Lexi whipped back round to Luke, just in time to see his
hand snake out from his body in the direction of the knife lying
on the floor. It was a small pocketknife, and the blade was short,
but it was still dangerous. Lexi threw herself down on Luke's
arm – she had to stop him getting hold of the weapon. She
shouldn't have looked round at Marietta.

Stupid. Stupid.

Despite her best efforts, she watched as Luke's large hand –
a hand that just a few days before had roamed up and down her
back as they had kissed – snatched up the knife. He had it by
the blade. Lexi grabbed for the handle and as she pulled it from
his palm it sliced into his flesh. He let out a roar of pain and
smashed the side of her skull with his other fist. The knife once
more clattered to the floor. Lexi saw stars. Aurora bellowed.

By the time she managed to shake her head and bring her

vision back into focus, she could see, using the phone torch still clutched in her hand, that Luke had the knife again. And this time he was holding it the right way around. She had no doubt that he would use it on her and on Marietta to make good his escape. She just prayed that he would leave Aurora unscathed.

It brought the Manchester image into her mind, that poor baby with blood on his hands from trying to rouse his dead mother.

'Why are you repeating history, Luke?'

'History? You'd call Bethany and Karolyn history?'

'Levenshulme. 1991.'

'I don't know what you're talking about.'

'I think you do.' She was desperately playing for time to get her addled brain in order and find a way out.

'1991? I was a baby then.'

'That's right. A toddler when your mother was murdered in front of you. Do you remember anything of that day?'

Marietta gasped from somewhere behind her.

'I was barely three years old – how could I remember it?'

'So you know what day I'm talking about.'

She knew what she was doing – delaying the inevitable. But why was Luke letting her? Had he lost his nerve?

Apparently not. He took a step towards her, and the blade flashed like molten silver in the air. She made her move fast. Muscle memory is solid. It doesn't succumb to the effects that capture the mind. Lexi's hours of self-defence training kicked in. She caught the wrist holding the knife, side-stepped towards him, shoved his shoulder down with her other hand, twisting his arm straight and then came down heavily on his elbow with her knee. Luke twisted sharply as he realised what was happening, but he wasn't quick enough to break her grip. They both fell to the floor as once again the knife flew free.

This time, Marietta was more alert. She snatched it up in one hand and grasped Aurora in front of her with the other arm.

Lexi gave her a small nod as she rolled away to escape Luke. But he was far bulkier than her, and lunging across, he pinned her to the floor. They struggled. He tried to get an arm across her throat. She scratched at his neck and tried to get her fingers close enough to his eyes to blind him. He pulled back and sideways. It relieved just enough pressure for her to raise herself on one elbow. Then she reached the other arm up and around his neck and pulled down with all the force she could muster, smashing his forehead against the floor of the cave on one side of her.

His grunt of pain told her he was down but not out. She wriggled violently and managed to shift the bulk of his body weight off her. As she stood up, he grabbed for one of her ankles, but it brought him into the range of Marietta and her blade.

With a sharp grunt, she stabbed him in the back of the hand and he let out a roar.

Lexi needed to incapacitate him thoroughly so she could get Marietta and Aurora out of danger. She needed another weapon. She cast her eyes around the tiny cave – there was nothing. But, of course, they were in the winery's huge cellar complex, and that was full of potential weapons.

Luke was pushing himself up on unsteady legs. He aimed a feeble kick at Marietta, but she managed to grab Aurora and scuttle out of range. Aurora was crying, Marietta was cursing in French, while Luke expressed his anger in a grim stream of expletives. But all Lexi could hear was a buzzing in her ears as adrenalin pumped her into full fight mode.

She ran through the larger cave and into the first cellar and, as she'd hoped, she heard Luke's footsteps hot on her heels. Good. She'd managed to draw him away from Marietta and Aurora. As she came to the first row of crates, she snatched up a bottle. It was sparkling wine – that meant thicker glass and a heavier bottle. Also good.

As Luke came into range, she drew her arm back, then smashed the bottle against the side of his head with a resounding crack. Her brain's instinctive split-second calculation of distance, trajectory and force paid off and he crashed to the floor.

The cacophony in her head stopped.

For a moment there was silence, then she heard Aurora's crying echoing through the caves.

But it was okay. Marietta and her daughter were safe.

FIFTY-SEVEN

Never in Lexi's life had she heard a sound as beautiful as the rattle of the opening of the cellar's security gate. She had dropped to her knees next to Luke's inert form, and just as she was about to search him, she heard the grate of a key in a lock and then, even better, Tom's voice, shouting from the far end of the larger cellar.

'Lexi? Are you down here?'

'Tom!' It came out cracked and broken – a call for help turned into a sigh of relief, and then she realised she was crying. She sniffed and passed the back of her hand swiftly across her eyes. She didn't want Tom to see. It was just the effect of the mushrooms, wasn't it? Swallowing down the lump in her throat, she stood up. The lights came on as Tom, followed by Will Steadman, came into the second cellar.

'Lexi, thank God – are you okay?'

She nodded. 'I think so.' She looked down at herself. She seemed to be in one piece, despite all that she'd been through. 'Luke Evans drugged me.'

Tom looked at where Evans was lying on the floor. 'This

guy? Isn't he your physio? What the hell happened?' Tom sounded furious.

'He put mushrooms in some brownies. I ate one before leaving the office.'

'Are you still tripping?'

Coloured lights flashed in front of her eyes. Bottles spun and danced on their shelves and in the wire crates. 'A bit.'

'That bastard.' He honestly looked as if he wanted to kick the living daylights out of Luke's unconscious body.

Lexi put a hand on his arm. 'It was nothing I couldn't handle.' She turned to Will. 'Marietta and Aurora are here, in the small cave.'

She needn't really have told him. They could all hear Aurora bellowing, and Will was already walking past her. Marietta appeared in the doorway between the caves and the cellar, baby in her arms, and Lexi was surprised to see Will sweep them into a wide embrace. Then she remembered, Marietta had been with Will the night Bethany had been murdered. There was quite a story still to be untangled, but she wasn't sure she could get her brain around it now. One thing was clear – she'd been wrong about the mushrooms having been given to her by Will in the coffee. They'd been in the brownie she'd eaten just before leaving the office.

Tom bent down and put a finger to Luke's throat. 'I can feel a pulse,' he said. 'I'll call an ambulance. What was he doing here, anyway?'

'I think he killed Bethany and Karolyn. Marietta was his next target.'

'And Johnny?'

'I don't know yet how it all fits together.'

'I've got Norris in custody for Johnny's murder.'

'Luke was also my physiotherapist.' She didn't see the need to add that she'd been out on a date with him, though no doubt that would come to light later. 'I think it must have been him who shut me in the sauna – he saw clients at the health club and had a staff pass to come in and out as he pleased.'

Tom was looking at his phone. 'No signal down here. We'll have to go upstairs.'

Shit! That meant her text to Ridhi about the brownies couldn't have gone through. They might still be on her desk, enticing anyone who dropped into her office.

'Come on, I need to call Ridhi urgently.'

The sun was dazzling outside. It seemed like she'd been underground for a lifetime, though it was probably less than an hour. She made the call, and averted the risk of Ridhi going through what she'd just been through, then closed her eyes to bask for a moment with the sun on her face.

Luke Evans didn't regain consciousness before being taken away in an ambulance, so Lexi and Tom were denied the satisfaction of arresting and cautioning him. However, they sent a pair of PCs to the hospital to stand guard outside his room, with strict instructions to let them know when he came round.

The paramedics checked Marietta and Aurora for injuries. Aurora was fine, apart from some bruising where Luke had stepped on her leg. Marietta was physically unharmed, but had swallowed a portion of the chocolate brownie before she'd been able to spit it out, and admitted that she was mildly tripping as a result. The medics wanted to send her home to sleep it off, but Lexi had other ideas.

'I'm afraid we're going to have to take you down to the station for a statement,' she said. 'We need to know exactly what happened while it's still fresh in your mind.' They were standing on the visitor centre deck, watching the ambulance containing Luke Evans disappear down the drive below. The sun was just dipping below the horizon, casting the vineyards in an amber glow.

Marietta looked affronted. 'I can't come with you. I need to take Aurora home and put her to bed. I can tell you everything tomorrow.'

'I'm afraid not,' said Lexi. 'There are some questions that need answering now. Perhaps you could call someone to come and fetch Aurora, or we can call in someone from social services to sit with her while you talk to us.'

Marietta's lower lip jutted out. 'I'm not handing my daughter to anyone. She can stay with me if you must ask your questions tonight.'

'That's fine,' said Lexi. After what had just happened, she could understand that Marietta would want to keep her daughter close.

They drove back to Canterbury and put Marietta and Aurora in an interview room.

'We need to wait a couple hours, I think,' said Lexi, 'to let the effects of the psilocybin wear off.'

'You or her?' said Tom.

'I'm virtually okay now,' said Lexi. 'Marietta got a smaller dose than me, but we should still wait. We can't rely on her answers if she's tripping. Let's get her some coffee and some food.'

'You don't think the psilocybin might make her spill something she wouldn't do otherwise? She could know more than she's letting on about Johnny and Bethany.'

'I'm sure it might,' said Lexi, 'but it won't do us much good in court if her lawyer casts doubt on a statement made when she was high.'

Lexi was starting to feel normal again. At least all the visual effects of the magic mushrooms had worn off. She made time to nip home for a shower and a change of clothes, and over fish and chips in her office, she debriefed Tom and Maggie with exactly what had happened down in the cave. The food made her feel immeasurably better.

'But you were hallucinating that whole time?' said Maggie, a look of deep concern on her face, when Lexi finished speaking and eating simultaneously.

'It was bloody weird,' said Lexi. 'Things would be fine for a minute or two, then everything would dissolve into patterns and colours. I don't think I'll be able to give evidence in court as to what happened – it's too subjective and distorted. We'll need to corroborate everything that I remember Luke and Marietta saying.'

'Did he definitely admit to killing Bethany and Karolyn?' said Maggie.

'Not exactly, but he implied it, talking about innocent and guilty angels. I have reason to believe that he's the baby, Baby D, in the Levenshulme case in 1991, though we'll have to confirm that.'

'What about Johnny Lycett-Boyd?' said Tom.

'I don't know – the subject didn't come up. We'll have to work out if he has the technical knowledge to have done it, and whether he was up at the track that morning.'

'Could he have done it when the Porsche was parked at the farmhouse overnight?'

'Not as easily.' Lexi wasn't sure at all. 'It would have been hard to do it with the Porsche parked on the drive, but up at the track, there were always people around and if he wasn't part of the regular engineering team, the chances are that someone would have noticed him working on the car. We might have to consider the possibility that Lycett-Boyd's murder was unrelated to Bethany and Karolyn's. The arrival of Ben Lycett-Boyd at the track a few minutes before his brother's death bears further looking into – he stands to benefit with Johnny out of the picture.'

'And what about Norris?' said Maggie. 'His prints on the wheel arch is strong circumstantial evidence.'

'We can keep him till tomorrow afternoon,' said Tom. 'Any longer and we'll have to apply for an extension.'

'Have you interviewed him yet?'

'No. I had him brought here from Elvington, and after that it all kicked off with Evans.'

'Along with the finger mark evidence, Norris had a strong motive for killing Johnny – at the time he might have believed that Johnny was responsible for Bethany's death.'

'Okay,' said Maggie. 'Question Norris and Evans, take Marietta's witness statement, then we'll meet again. And hopefully we'll be ready to charge someone for each of the murders.'

Tom's phone sounded a text alert and he glanced down at its screen. 'Evans has come round, but he suffered a serious concussion. The doctors won't let anyone in to see him until they've checked him again tomorrow morning.'

It hardly came as a surprise.

'Right, we'll talk to Marietta first,' said Lexi. 'See if she can give us anything that would be useful for when we talk to Luke.'

FIFTY-EIGHT

It was close to midnight by the time Lexi and Tom faced Marietta across the table in an interview room. Aurora was sound asleep in her mother's arms and Marietta looked exhausted. Her complexion was pallid and her eyes bloodshot. Dehydration made her features look pinched and her skin dry.

Lexi poured water into a paper cup and placed it in front of her.

'I'm sorry for keeping you waiting, but it's important that we get your side of the story straight away. Have you had some food?' she said.

'I couldn't,' said Marietta.

'And Aurora?'

'Yes, she's okay. She had something to eat.'

Lexi turned on the recording device and introduced herself and Tom for the record.

'Please state your name,' she said to Marietta.

'Marietta Lycett-Boyd.' She took a breath. 'Can I just ask, are you allowed to record what I say?'

'Yes,' said Lexi.

'I thought that was only for suspects?'

'No, we're allowed to record witnesses as well.'

'But surely only if you have my permission?'

'Marietta, the recording is to protect you. It will provide an accurate record of what you say.'

Marietta pursed her lips. She looked far from convinced. But Aurora stirred in her arms, and she looked down at the sleeping child. 'Okay, let's do this as quick as we can. I need to get my daughter home.'

Lexi sent out a silent vote of thanks to the universe – as a witness, Marietta would have been quite within her rights to say no – to both the recording and the interview.

'Great,' said Lexi. 'First of all, how well did you know Luke Evans?'

'He was my physiotherapist. A friend recommended him to me last year for treatment of a frozen shoulder.'

'So you've known him for about a year?'

'I wouldn't say I knew him. It was just a professional relationship.'

'Nothing more than that?'

'For a few months, I was seeing him twice a week. And I think I went for coffee with him once. He wanted to pick my brains about a holiday in France he was planning.'

'Would you say he was physically attracted to you?'

Lexi noticed how Marietta's body tensed up at this question. Her shoulders came up and her arms tightened around Aurora's back.

'You're talking about a man who abducted my daughter and was presumably going to kill me the same way he killed Bethany and Karolyn.' Her voice was tight with compressed fury.

'How do you know he killed them? Had he told you?'

'Before today? Of course not. But in the cave? I quickly realised what was going to happen.'

'But before this afternoon, you had a certain level of intimacy with him?'

Marietta's face crinkled with disgust. 'No sexual intimacy – that's what you're implying, yes? He was my physio. It was just professional.'

'Okay.' Lexi needed to dial back a bit. They wouldn't get anything useful from Marietta if she was angry. 'Tell me about what happened this afternoon. Who was looking after Aurora, and where was she?'

Marietta's back slumped and she stared down at her daughter's head sulkily. 'She was at the farmhouse with our cleaner, Mrs Goddard. Johnny's parents were too upset by Johnny's death to cope with her. I still had work to do at the winery, so I asked Mrs Goddard to watch her.'

'But somehow Luke managed to take her. Did Mrs Goddard know Luke?'

'He treated me at the house always so, yes, she was familiar with him. She opened the door to him sometimes.'

'Did she call you to say Aurora was missing?'

Marietta shook her head. 'I spoke with her an hour ago. She said Luke had come to the house and told her I'd asked him to pick up Aurora and bring her to me.'

Lexi put up a hand. 'Okay. We'll talk to Mrs Goddard and get her statement.' Second-hand hearsay wouldn't be allowed into the case – they needed to hear it from the cleaning woman first-hand.

'Was that something you'd ever asked him to do in the past?' said Tom.

'No.'

'But Mrs Goddard didn't think to ring you and check it was okay?'

'I suppose she had no reason to doubt it.'

Lexi was thinking the scenario through. The winery would have been busy, so Luke must have taken Aurora into the caves unseen, using the tunnel. How had he known about the existence of the tunnel? From Bethany, who presumably knew about it from her liaison with Johnny?

'You were working up at the vineyard. Did Luke come and seek you out?'

Aurora became restless on Marietta's lap. Marietta stroked her hair and whispered softly in her ear. The baby quietened, and Marietta looked up to meet Lexi's eyes. 'I bumped into him – or at least that's how it seemed at the time. I'd been to Will's office for something and I was walking back up to the winery and I saw him coming down the track towards me. I asked him what he was doing at the vineyard.'

'You confronted him because he shouldn't have been there?'

She shook her head. 'Not confronted – it was fine that he was there. I just wondered if he was looking for me. He told me he had something to show me in the caves.

'I asked him what. It felt odd to me. I didn't understand. He was being... I would say he was being secretive.'

Lexi remembered walking up the track to the winery behind them, her brain scrambled. She hadn't been able to hear their conversation.

'But you went along with him?'

'I wanted to know what he was talking about.'

'What happened next?'

'We went into the winery and through the fermentation hall to the cellars.'

'Did anyone see you?'

'I think so. There were people working there. I might have said hello or waved at someone.'

Tom made a note in his pad. He would follow up with any witnesses.

'We went down the stairs into the cellar, and that's when I heard Aurora crying. I knew it was her straight away – as a mother, you know your own baby's cry, and it pierces your heart. I ran to her. That's when I got scared. She was alone in the cave, in the dark.'

'Did you realise then that Luke had locked the gate behind you?'

'No. All my thoughts were for my baby. Luke followed me to the cave, and I asked him why she was down there. He lit a candle and I saw a bag, a clear plastic bag, with wings in it. That's how I knew he had killed Bethany and Karolyn. I was terrified. He wanted me to undress. He picked up Aurora and threatened to hurt her if I didn't do what he said. I thought I was going to die.' Marietta's breathing had become so fast she could hardly get the words out.

'It's okay,' said Lexi. 'You're safe now.'

'Thank God you came,' said Marietta. She was crying now. 'You saved my life.'

Lexi waited for a few moments for her to calm down. She had one last question.

'Marietta, do you think Luke could have come to the farmhouse during the night and tampered with Johnny's car on the drive?'

Marietta looked up, swiping her wrist across her eyes to clear the tears.

'On the drive? No, no, the car would have been in the garage. Johnny never left it out on the drive. There have been lots of expensive cars stolen in this area, so he always locked it away at night.'

And with that one statement, everything changed. Lexi clearly remembered Marietta saying that she didn't know where Johnny's car was parked. Now she did. It was an error that told Lexi everything. She knew who'd tampered with Johnny's car and who was responsible for his death.

FIFTY-NINE

SUNDAY

Despite being well past one in the morning, the lights were still burning in the police station. Maggie was pacing Lexi's office with a face like thunder.

'Why in hell's name are you still detaining that poor woman with her child? She's a witness in the case, not a suspect.'

Lexi sat behind her desk. With the realisation of the previous hour, a sense of calm had washed through her. The quietude she always felt when she'd solved a case and it was just a matter of gathering in the loose ends to make sure they had a watertight file to present to the prosecutors.

'I can explain, but I've just asked Tom to confirm something for me. I need to make sure I'm right. He'll be back soon.' She got out her decision log and started making notes on everything that Marietta had said and how it had blown the case wide open for her.

Maggie continued pacing. Then she stopped in front of Lexi's desk and leaned on it, glaring down. 'This could look really bad for us if Marietta lodges a complaint about being detained unlawfully.'

Lexi took a deep breath. 'She's not being detained unlawfully. I simply asked her to wait a little longer. She's within her rights to leave if she wants.'

'Which I'm sure you haven't made glaringly obvious to her.'

'Maggie, honestly, you know I wouldn't do this without reason.'

What was keeping Tom?

The tension rose gradually for another ten minutes, then Tom appeared in the doorway, out of breath from running up the stairs.

'You were right, boss.'

'I thought so,' said Lexi.

Maggie turned sharply to face them. 'What is it?'

'Marietta told me that Johnny garaged the Porsche at night, as there had been a problem with car theft in the area.'

'Lexi asked me to go to the Lycett-Boyds' house and check a couple of things. The garage doors are kept locked, but the garage can be accessed from the house. It looks as if Johnny used to work on his car there as well as at the track – there's a large grease pit for accessing the car from underneath and a workbench with a full set of mechanic's tools.'

'And all this means?' said Maggie.

'The Porsche was locked in the garage that night. The footage from the track only ever shows Johnny working under the bonnet of the car, and no one else touching it. We thought Norris had done it – his prints were on the car – but CCTV confirmed that he didn't go near it that morning. That means that there were only two people who could have tampered with the rear springs – Johnny or Marietta. While the car was locked in the garage, they alone had access to it.'

'So you think Johnny adjusted them and it was suicide?'

'Not at all. I think Marietta adjusted them and it was murder.'

She heard Maggie's quick intake of breath as she processed the suggestion.

'Johnny wasn't suicidal,' Lexi continued. 'He was thinking of selling the vineyard, he was about to start a custody battle for Scarlett – there was nothing to suggest he wanted to end it all. We know now he didn't kill Bethany or Karolyn, so he couldn't have been feeling guilty. And if he was going to commit suicide by car, he could have just driven it into something at speed rather than make an adjustment that wouldn't guarantee death anyway.'

'Fair point,' said Maggie.

'Marietta had the means,' said Tom. 'The necessary tools were to hand. She had the motive – Johnny had betrayed her, and if he died, she would presumably inherit his share of the vineyard and could play house with her vintner. And she had the opportunity – the car was in the garage, out of sight of anyone else.'

'But does she know enough about cars to have done that?' said Maggie.

'I've asked Emily to check any unidentified finger marks taken from the car against her prints, which we took as a matter of elimination for the winery crime scenes. If they show up on the car's moving parts, I think we can assume she has.' Lexi was one hundred per cent certain Marietta's prints would show up, either under the back wheel arches or on the springs themselves.

'Tom, did you confiscate the spanner wrenches from the Lycett-Boyds' garage?'

'Yes. I'll get them over to Emily first thing in the morning.'

'What does this mean for the rest of the case?' said Maggie. 'Didn't you think the murders were at least linked, if not done by the same killer?'

It was something that swirling around in Lexi's mind, too.

'Marietta knew Luke – he was her physio. He came to her house often, which was why Mrs Goddard trusted him with Aurora. Marietta claims it was nothing more than a professional relationship, but I'm beginning to wonder.'

'So now what?' said Maggie.

'I want to confront her and see if we can elicit a confession of tampering with Johnny's car. With or without it, I think we'll be able to make a case for either murder or manslaughter.'

Maggie frowned. 'It'll be up to the CPS to decide which. Charge her with manslaughter. We can always add an additional charge of murder later.'

'I think it's definitely murder,' said Tom. 'There was an intent to harm in some way, and it resulted in Johnny's death.'

He was probably right, but the main thing was to get Marietta processed and into a holding cell, ready for an appearance at magistrate's court in the morning.

Lexi went back to the interview room, where Marietta was still sitting with Aurora on her lap. Her face was puffy and red, though a listless exhaustion had taken the place of her earlier crying.

Lexi sat down opposite her. 'Marietta,' she said gently. Marietta barely registered her presence. 'I need to call someone to come and fetch Aurora.'

This caught her attention. She straightened up in her chair and hugged the little girl so tightly that she whimpered in her sleep. 'Why? What are you talking about? I was going to take her home, non?'

'I'm afraid we're going to place you under arrest for the manslaughter of your husband.'

'No. What are you saying? What are you accusing me of?'

'Isn't it true that you adjusted the rear spring rates on Johnny's Porsche when it was locked in the garage the night before the crash?'

'Not at all.' Her lip twisted and her brow lowered. 'I wouldn't even know how to do that.'

'You and Johnny were the only people who would have had access to the car that night.'

'So? Someone maybe did it up at the track.'

'We've ruled that out.'

'*Putain!*' Marietta wasn't quick enough to conceal her anger.

'I believe we'll find your fingerprints on the spanner wrenches we retrieved from your garage, and on the car itself.'

'You can prove nothing.'

'I think we can. You'll have to remain in custody, at least until you've been arraigned in court on Monday morning. The magistrate will decide whether or not to give you bail. Aurora can't stay in custody with you. Who can I call? Didn't you say Johnny's parents looked after her sometimes?'

'No.' Marietta shook her head frantically. 'I don't want her to go to them. They'll never hand her back to me. I don't trust them.'

'Do you have any family in this country?'

'No.'

'Then I'll have to call social services. They can look after her and place her with a foster family if need be.' Lexi hoped it wouldn't come to that, but there was no point in sugar-coating what might be coming down the track.

Marietta rubbed her eyes with her thumb and index finger. They came away wet. 'Perhaps you could call Ben?'

'Johnny's brother?'

'Yes. I think he's still in London. Aurora is his niece, and he has children of his own...'

'Of course, if you'd rather that than Johnny's parents.'

Marietta sniffed and nodded. 'Can she stay with me until he arrives?'

'Of course.'

After Lexi had made the arrest and given the statutory caution, she went back up to the incident room.

'Tom, what are you doing still here?'

'Waiting to drive you home.'

Lexi crinkled her nose. 'Come off it.'

'I'm not letting you drive after what you've been through. You must be exhausted. Anyway, your car's still at the vineyard.'

He was right – she was absolutely knackered. She gave him a grateful smile. 'Just a couple more calls then,' she said.

It felt good to be wrapping up the case. She found Ben Lycett-Boyd's phone number in her notebook and called him. It took a while for him to answer – of course, he was asleep – but as soon as he heard that Marietta was under arrest and that someone was needed to take charge of Aurora, he said he would drive down first thing in the morning. They decided to let Marietta keep Aurora with her in the custody cell until he arrived.

'Home now?' said Tom, stifling a yawn.

'One more thing,' said Lexi, with a grin. There weren't many moments in her job that involved giving people good news. 'Liam Norris.'

If Liam didn't take the news that he was free to go exactly gracefully, Lexi could at least sense the relief that swept through him when she told him he was no longer being considered a suspect in Johnny's death.

'How am I supposed to get home?' he whined, consulting the watch he'd just got back from the custody sergeant.

'We'll sort out a uniformed officer to give you a lift,' said Lexi. It was the least they could do, having held him for almost eight hours without charge for a crime he hadn't committed.

As they watched him pull away in a marked police car, Tom marched Lexi across the car park to his Jeep.

'No argument now,' he said. 'We need to be back here in a

few hours to write all this up and, hopefully, take Luke Evans into custody when the hospital releases him.'

'No argument from me,' said Lexi. 'Dead on my feet.'

She settled back in the passenger seat, and when Tom woke her they were outside her cottage.

'See you tomorrow,' she said, getting out.

'Today, in fact,' said Tom.

SIXTY

Lexi's work wasn't over by a long shot. She made a start on the mountain of paperwork the two arrests had generated while she waited for Ed Harlow to arrive, though she'd hardly got through a fraction of it by the time he did.

He smiled at her from the doorway, holding out a takeaway coffee from Lexi's favourite café.

'You're a saint, Ed,' said Lexi, saving the document she was working on. 'Come in.'

'I could say the same about you. You've rescued me from a morning of doing battle with insurance companies and banks.' He looked tired and he'd lost weight over the past few weeks, making Lexi wonder if she was doing the right thing by involving him. But it was what Charlie had wanted, and it seemed to please him.

'As long as I'm not taking up too much of your time.'

Ed's smile was wistful. 'Like I said before, sometimes it's all a bit much. It's good to get my head into a different space for a few hours.'

Lexi nodded. She understood. When she and Amber had come home after being abducted, while the police were still searching for Rose, their parents' attention had been over-whelming. She'd felt suffocated in those weeks, but at the same time guilty for wanting to get away from it all and not think about what had happened.

She quickly filled him in on the events of the previous twenty-four hours.

'You're joking! That guy gave you a spiked brownie?' Ed was furious. 'If I hadn't interrupted you that night...'

It was a thought that Lexi had been pushing out of her mind since the moment she'd realised it was Luke that had given her psilocybin, rather than Steadman. What exactly had Luke's plan been for that evening if Ed hadn't turned up?

'Let's not go there,' she said, feeling a little shaky. 'It had to have been him that locked me in the sauna, as well. I can't believe I was taken in by him.'

'You think you should have seen through him?' He looked sceptical.

'Of course.' She paused. 'No, you're right. The charming psychopath. He could take anyone in.'

Ed pursed his lips. 'Thank God he's in custody now.' He took a sip of his coffee. 'So with him and Marietta under arrest, what do you need me for?'

'The easy option would be to simply refer both arrests to the Crown Prosecution Service for prosecution. We can put together the evidence and make a compelling case against both Luke and Marietta. But I believe there's more to it.'

'What do you mean?'

'Luke was Marietta's physio. She recommended him to me and subsequently he made two personal attacks on me. Can we really just take the line that the murders of Bethany and Karolyn were in no way linked to the murder of Johnny Lycett-Boyd? It's too much of a coincidence. I believe Luke and Marietta were in this thing, whatever it was, together.'

'I agree. And you want to untangle what's going on?'

'The relationship between them makes me believe that Marietta was somehow involved in the girls' deaths, and achieving justice for Bethany and Karolyn means winkling out the truth of what was going on between them. That's what I need you for. Luke's been released from the hospital, and I've got them both here in custody. This might be my only chance to play them off against each other.'

'I'm in – what do you need me to do?'

Lexi called Tom into her office and laid out her plan.

'Luke in one interview room with you, Ed, and Marietta in another with you, Tom. I'll go between the two and ask the questions, and we'll see who trips up first.'

Now it was lunchtime, and she, Ed and Tom had worked out a series of questions, just breaking off to talk briefly to Ben Lycett-Boyd when he arrived to pick up Aurora.

Linda Ellis had attended to oversee the handover, and Lexi had been surprised to learn from the way the two of them greeted each other that they already knew each other.

'I'm going to apply to adopt Scarlett Glover,' Ben had said, by way of explanation. 'Both her parents are dead, and she's first cousin to my boys. It makes sense for her to be with family. My wife is flying over from Australia, and I think we're going to look into moving back here.'

'That's wonderful to hear,' Lexi had said. 'Of course, Scarlett and Aurora are half-sisters, so it will be even better if they get the chance to spend time together. It'll be a safe family environment for her while Marietta is in custody.'

'I can't believe she killed Johnny.' Ben's eyes were wide. 'She loved him so much. I know they'd been having problems, but truly, she wouldn't have hurt him on purpose. You've got it wrong, Detective.'

Lexi couldn't agree with his interpretation, but she didn't comment. She just hoped that Scarlett and Aurora could stay in each other's lives whatever happened.

As Ben left, a text came in from Emily Jordan.

'Yes!' Lexi punched the air. 'Marietta's prints matched finger marks on the spanner wrenches and on the rear springs. We've got her. Now let's finish this thing off.'

As the three of them made their way down to the interview rooms, Lexi could feel the energy coming off Tom and Ed. They were on the home straight, coming in for a win.

Luke Evans looked bruised, battered, and crumpled. There was a square bandage over the spot on the side of his head where Lexi had hit him with the bottle, and a bruise on his cheek. The hospital had released him and he was back in the clothes he'd been wearing the previous day. They still bore the evidence of what had happened. Chalk dust, blood stains, white rings of sweat. He didn't smell good either.

He stared at her across the table, sitting in exactly the same chair Marietta had vacated a few hours before. His gaze was hostile, and he seemed a different man to the one that she'd spent an evening with. Her face burned at the thought of it and she desperately hoped he couldn't read her emotions.

The tension in the room ramped up as Luke recognised Ed. His eyebrows went up and he leaned back theatrically in his chair, looking from one to the other of them.

'Well, well, well, who have we here? The original love triangle, all reunited.'

Lexi thanked the heavens that she hadn't switched on the recording device yet. She didn't need this exchange to be played in open court when Luke came to trial. It would be bad enough that the defence would try to make something of their personal relationship, even though it was clear that he had targeted her to find out about the investigation. However, she couldn't delay things, and she leaned across to the side of the table to press the button. After the long bleeping tone which signalled the start of recording, she stated the date, time and place and introduced herself.

'Please state your name and your job title,' she said to Ed.

'Ed Harlow, forensic psychologist.'

'And I'm Luke Evans, psycho in need of his evaluation, apparently.' Lexi and Ed ignored the bark of sarcastic laughter that followed this.

'Would you like a lawyer present?' said Lexi.

'No. I don't need direction from a man in a suit. I'm quite capable of advocating for myself.'

Lexi and Ed exchanged glances. So far, so typical – arrogance was a trait they came across time and time again in men who killed. What was interesting was how well he'd covered it up during the time Lexi had spent with him. He was able to wheel out the charm and humility when it served his purposes. It was as if she was sitting opposite an entirely different person. Even the way he looked at her was different, an expression of contempt plastered across his face as he let his eyes roam up and down her body.

She felt a surge of hate and anger course through her which was anything but professional.

Lexi took the role of interrogator. Ed was present to observe, and she'd get his impressions after the interview was over.

'Mr Evans, what do you do for a living?' A few base questions to lead off with, so Ed could establish a benchmark for Evans's voice when he was telling the truth.

'Mr Evans? Last time we met, you called me Luke.'

Lexi had been expecting this type of answer, and she'd already steeled herself for it. She certainly wasn't going to rise to the bait.

'Please answer the question.'

'You know the answer.'

'For the recording. Answer the question.'

'I'm a physiotherapist. A good one, wouldn't you agree, Lexi? As you have first-hand knowledge of my skills.'

'Please state your home address.'

'You know my home address, Lexi. You've spent the night at my flat plenty of times.'

Lying bastard.

As the spring inside her coiled tighter, Lexi had to concentrate hard on not letting her emotions show on her face. She hoped that Ed was tracking this as a lie.

Her phone buzzed with the arrival of a text. She glanced down to see it was from Tom.

A word?

'Give me a moment,' she said to Ed.

She went out into the corridor and found Tom waiting.

'I was listening in while I wait for Marietta to be brought up. What the hell was all that about?' he said, as soon as the door to the interview room was closed. 'You were dating him?'

'No. I had a couple of physio sessions with him and we went for a drink. Once. Nothing happened and that stuff about staying at his flat is a lie. His little fantasy, no doubt, which he's happy to use to derail the interview.'

'Don't you think you should have said something? A personal relationship with the suspect you're interviewing? They'll rip this to shreds in court.'

She knew he was right, but she wasn't prepared to let go. 'Don't you think I'm fully aware of that? But it's my call, Tom. You need to understand why I'm doing it. He thinks he can rattle me. He thinks he's got the upper hand, and that by embarrassing me, I'll have to pull back rather than go hard on him. And that's when his arrogance will lead him to make mistakes.'

Tom glowered at her. 'His arrogance? Or yours?'

It was the first time he'd ever directly challenged her, and she didn't like it, but now wasn't the time to deal with it.

'When he makes a mistake, we'll be able to ask Marietta for her version of the story. They'll practically convict each other.'

'Talking of which, Marietta wants to lawyer up.'

'Her prerogative. Hopefully they'll advise her to work with us rather than against us.'

Tom nodded.

'I need to get back in there,' said Lexi.

As she opened the door to go back into the interview room, she overheard Luke say something.

'Sorry, I didn't catch that,' said Ed.

'How's your wife, Dr Harlow?'

Lexi couldn't believe what she was hearing. Luke knew Ed's wife had just died. As a police officer, she knew she was fair game for Luke's jibes, but this was unconscionable cruelty, and anger bubbled up inside her like lava. And it was her fault that Luke knew about it. Tom was right – maybe she shouldn't be doing this. It was incredibly risky.

However, Ed was cool. 'Her funeral is next week. You'd be welcome, but I suspect you'll still be in custody.'

A muscle in Luke's cheek twitched. He didn't like someone getting the better of him.

Lexi sat down.

'Everything okay, Lexi, or are you in trouble?'

'Please tell us where you were on the night of Saturday 23rd September. That's Saturday a week ago, the night Bethany Glover died.'

'I was with Marietta Lycett-Boyd.'

He didn't miss a beat. No pause for thought, which suggested to Lexi it was a prepared answer. He'd gamed out how he would answer their questions. But what he didn't realise was that Marietta had already told them where she was the night Bethany died. Twice.

'Where precisely?'

'In my flat – you know, the one you've visited often.'

'All night?'

'All night.'

'And how would you react to the news that Marietta has confirmed to us that she was with Will Steadman that night?'

'I'd say she was lying.'

'Why would she lie about that?'

'To protect Will Steadman. She told me that he killed Bethany. But with Johnny gone, Will Steadman might become an attractive prospect to a woman in possession of a vineyard.'

She didn't need Ed's input to know this was a lie. Had Evans blanked out the fact that they'd taken him into custody having discovered him in the cellars with Marietta and Aurora?

'Were you and Marietta having a relationship?'

'She's not a threat to you, Lexi.'

'Were you and Marietta having a relationship?'

'She wanted one. I was her physio – like I was yours. She kept coming onto me during appointments.' He shaped his face into a look of regret that didn't take Lexi in for a moment.

'How long have you known Marietta?'

'She became one of my clients about eighteen months ago.'

'Was it a purely professional relationship at the start?'

'Of course it was. It would have remained that way if I hadn't been so stupid.'

'What do you mean?'

'Unfortunately, I let her seduce me, and after that she wouldn't leave me alone.'

'What did she do?'

'She was demanding. She expected sex every time I saw

her. She kept calling, leaving messages. Basically, she was obsessed with me.'

'This was a one-sided thing?'

'There was nothing I could do to put her off. She started stalking me, hanging around outside my work. Turning up at my house. I tried to end it countless times, and when I told her I wasn't interested in having a relationship with her, because I was in a relationship with you, she became utterly infuriated. She stole my pass to the health club. I found out the next day that someone had trapped you in the sauna. It was her. She wanted you out of the way so she could have me to herself.'

'But you didn't see fit to tell the police this when it happened?'

'I was scared of her. What she might have done to me in retaliation. She could have ruined my career.'

He'd done a pretty good job of that himself.

Lexi stood up. 'Time to hear Marietta's version of your relationship.'

The look of horror on Luke's face was priceless.

SIXTY-ONE

Ed followed her out into the corridor.

'You know, virtually everything he said in there was a lie.'

'I agree. I've never been to his flat, for starters.' She didn't know why she needed to make this specific point – it just came unbidden out of her mouth.

'I didn't think you had.' There was a note of concern in Ed's voice that caught Lexi by surprise. 'He's using a classic tactic – finding someone else to blame for everything he did, raising enough doubt to send you off down a rabbit hole.'

'It's not going to work, though. With the charge against her, we've got some leverage to encourage Marietta to tell the truth.'

She went into the second interview room and Ed returned to keep an eye on Luke.

Lexi recognised the man sitting next to Marietta. It was the lawyer she'd briefly glimpsed at the farmhouse a few days previously. He was whispering in Marietta's ear in rapid-fire French, which made Lexi wonder if he had legal standing here.

Her question must have shown on her face, as he stopped talking and looked up at her. 'Good afternoon. My name is Jean

Bastin. I will be acting for Madame Lycett-Boyd. I'm registered with the SRA, so allowed to practise in the UK.'

Lexi gave him a nod of recognition as she took the chair next to Tom.

'Marietta, you've been charged with the voluntary manslaughter of your husband, John Lycett-Boyd. We believe we have enough evidence against you to secure a conviction. Do you understand?'

Marietta nodded. Her eyes were wide with fear, and her hands, resting on the table in front of her, were shaking. She looked, if anything, a little worse than when Lexi had seen her a few hours before, when Ben came to fetch Aurora. The little girl had howled at being prised away from her mother, and it struck Lexi that Aurora didn't know who Ben was. He'd been away in Australia for most of her short life. Lexi's heart went out to Marietta as a mother, but she couldn't afford to show her sympathy in the room. She had a job to do, and it was beginning to look as if Marietta was even more deeply involved in the case than she had previously suspected.

Bastin glared at her. 'My client is innocent, and we will test your evidence robustly in court.'

'It's right that you should do that,' said Lexi.

'It could only be involuntary manslaughter at worst,' said Bastin. 'There was no intent to cause death.'

'That will be for a jury to decide. However, if you're co-operative with us now, you might be able to look forward to a better outcome at trial or sentencing.'

'What do you mean?' said Marietta.

'We're currently questioning Luke Evans about the murders of Bethany Glover and Karolyn Small. I believe that you have some knowledge of these crimes that might be useful to us in building our case against him. So if you help us, we will do what we can to help you.'

'If you want to help my client, you would drop these bogus charges against her and release her.'

Bastin was going to be a hindrance to his client if he continued in this approach, but that wasn't for Lexi to say out loud.

Marietta put a hand on his forearm, possibly to rein him in. He said something to her in French and she answered hurriedly in a low voice. Not that they needed to whisper. Neither Lexi nor Tom spoke French, and what was said between them was privileged.

'Okay, my client will answer the questions you have. But first I want assurances that the charge will be lowered from voluntary to involuntary manslaughter.'

'I can't make any promises on that. It's the CPS who'll ultimately decide the charge, but I'll make sure to tell them that your client has been co-operative.'

'What are your questions?' said Marietta.

'I just need to go over a few details about your relationship with Luke Evans.'

Marietta nodded, but then looked away, unable to make eye contact. That told Lexi a lot.

'How long have you known him?'

'I first started seeing him as my physio just under eighteen months ago.'

This time Marietta made eye contact. She was telling the truth. Lexi started a mental score card – Marietta, one, Luke, zero.

'For how long was the relationship purely professional?'

Bastin murmured something. Marietta's eyes skittered from side to side as she considered her answer.

'There was a mutual attraction from the start... but things changed quickly. He flirted with me. I was unhappy with Johnny and Luke's attention made me feel good about myself.' She spoke with increasing confidence, but that didn't make Lexi believe what she was saying. Luke had put the blame for their relationship on her. Now she was putting the blame for their relationship on him. Lexi suspected they'd been as keen as each other.

'When did the relationship become sexual?'

'He seduced me last Christmas, but I told him it couldn't happen again. I stopped seeing him for a while.'

'Professionally or personally?'

'Both.'

Lexi was certain she was lying, and as she finished speaking, she slipped her hands from the table onto her lap. It was a classic 'tell' that someone was being less than truthful. Time to apply more pressure.

'Where were you on the night Bethany Glover died?'

Marietta's nostrils flared. 'I told you, I was with Will Steadman that night.'

'Luke Evans claims that you were with him.'

'*Non.*' She shook her head vehemently.

Bastin fidgeted uncomfortably.

'I believe that Will asked you to give him an alibi for that night, and it suited you very well to do so, because it also gave you an alibi. But in reality, you were with Luke.'

Marietta's whole body tensed. 'He's lying.' The words emerged from her mouth like bullets.

'Were you in the cave with him when Bethany died?'

'No.'

'Were you with him at the pergola when Karolyn died?'

'No. Whatever he's told you, it's all lies.'

Lexi glanced at Tom and could tell by his expression that he didn't believe her either.

'So why would he say these things about you?' In fact, he hadn't, but Marietta wasn't to know that. It wasn't something that Lexi liked to do, but sometimes it was necessary.

'He wants to blame someone else for the murders. He'll tell

you that they were my idea, that I suggested he should get rid of them.' Flecks of spittle gathered in the corner of her mouth and her breathing suggested that her heart rate had elevated.

Suddenly Lexi knew that she was telling the truth. She *had* suggested that Luke get rid of her rivals. She was trying a double bluff, but under the circumstances, she couldn't pull it off.

'Are you in love with Luke Evans?'

Marietta recoiled at the question, shaking her head.

'He says you were obsessed with him.'

'He's lying – everything he says is a lie. He became obsessed with me. And with Aurora. He was always asking about her. It made me uncomfortable. It made me scared of him.'

'I don't believe you, Marietta.'

'Stop,' snapped Bastin. 'You are pushing my client too hard.'

But Marietta had revealed enough. The balance on Lexi's score card had swung the other way. Her suspicions that Marietta had been involved in Bethany's and Karolyn's deaths appeared to be correct. Why else would Luke have selected two women that were potential love rivals to Marietta? Bethany threatened her marriage to Johnny, while Karolyn was proving a threat to her burgeoning relationship with Will. It was too much of a coincidence that they both became the victims of a serial killer who Marietta knew personally.

Now Lexi's only problem was how to prove it.

SIXTY-TWO

Lexi convened with Tom and Ed in the corridor. Once she'd updated Ed on what Marietta had said, they deliberated on how to proceed.

'They both lied,' said Lexi, 'but Marietta's claim that Luke would suggest killing the girls was her idea actually revealed the truth of what happened. I could tell from her body language.'

'Is the interview on video?' said Ed.

'Of course, and I'd like you to take a look at it and see if you agree with my assessment.'

Ed nodded.

'What next?' said Tom.

'We need evidence.'

Lexi called Emily Jordan and explained her suspicions. 'Can you do another check for matches with Marietta's prints? Of course, any that you find in the cellars and the caves can be explained away by the fact that she worked there and that Luke took her down there with intent to kill her. But if you can find a match on the evidence from the pergola, or any of the sets of wings that Bethany, Karolyn, Scarlett or Ronnie were wearing, then we'll have our proof that she was involved with the murders.'

'I'll get right on it,' said Emily.

'Thank you. I really appreciate it – I know I keep coming back with urgent demands, but it could be make or break.'

'No worries – you'll hear from me soon.'

Lexi turned to Tom and Ed. 'If Emily can find evidence which confirms her presence at at least one of the murders, we've got her. It'll be for the courts to decide who was more culpable, but I want to see them both going down for all three murders.'

'What do you need from me?' said Tom.

'Can you get Marietta back to her cell? I've finished with her for the moment. But I want to talk to Luke once more. We need to probe the reason he killed women and left their children alive. Marietta may have been pulling his strings, but his signature was all his own and I need to understand what made him so pliant to Marietta's wishes.'

'You're right,' said Ed. 'She wound him up like a toy mouse and pointed him in the right direction. But he had to have his own motivations or he wouldn't have gone through with it.'

They went back into the interview room.

Luke straightened up in his chair as they came in.

'She denied it all, didn't she?' he said. 'But you have to know, she pushed me into doing it.'

Lexi sat down without speaking. Did Luke realise he'd just given them the confession they needed? But the recording device had been switched off when they left the room, so they didn't have it on the record.

Damn!

She would need to elicit it again. She quickly pressed the button to resume recording.

Evans's face clouded with anger at her lack of response. 'She said she'd accuse me of rape. It was her word against mine.

Who do you think would be believed, would be listened to? They had money, the Lycett-Boyds. I had to do what she said.'

Lexi somehow doubted this scenario. Luke Evans had shown himself as someone highly manipulative already, perfectly capable of squirming out of Marietta's clutches. He went along with it because he wanted to. His need to kill women was as great as Marietta's desire to be rid of Bethany and Karolyn.

'Are you in love with her?'

The shock that registered on Evans's face at this question was genuine, and Lexi had to wonder why. Was it so outrageous a proposition?

'No one could love her,' he said. 'She's an evil bitch. Only interested in what she could get for herself. That's why she wanted Johnny dead – to give her control of the vineyard.'

'She told you that?'

'She wanted me to kill him. Threatened me if I didn't do it.'

'But you didn't do it, did you?'

He shook his head.

'What happened to the threat?'

'That's why I took her and Aurora down into the caves. To persuade her not to act.'

'You threatened her child?'

'No. I would never hurt a child.'

Ed slid a folded note across the table to her.

Ask him about the woman in Bromley. And then Levenshulme and what happened to his mother. That's where he's vulnerable, that's where he'll break.

Ed was right. Luke would go on trying to deflect the blame onto Marietta, using her as a shield and a distraction. But she needed to slip a blade between his ribs and catch him where he was vulnerable – his heart.

'You would never hurt a child,' said Lexi slowly. 'Is that why you left Scarlett alive? And Ronnie? Was it your plan to kill Marietta and leave Aurora by her body?'

'I didn't want to kill anybody. It was Marietta who insisted the women had to die. And that I had to help her. The cave was her idea – that way we'd be able to frame Johnny for the murder as he was one of the few people who knew about it or had access to it.'

'Was she there with you when the women died?'

He didn't answer. The lie not tripping so readily to his tongue?

'Was Bethany the first, or had you killed other women before her? That poor woman in Bromley, for instance.'

'What woman?'

'Her name was Susan Gibson.' Lexi opened the briefcase that stood on the floor by her chair and extracted a plain blue folder. She slid a photo from it, being careful not to let Luke Evans see anything else inside. It was a picture of the dead woman in question, taken when the body was first discovered. 'Maybe this will jog your memory.'

'No.' But his body language said that it did. His muscles tensed, his posture become tight and defensive, and he couldn't take his eyes from the image.

'Was she your first kill? Before you'd even met Marietta?'

Luke Evans continued to stare at the photo but said nothing.

'I've got something else that might jog your memory.' She slid a second picture out of the folder. The Manchester baby. She turned it round so it was the right way up for him and pushed it across the desk.

'That's you, isn't it?' Even she could see a ghost of a resemblance between the man opposite her, in his thirties, and the infant in the photo. Something familiar about the eyes.

Evans looked at the photo for a long time. Lexi studied the

play of emotions across his features. At first, he glanced at it dismissively, then his eyes widened as, perhaps, he saw what she'd seen. And then the pain rushed in – his jaw tightened, his lips compressed, his eyes narrowed, as his head came forward, staring harder and harder at the baby and the body beyond it.

'That's your mother, Luke. And you. Do you remember?'

He took a gulp of air. Lexi wondered if he had an image of his mother in his mind. Of how she looked when she was alive. Not that this picture would enlighten him. The woman's head was turned away from the camera – all that showed was a tangle of long, dark hair.

'I've never seen this photo before,' was all he said.

And then the dam burst. It all spilled out of him, the things he couldn't keep inside any longer. Years of pent-up emotion finding release. Lexi had seen it happen before – a killer freeing himself from the shackles that kept him killing.

'I remember the blood on my hands,' Luke said. His voice was stilted and he spoke slowly. Uncoiling the memory with dread. 'It was sticky. It stank. My mother was asleep and I couldn't wake her. Then a man came, and another, with cars and radios and flashing lights. They took me away from her.' He rubbed a hand across the bottom of his nose. 'I never saw her again. I didn't know she was dead – I didn't even understand what dead was. But I saw my bloody hands at night in dreams. Always. And later, when I was seven or eight, for a while, I believed that I'd killed her. I knew it was her blood on my hands, but I didn't know how it had got there.'

Lexi stayed quiet, giving him full rein to continue.

'Of course, I didn't kill my mum. I was a baby. But I can't forgive her for what she did to me.'

'What was that?' said Lexi softly.

'She left me alone.' He could barely speak.

'But that wasn't her fault.'

'She did it to herself. She was a whore. She put herself in harm's way, and she should have kept herself safe. For me.'

It was a tragedy and he'd grown up broken.

'For a long time I thought she was an angel watching over me. Believing that helped me feel better. But one day I realised it wasn't true. That's when it all started.'

'What started?'

'The urges. I couldn't bear to see mothers with little kids. I knew they'd end up hurting their own children.'

'So you killed them?'

'The angels do better than the real mothers.' A vein pulsed at his temple. 'Those women were better off dead.'

Inside, Lexi breathed a sigh of relief. She had her confession, this time recorded.

'Where did Marietta fit in all of this?'

'At first, I thought she cared for me.' His eyes were vacant. 'But then I understood I meant nothing to her.'

'So you were going to kill her, like you killed Bethany and Karolyn?'

'Things went wrong between us... Asking me to kill Johnny was wrong...' A single tear rolled down his cheek.

The man in front of Lexi had become a vulnerable child. She pushed her chair back and went to the door. Ed followed her, leaving Evans weeping softly at the table.

Outside, Lexi was able to vent some of her anger. 'He didn't stand a chance, did he, after what happened to him? And like always, he pays it forward and starts another cycle of suffering. But her—' she pointed to the room where they had spoken to Marietta '—she has no excuse. Some sort of perfect storm brought the pair of them together and Marietta realised she had found a man who'd do her bidding, no matter how evil or destructive it was.'

'A man who'd kill women for her, but not men,' said Ed. 'If she wanted Johnny dead, she was going to have to do it herself.'

'And she did.'

'You've got them both. And if the prosecution lawyers do a proper job of it, they'll end up incriminating each other.'

'There's just one more thing I need to ask him about.'

They went back into the interview room. Luke Evans looked up at them as they came in. His face was red and wet.

'You said Marietta shut me in the sauna. That was a lie, wasn't it?'

He nodded. 'Marietta was scared that you were going to realise it was her that fixed Johnny's car. I saw you going into the sauna and I wanted to please her. I jammed the door shut and waited. Once you passed out, I was going to remove the bar so it would look like an accident.'

A shiver ran up Lexi's spine. Luke Evans had been lurking outside the sauna as she'd gone through hell trying to escape. Her anger knew no bounds. But she was as angry with Marietta as she was with him. And they were both going down.

She flipped off the recording machine.

'That's enough for now, Luke. We'll talk some more later.' Now she needed to update Maggie and get the green light to charge him and Marietta with murder and attempted murder.

Lexi's phone rang as they came out into the corridor. It was Emily Jordan.

One sentence sufficed.

'I've found a match to Marietta's prints on the set of wings that Bethany was wearing.'

They had her.

Lexi went up to her office and sat at her desk. Ed stood by the window, stretching his arms to release the tension in his shoulders. Lexi felt just as tense.

'I just can't get over it,' she said.

'What?' said Ed, turning back to her.

'The fact that Marietta was there when Luke killed them. That's what the fingerprint evidence tells us. She watched

Bethany die. And presumably Karolyn, too.' The thought of it made Lexi feel physically sick.

Ed grimaced, but didn't speak.

Breathe. Just breathe.

The case was done and dusted apart from the paperwork. Luke Evans and Marietta Lycett-Boyd would go to prison.

And she'd move on to the next case. Because, somewhere out there, another killer was making his plans, stalking a victim or hiding the evidence. Her job was never done.

Her phone rang again. More evidence come to light? But it was Amber, and she remembered she'd promised to go round to her sister's house for Sunday lunch.

'Where are you?' said Amber. 'The beef's going to be overcooked.'

'God, I'm so sorry.' She absolutely meant it. 'The case has broken – I'm stuck at the station wrapping it up. Honestly, I'd come if I could...'

'How long will it take?'

'Probably another couple of hours. Sorry.'

'The kids will be so disappointed. Never mind – come round later. There'll be plenty left.'

The old Lexi wouldn't have been so apologetic. The old Amber would have taken it personally. Their relationship had definitely improved.

Damn it!

'Give me a moment.' She put the call on hold, and turned to Tom who'd appeared in her office doorway. 'Tom, can you check in with Maggie and then charge the bastard?'

'Sure, but I thought you'd want to.'

'I've got something more important to do.' Tom hurried off and she turned to Ed. 'Want to come with me for Sunday lunch at my sister's?'

Ed smiled – the first proper smile she'd seen on his face in a long time. 'I'd better not. I told my brother I wouldn't be gone long.'

'Fair enough.'

'But if the invitation ever came up again...'

'It will.' She reconnected to the call. 'Amber, I'm on my way – keep a plate warm for me.'

Just sometimes, there were things that were more important than work. And today, her family was one of them.

A LETTER FROM ALISON

Thank you so much for reading *The Innocent Angels*. Whether you've read the first two books in the series before this one or whether this is your first encounter with Lexi, I hope you've enjoyed it.

If you're interested in hearing about the next titles in the Lexi Bennett series, please sign up using the link below for details of forthcoming releases. Your email address will never be shared and you can unsubscribe at any time.

www.bookouture.com/alison-belsham

I have one small favour to ask of you. If you've enjoyed reading about Lexi and the team, I'd be hugely grateful if you'd write a review of *The Innocent Angels*. I'd love to know what you made of Lexi's latest case and how she and the team are getting along. Reviews are also important to help new readers to discover the series for the first time.

If you want to know what I'm currently up to, you can follow me on Instagram, Facebook, Twitter/X, Goodreads or my website.

Alison

KEEP IN TOUCH WITH ALISON

www.alisonbelsham.com

 facebook.com/alison.belsham.3

 twitter.com/AlisonBelsham

 instagram.com/alisonbelsham

ACKNOWLEDGEMENTS

Writing the Lexi Bennett series is a great pleasure, but it wouldn't be possible without the help of many other people, from researching the story before I start writing to the point of publication and beyond.

Naturally, I'm enormously grateful to my editor Ruth Tross, who made *The Innocent Angels* immeasurably better at every stage of the manuscript – an expert on structure and pacing, characterisation and suspense, while at the same time keeping me up to date with the publishing and marketing plans for the books.

Thanks are also due to the rest of the brilliant Bookouture team – in particular to Richard King, Head of Rights, Melissa Tran on production, Mandy Kullar in managing editorial, Melanie Price in marketing and the wonderful PR team, Kim Nash, Noelle Holten, Sarah Hardy and Jess Readett. Thanks also to copyeditor Dushi Horti and proofreader Shirley Khan, and to Lisa Brewster for designing the glorious cover.

I'm also grateful to my agent Jenny Brown, for her sage advice and steadfast encouragement of all my writing endeavours. Since our first encounter at Bloody Scotland in 2016, she's been a supportive presence and instrumental to any successes I can claim.

My research for *The Innocent Angels* was enabled by a fascinating tour of Hambledon Vineyard – huge thanks to Katherine Fromm for showing me around and answering my questions, and thanks are also due to Davy Zyw of Berry

Brothers and Rudd for the introduction. Any errors in the descriptions of winemaking are entirely my own.

Thanks to my writing group colleagues Jane Anderson, Kristin Pedroja and Hannah Kelly for making the solitary process of writing less solitary than it otherwise might be, and to the wider writing community of Edinburgh for making me feel part of a wonderful fellowship.

Thanks again to Mark, my travel companion on research trips to Kent and beyond, for relentlessly instructing everyone he meets to buy my books.

And finally, thanks to you, the reader. Without readers, there would be no reason to write, so you're maybe the most important element in the whole process!

Printed in Great Britain
by Amazon